Also by Co

NANTUCKET

If For Any Reason
Is it Any Wonder
A Match Made at Christmas
What Matters Most

HARBOR POINTE

Just Look Up
Just Let Go
Just One Kiss
Just Like Home

LOVES PARK, COLORADO

Paper Hearts
Change of Heart

SWEETHAVEN

A Sweethaven Summer
A Sweethaven Homecoming
A Sweethaven Christmas
A Sweethaven Romance (a novella)

STAND-ALONE NOVELS

Things Left Unsaid
Hometown Girl
A Cross-Country Christmas
Merry Ex-Mas

A HOLIDAYS WITH HART ROMANCE

COURTNEY WALSH

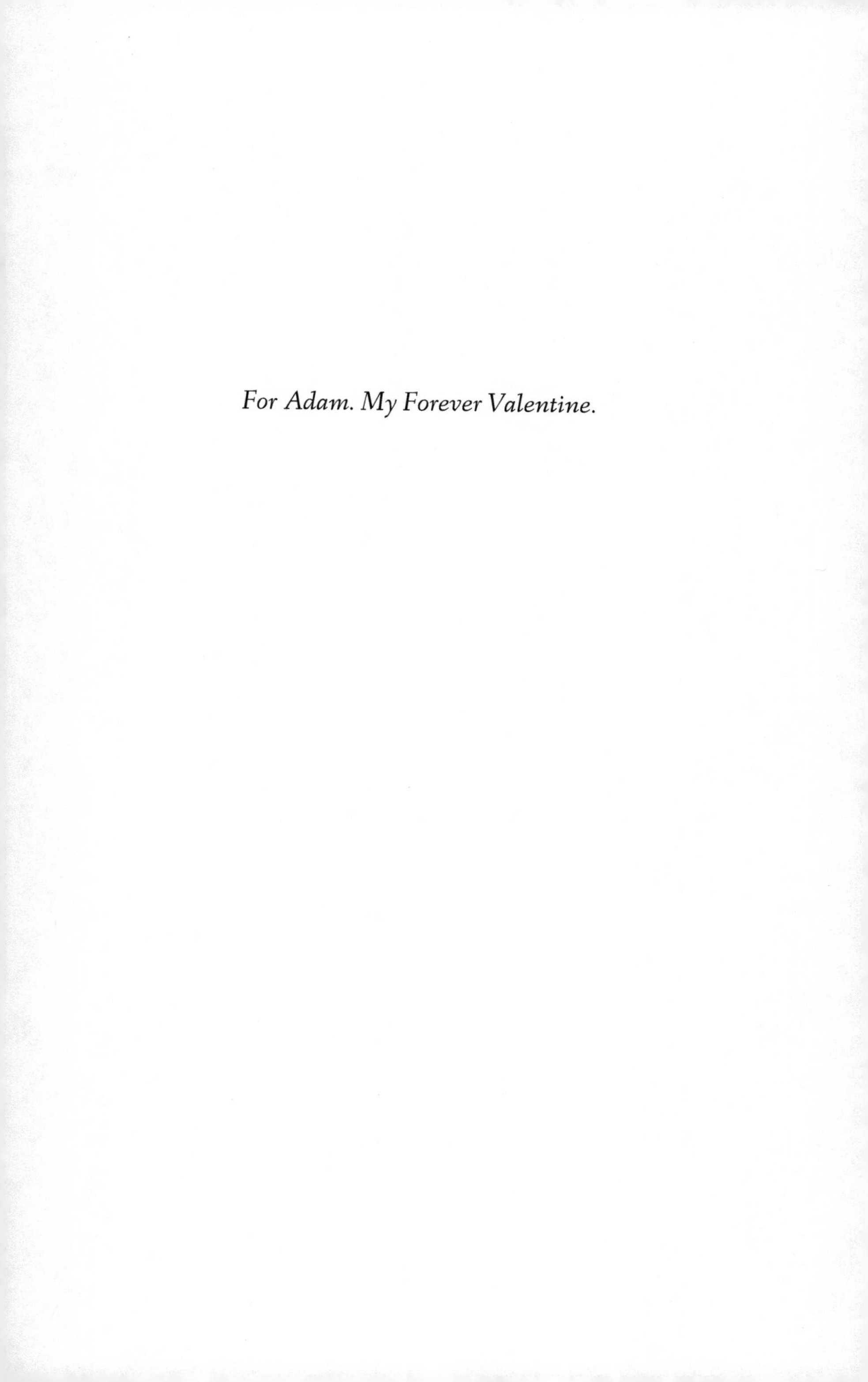

For Adam. My Forever Valentine.

Chapter One

Poppy

I don't know why I did what I did.

I mean, I *know* why I did it—I just can't believe I *did* it.

It was a knee-jerk reaction. A rash decision. An instinctive reflex, not unlike that decision you face when you're waist-deep in the cold water of the swimming pool, and you have to tense up and plunge yourself under the water.

Or when you're twelve and you're in the circle and the bottle you've just spun lands on that boy you've been doodling about in your notebook for a month.

I just. . .went for it.

And now I'm arm in arm with a complete stranger.

But I'm getting ahead of myself.

Twelve and a Half Minutes Earlier

Some voices just have that knack of making the muscles in your neck cramp when you hear them. Like dragging a rake across a chalkboard.

I don't have to turn around to know who's behind me in the line at the coffee shop. What are the odds?

"*Poppy Hart*, is that you?"

Actually, considering how small of a town Loveland is, the odds are pretty good that if I leave the house I'm going to see someone I know.

But why does that someone have to be Margot Richards?

I do a slow turn and force myself to be nice. "Sure is, *Margot*." Even her name in my mouth tastes like week-old milk.

"It sure is!" she repeats back, as if she didn't hear me at all. "Poppy Hart. You look—" she gives me a familiar once-over, as if searching her Rudeness Rolodex for the perfect insult—"healthy."

Margot Richards, everyone.

I shake my head slightly. "Uh. . .Thanks?"

She continues, unabashed. "Amazing your little restaurant is still running after everything that happened with that *boyfriend* of yours," she says, emphasizing boyfriend as if it's bolded in a *National Enquirer* headline. "Wait. Was it. . .boyfriend? Business partner?" She waves a hand in the air. "I never was sure of the relationship." She smiles one of those *I'm being friendly but really insulting you* kind of smiles. "But then, apparently neither was he," adding a "right?" with a head tilt.

People don't really speak like this in real life, do they? As if their rear ends were planted squarely at the top of their neck and talking out of the hole that's there?

"It doesn't really matter," I say, desperately wanting to run down to the river and jump in, or, at the very least, push Margot in.

Her laugh is humorless. "Doesn't it?"

"I just meant—"

"Oh, I know what you meant, Poppy." Another dismissive

wave. "I *was* sorry for you though. Such a pity to waste so much time on someone who turned out to be such a disappointment."

I turn away, but then double-take. "Are you talking about him or me?"

She just smiles back.

I glance at the line. It's moving as fast as a sloth on Benadryl.

"And *The Mill*," Margot says. "Ugh. That article?" She places a hand over where a normal person's heart would be, as if there wasn't just a gaping black soul-sucking cavity there. "I really felt for you."

"Yeah. That was. . ." I stiffen. "That was some post." I shift my weight to stop from kicking her. "I doubt anyone really visits that site anyway."

I know absolutely everyone in town visits that site anyway.

It's the website that Loveland locals had been getting their daily dose of town chin-wagging from ever since the *Gossip Girl* wannabe site popped up online.

I thought someone like me was exempt from rumors. And I was, until Avi blew up my life.

"Oh, Poppy." Margot lays it on thick with a sardonic laugh. "Everyone reads *The Mill*. You know that."

I just stare at her, and she nods over my shoulder toward the line, which has moved three millimeters. I turn, take a step forward, and face the front, but Margot isn't done humiliating me.

It's her favorite pastime.

"It is *so funny* seeing you here. I haven't seen you around town for so long."

"I work down the block," I say.

She ignores me. "You know, I just ran into your mom at the store the other day. She mentioned she's worried she's never going to have grandkids at the rate you and your sisters are going. I guess some people bloom late." I turn to her just in time to see another pointed look from my feet to my face. "And some people never bloom at all."

Most people outgrow their bullying once they graduate high school, but it turns out that's not true for boxed-wine sociopaths like Margot.

Some people are mean no matter how old they are.

Oh, look. She's still talking.

"Though, with everything that happened. . .I can see why you'd want to avoid the male species at all costs," Margot says. "There is absolutely nothing wrong with being single, Poppy."

My stomach twists. I don't know why Margot chooses to be the way she is or why she seems to focus her energy on humiliating me, but I do know that I'm tired of it. Tired of *The Mill.* Tired of the town looking at me with a strange mix of pity and judgment.

Still, a smart person would turn around and ignore her. A smart, *mature* person would let Margot be her typical unhappy self and pity *her* for it.

Today, I am not a smart person.

Today, I'm waist-deep in the pool, and I tense up my muscles.

Today. . .I just go for it.

I turn to let loose a barrage of pent-up vitriol, when at that precise moment, my shoulder bumps into the man in front of me. A tall, solid man.

A man who I decide in an instant would make an excellent visual aid.

I turn to face her full on. "Actually, I haven't gotten around to telling my mom yet, but I am, uh, dating someone."

Margot's face looks like the *eyes wide emoji,* but quickly disintegrates into disbelief. "Oh, you are?"

—the water's not THAT cold, just take a breath, plunge

deep, it'll be fine—

"Yep."

I turn and I grab onto the arm of the man I just bumped into. "So, sorry, Sugar Bear."

Now We're Caught Up

He's talking on his phone, and when he realizes I'm talking to him, he gives me a confused look.

My eyes go wide at him.

Telepathy, don't fail me now.

I look at Margot. "So sorry, he's on an important call." I turn my attention back to Margot. "It's new, so I haven't even told my sisters yet."

"*HE* is your boyfriend?"

I squeeze the man's arm, hoping he'll take pity on a perfect, albeit crazy, stranger. Also hoping he doesn't look like Gomez Addams or worse, Uncle Fester. "Yep."

I am not a smart person.

At that, the man turns around, giving me the first real look at his face. His beautiful, chiseled face. He's got dark hair and blue eyes, a traffic-stopping combination. And while I typically don't like facial hair, his neatly trimmed beard is working for me.

Definitely not a member of the Addams family. He'd be better suited as an honorary Hemsworth. A dark-haired Hemsworth.

Wait. . .*is* he a Hemsworth? There are a lot of them, you know.

Margot's eyes widen, and I delight in her surprise, even though part of me is aware I could be heading for even worse humiliation.

"Dallas *Burke*." Margot says the name on an exhale.

Dallas Burke? Why is that name familiar?

The man—Dallas Burke—straightens.

The heartless cow—Margot Richards—muses. She flicks her eyes to mine. "*Dallas Burke* is your boyfriend? Sure, Poppy."

I look up at him. And I do mean *up,* because he's a good foot taller than me, and I want to hide. To crawl under a rock and stay there, sealed deep in the dirt. I could live out the rest of my days in darkness, the worms and I.

"Poppy, next time you fake a boyfriend, pick someone a little more in your league."

Margot twists a curl around her finger and eyes Dallas like he's a giant cupcake and she hasn't had carbs in ten years. She leans around me. "*So* sorry to bother you, Mr. Burke."

I'm about to go find a building to jump off of when a thick, muscular arm lands on my shoulder, anchoring me into place. "Hey, sweetheart, did you want a scone with your coffee today, or are we just doing drinks?"

I look back at him, jaw fully slack.

Is this. . .are we doing this? Oh, my Dear Lord, we're doing this.

He smiles at me and I feel it in my knees. They actually go weak for a moment, and I'm thankful for that beefy arm that seems to be holding me steady. He gives my shoulder a soft squeeze, probably meant to remind me that a question has been asked and I'm expected to answer. For the life of me, I can't remember what that question was.

"Pops?" Dallas says.

"Huh?"

"Are you hungry?"

"What can I get for you?" The barista behind the counter smiles at Dallas.

He smiles back. The power goes out on three city blocks.

"I'm going to have three of those egg bite things, two blueberry muffins, and a black coffee, and my girlfriend will have. . .?" He looks at me, smiling, and all I can think is, *Wow, his teeth are so white.*

"Poppy?"

"Right! That's me!" I finally find my voice, slapping the counter like a sailor asking for another. I point at the barista, trying to speak, but forget how to for some reason. I glance at Margot, who stares at us both in disbelief. She's clearly as confused as I am.

I realize I'm still pointing, so I thrust my finger again at the poor barista, a bystander to this mental breakdown, hoping the movement will dislodge the twenty-car pileup in the speech center of my brain. "I'll have a peppermint mocha."

"Anything to eat, babe?" Dallas asks. Then, he looks at Margot. "I'm always trying to get this one to eat. She knows I love her curves."

I'm almost certain my eyeballs just bugged out of my head and are now rolling around on the floor. He flashes that ultra-white smile at me.

"Ha. . .ha ha. . .you know I love you. . .loving my curves. . .!"

I'm an idiot. A blathering, nonsensical idiot.

"I'll just take the drink, uh, sweetheart." My mouth goes dry. "Thanks."

He takes my hand and squeezes it, sending a pulse of electricity straight to my gut. "You're sure?"

"Yep." The word comes out like air from a squeaky toy that's been stepped on.

The barista gives Dallas the total and he pays, stuffing a twenty into the tip jar.

A beautiful man named Dallas Burke just bought me coffee.

I'm still trying to place him. *Where do I know him from?*

Margot's snotty voice from behind reminds me that yes, there really are terrible people in the real world, and not just on Twitter. "*You* are dating the *star* of the Chicago Comets." There's an insulting amount of disbelief in her voice, but I can't even be offended because I'm equally shocked by this turn of events.

It clicks. The Chicago Comets.

Dallas Burke is a hockey player.

I think he'd been in the news recently, but I can't for the life of me remember why. At this moment I can't even remember my own name. I don't follow sports, especially not hockey. I don't even know the rules of the game.

Dallas slides his credit card into his wallet and tucks it in his back pocket. I wish I was that wallet right now.

"Is this for *real*?" she chirps.

"Oh, it's for real. . ." His arm is back around my shoulder, pulling me closer into him. He smells like a forest and I want to get lost in the woods. He studies Margot. "I'm so sorry, what was your name again?"

It's an honest question, but the look on Margot's face tells me it felt like a burn.

Good. I shouldn't relish that fact, but I do. Just a little. Or a lot.

"Margot Richards."

"Good to meet you, Margot, but we should go. Busy day."

Margot's eyes narrow. Dallas flashes a smile. I'm a statue afraid if I move I'll wake up from this pine-scented fantasy.

Margot turns her attention back to me. "So, we'll see you both at the Festival of Hearts then?"

Dallas answers for me. "We'll be there."

She looks incredulous. "I find it hard to believe a big hockey star like yourself wants to spend the week of Valentine's Day at some festival in our little town," Margot says.

Dallas puts both his hands on my shoulders and says, "I want to spend Valentine's Day making my girlfriend happy." I look up at him, and he looks down at me, and I swear there is a moment. He tilts his head, almost imperceptibly, as if considering it for real.

A moment.

The moment's gone, quick as a rumor, and he says, "So, I'll do whatever she wants to make that happen." His hands slide all the way down to mine, so slowly it sets off a chain reaction inside my body.

And then he's standing next to me holding my hand.

I let out three quick, sharp, high-pitched sounds that can only be described as a "titter."

Margot eyes me, suspicion on her face, then finally turns on her heel and walks away.

I guess she didn't want coffee after all.

Dallas is still holding my hand when the barista slides our drinks across the counter. We each pick up our cups with our free hands, and then he leans toward me. "Is she gone?"

I peek back just in time to see Margot's blond head disappear out the door. I let out a heavy sigh. "Yes, thank God." A pause. "You really didn't have to do that."

"No big deal." He waves me off like he didn't just save me from utter humiliation. "Besides, it's been a long time since someone called me 'Sugar Bear.'"

I groan.

"You know that's not an acceptable nickname for a grown man, right?"

"But 'Pops' is perfectly fine for a grown woman?" I smile at him, some of the embarrassment starting to wane. "Sorry. I panicked. I froze. I owe you big time. How can I return the favor?" I glance down and realize he's still holding my hand. When I do, he slowly lets it go.

Darn my eyeballs for zeroing in.

"No need," he says. "I was happy to help." He grabs the bag of food he ordered.

I stare at him, mostly because I still can't believe he's real. Or that anyone looks this good in person.

I always wondered how I'd act if I ever met a celebrity. Now I know.

Mouth agape. Stuttering for words. Making a fool of myself. And I'm not even really a fan.

I stand awkwardly, clinging to my mocha like it's the only thing keeping me upright.

Dallas looks around the coffee shop. I'm thankful there aren't many people here today and curious what he's doing in town, but it's none of my business.

"I should probably go."

What? Why did I say that? I don't want to go!

I want to stand and stare. And I do, until, "Oh, shoot."

"What?" He seems legitimately interested.

"The Festival of Hearts. You said you'd go, but you obviously aren't going to do that, so don't worry, I'll make up something."

He looks at me and I just keep right on talking.

"I'll tell everyone you let me down easy, or it didn't work out, or whatever. I won't make you sound like a jerk or anything." I try to smile. I wonder if it's as weak as it feels.

"Why don't you tell them *you* let *me* down easy?" He smiles. I hear an angel getting its wings, I swear it.

"Ha. That's funny." I'm staring again. In an effort to stop, I say the only thing that comes to my mind.

"Poppy."

His expression turns quizzical.

"My name, it's my name, it's what people call me, it's. . ." I shake my head to stop talking, and stick out my hand for him to shake. "Poppy Hart."

I'm wholly unprepared for the zinger that shoots through me when he takes my hand in his.

Is this lust? Am I going to have to repent? How many deadly sins am I committing?

"It's good to meet you, Poppy Hart," he says.

"Good to meet you, *Dallas Burke*." I'm certain my smile pales in comparison to his. Margot was right to be gobsmacked by the whole idea that I even have a boyfriend, especially after the embarrassment of my last relationship. But Dallas Burke? Ludicrous.

I can't believe I'm standing here talking to one of the most successful professional athletes of our generation.

And he's not running away.

"You have no idea who I am, do you?" He grins.

"Sure I do." I smile back. "You're the star of the Chicago Comets."

"Do you know what sport that is?"

"Um. . .ice dancing?"

He laughs. I find myself wanting to make him do that more.

"Thanks again for the save," I say.

He nods at me. And as much as I wish he'd ask me to stay and drink coffee with him *for as long as we both shall live,* I know this surreal interaction is all I'm going to get.

I smile again, wave, and turn to go, bumping into a rack of granola bars as I do.

I slowly turn back to look, and yep, he's totally standing there, still watching me.

Solid.

Not exactly the impression I was hoping for, but hey, at least I'd made myself hard to forget.

For once.

Chapter Two

Poppy

I'm still feeling slightly dazed.

I'm also kicking myself for not getting a photo with Dallas Burke because there is no way my sisters are going to believe that just happened.

Or that I told Margot I was *dating* him.

I'm not delusional enough to think I'm going to get away with my little white lie, of course. Knowing Margot, half the town probably already knows I've made this ridiculous claim, and it's only a matter of time before the truth comes out.

I'm okay with that.

I'm used to being the butt of the joke. I'll laugh it off like I pulled one over on Margot and try to save a little face.

I get in my Ford Escape and take the first sip of my peppermint mocha, but the second the warm liquid hits my tongue, I realize there's no peppermint in this cup.

There's also no mocha. It's straight black coffee.

I spin the cup around to read *#DBhotguy* scrawled on the side. Guess Mindy read my mind when she made this drink.

Unfortunately, with the day I'm set to have, this isn't going to cut it. At all.

I glance up at the coffee shop just as the door opens and the rock solid professional hockey player steps out onto the street. His beautiful hand is holding my beautiful mocha, so I open the car door and call out to him.

"Dallas!"

He spins toward me, a shocked look on his face, almost like he was expecting a bounty hunter to take him in and collect a giant reward.

When he sees me, his features soften, and he lifts a hand in a wave.

I cross the street to where he's standing. "They gave me your drink."

He looks down and reads the label on the cup in his hand.

"Oh, good, you saved me from getting a toothache from the sugar."

"Ha, ha," I say. "Unfortunately, I did get a taste of your drink of choice and one hundred percent do not recommend."

We exchange cups and he laughs. His smile is so bright and shiny I'm hoping it doesn't cause a car accident.

"Thanks," he says.

"Of course." I stand there, staring at him, aware that I should really just walk away now. I will not be one of those people who asks for a photo, no matter how curious I am about him. I've never met a real-life celebrity before. "What are you doing in Loveland?"

He looks around. "It's quiet here."

I laugh. "You can say that again."

"Yeah." He looks away. "No cameras."

I tilt my head to try and decipher what it is he isn't saying. Then, I lift my phone and take a photo. "Wrong about that, mister. There are cameras everywhere."

He watches me for a few seconds and I'm painfully aware how awkward I am.

"Sorry, I was just. . ." I trail off. "I'll delete it."

"It's fine," he says. Then, abruptly, he holds up a hand. "Your camera doesn't have a direct link to any major news outlets, does it?"

For a moment I feel heat rise on my neck as if I did something wrong, but then he smiles. "It's okay," he says, "I'm just kidding."

"Oh, good," I breathe, relieved. A nudge in the back of my brain tells me he isn't kidding. Not really.

I take a sip of my mocha. Could I have an actual conversation with a man that looks like a walking advertisement for teeth whitener? *I guess we're going to find out. . .*

"So, you're hiding out?"

"Yes." A beat. "No." He shrugs. "Not exactly."

I realize that it's cold on the street, but also that anyone in town could walk by and see me—*me, Poppy Hart!*—talking to hockey superstar Dallas Burke.

"Do you. . .want to go sit?" I motion back into the coffee shop. "You're probably used to the cold, being a hockey star, but for the rest of us. . ."

He looks at me for a moment, then nods. "You know what, that actually sounds kind of nice."

This feels. . .oddly familiar. Yes, he's built like a statue, and yes, he's insanely attractive, and yes, I should be a blubbering puddle of nonsensical words—but I'm not.

I'm a bit shocked, if I'm honest.

"So you do know what sport I play." He grins, but for the first time, I can see there's some level of sadness in his eyes.

"I do, yes—but don't ask me how to play. I'll fall down just thinking about it." I follow him back inside and we find a table in the corner. It's quiet and a little dark, one of those cold winter days where the sun is peeking out from behind a slate overcast sky.

Once we're seated, I stare at him. Again.

He pulls the egg bites out of the bag and unwraps them. "Do you know anything about me?"

I laugh. "No, actually. If Margot hadn't said your name, I wouldn't have known who you were."

He nods. "Good. Then can we pretend I'm just a guy?"

"Ha." I half-laugh to myself. "Just a guy. . ."

He smiles, swallowing his bite. "A guy who doesn't play professional hockey."

"Right, got it. Sure, let's pretend that for a minute."

As if on cue, a little boy appears at our table. He's holding a notebook and a pen. "Mr. Burke? Could I get your autograph?"

Dallas smiles, but it looks slightly forced. "Of course, kiddo, what's your name?"

"It's for my dad," the boy says. "He's too chicken to come over here." He nods over two tables to where a man is sitting, watching, sending his kid to do his dirty work.

"Ah, so you're the brave one," Dallas says. He scribbles something on the paper and hands it back to the kid. "Have a great day."

He turns his attention back to me.

"So. . .just a guy." I smirk at him, and he looks away.

"Yeah, probably not something I should be wishing for. I know how entitled it sounds." He continues eating.

"I think it's okay to want to escape a life like yours for a little while," I say. "Or what I imagine is a life like yours. I really wouldn't know."

He looks back at me, eyes full of hope. "You're the lucky one."

I take a sip of my drink, savoring it. I sure haven't felt like the lucky one.

But here? Now, at this table with him? Maybe for the first time in my life, my luck is starting to change. "I mean, I've never been a rich, famous, playboy hockey player, but I can imagine it's exhausting." I take another drink.

"I thought you said you didn't know who I was?" He says this a little defensively, raising one eyebrow.

I choke, horrified that I've offended him. "Oh, my goodness, is that all true? I was just guessing, I didn't mean anything by it, I'm not. . ."

He smiles another half-smile, but I can't quite tell what's behind it.

"Well, you've almost got it right," he says. "I'm no playboy."

I narrow my eyes, sizing him up, thinking what every woman in the world would be thinking hearing *those* words come out of *that* mouth. "Sure you aren't."

He holds up his hands, as if I just told him this was a stick-up. "I swear."

I can't tell if it's a line. I don't know him yet. But for some reason, I feel comfortable enough to be bold. And a bit vulnerable.

"Look, I know I'm not the one the group of guys buys the drinks for. I'm the one who gets comfortable standing off to the side at the dance. I'm clearly not a woman you need to impress," I say, "so, you can save the lines for someone who might buy them."

That felt—good. I'm not usually one to speak my mind.

Maybe I should consider changing my entire personality.

He sits back in his chair, taking a moment. "That, 'Pops'. . ."

I tingle inside when he says that. It already feels like an inside joke.

". . .is incredibly refreshing." He shakes his head. "I'm not really into the party scene. At least, not anymore."

I believe him.

We sit in silence for a few moments, and I notice people in the coffee shop are staring. And not at me. I feel a little self-conscious, but Dallas doesn't seem to notice. Maybe he's conditioned himself to ignore this sort of gawking.

"So, if you're not hiding out," I say, "what are you doing in Loveland?"

His phone buzzes with a new text, which pulls his attention. He reads it, frowns, then looks up at me. "Sorry, Poppy, I need to go take care of something."

I nod, resigned, and sit back in my chair. "Of course."

For a flicker of a moment, he almost looks disappointed. "Maybe I'll see you around town."

I know he probably won't, but I nod anyway. "Thanks again for the coffee. And the save."

He stands. He's wearing Nike track pants and a hoodie, one of those expensive ones I only buy when they're on sale. Somehow, he makes this outfit look *good.* He turns to leave, then stops. "Hey."

I look up at him.

"Thanks. Really. I wish I could stay."

And just like that, he leaves, and the prying eyes turn their attention to me.

I'm used to hiding in the background. Strike that—I'm used to *existing* in the background, because that's often where others put me—and as much as I thought a change might be nice, I realize almost instantly, I don't like it. Everyone watching me. Probably speculating about me. I'd had my fill of that after Avi, which was only now starting to die down.

Living in a small town, there is some level of everyone knowing your business. It's in the bylaws, probably. But when you're trying to process your emotions, difficult ones, it's hard to hear—and read—everyone else's opinions about them.

Sometimes I wonder if I've absorbed *what everyone else thinks* and made their feelings my own.

It must be ten times worse for someone like Dallas.

I glance out the window and see him get into a fancy sports car. If anyone asked me what kind of car it was, I'd say "black" because I have no idea. I've never seen a car like that before. I bet it cost more than my house.

He's on the phone as he gets inside, disappearing behind the darkened windows.

And I can't help but feel a little bit sorry for the man who has everything. Because that everything includes a whole lot of things I would never, ever want in my life.

My phone buzzes on the table with a text from my oldest sister Raya, in our *Hart Sisters Group Chat.*

RAYA

Poppy. . .I think you have some explaining to do.

A photo appears on the screen. And not some silly meme or the latest Siberian husky video Eloise thinks is so hilarious. This photo is of me and Dallas Burke, sitting at this very table, staring at each other like we're, well, a little more than strangers who met in line thirty-three minutes ago.

Then, a buzz from Eloise.

ELOISE

Poppy Hart! What is the meaning of this?

And when can we meet him?

A succession of buzzes forces me to pick the phone up off the table—they're now texting in tandem.

RAYA

How did this happen?

ELOISE

And why haven't you told us about it?

RAYA

Poppy, where are you?

Are you DATING Dallas Burke?

POPPY

SLOW DOWN! I will explain everything later.

RAYA

Not good enough, sis.

We need to hear this NOW!

POPPY

I'm late for work. I promise, there's no story here.

I glance around the coffee shop, wondering who might've sent the photo to Raya, knowing that it could've been anyone. And that meant it will probably end up in *The Mill* later on today.

Fabulous.

I groan. Just when I'd gotten my name off of that trashy gossip site.

I stand and walk out onto the sidewalk.

If this is my brush with fame, I hope it's over in the prescribed fifteen minutes.

Chapter Three

Dallas

I connect the phone to the bluetooth in my car.

"Okay, slow down, Gram, what's going on?"

"There's a young man here holding a card with my name written on it," my grandma says. "He says you sent him to the airport to get me."

"That's right, Gram. He's going to bring you here."

"But, Dallas, my name is spelled incorrectly on this card, and I don't know if he can be trusted. What if he is trying to kidnap me? I watch TV. They'll kidnap me and then send you a ransom letter. You are quite wealthy, you know."

I drive toward the house I've recently purchased at the edge of town, wondering if my grandma is going to demand that I make the trip to O'Hare to pick her up.

O'Hare is a nightmare, even at this time of day.

"That's Gerard, Gram," I tell her. "He's my driver."

"You don't drive yourself?"

"I do sometimes, but a lot of the time, I have Gerard drive me."

"Because you're Mr. Fancy Pants," she says.

"Because. . ." I stop. I don't really know why Gerard drives me. Because I've gotten used to being carted around like I'm too precious to drive myself? "Sometimes I have work to do in the car." That was true. Interviews. Meetings with my manager. Watching game tape on my phone after we've already gone over it at practice. So much happens on the go. Enter Gerard.

She pauses, probably giving my poor driver a suspicious look of death. "How do we know that this is the real Gerard?"

My grandma isn't delusional. She's not suffering from anything but a bum hip that needs replacing. She's perfectly lucid. She simply loves to be melodramatic, and she loves pushing my buttons. Always has.

She also subscribes to just about every conspiracy theory that's ever been written down. And every one that hasn't been written down.

I'm not convinced she hasn't started some of them herself.

"Put him on the phone," I say. Why I'm humoring her I have no idea.

I hear Gram shuffling the phone around, then, faintly, "He wants to talk to you."

Some noises on the phone as it's being handed off, then: "Sir?"

"Gerard, I am confirming your identity."

"It's me, sir," he says.

"She's a sweet old lady, but a little melodramatic," I say. "Actually, she's probably just bored." I wasn't buying for a second that she actually thought Gerard had been replaced by some strange kidnapper who wanted to hold her for ransom.

Though, if someone did, I'd pay whatever I had to to get her back. I owed everything to Gram.

"Is she glaring at you right now?"

"She is, sir."

"Staring you down, like she's got your deepest, darkest secret all figured out?"

"That's right, sir."

"She's got a mean stink eye."

He laughs. "I agree, Mr. Burke." A pause. "Have I satisfied your identity check?"

"Yes, Gerard," I say. "You can put her back on."

More shuffling, then Gram's back. "You gave him the all clear?"

"Yes, Gram, he is who he says he is."

I imagine her giving him a once-over. "Let's hope he's not masterminding a plot. He'll sell me to some foreign land and I'll be forced to cook and clean for a tyrant!"

"Yes, but at least the tyrant will be well fed," I say dryly. "I'll see you soon."

"See you soon, Dally."

I wince at the horrible nickname. Most people call me "Burke," and if anyone else called me "Dally" I'd probably clock them, but Gram's been calling me that since before I could talk, so she gets a pass.

I drive out to the new house. It's a ranch style, so it'll be easy for her to get around after the surgery, and it's got a nice, big yard with lots of privacy.

I've had everything set up just how I think Gram will like it, and my commute to the city and back shouldn't be unbearable.

About an hour later, Gerard pulls into the driveway, and I'm standing on the sidewalk waiting for them. I open the back door of the SUV, and Gram stares at me.

"Have you just been standing out here waiting for us to get home?"

"Gerard called to let me know you were close," I say.

"Would you stop being so testy and let me help you out of the car?"

"This isn't a car, Dallas, this is a mansion on wheels. Why do we need all these bells and whistles in a vehicle?"

"I'm so happy you like it," I say, ignoring her feisty tone. "I'm sure you're going to love your room, too."

"Is there a bar in there as well? Because there's one in this car."

"I could put one in there if you're feeling saucy," I say.

She scrunches up her nose and smiles at me. I smile back and hold out my hands to help her out of the car.

This is our relationship in a nutshell.

"This is all very unnecessary," she says, finally letting me help her out of the car and onto solid ground. "It's a hip replacement, not brain surgery."

I open my mouth to say something smart and she stops me mid-breath by raising a finger and cracking, "Not a word out of you."

Gerard grabs Gram's bags and I lead her up the sidewalk and into the house. Ramp, minimal stairs, most living done on one level—all requirements. Thankfully, my real estate agent found the perfect house in what I think will be the perfect location. I knew Gram wouldn't do well in the city, not after living her whole life in a small town.

"But this way, I can make sure you have everything you need," I say.

She hobbles inside the ranch and looks around. "How much did this place cost you?"

"That doesn't matter," I tell her.

"And you've still got your own place in the city?" She waves her hands in the air as if to say *this is ridiculous.* "It's too much."

"Well, you're worth it."

Gerard walks in behind us with the bags. "I'll take these into the bedroom."

Gram looks slightly overwhelmed, and for a minute, I wonder if I've made a mistake. But how else was I going to make sure she was okay? There's the whole post-surgery PT regimen, plus the driving to and from follow-up appointments, not to mention the day-to-day. And while Gram has friends, I know she won't ask for help if she thinks she's being a burden. I've found in these situations, it's best to simply take charge. It's what I do.

So, that's what I did.

I bought the house. I arranged for her things to be shipped. I researched surgeons in the city and physical therapists that would make house calls. After everything this woman has done for me, this is the least I can do for her.

And it would never be payment enough.

"So, you can come in, get your bearings, rest a little, and then tomorrow we'll meet the surgeon and the physical therapist who is going to help get you back into fighting shape."

"Ha! Fighting shape? At my age?" She rolls her eyes. "You have a lot of faith in those doctors."

"I have a lot of faith in you," I say.

"Well, you're sweet to say so."

We're still standing in the entryway, and I realize I need to give her a tour of our new home. But when I turn around, I find her holding up a tabloid magazine with my photo on the cover. "You want to explain this?"

I take it, wondering how these people manage to always find the least flattering photos for the covers of these magazines. Over a photo of me yelling at a ref during a game, is the headline: "Hockey's Bad Boy in the Penalty Box Again" in blocky yellow letters. Underneath, the subtitle: *The Rise and Fall of Dallas Burke.*

"What's to explain?"

"Don't tell me this fight with Mulligan was over that singer," Gram says, doing nothing to hide the disgust in her voice.

Mulligan and up-and-coming rock star Jessie DeSoto met at some party I refused to go to. It was easy for him to exact his revenge on me by sleeping with the woman I was dating. She didn't want a relationship, it turned out. She wanted fame. Fortune. And a man who would do whatever she said.

That wasn't going to be me.

"We broke up."

"Thank goodness," Gram says. "I never liked that little tart."

I laugh. That's such a Gram thing to say. I fold the magazine in half.

"Aren't you going to read what they said?"

"No," I say. "I don't need to discover all the ways they got this wrong."

"They didn't get everything wrong," Gram says, leveling her gaze at me. "Did they?"

No. I'm sure they didn't.

My fight with Aaron Mulligan had very little to do with my ex. Yeah, she cheated on me with him, but that was weeks ago, and honestly, it had been easy to move on. From her, at least. The truth is, that's not the relationship I regret losing. It's the ones with my teammates.

I could blame the division on Mulligan, but that would be a cop-out.

"It's garbage," I say.

"But you did get in a fight," Gram says.

"Yeah, but it wasn't about Jessie," I say. "Not really."

I can see disappointment on Gram's face, and I hate that I've let her down.

"Dallas, I know it's been a rough few years," Gram says. "But this," she takes the magazine from me and holds it up, "isn't going to help. You know that."

"All due respect Gram, but you weren't there. You didn't hear what he said."

My mind twists at the memory of the way Mulligan incited the fight. Sure, he said inappropriate, even vulgar things about Jessie, but that wasn't what set me off. I wasn't protective of her.

"He had it coming."

"I'm sure he did," Gram says. "That boy has always been a first-class jerk. But Dallas, this is your career on the line. Your future. You're hanging by a thread and you're trying to hold on with a pair of scissors."

She studies me for a long moment. "A good woman is what you need."

I scoff. "That's the *last* thing I need," I say. Even if I had time, I don't have the emotional capacity for a relationship.

Gram walks crookedly toward the kitchen, wagging her finger in the air. "A good woman would keep you out of trouble. All of this hotheaded fighting isn't good for your image."

"I don't care about my image," I say.

She turns and faces me. "Well, you should. You've got all the talent in the world, but how are you going to keep endorsement deals with stuff like this following you around? I know the shoe company dropped you after the accident."

How she knows this, I have no idea. Gram is whip smart, but she usually leaves this kind of thing to my business manager, Alicia. I should've known she had her finger on the pulse of my career. She is the reason I was playing, after all.

"And if you're serious about the foundation, you need to get serious about repairing your reputation."

I want to groan. I never should've told Gram my idea to

start a nonprofit. She loved it, which meant she wasn't going to let it go, even if it was illogical for me to think I could pull it off.

She faces me. "Your name is what matters."

"I think my slapshot is what matters, Gram," I say.

She opens the refrigerator and does a quick check of the groceries I've stocked inside. She turns to me, face beaming with approval. "I taught you well."

"Well, you did send me a list."

She grins. "And your stomach will thank me for it. Tonight I'm making manicotti."

Let's. Go. Gram's manicotti is the stuff of legend.

I stretch my arms out wide then pat my stomach. "I eat a lot. You sure we've got enough?"

"Oh, don't you worry. I've got it covered."

"I don't want you slaving away in the kitchen for the rest of the afternoon and evening, Gram. You need to rest."

She blows a raspberry, throws a dish towel at me, and immediately starts pulling things out of the fridge, setting them out on the counter. Then she pauses, looks at me, and relaxes her shoulders. "Thank you. For having me. I promise not to be too much of a pain."

"I think I said that to you once upon a time."

She covers my hand with her much smaller, much frailer one. "Let's see if I do a better job keeping that promise than you did."

I laugh. "Put me to work, old lady."

She starts barking kitchen orders, just like old times, and I can't help but think how nice it is to have her here.

It'll be nice not to come home to an empty house.

The {Rumor} Mill

Spotted at Mo's Coffee Shop: *Local chef and jaded lover Poppy Hart with a new flame! And you aren't going to believe who it is.*

This *Miller* didn't think the middle Hart sister had it in her to start dating after what happened with *he-who-shall-not-be-named*, so imagine my surprise when this photo hit my inbox this morning.

<Photo of Poppy Hart and Dallas Burke at a cozy back table in Mo's Coffee Shop.>

I have it on good authority that Poppy has claimed she is dating the smokin' hot right wing of the Chicago Comets, and while we were skeptical, you can't deny they looked awfully cozy this fine January morning.

Which begs the question. . .how did local wallflower Poppy Hart score the likes of Dallas Burke? Only time will tell if this unlikely match is real, or if Poppy is just another notch on the hockey star's bedpost.

Chapter Four

Poppy

"Spill it, sister."

Raya doesn't look happy.

Eloise, on the other hand, looks positively giddy. We're sitting in our parents' kitchen, and she's staring at the photo someone snapped in the coffee shop, which was posted three minutes ago by The Loveland *Miller.* As in, the writer of *The Mill.* As in, the rumor mill.

Not the cleverest title, but it does its job.

They're basically a gossip monger who has nothing better to do with their time.

My little white lie is big fat news, apparently. I'm sure it's all over town by now, made more believable with photographic proof.

"Is he really as good-looking in person as he is in these pictures?" Eloise asks.

"Yep," I say. I did a little googling after my run-in with Dallas. The restaurant was depressingly slow, and my fingers—and eyes—were itching to look him up.

"*The Mill* says you claimed you're dating," Raya says matter-of-factly.

Margot.

Clearly she's been busy. She must've texted the story to the gossip site's tip line (dubbed *Text the Tea*, another subpar title) the second she walked out of the coffee shop. That or she's the author of the site, though I doubt it.

Whoever writes *The Mill* actually understands how to use the English language. Margot only has an innate understanding of one thing: herself.

"It's not what you think," I say, trying to downplay the drama.

"What's not?" Mom walks in from the other room. "The rumor about you and that fine-looking hockey player?"

I groan. "You, too?"

Mom walks over to the pot of chili on the stove and gives it a stir. "There are photos. But as exciting as it is, I'm not happy about it, Poppy. He is not someone to get mixed up with."

"Aren't you tired of being the subject of town gossip?" Raya asks.

"Yeah, give me a turn, would ya?" My little sister pops a cracker in her mouth and chews it obnoxiously with her mouth open. "I'm a catch."

I know I need to come clean with them, but a part of me loves that even my sisters are wondering if I, Poppy Hart, have somehow managed to snag the ultimate catch—Dallas Burke.

I must be smiling and zoning out because when I drop back in the conversation, my mom and sisters are all staring at me.

"Poppy. Jane. Hart." Raya is the impatient one.

"It was nothing," I elude, trying to physically shrink at the same time. "He. . .sort of. . . came to my rescue is all. With Margot."

A collective groan. Everyone in this room knows all about Margot Richards.

I tell them the whole story about bumping into Dallas, making my split-second decision, and then claiming him as my new boyfriend.

When I finish, I'm peppered with overlapping questions.

Raya: "Why is he even in Loveland? We're an hour from the city."

Eloise: "Was he visiting someone? Does someone here know Dallas Burke?"

Raya: "He's *such* a player. And the fighting! Did you see he punched one of his own teammates last week at practice?"

Eloise: "And that accident last year? Ended Ricky West's career?"

Raya: "You know he was drunk."

Mom: "Is he really going to take you to the Festival of Hearts? I thought you hated that whole thing!"

I hold up my hands in surrender. "I have no more information! That's all I know!"

"Did you get his phone number?" Eloise asks. She reaches for another cracker, and Mom moves the bowl out of her reach.

"Those are for the chili."

"But I'm hungry *now*."

Eloise leans farther over, but Mom comically slides it slowly away without looking at my sister.

"No, I didn't get his phone number." Then, after a thought, I add, "Honestly, I think he just wanted to feel normal. That could be why he's here. Maybe we should all stop speculating about him because really, none of us knows the truth."

"We know he likes women and fighting." Raya, ever the compassionate one.

I groan. "My own family, passing judgment before they've ever even met the guy."

Mom slides into her familiar role as Switzerland whenever we sisters are together. "You're right, Poppy. I don't think he'd be the first person to be unfairly crucified in the media."

"*Thank* you," I announce to the room, unsure why I'm defending a man I don't even know.

Yes I do. We had a moment.

There was a moment, right?

"But," she continues, "I would be more comfortable if you didn't make it your mission to find out everything about him."

I wish my dad wasn't still at work. He'd be on my side—he loves the Comets.

I stand and pull the bowls from the cupboard for dinner. "I'm pretty sure my path won't cross with his ever again, but if it does, you guys'll be the first to know."

They don't believe me.

And neither do I.

Early the next morning, I make my way through town. I notice the swaths of hearts beginning to line the cozy streets of Loveland. The lamp posts will all be decorated with various shades of pink, red, and white, and local artists will come out to paint the windows of the businesses that line Cupid Lane. Residents paint hearts on the sidewalk, and our local post office prepares for an influx of love letters, all needing to be stamped with our special heart-shaped Loveland stamp.

Valentine's Day here is a big deal.

The residents go romance crazy, which has always been, you know, *super* fun, as a single woman.

It starts in early January, barely after Christmas, and it all leads up to a big week-long festival, which culminates in a formal Valentine's Day dance. It's the one time of the year everyone in Loveland gets fancy. Kids, adults, retirees. . .everyone gets in on it.

I'd skip the whole thing altogether, like I usually do, but my restaurant has a booth at the Taste of Loveland, and this one week could bring in more revenue than a typical month.

I have to hand it to whoever decided to lean into the Valentine's Day branding. Granted, the town's name lends itself better to a V-Day celebration rather than, say, Fourth of July, but kudos to the genius city employee who basically created a whole tourist destination based around a holiday most people write off as a consumerist frenzy.

And though I rolled my eyes when they unveiled a new name for Main Street (which I personally found straightforward and functional), Cupid Lane has turned out to be beneficial for many of the businesses downtown.

It's good marketing. Never mind how I feel about it personally.

Our town has become known for its romantical tendencies. Over the years, we've seen proposals, vow renewals, baby reveals (until some expectant couple's exploding balloons coated all the trees in the square with a fine pink mist. After that it was forbidden by city ordinance), and more than our share of weddings.

It's a whole deal.

And this year, my restaurant is going to be right in the middle of it all.

Which is important, given the current financial state of Poppy's Kitchen. One would think having lived here my whole life would warrant me some foot traffic other than my immediate family, but unfortunately there's a lingering truth that explains why many people stay away.

Would the town ever stop treating me like an outcast?

I swing through the same Dallas-Burke-Incident coffee shop, even though I have a perfectly functional espresso machine in my kitchen. I can't explain it—coffee tastes better when someone else makes it. Besides, I like to support my fellow small business owners.

Mindy, the barista who works the morning shift, hands over my peppermint mocha with a knowing glance. "You've been holding out on us."

I frown. "Me? Never!"

She leans over the counter. "I saw the photos on *The Mill.*"

"Yeah, and do we know who took those photos, Mindy?" I ask with intention.

"Oh, it wasn't me. I swear."

"Uh huh."

"Whoever did, I hope they're not going to sell them to one of those tabloid magazines."

I wave her off. "That won't happen." But then, I'm struck with slight panic. "Right?"

She shrugs. "He's a star. And he's got quite a reputation." She grins at me. "What's he look like with his shirt off? Are those abs photoshopped, or are they the real deal?"

My eyes go wide, and I take a step back. "I'm going to go now."

"Oh, I get it. Keep the good stuff to yourself. That's fine. Hey! Maybe you can get him to volunteer for the kissing booth at the festival. The line would be around the block."

I grimace. I've always thought that kissing booths were so unsanitary. And that kissing should be reserved for two people who at least know each other's names. And preferably their height, weight, food allergies, and maybe social security number.

Unlike my youngest sister, I have a tendency to be a little

less *open* when it comes to relationships. Eloise has been enthusiastically kissing boys since kindergarten.

I'm backing away from Mindy, who calls out, "Just think about it, okay? It's for the good of the town!"

I toss her a pathetic wave and push my way out the door and onto the street, hoping Mindy doesn't bring that idea up at the next planning meeting for the festival.

I give a cursory glance both ways down the street—for what, I'm not sure. Knowing that someone photographed me without my knowledge yesterday has me on edge. Also knowing that half the town thinks I'm actually *dating* a famous hockey player has me. . .what? Slightly paranoid or slightly amused?

My thoughts of secret photographers are interrupted by another more horrifying thought—the stacks of bills on the desk in the office of the restaurant. I try to shake the weight of that picture, take a sip of my mocha, and inhale the chilly morning air.

Most of the town isn't up this early, and because of that, it's easily my favorite time of day. Probably why I chose to open a restaurant that serves breakfast.

Thinking of that makes me think of Avi, which floods my skin with hot anxiety. There is just so much to face, so much to figure out, so much debt to. . .

No.

Coffee. Morning. Breathe. Just. . .breathe.

I turn to walk the block to Poppy's Kitchen when I see him. *Dallas*. He's running, and he's making it look easy.

How anyone can make running look easy doesn't make sense to me, but Dallas Burke sure does. His stride is long and easy, and his face is relaxed and all at once, I'm a smitten teenage superfan at a boy band concert.

I'm frozen. I can't move. His beautiful form deserves to be admired.

And, thanks to Mindy, I'm wondering if I should check if his abs are photoshopped. Like, hands-on.

To my absolute shock, he slows his pace when he sees me and removes his AirPods from his ears. He flashes me that smile that knocks me flat. "Poppy."

And he remembers my name.

"Hi," I say.

He nods at my coffee. "I take it you're a regular."

I smile dumbly. *Words gone. Head empty. Heart racing.*

"I was looking for the bike path," he says, thankfully ignoring my stupor.

"Oh, you want to go two blocks over." I point. "That way."

He nods. "Great." He turns to leave, and I blurt, "Hey!"

I mentally facepalm.

He stops and laughs. "Dallas. . .?"

I chuckle, awkwardly. "Right! Yes. '*Dallas*.'" As if I could forget. "Hey, there's a photo of us floating around I thought you should probably know about," I say. "Someone took it when we had coffee yesterday."

He's not even out of breath. If I ran the length of one single block, I'd need an oxygen tank, and this guy is completely unfazed. He sticks his hands on his hips and looks past me. "They have a tendency to pop up like that."

"Well, that must be horrible," I say.

His gaze meets mine, but he doesn't answer.

I feel the need to fill the space with words. "I mean, I feel violated after just one photo. I can't imagine what it's like for you."

He shakes his head. "You get used to it."

There it is again. There's something else there. It's not exactly sadness, but it's something.

"Do you, though? Does anyone, really?"

He smiles, resigned. "It's what I signed up for, right?"

I shrug. "I think you signed up to play hockey."

He lets out a single laugh, a real one. "Tell that to my manager."

I imagine it for a moment—the life he must live. The cameras. The expectation to perform. The rigorous training schedule.

It dawns on me that it's not that different from what I do.

Minus the rigorous training part—although a case could be made that unloading ten 25-pound bags of potatoes from the back of a delivery truck counts.

I'm staring again. And I'm feeling. . .*sorry* for him. It makes no sense given the fact that he is Dallas Burke and I'm a lowly, struggling, small town chef. Between the two of us, I think we know who warrants more pity.

And then, I find myself waist deep in the pool again. Faced with a decision, I take a breath and prepare for the cold shock to my system.

"Hey, this is kind of crazy, but could I cook for you?"

His life seems perfect, but I can see something weighs on him. There's stress etched in a line across his forehead, and I imagine he doesn't have many people he can trust. I know something about that.

I also know that I can cook. And food brings people together in a way that other things can't. With food, cultures are transcended, walls are broken down, heartfelt stories are seasoned and salted.

There's a reason that the kitchen is called "the heart of the home."

It's where love is blended.

At his silence, I start to fumble again. "That's stupid of me. . .I mean, I just thought. . .you did something really nice for me yesterday, and I'd like to return the favor, and food is my love language. Wait. I didn't mean *love*, of course, I just—"

"Promise me you're not secretly a reporter working some sort of angle."

I laugh, willing away the hot flush in my cheeks. "I'm a chef." I nod in the direction of my restaurant. "I own the breakfast and brunch place down the block. Poppy's Kitchen."

He looks down the block. "I didn't make the connection."

"Well, you've known me for about five seconds."

He smiles. "True."

This is an actual conversation. And it's easy. Way easier than I thought it would be.

"You can come in and I can cook for you there, but I was thinking if you're trying to avoid prying eyes, you know, like away from people, I could come to you." I pause, trying to get a read on his bemused face, then add this gem: "Wherever. . .you are. . .living. Currently."

I can make ricotta pancakes with bananas and creme fraiche, but apparently I can't form a coherent sentence. A good reminder not to get cocky thinking conversation with an attractive man is easy. It never has been before, so why should now be any different?

"Poppy, are you asking me out?"

What?!

My eyes widen and on a gasp, I say, "No! Oh, no. Not at all."

Mortification washes over me. I cover my face with my gloved hand, hoping it will teleport me to a deserted island somewhere.

A miniscule part of me, though, imagines *what if I was? And what if he said yes!?* I shut that part up *very* quickly.

"I'm so sorry. I was just thinking, it must be hard, you know?"

"What must be hard?"

"Being famous."

He watches me for a few seconds, and there's a strange expression on his face. He looks away. "Most people want the life I have."

"I don't." I say this a little too quickly.

He looks surprised, like it wasn't what he expected to hear.

"Sounds like a lot of stress to perform. To be on. So much emphasis is put on what other people think." I shrug and look down at my storefront. "I kind of love that when I make a dish and it bombs, I can take something out or put something else in. And there's grace to try again."

I half-believe what I'm saying, preaching to myself. Being a chef is pretty stressful, owning a restaurant, doubly so.

Especially now.

The drop in his shoulders is barely detectable as he seems to contemplate that. "All right, *Pops*."

I make a face. "That nickname doesn't have to stick. Unless you want me to call you Sugar Bear."

"I could get used to it." He grins, then inhales a deep breath. "If you promise me you're not a secret tabloid spy, I'd love for you to make me dinner."

"Great," I say, and then repeat it. "Great."

I pause.

I realize I didn't think I'd get this far in my plan. Because in typical Poppy fashion, there was no plan to begin with. My method tends to be more *open mouth, say stuff*.

"Any food sensitivities I should know about?"

"No," he says. "I'm a carnivore and eat just about anything."

I smile just thinking of the possibilities. "Ooh, my favorite type of person to cook for."

"Are you okay making dinner for three?" he asks. "I've got, uh, a house guest."

I pin my smile in place. "Of course!"

What did I think, I was going to have a secret romantic meal with a famous hockey player? I am seriously out of my league here, and I know it. But I can't help but feel that Dallas Burke needs a friend. Maybe I'm wrong though.

Maybe he already has a friend.

No going back now. "Are you and your house guest free tonight?"

He nods. "Yep." He hands over his phone. "Put your number in here, and I'll text you the address."

I'm giving Dallas Burke my phone number. So he can give me his address. I'm going to his house.

I do as I'm told and hand the phone back to him.

"I've got to get to practice—but I'll plan on seeing you tonight?"

I smile and nod.

He tucks the phone in his pocket, puts the AirPods back in his ears, gives a small wave, and runs off.

As I watch him go, I notice a few people who have gathered inside the coffee shop, staring out through the front windows. They're all watching me with a strange curiosity.

I can imagine their conversations.

What is he *doing with* her?

I take a sip of my drink and start off toward the restaurant, wondering the exact same thing.

Chapter Five

Poppy

"What is going on?" Miguel, my other chef, is whipping up the third batch of French toast, wiping sweat from his brow. It's the same question that's been racing through my mind since I came in the back door to the kitchen this morning.

Selena, one of my best servers, pushes through the door to the kitchen. "Poppy, did you start dating a famous hockey player without telling anyone?"

I groan. "No, it's. . ." I stop. "Wait."

I peek out the door from the kitchen to the dining room. There's only one table that's empty, and there are four more people waiting by the check-in.

"Why are there so many people here?"

I don't wait for an answer because I know what it is, and I say the quiet thing out loud.

"Because people think I'm dating Dallas?"

Selena gives a sly smile. "First name basis? Huh."

I check the temperatures of the ovens and wipe off the wait station. "It's not a thing!"

"Sounds like it is," Selena says. "They're all asking about you. And Mrs. Warren wants me to tell you to be careful because 'that boy is a womanizer who is going to break your heart.'"

I shake my head. "Unreal."

"What do you want me to tell them?" Selena hands over an order to Miguel.

"Nothing," I say. "It's nobody's business who I date."

"Except the entire nation when it ends up on TMZ," Selena says.

"It won't," I say. "It's nothing. It'll blow over when he leaves town." Though, I have no idea when he's leaving town. Or *if* he's leaving town. I've really made a mess of things.

"Well, play it up now," Miguel says. "We haven't had this kind of business in months."

This hits me.

He's right. We haven't. My restaurant has struggled here in Loveland. After everything that happened with Avi, the truth is, I'm completely upside-down. Restaurant margins are slim at best, and I can't bring myself to even consider how red my bottom line is.

If I really have a fake romance with Dallas Burke and a mention in *The Mill* to thank for a full house and a line waiting to be seated, it's not something to just brush off.

But good gravy, that's selfish and deceitful and about fifteen other horrible things.

The bad thing about debt is that the anxiety makes you compromise.

I really thought our town would do better at making a celebrity feel normal. Apparently, I gave us all too much credit. Myself included, because I'd been tripping all over myself since I first bumped into Dallas. I'm shocked I didn't actually drool on him.

The door to the kitchen flings open and Raya walks in. She's dressed for work in a sleek pair of high-waisted, wide-leg black dress pants and a red, cowl-neck sweater peeks out of her chic black coat. She's wearing red heels, which are wholly impractical in this weather, but I don't think she's in the mood for my opinions on the subject.

Raya is stunning. Her hair is two shades darker than mine and two times as shiny. It's long and silky, like the women in shampoo commercials, and she might be the only person I know who can pull off bright red lipstick.

I table those thoughts the second she stomps over to the stove where I'm cooking and shows me a new photo. This one was taken this morning, right outside Mo's. The caption reads: *"New romance for Playboy Dallas Burke?"*

"Explain, please." Raya's pointed brow tells me she means business. "You said this was nothing."

In the image, posted on *The Mill's* Instagram account, I'm handing Dallas's phone back to him. He's wearing that trademark smile. My hair is in a messy bun, and I'm dressed for work, because if I'm going to have any moment in the spotlight, of course I'm not going to look good doing it.

"I bumped into him on the street this morning," I say.

"And his phone accidentally fell into your hands, where your fingers randomly hit the numbers of your phone number, in order, and it was saved in his phone?" Raya is on a roll this morning, and it's not even nine. "That's what you're going with?"

"Well, no. It wasn't random."

She follows me around the counter in the middle of the kitchen, even though I'm trying my best to scoot away.

"So you did give him your number."

Was this a test? Had I just failed?

She stops. "Wait. Did he *ask* for it?"

I grab a spatula and slide it under a crackling slice of French toast on the griddle top. "Yes, I gave him my number." I flip the French toast, and it sizzles in the hot butter. "And yes. He asked for it."

Raya's face looks as though the government just announced aliens are real and some of them are planning to try out for the Olympic downhill skiing team.

"I'm cooking him dinner tonight."

"You're *what*?!" Selena gasps. "So this is legit? You're *dating* Dallas Burke?"

"No," I say, calmly, even though there is a very real part of me that wants to squeal like a middle schooler and jump around in a circle. I never understood why girls did that. But now I get it. "It's just dinner." I don't mention it's dinner for three. I should, but I don't.

"Poppy." Raya walks over to me and puts a hand on my shoulder, turning me to her. She has slipped into big sister mode. I hear it in her voice. "This man is not someone to get hung up on."

"Raya." I mock her tone and take her hand off my shoulder. "I am not hung up on him."

And I'm really not. Yes, he's very pretty to look at, but the truth is, my offer to make him dinner had nothing to do with me at all.

I want to try to explain how he looked, and how I felt, and. . .that I just thought he would appreciate it. That there are no ulterior motives or shady desires or anything like that.

I make good food, and good food is what he needs.

But I don't say that, because I know she won't buy it.

I want Dallas to know there are good people in the world. People who won't ask him for favors or try to sponge off of him or take his photo and sell it to the highest bidder.

Besides, he has a *house guest*, who I assume will knock me back down to Earth without so much as a word.

"This really is nothing," I say, hearing a little too much protest in my own voice.

She pulls away from me. "You've got a whole restaurant full of people who disagree."

The fact that I am profiting off someone else's fame—or an outright lie—does rub me wrong. I need to clarify the situation, and if that means making an announcement to a room full of paying customers, that's what that means. Even if it costs me their business. I pull a dish towel from a hook nearby and wipe my hands on it. "Fine. If I need to set the record straight, I will."

I whip the towel absentmindedly over my shoulder. "Miguel, can you watch these?" I nod to the stove, and Miguel gives me a quick salute.

I push through the kitchen doors and out into the dining room. The buzz in here is electric. Every table is full. The wait is out the door.

In my periphery, I notice a few people at tables near me try to discreetly point in my direction—unsuccessfully. I look at them full on, and they go back to their conversation, trying to look innocent.

Selena and Raya come up behind me.

"You were saying?" Raya asks.

"I've never seen it like this in here, " I say. "Ever."

"Go ahead," my sister says, putting a sarcastic hand on my shoulder and motioning to the room. "Set the record straight."

I scan the crowd. This was what I'd always dreamed of for Poppy's Kitchen. A place where people would spend their mornings, eating my food, catching up with friends, just being. . .comfortable. The low hum of chatter just a little louder than the music coming through the speakers.

It's wrong of me, but I can't bring myself to tell everyone

that if they're here because of Dallas, then they're here under false pretenses.

If I do come clean, all it will do is prove that I'm not trustworthy.

Again.

That label is what I've been trying to shed ever since the whole debacle with my ex-boyfriend.

I turn and push back into the kitchen. "This is crazy."

Raya follows me. Selena, thankfully, doesn't. "It *is* crazy. Especially given everything that's been in the news about your new boyfriend."

"Like what?" I ask, not because he's my new boyfriend, but because I'm genuinely curious.

She pulls out her phone and types in what I can only assume is Dallas's name.

"He's got a new girlfriend every week, for one thing," Raya says. "Supermodels, Poppy. Actresses. Rock stars." She scrolls. "No serious relationships. Involved in a suspicious car accident. Very hot-tempered on the ice."

"And off the ice?"

Raya's eyes jump to mine. "He is not a good guy, Poppy. Not for you."

I clamp my jaw shut so tightly I think I might chip a tooth. I feel like I'm being reprimanded, and I didn't even do anything wrong.

"Well, then it's a good thing he's not my boyfriend, isn't it?" I say. "I hardly even know him. I already told you this."

She gives me a stern look. "Please. I'm your sister, and I care about you. So please." She stares right into my eyes. "Keep it that way."

Raya holds my gaze for three very long seconds, then leaves, and I'm still for a moment. Then, my owner-chef brain kicks in, and I take over the kitchen. For some, the choreographed chaos that happens behind the kitchen doors at a restaurant would be completely overwhelming, but for me, it's where I come alive. As I go back to cooking—certain that I'm going to collapse when this morning ends—my thoughts are conflicted.

I know Raya is right about Dallas. His life and mine would not complement one another. And I know it's dishonest for me to let people believe we're together.

I know I should stay away from him.

There's just one problem. I don't want to.

Chapter Six

Dallas

After practice, I find Alicia waiting for me in the locker room.

"You know this is a men's locker room, right?" I ask.

"You know I couldn't care less, right?" She gives me a wry grin. I know this is true, because my manager would eat any of these guys for lunch. "When you bought that house in the country for your grandma, I thought it was sweet. I tried to float the story to the press, but nobody picked it up. All anyone wants to talk about is your ongoing feud with Mulligan and what it's doing to the team."

I tug my shirt up over my head and toss it in the bin. "Good. I don't need the press knowing about anything that has to do with my grandma. I didn't do it so they'd write about it."

"I know, Dallas, but you could use some good PR right now."

"Nobody is going to believe a feel-good story when it comes to me," I say. "You know that."

I've known that for years. When I started in the league, I

was hotheaded and made some bad choices. Okay, a *lot* of bad choices. I hurt people, broke a lot of hearts, and an equal number of jaws. Didn't matter who it was, I treated them people equally horrible.

When some reporter dubbed me the "bad boy of hockey," the name stuck, and it's been my public persona ever since.

Then there was the accident nine months ago that nearly ended my career. Funny thing is, it probably saved my life. It was the wake-up call I needed to get my life on the straight and narrow. A stark reminder of my own mortality.

Of course, that wasn't the story the media wanted to tell. Not when one of my teammates lost his career as a result of that crash. Not with all the speculation that I'd been drinking, that I'd somehow paid off the cops to look the other way, as if that would even be possible. Not when it was my own teammate leading the charge in the smear campaign against me.

It was perfect fodder for the press, who wanted to focus on my failed relationships and my short fuse to feed into the image that I used to deserve.

Redemption, it turns out, is a fairy tale.

Alicia had tried harder than anyone to help people see that I'd changed, but often, any progress she made would be undone. Usually by me. I still had a temper, I still made the occasional poor choice, and I still found myself in the wrong place at the wrong time.

For instance, letting Mulligan get the better of me.

Alicia called the fight "career threatening." But I was only defending myself. No sense explaining that to anyone, though. People believe what they want to believe.

"What's the deal with this woman?" Alicia flips her phone around to face me, revealing a series of photos of me in Loveland. In the coffee shop. On the street. All with Poppy.

"There's no deal," I say. "She's just a girl I met at a coffee shop. Helped her out of a little situation."

Alicia turns the phone around and reads, "Local sources say hockey's bad boy Dallas Burke is spending time with small town chef Poppy Hart. Is true love blooming or is Hart destined for another broken heart?"

"Once again, they're getting it wrong," I say. "And that's a terrible sentence."

Around us, the guys start the process of showering, nobody even slightly fazed by Alicia's presence in the locker room. Everyone is used to her by now. Jericho Stephens walks by, completely naked. Oh, he has a towel. In his hand.

Alicia doesn't even bat an eyelash.

I point in his general direction. "That really doesn't bother you?" I ask. "I'm bothered on your behalf."

She shakes her head. "If the world knew what a prude you were, they'd be shocked."

And it's true. When I made the decision to change my life, I changed it completely. Gave up alcohol. Gave up the parties. Gave up the nameless, faceless women. When I met Jessie DeSoto, an up-and-coming rock star, I was actually drawn to her. She had that "tortured artist" thing going on, and I thought we might have a future. I had no idea she was just using me, which made me a first-class idiot because all the signs were there. I thought we were in a real relationship.

Turns out, I was nothing more than a publicity stunt.

I chalked it up to karma paying me back. But it made me realize that right now, a relationship is not what I need.

"Look, you need to be careful," Alicia says. "We don't need any more public displays of aggression, or fighting with fans, or anything else. And you especially don't need to drag this girl into your mess. She seems really girl-next-door, she'd be totally overwhelmed by"—she holds out her hand and indicates to me, up and down—"all of this. You need to lay low."

"I am laying low," I say. "I'm taking my grandma to get her hip replaced. I bought a house in the middle of nowhere, for crying out loud. How much lower can a guy get?"

"And yet. . ." She holds up the phone again.

I sigh. "I could never go outside. Would that make you happy?"

"Just don't hurt this girl or give her any reason to come after you in the press."

I shake my head as I sit to pull my socks off. "It's not like that."

"It better not be," she says. "I'm having a hard enough time cleaning up last month's mess. We're so close to a huge deal with HydroIce. And you aren't getting any younger, so securing these deals is important."

"Boy, you're just a breath of fresh air in here today, Alicia." I give her a mocking smile, and she rolls her eyes.

"*HydroIce*, Dallas," she says, like I didn't hear her the first time. "They want to position themselves as the top sports drink on the market. We want this. So you need to stay focused."

"I'd be a lot more focused if you'd stop showing me pictures like that," I say.

She waves me off as she turns to go. On her way out, she tosses back, "Hey Jericho, if you're not going to cover anything up, can you at least try to cover your guy on defense so he doesn't score a pair of goals in 58 seconds? How about a little hustle, big guy?"

The locker room erupts with collective hoots and hollers, followed by several guys chucking their shirts and towels at him. She's a piece of work, that one. I'm glad she's on my side.

An hour later, I'm pulling into the parking lot of the hospital in the city. Gerard is bringing Gram to her appointment to meet the surgeon, and later, she'll head back to Loveland to meet with a physical therapist who will come to the house to work with her. I've also got an overnight nurse who'll be there when I'm traveling. I think I've covered all my bases, but I hope I'm not forgetting anything.

I want Gram to feel like a queen. She deserves it.

She was the worst casualty of my poor choices. Of all the women I've disappointed in my life, she was the one I regret hurting the most. She always believed in me. Always.

I needed to prove to her that I'd changed. That I was committed to being the man she'd raised me to be. I know there's a part of her that blames herself for the way my father turned out—and I often wonder if I'm her chance at redemption.

I cannot let her down again. I want to make her proud. The fight last month certainly didn't do the trick.

While nothing bad has been written about me and Poppy—yet—I just want to stay under the radar. It's part of why I subleased my apartment in the city and moved to Loveland. The other part, of course, is Gram. She's going to need help recovering, whether she wants to admit it or not.

I can't put my career on hold, not in the middle of the season. But I'll be there for her when I can, and that's better than nothing. I couldn't stand the thought of her going through this alone, trying to get around her house in Florida, refusing to accept help from anyone.

We meet the doctor, a man I've researched extensively, and Gram, of course, gives the guy the third degree—*How many of these surgeries have you done? How much gas are you going to give me? How many people have died?* He's brusque with his answers, and she lectures him on his bedside manner. I laugh to myself, because you just have to know her to understand her. I try to explain that he doesn't need to be friendly. He needs to be good at his job. And he is. The best.

"Well, he can still be nice," Gram hisses at me, as if the surgeon isn't sitting right there.

I can tell she's nervous. She'll never admit it, but a lot of her fear comes out in inane questions and crankiness. It's part of her charm.

As we leave the hospital, I tell Gram she's off the hook for cooking tonight.

"Oh?" she says. "You don't want my fried chicken?"

I love her fried chicken, but I don't want her to feel like she needs to take care of me. For once, I want her to be waited on, fussed over, looked after. I want her to relax. I know it's against her nature, but a guy can hope.

"I have a friend who offered to come cook for us," I say.

Gram raises a single eyebrow. "A *friend*?"

"Someone I met in town."

"A woman."

"Yes, but just a friend."

Gram stares me down. "I told you last night you needed a good woman, and you said nothing about already having one."

"It's not like that, Gram."

She *tsks* as she clambers into the back seat of the black SUV. "It's never like that, Dallas." She looks at me. "Until it is."

"I'll see you tonight." I go to close the door, but stop short and give her a pointed look. "Promise you'll be on your best behavior."

"I can't do that," she says, then breaks into a wicked smile.

Poppy is going to have her hands full of more than just dinner tonight.

I have a feeling, though, she just might win the old lady over.

Chapter Seven

Poppy

"I need to be straight with you," I say the second Dallas opens the door to his massive, sprawling ranch house at the edge of town.

He grins. "Why don't you come in first?"

My arms are loaded with supplies. I'm a one-trip person. I'll cut off circulation in my forearms before I make a second trip.

Dallas reaches out to take a tote, but I step back. "This is like Jenga. If you pull the wrong bag, it's all going to come down."

He steps back. "I feel like I should help."

"Just point the way to the kitchen."

"Follow me." He starts down the hall from the entryway.

"What, no butler?" I tease.

He shoots me an amused look.

"Sorry," I say. "This mansion life is all new to me."

He chuckles. "It's not a mansion."

"Uh-huh."

"It's a one-story ranch."

"A *sprawling* ranch. And three times the size of the house where I grew up," I say.

"It's just a house." He leads the way to the most beautiful chef's kitchen I've ever seen.

"Right," I say under my breath. "Just a house." I want to ask why he bought it, what he's doing here, and can I move in and make this kitchen my own personal haven, but instead, I snake my hands through the loops of the tote bags, setting them on the counter.

"Do you cook?"

"Unfortunately, no," he says. "The kitchen came with the house."

"What. A. Waste." I smile at him and do a slow turn around the space. "This is unbelievable." I'm not sure what I like best—the double oven, the large gas stove, the side-by-side oversized refrigerator, or the giant island at the center of the room. The cabinets are a mix of black and white, with gray-and-white marble counters and a white tile backsplash. Empty wooden shelves on the wall flank a large, stainless vent hood over the oven, and there's so much space to move around, I'd be happy to grab a cot, pitch a tent, and live out the rest of my days in this one room.

"You like it?" Dallas asks.

I shake my head. "I love it. It's incredible." I'm still trying to process what it would be like to have access to a space like this at my fingertips when my eyes reach Dallas, and I remember why I'm here.

"What was the thing you wanted to be straight with me about?" he asks.

"Oh, right," I say. "The whole town thinks we're dating. There's this local gossip website called '*The Mill*,' where someone who thinks they're Gossip Girl or Lady Whistledown or TMZ or whatever shares *fun little tidbits* about people's lives, and, well—" I open my phone and show him the photo of us. He doesn't look all that surprised.

I go on. "And. . .they all came into the restaurant today, probably hoping to see you or something. I had more customers today than I've had in the last three months."

He stares at me, clearly not bearing the weight of my confession.

"I just wanted you to know that I'm profiting off of a pretend relationship with you. Because I feel shady about it. I mean, you did me this great service of helping me with Margot, and now everyone thinks we're actually a couple."

"And you didn't want to tell them the truth?" He asks this lightly, but I still feel a little embarrassed.

My eyes go wide. "No! I haven't had that many people in the restaurant at the same time since we opened."

He laughs. "So, you're telling me now so you can ease your guilty conscience."

"Yes," I say, then, a groan. "See? Shady! I *will* set them all straight. I just. . .kind of. . ." I wince, "need the business."

He holds up a hand. "It's fine. I'm actually surprised anyone can benefit from using my name at all anymore."

"Because of your sordid past?" I start unpacking the groceries, not realizing that I'm unpacking words from my mouth in the same haphazard way. "The partying. The fighting. The *women.*" I pause. "The accident."

I set out the meat, still wrapped in brown butcher paper, and realize that it's been silent for a good ten seconds. Upon this realization, I don't look up. I just stare at the potatoes.

I hazard a glance, and he's just watching me. I wonder how to extract my foot from my mouth.

"Yeah, because of that." He tilts his head slightly. "Nobody's ever come right out and, you know, said the quiet thing out loud before."

"Sorry," I say. "I blurt when I'm nervous." Not like I have any room to talk. My past was almost as sordid as his.

Okay, not really, but I have my share of skeletons. Or rather, one very prominent skeleton. Named Avi.

"You googled me, huh?" he asks.

I cringe. "Guilty."

"So, you went from not knowing who I am to knowing everything the *press* says I am in one single day."

I hear his disdain for the media in his voice. "I take it they got some stuff wrong?"

"They got all of it wrong." The voice comes from behind me, and when I spin around, I see a short, older woman standing in the doorway. Her short hair is dark with flecks of gray, and she wears glasses.

This is his houseguest?

My eyes flick over to Dallas, who suddenly looks shy and boyish. It's a completely different version of him than the one I've seen online, that's for sure. It suits him. "Poppy, this is my Gram. Gram, this is my friend Poppy."

Friend? I'm Dallas Burke's *friend*? It's not as great as *my girlfriend*, but I'll take it. I've never been friends with a famous person before.

"The woman in the photos," his grandma says.

"The photos on the internet?" Dallas asks. "When did you see those?"

"I'm old, I'm not stupid. I have TikTok."

I laugh. *I* don't even have TikTok.

She limps toward a chair around a large kitchen table and Dallas moves to help her. She holds up a hand that stops him. "I'm not an invalid yet."

Dallas glances at me. "Gram's having her hip replaced."

"Ah," I say.

"It's why we're here," he says. "In Loveland."

My eyes drift from Dallas to his grandma, and I start to see what's happened here. Dallas Burke, the rogue hockey player, has bought a house in a small town so he can be close to his grandma while she recovers from surgery.

Google didn't mention that.

His grandma must see the moment it all makes sense, because she nods and points a finger at me. "Like I said, they got it all wrong."

"Not all of it, unfortunately," Dallas adds, a tinge embarrassed.

I glance at him, and he looks away.

"But it doesn't matter," he says. Then, to his grandma, "Are you comfortable? I think you should sit in the living room."

He reaches out to help her and she smacks his hand away. "I think you should go sit in traffic."

Oh my goodness, she might be one of my favorite people on this planet and I've known her for all of four minutes.

She looks at me. "Do you see what I have to put up with? So much fussing."

I laugh and tuck the reusable tote bags away as I sort through the ingredients.

"I'm going to help the chef," she says.

Dallas glances at me and shakes his head so subtly I almost miss it.

"Actually, I'd love to cook for you both," I say. "You can pretend I'm not even here."

She frowns. "Why would we do that? You're our guest."

"I'm paying Dallas back for doing me a huge favor." I glance at him. "Which has turned out to be more than one favor, if the business at my restaurant today was any indication."

"It's fine," he says. "I'll happily give you my endorsement."

"For a fee," Gram says with a wink.

I get busy preparing the food, and I have the distinct impression the older woman is sizing me up.

"Is your restaurant in trouble?" she asks.

"Isn't that kind of a personal question?" Dallas asks.

I give a slight wave. "It's okay. I don't mind." Then, to his grandma, "Yes. It's. . .struggling a little." It's an understatement, but there's no sense letting on just how bad things are.

Dallas doesn't need to know I'm a complete failure as well as a social pariah.

"Restaurants are a hard business," she says. "I had a friend who had a restaurant for years and never turned a profit."

I try to hide a shock of anxiety. "That sounds regrettably familiar." My stomach drops, because I'd been *so sure* mine wouldn't fail. Dallas must notice—because I'm terrible at hiding things—and he puts a hand on Gram's shoulder.

"Gram, bedside manner, huh?"

I don't like the thought of my place being a complete failure, but I do like his grandmother's directness. I straighten and say, "Well, I got a little boost this morning, thanks to Dallas." I think of the line of customers waiting to be seated. I imagine a few more weeks with that kind of business. I'd have to hire more staff to keep up, but I'd have no problem paying my rent this month, which was saying something since I still owed a piece for last month.

"I. . ." I gingerly step into this part, "sort of told someone we were dating yesterday." I smile weakly at Dallas, then turn the knob on the stove and hear it *click click click* before the flame pops on. "It was not my finest moment."

"Ah," Gram says. "So, this is a guilt dinner?"

I laugh. "Yes! And I will come clean. I promise."

But how?

This town needed reasons to believe in me—to support me. Revealing that I concocted a fake relationship with a huge hockey star was going to accomplish exactly the opposite of that.

"Well, I thought you two looked cute together in those photos," Gram says.

I feel my cheeks heat—and not because of the stovetop.

"I have an idea," she says.

"Poppy, beware. That's never good." I think Dallas is kidding when he says this, but then I look at him and see that he's semi-serious.

"The way I see it, you two can help each other out," Gram says.

I frown. "Dallas can help me, but I have nothing to offer him."

"Oh, don't be so sure," Gram says. "Dallas could use someone like you in his life."

"Gram, I told you—"

"You're not dating, I know, I know. . ." Then, to me with an eye roll, "Apparently he's sworn off women." She huffs. "He's not interested in romance."

Then what is *he interested in?*

My mind is working overtime not to have impure thoughts. Mostly I'm wondering if he always looks this good. And smells this good. Yes, I am this shallow.

"People are obviously already interested in you two," Gram says. "I see an opportunity here."

My eyes dart to Dallas long enough to see skepticism on his face.

"Gram, what are you getting at?" He crosses his big, beautiful arms over his chest, and I forget for a moment that I'm holding a knife.

"I know Alicia has been trying to repair your reputation for months," Gram says. "But she sucks at it."

I can't help it. I laugh.

Gram looks at me. "Well, sorry. She does. A few hours with Google and the photos of you two floating around the gossip sites, and it's pretty clear to me what needs to happen."

"What are you suggesting?" Dallas asks.

Gram waves her hand between Dallas and me. "You two date. For real."

I inadvertently chop a head of lettuce in half *way* harder than I intend, landing the knife on the cutting board with a loud *ka-CHUNK*.

"I'm sorry, what?" Me? Date Dallas Burke? For real? His grandma was off her gourd if she thought he'd go for that.

"It'll be like Richard Gere and Julia Roberts in that hooker movie," she says.

"Whoa!" Dallas shakes his head, then looks at me. "I'm sorry."

"What? I'm not saying you"—she indicates to me— "are a hooker."

"*Gram.*" He looks mortified. "I don't think that's what they're called anymore."

She continues, unabashed. "I'm saying you date Dallas to help your restaurant and you date Poppy to help your image."

"You just met her," he says. "Heck, I just met her. What makes you think this is a good idea?"

I numbly reach over and turn off the burners. I have a feeling if I don't turn them off now I'll forget about them completely.

Gram slowly turns and cocks her head at Dallas. "You actually think she's got some underhanded motive?"

"Well, no, I. . ."

"You think she's going to stab you in the back?"

He's on his heels. "I mean, no, I don't think..."

"You think she's pretty?"

"Yes, she's beautif. . ." he blurts that out, and abruptly stops, caught.

My brain is glitching right now. Like trying to find the sailboat in the stereographic picture, or when you use the word *slacks* so often it stops feeling like a real word.

She shrugs, palms up, as if to say *I rest my case, Your Honor.*

He looks at me.

I look back.

He makes a face, as if to ask a silent question.

I make a face, as if to say *I don't understand what's happening right now.*

He hesitates, and I think it's an okay time to start talking—but he starts talking at the same time.

Him: "I'm not sure. . ."

Me: "I don't think. . ."

Together: "I'm sorry, go ahead."

We go back to staring.

"Good grief, you're already acting like a married couple, for Pete's sake."

Like smacking the steering wheel in horror movies finally gets the sputtering car started, my brain decides to jumpstart and focus.

I start chopping the remaining lettuce. "It's. . .an idea. A good one, maybe, but this kind of thing never ends well."

"Oh, sure, Richard Gere on the fire escape is a terrible ending," Gram says with a huff.

"This isn't a movie, Gram," Dallas says. "In real life, there's no reason for two people to fake a relationship."

Gram laughs. "That's funny. And false. You know half of the people in Hollywood are in relationships for publicity's sake."

"Well, we're not in Hollywood." He looks at me.

"And I'm a *terrible* liar," I say.

"But it wouldn't be a lie," she says, "not *really*. You would actually go out on dates. Public appearances. That Valentine festival thing this town is so big on."

I glance at Dallas. "How long has she been in town?"

"Hours," he says.

"Impressive," I say.

"It's a good idea, and you both know it," Gram says. "If you think about it for two seconds, you'll agree."

But I won't. Already, people are asking why in the world Dallas would be dating someone like me. He is a man who dates supermodels and rock stars. I'm about as plain as they come, and my size two has a one in front of it. Dallas doesn't need to pretend to tell the world he's slumming it with a townie.

I'm mortified this lie has blown up as much as it has, but what Gram is suggesting would put everything on a whole other level.

I try to get back to the food. "Besides, I still don't think this plan is mutually beneficial," I say. "I'm not. . .his type." I really don't want to spell it out.

Gram looks at me. "Not his type? His type is airbrushed."

I look at Dallas, who looks equal parts embarrassed, ambushed, and like she's not wrong.

"You're smart. You're pretty. You've got your own business. And you've got that girl-next-door thing going on," she says, and then turns to Dallas, "which is exactly what my grandson needs."

Dallas looks a little like he'd rather be having a root canal. It's probably preferable to having people think he's dating someone like me. Gram might not see it, but Dallas does. I would embarrass him, or at the very least, not live up to the standards of everyone else he's dated. Can you imagine the talk in the locker room if he showed up somewhere with *me*?

I open the bag of potatoes and begin washing the dirt off of them.

Gram continues to needle. "This would be good for you, Dallas. The accident cost you a lot."

He looks away at the mention of it.

I know all about the accident thanks to an article Raya sent me on her lunch break. Dallas was driving home from a party with his teammate Ricky West when they were hit by a truck that blew a stop sign. Because they were coming from a party, there was a lot of speculation as to whether or not Dallas had been drinking. Especially because Ricky was plastered.

I don't know the whole story, but some people believe that Dallas had handlers pay someone off to avoid a DUI. With his alleged history, it wasn't a far stretch.

Looking at him now, I have no idea where the truth lies. But I can tell there's a lot of guilt and shame around his broken reputation.

"You know it's true," Gram says. "Nine months, and they're still talking about it. Maybe this would give people something else to yap about."

Locally, yes. But on Dallas's level? Unlikely. Unless it was to marvel at how far the hockey superstar had fallen.

Dallas must feel cornered, because he stands and says, "Gram, let's get you set up in the living room so Poppy can cook." He helps her to her feet, and as they leave the kitchen, she stops and looks at me.

"Think about it, " she says. "This would be good for your business. And you two wouldn't even have to get it on." She wags her eyebrows. "Unless you want to, of course."

"Okay, that's good, let's go." Dallas shakes his head and they exit the room, which is, I think, the first time I exhale since Gram proposed her crazy idea.

I came here trying to figure out how to make up for a

momentary lapse in judgment. Now she wants me to expand on it?

Dallas returns a few minutes later, just as I'm turning the burners back on when I should really be sticking my whole head in the freezer.

"I'm so sorry." I fall into the familiar stream of opening my mouth and letting whatever pour out like a faucet. "I am totally willing to admit that if I'd never grabbed your arm in that line, and if I never told Margot we were dating, your Gram never would have had this idea and we wouldn't be in this mess at all."

"Don't give it a second thought," he says. Then, after a moment, he adds, "It's not the craziest idea I've ever heard."

Surely, he's just being kind.

"I really hate to think that your restaurant isn't going as well as you hoped. I'll give it a glowing endorsement anytime you want me to. Would that help?"

Yes! *Way* easier. He doesn't need to pretend to date me. Pssh.

But then, what does he get out of it?

"You don't have to do that," I say. "I'm honestly just so thankful for the save yesterday, and happy to cook for you and your grandma."

I pause. And then, after a beat, I glance at him, aware that I'm about to ask a crazy question. "Would it. . .I mean. . .would it really help you? Like with the press, or the fans, or whoever?"

"No. Don't even go there. We don't need to turn this into *Pretty Woman*," he says.

I stop moving and look at him. "I think the media got it wrong about you."

He looks away. "It doesn't matter."

I pull a face. "It kind of does."

"The truth is, Poppy, I'd consider doing this as a favor to you, but I don't want you to get dragged into my mess."

At that exact moment, his phone buzzes on the counter. He groans. "It's my manager. Sorry." He takes a step toward the living room. "Gram, did you tell Alicia about your crazy idea?"

No response.

He looks at me. "She texted Alicia."

I can't help but smile. I lean toward him and whisper loudly, "I like your grandma."

With a shake of his head, he steps out of the room to take the call from his manager, and I try to concentrate on cooking and not on the fact that I feel like Alice discovering Wonderland for the first time.

Maybe Lewis Carroll should've tried fake dating a hockey player instead of psychedelic drugs.

If we pretended to have a relationship—me and *Dallas-for-the-love-of-all-that-is-holy-Burke*—it *would* be excellent for my business, which, let's be honest, really needs a miracle to survive. But I'm not convinced dating an ordinary girl is going to have any effect on his reputation at all.

Why would anyone outside of Loveland even care?

Maybe an endorsement from him would keep people's interest long enough to make a dent. Though, let's be honest, the second it comes out that we aren't dating, I'm going to look so incredibly foolish, and that will undo any attention Dallas gave me or the restaurant.

Chapter Eight

Dallas

For the first two years of my pro career, Gram was involved in every single decision I made.

She helped me with my agent. She vetted a nutritionist. She found Alicia. And she told them all how it was going to be. Gram was whip-smart, and almost always right.

Drove Alicia crazy.

As she got older and my career took off, Gram started to step back. She said it was getting to be too much, and I was smart enough to make my own decisions, for better or worse.

Apparently, she's just stepped right back in.

Because the second she saw the photo of me and Poppy, I could see the twinkle in her eyes again. And, like a dog that's locked on to the ham sandwich you absentmindedly set on the edge of the counter. . .she was going to get what she wanted.

Alicia confirmed my suspicion with her phone call, telling me she'd had a change of heart and thought the idea of fake dating a small town restaurant owner was, in her words, "a brilliant one." She had a whole pitch prepared in a matter of about ten minutes, and she was pulling out all the stops.

This was exactly the kind of thing I should've expected, but also something I never saw coming. That's Gram in a nutshell.

She set the wheels in motion seconds after she got the idea, and now they're tag-teaming me. According to Alicia, she and Gram both believed this, in her words, "could do wonders for my *challenging* reputation."

I couldn't give a rip about my image. I don't care. I do what I do, and people say what they want. I could be a saint that just saved a basketful of puppies from a burning building and people would still find a way to call PETA on me.

I have catered to people long enough, and it's clear I'm not going to change anyone's opinion of me any time soon.

Then why on earth am I thinking about doing this?

Earlier, on the street, Poppy mentioned grace. From what I understand, grace is being forgiven for messing up—even when you don't deserve it.

I can't relate.

I don't even understand the concept.

My mistakes are played over and over in high definition, on a 24-hour news cycle, on a national stage. There is simply no grace for someone like me.

And I'm not looking for pity from anyone, either. The things I did in my past were decisions that I made; it wasn't like someone made them for me, or I was an innocent bystander caught up in the shrapnel of the blast.

It just is what it is. I get it.

My thoughts turn to Poppy. Gram's idea could help her.

I could help her. What a departure from my normal M.O. of just helping myself.

Still, the woman was a stranger. A beautiful stranger, but a stranger nonetheless. It's not like I owe her anything. She pretended to be dating me to shut up a loudmouth—*that's* something I can totally relate to and fully support.

She could turn out to be a crazy stalker.

Even as the thought enters my mind, I know there's no way it's true. I have a sense about Poppy. She's just. . .different.

And Gram agrees.

After my call with Alicia, in which I remind her that earlier she told me to stay away from Poppy, I return to the living room and find Poppy sitting on the edge of the couch. Gram has obviously pulled her in here to drive home her point, and from the look on her face, I think Poppy is buying it.

Somehow, in the five minutes I was on the phone, Gram has flipped this idea around and is convincing Poppy this would be good for me.

But I know my grandma. And she has ulterior motives. She either sees a way this plan would benefit my career, or she genuinely thinks I'm going to end up falling in love with the girl next door and living happily ever after. I haven't worked out which.

Either way, it's a dumb plan that only ends one way.

My world is all wrong for a woman like Poppy. Of all the people I've met over the course of my career, she may, quite possibly, be a real life, honest-to-goodness genuine person.

There are so few left on the earth. Do I really want to risk that?

Gram sees me standing there, and my head starts shaking before I even try to speak.

"Just hear me out, Dally," Gram says.

Poppy looks at me. She's wearing an apron and holding a dish towel, and now the open-mouthed expression on her face taunts. "Yeah, *Dally*. Hear her out."

"Don't you have a meal to cook?" I tease.

"Oh." She holds up one finger and stands. "You have *no* idea how good this is going to taste."

I fold my arms. "Is that right?"

She moves a bit toward me. "This is going to ruin you eating anywhere else ever in your whole entire life."

I lean in a bit closer and lower my voice slightly. "I'll be the judge of that."

She points an *I'll-hold-you-to-that* finger at me and holds it there as she grins and backs out of the room into the kitchen. I really don't hate watching her go.

For a stranger, she sure is easy to flirt with.

"Yeah, you two would be terrible together," Gram mutters under her breath. "I wish people would just listen to me and do what I say."

I sit in the chair opposite her. "Gram—"

"When have I ever steered you wrong?" She cuts me off, staring me down with that single pointed eyebrow.

"This is not a good idea," I say, keeping my voice low.

"Why not?" Gram leans over and smacks me on the arm. "She's a lovely girl. Don't you want to help her out of this jam?"

"I could just pay off her debt," I say.

"She'd never let you do that."

I narrow my gaze. "And neither would you because you're clearly up to something."

Gram waves me off. "I have no idea what you're talking about."

"Just tell me which it is—my career, or my love life?"

Gram barely glances at me. "A bit of both, actually."

"No," I say.

"Ugh, you're so stubborn." She raises her hands like she wants to grab the sides of my head and rattle my brain around. "Fine, then look at it as a good deed." She leans over the armrest of the chair and glares at me. "That girl is in dire straits."

I frown. I'm genuinely concerned, but I don't know why, exactly. I shouldn't be. I don't even know Poppy. "She told you that?"

"She didn't have to," Gram says. "What if your name helps boost business? It's not like your endorsement hasn't moved markets before."

"Posing for a photo shoot with a protein bar in my hand isn't the same thing as claiming to be dating someone."

"You're right. It's not. The fact that it could also be good for your reputation is just a bonus." She leans back, shaking her head.

"You know I really don't care about that."

She groans. "Believe me, I know."

It wasn't exactly true though, was it? Maybe a year ago, I didn't care. But the accident was a turning point. One of those moments that shapes your life. Now, living in the *after*, I look back on everything I had done up until that point and think none of it mattered. Selfish, self-seeking, egotistical.

Now I want to do more than just play hockey. I want to leave a legacy behind. Do some *real* good, off the rink and out of the spotlight.

But still. . .was staging a romance with a woman I barely know really going to help?

"Shouldn't I just lay low? Concentrate on the game?" I ask.

"Sure, you can try that," she says. "How's that going so far?" She studies me from the couch the way she did when I was a kid.

I groan. "Can we just table this discussion?"

"Until when?" she asks.

"I don't know," I say, feeling cornered. "Later." I lower my voice as I continue. "Poppy and I don't even know each other."

She shrugs, flicking a hand in the air. "So you'll get to know each other. Heck, it can't hurt. She's nice. You could *use* a bit of nice, Dallas."

She's not wrong.

She continues. "If it bothers you that much, look at it as a business contract. Think of her like any other business partner you have."

"Okay, this is *completely* different," I say.

"Doesn't have to be. We can draw up a contract. Pay her a fee, if you want to."

"Pay her a fee?"

"For the cooking."

"So, now you want me to pay her on top of fake dating her?" I shake my head.

"It's not like you can't afford it." Gram folds her hands across her midsection, case closed.

She knows she's winning. I can see it on her face, darn it.

I groan. Gram knows I'm done with women, for now, at least—but that doesn't stop her. She'd been talking for years about me finding a good woman and settling down. "It would be good to have a safe place to land," she'd say. But nothing about my relationships had felt safe.

She lands the plane. "We both know you'd happily lend your name to Poppy if it will help her, and there's no way you're going to let her cook for free."

She's right.

I know she's right.

She knows she's right.

I also know resistance is futile. Gram and Alicia are going to make this happen, no matter what I think of the plan.

I stand. She raises her eyebrows, and I sigh my surrender.

I walk into the kitchen and see Poppy preparing the food. I watch her for a few seconds, as she rubs fragrant spices into the steak, then transfers the meat to a hot pan on the stove. She situates them in the pan with a pair of tongs, and the sound and smell of searing meat fills the room. She's confident and graceful as she cooks, and I start to feel bad for watching when she has no idea I'm here.

I clear my throat, and she glances up at me and smiles.

"*DAL-ly!* So nice of you to join me!"

I bite the inside of my bottom lip to keep from smiling. "So, this is how it's going to be?"

She nods, her smile wide, like she just turned over pocket aces. "Yep. You're *never* living that one down."

It's not the kind of smile that would alert the paparazzi, but it's the kind of smile that a person could hold onto. The kind that could make, say, a man in a tough spot hope that things could turn around again. Like an anchor.

A safe space to land.

Did Gram really sense this seconds after meeting her?

"You okay?" Poppy asks, a slight frown playing at the corners of her lips.

"Great," I say, forcing my face to behave. "Can I help?"

She grimaces. "Ooh. I don't know. I'm bossy in the kitchen."

"Good, because I have no idea what I'm doing."

She watches me for a long moment, then finally nods. "Okay, you can cut the potatoes."

"What are we making?"

"Steak frites with homemade fries and a fresh green salad. And I'll make a hollandaise sauce and a salad dressing to go with it."

"Sounds amazing," I say, realizing just how hungry I am.

"I told you this is going to ruin you. You're going to want to hire me full time, buddy."

Funny you should say that.

I round the island and scan the food on the counter. "So I'm. . . ?"

"Cutting the fries." She nods to a deep fryer. "And they'll go in there."

I start to cut odd shapes, and then look up at her, trying not to seem helpless.

"Wow. You weren't kidding about not being able to cook." My face must've betrayed my embarrassment, because she quickly says, "Sorry, I was just kidding! Here, I'll show you the quick and easy way to slice these."

She comes around my right side, wipes her hands on a towel, then takes the knife, gently touching my hand for a split second.

She doesn't seem to notice, but I do. I look at her, noting the slope of her cheek.

She slices longways, then in half and in half again, and after a few seconds, slides the perfectly cut fries to one side of the cutting board.

"See? Just try to keep the sizes as uniform as you can, that way they'll cook evenly."

I reach out and take the knife, making sure to touch her hand again. "Got it, boss."

She smiles, and I think I'm imagining it, but she leaves her hand there a little bit longer this time. "That's. . .um. . ." she clears her throat. "'*Chef*,' actually," she says, a little breathless.

I feign being caught. "Ah! Yes. Right. Thank you, *chef*."

Neither of us speaks for what feels like a year. I try to concentrate, but potatoes are the furthest thing from my mind right now. I steal quick glances at her, wondering if her embarrassment over this whole situation has died down. No matter how her restaurant benefited, I know she never meant for any of this to happen. A lesser woman would never have confessed it all.

"Can I ask a question? I don't want to be too personal or make you uncomfortable, but—"

She cuts me off. "Is my restaurant really in trouble?"

She knew what I was going to ask without me even hinting at it. "Well. . .yeah. I'm sorry. Is it. . .bad?"

She doesn't look up. "Not 'in trouble' exactly. Just not great." She meets my eyes. "Not as well as I'd hoped."

I get the feeling she's holding back, but I don't say so. "Tell me about it. The restaurant."

"Oh, I don't want to bore you," she seems a bit uneasy—maybe talking about herself doesn't come naturally.

Another thing that makes her completely different from all of the women I've known.

"No, really. I'd love to hear about it," I nudge.

She looks at me for a moment, then shrugs an *okay, here goes*.

"I opened it about a year ago. Poured all of my savings into it, took out a loan to cover the rest, and had to. . .borrow from my folks and some other wealthier families here in town. And now, it's. . ." she pauses, and then looks at me with eyes that are just a touch glassy. "It's not giving them a great return on their investment, you know?"

I nod, but I don't interrupt.

She goes on. "That's the real kicker—I have to pay them all back. My own parents used part of their retirement to help me. I couldn't live with myself if they lost that money because of me. Especially because they said I was worth investing in. I want to prove them right."

She glances down at the potato I'm pretending to know how to cut. "Not bad. I mean, not *great*. I would never hire you, but it's not a total hack job." She smiles with a glint, grabs a potato, and within three seconds has it sliced perfectly. Her confidence and skill are surprisingly sexy. When she finishes, she looks at me. "I told you I'm bossy."

I laugh. She has clearly gotten over the initial shock of

claiming to be dating a famous hockey player. She's in her element, and that means her real personality is coming out.

I like it. A lot.

I finish cutting the rest of the potatoes at a snail's pace while Poppy moves the steak to the oven. She then turns her attention to the salad and dressing.

"I wanted to bring the whole farm-to-table concept to Loveland," she says. "Partnering with local farmers, growing our own organic produce. I thought the local angle would be something people would grab onto, but I don't know. . ." She pauses, as if she's deciding how much to say. "It's taken some of them a bit to warm up to it, I guess. Everyone has their favorite places. And diner food is really popular here. Midwesterners love their comfort food."

"Well, I'll definitely be in while I'm here with Gram," I say.

She holds up a knife. "I haven't scared you off?"

"Okay, maybe I won't come, psycho."

We smile at each other—and this feels *so* easy, and familiar. Old friends, even. It's weird.

There's a slight wince on her face. "I would understand if you wanted to take out a restraining order after the way I behaved, but I promise I'm not a threat."

I laugh. "The jury's still out on that, but if the smell in here is any indication, you definitely know what you're doing in the kitchen."

"I *do* know what I'm doing in the kitchen," she says quickly. "It's the place I feel the most at home. Probably like you on the ice, right?"

I nod. "Yeah, actually. Ever since I was about twelve, hockey was always the only thing that mattered. I was obsessed. It was all I cared about. My friends thought I was nuts."

"I know how that feels. Like you'd try to talk to someone

else about it, because you're so passionate—and they look at you like you're crazy."

I can relate, and it's nice that I can. "So, how'd you end up cooking professionally?"

"I used to make big spreads for my college roommates. I loved it, but I never considered it as a career. Then I graduated from the University of Illinois and got a job in one of those corporate businesses downtown. After a year, I realized I hated going to work, and since it was such a huge part of every day, I started to hate my life."

"So you changed it," I say.

"So I changed it." She gives a definitive nod. "And off to culinary school I went."

"That's brave," I say.

Her forehead scrunches. "Is it? At the moment, it just feels kind of. . .misguided."

"No way." I face her. "To change course after you've already set out in one direction? That takes guts."

"I never thought of it that way before." She wipes off her knife and sets it down. "So, what about you?"

"What about me?"

"Who is the Dallas Burke the paparazzi doesn't know?"

I slide the misshapen potato slices toward her. "I'm afraid he'd be a terrible, boring disappointment."

"Aw, come on!" She grins as she opens the top of the deep fryer.

"I'm just a guy, trying to make a living doing what he loves and really wanting the chance to start over." I shrug. "I don't know, I guess I just want to make Gram proud. She believed in me long before I did."

She meets my eyes, and there's something there—a spark that I haven't felt in a long time. Or maybe more like a light switch that's just been turned on.

My staring must unnerve her, because her laugh is nervous and she seems uncertain all of a sudden, which is not how she's been acting since she took over this kitchen.

"So, what now?" I ask.

"Now, I clean up this mess," she says. "Unless you have people for that?" There's a glimmer of mischief in her eye, and she adds, "*Dally.*"

And I note the comfortable ease of talking with a woman who isn't feeling at all like a stranger anymore.

Chapter Nine

Poppy

I pull the steak from the oven and finish it in a pan. I'm picky when I cook. Everything needs to be perfect. To be honest, the kitchen is just about the only place in the world where I feel like I have any control.

Anywhere else I have a tendency to mess things up.

Everything, really.

I'm in debt from earning a useless college degree in Communications, not to mention the money I have to pay back from getting the restaurant started.

Avi. Even in my head, his name sounds like a swear word.

Thankfully, I never let myself dwell on that topic for very long.

I'm supposed to be digging my way out of this hole, but in truth, I'm in deeper than ever.

As I cooked, I tried to pretend Dallas wasn't watching me. I did a terrible job and finally asked him to leave.

It sounded nicer in my head than how it came out of my mouth.

He stared at me, chagrined, for a few seconds because

really, what right do I have to ask the man to leave his own kitchen? But then, as he pushed his beautiful body up off that stool, he said, "Yes, Chef," and strode out of the room.

I feel confident that ninety-seven percent of him has no idea the effect his nonchalance has on a girl like me.

The other three percent knows exactly what it's doing.

After ten minutes, he returns, claiming he needs a drink.

A part of me thinks he wants to make sure I'm not snooping around in here.

In other news, I was totally snooping around in here.

He just moved in, so there isn't much evidence to piece together—but I've also never been inside the house of a famous person. Maybe this is how they all live. Spartan, simple, untethered.

He walks over to the refrigerator and glances quickly at the table. It's set with two place settings, one for him and one for his grandma. The drinks are already poured and the salad is at the center of it. The presentation looks inviting, and I'm proud of it.

"There are only two plates," he says.

I feel caught. And confused. And. . . "What?"

"Dinner for three, remember?" He opens a bottle of water and takes a long drink. I watch his Adam's apple bob as he swallows. I've never noticed an Adam's apple before, but I suppose even this part of Dallas Burke's body is more fascinating than most people's.

"I thought I'd make this for you two," I say. "Sort of a. . . good luck with the hip replacement kind of meal. I don't want to intrude."

He walks over to the cupboard, takes out a plate, walks it back to the table and sets it down. "You're eating with us."

I don't like being told what to do, so this throws me.

Raya would definitely not capitulate, either. She's fiercely independent, and she's always taken care of herself. She's tried to pass that on to me and Eloise, but the truth is, most days I wouldn't mind someone taking care of me a little.

Adulting is hard. Even at twenty-eight, I haven't mastered it. There are moments when I don't want to be strong, or independent, or responsible. There are moments I want someone else to take the risk, or make the decision, or tell me what to do.

And at this moment, I'm totally fine with a handsome hockey player telling me to sit and eat.

"Poppy?"

I realize I'm staring. Because, of course I am.

"So you'll stay?" There's a hopefulness in his eyes that I'm unsure how to interpret. Why in the world does he want to spend any more time with me than he already has? I just barked at him for being in his own kitchen.

"Of course," I say dumbly, only then realizing that I'm equal parts nervous and hungry. "I'll stay."

"Of course she'll stay," Gram says, entering the room. "We have details to sort out."

"No, Gram," Dallas says. "We don't." He looks at me. "I'm sorry that she's on about this. She doesn't like to take 'no' for an answer."

"Not when I'm right, I don't," she says.

Dallas glances at me, and I can see his jaw muscles working to hold in whatever he wants to say. It's a bit fun to see someone like him helplessly and hopelessly losing an argument to a senior citizen.

As I plate the meal, Dallas moves to help his grandma into her chair. He's trying to be supportive and gentle, and she's fighting him to do it herself the whole way.

She and Raya would get along well.

Unlike me, Gram doesn't like to be fussed over. He eventually gives up and turns to me. "Can I help you? Because this one insists on doing everything on her own."

I'm tempted to tell him to sit and relax, but I get the sense he's not good at either one of those things. "Sure, you can take this to the table." I hand over the platter of steak, and he inhales the aroma of it, an appreciative look washing over his face.

He looks at me, and I smile. "Right?" I say and nod.

"This smells amazing," he says.

"It tastes even better. It's one of my favorite meals."

We sit, and there's a lull. Dallas meets my eyes from across the table.

Gram smacks him on the arm, and he says, "Oh, right. Sorry."

He folds his hands and closes his eyes. *Is he going to pray?*

"Lord, thank you for—" he is, and I quickly close my eyes— "this meal and this company. Thank you for Gram, and I pray that you convict her about her poor interpersonal skills."

I hear another smack.

"I ask that you bless this food, and bless the hands that made it."

Are famous people's prayers on a fast track to God's ears? If so, I'll take it, Lord.

"Bless our time and conversation, and," he slightly pauses to clear his throat, "thank you for bringing Poppy into our lives."

Wait. What?

He finishes his prayer and opens his eyes to find that mine are wide open and staring at him.

Total prayer etiquette fail.

He chuckles to himself and then says, "I can't wait anymore. This smells way too good. Can I. . .?" He slowly starts to reach for his fork and knife.

The stupor I'm in begins to fade and I stammer, "Uh. . .yeah. Yes. Dig in."

That brief, forty-five second prayer makes me see Dallas Burke in a totally different light. Not that I believe people like him don't believe in God, but I really thought that people like him didn't believe in God.

Also, it's rare for me to sit and eat with the people I cook for. Rare, but nice. It gives me a chance to experience my food through their reactions. While I feel slightly self-conscious about it, it's good for me. Sometimes it's easy to forget this part for all the day-to-day business busy work nonsense that rules most days.

I don't ever want to lose sight of why I love to cook in the first place just because it doesn't exactly pay the bills.

"This is delicious," Dallas says. "How are you not turning people away every day?"

At least I know better than to confess *that* to him. Instead, I shrug. "Like your grandma said, it's a tough business."

Dallas shakes his head. "People have no idea what they're missing."

I don't get the sense he's the type to blow smoke. I think he genuinely likes my food, which is a kind of validation I could get used to.

"Tell me about the surgery," I say to his grandma so I can stop my mind from spinning out of control.

She rolls her eyes. "Oh, it's ridiculous. My hip is bad, probably from years of kicking this one's behind six ways to Sunday."

Dallas, mouth full, nods his agreement.

"And so they're turning me into a bionic woman."

"How long is the rehab?"

"Two to four weeks," she muses, "but I'll be done with it in a week and a half. I'm not rolling around on some stupid inflatable ball for a month."

I laugh out loud.

"It'll all be done here," Dallas says. "I hired a physical therapist to come to the house and work with her. And a nurse to help on the days when I'm on the road."

"He's thought of everything," Gram says.

Everything but a cook. I almost blurt this out, but thankfully have the good sense to keep this to myself.

I glance at Dallas. He might've earned himself a very specific reputation, but the man in front of me is contradicting it at every turn. In this one interaction, I can see how much he loves his grandma. He may be a womanizing playboy with a bit of a temper, but if he is, at least he's one with redeeming qualities.

After we eat, Dallas helps Gram get situated in the living room, where she turns on *The Great British Baking Show*, and I start to clean up the kitchen, rolling up my knives and packing away the leftovers.

"Leave the mess," he says. "I can get it."

"Don't be silly," I say. "I could never."

"You cooked. I clean. Gram would need another hip replacement if she heard I let you do this."

I smile, thankful for the help.

We finish cleaning, working wordlessly but anticipating each other's moves like we've done this a thousand times. Even Miguel and I struggle with this. Once the dishwasher is clicked shut and humming, the bowls are stacked, and the extra ingredients are packed in the tote, Dallas says, "Thanks again for dinner. Expect a glowing endorsement from me via social media later tonight."

I smile. "That's appreciated—but not necessary. I really did just want to thank you. For what you did for me yesterday with

Margot." I smile when I say this, but it still pains me a little to think that the first time I met him, he saw behind the curtain and witnessed a tiny piece of what my life is like. It's hard to change your reputation.

However, in one evening, didn't Dallas do exactly that?

"Small towns have long memories, don't they?" He says this with a kind of authority I'm not sure he has.

Instinctively, though, I know what he means. People don't always let us become who we are. They try to keep us in the box of who we *were*.

We're all on our way to becoming someone new, aren't we?

I wonder who Dallas Burke is becoming.

I wonder who I am becoming.

I'm staring again. I quickly right myself, heave the tote over my shoulder, and give a single definitive nod. "Well, I should go."

"Thanks again, Chef," he says. "It was really great." He extends a hand.

I instinctively slip my hand into his, and as his fingers wrap around it, I let myself imagine that this isn't the last time I'll see him. That this evening might be the first of many intimate dinners right here in this glorious kitchen. It's a ridiculous thought, of course, but I'll freely admit that when it comes to Dallas, I'm a ridiculous girl.

I could be imagining it, but I think he's holding onto my hand a little longer than a normal handshake would warrant. I think he's *lingering*.

He's LINGERING.

But then he smiles, and I realize it's more likely me who's lingering, and I quickly pull my hand away.

I poke my head into the living room and wave at his grandma. "It was wonderful to meet you!"

She's sitting in a recliner with an afghan on her lap. She barely glances at me as she waves and says, "You'll be back."

I smile at her, then turn to Dallas. "Have a great night."

And with that, I step out into the chilly winter air.

Here's hoping the cold brings me back to my senses.

The {Rumor} Mill

Spotted on Dallas Burke's social media: *Hockey's favorite rebel shares photos of an intimate at-home dinner cooked by none other than local chef, Poppy Hart.*

Apparently, Miss Hart cooked quite the meal for Dallas, who had this to say about it:

Enjoyed the most delicious steak frites with homemade fries and a salad I could eat every day courtesy of the owner of Poppy's Kitchen, a farm-to-table restaurant in downtown Loveland. Do yourself a favor and let Poppy cook for you as soon as humanly possible. Thank me later.

They do say the way to a man's heart is through his stomach, so, what do we think, Millers? Is Poppy Hart courting the Comet with kisses and prime cuts? And is anyone else salivating after seeing the photos of this food?

You "butter" believe it!

Chapter Ten

Poppy

The next day, Margot comes in for breakfast.

She's got the entire Festival of Hearts committee with her, and they're taking up the big table in the back. My restaurant is now her conference room.

Margot has never eaten here. Her friends have never eaten here. I can only assume they're here now out of morbid curiosity, or to catch me in my lie. I should set the record straight, but I don't have time. There are too many orders piling up.

How often have I been able to say that?

As before, the restaurant is bustling, and I know who I have to thank. Dallas's post about the meal I cooked him last night has only stirred up more rumors. I'm trying to feel bad about it, but honestly, it's such a stroke of good luck I'm mostly just feeling grateful. And a little like a fraud, though I was straight about it. At least he knows the truth, and he's really the only one I care about not hurting.

"Can we handle this many people?" Miguel asks, beads of sweat dotting his forehead.

"We're sure going to try," I say. "I'll call Kit and see if she can come in today."

Thankfully, Kit, one of my servers, is free, and when she arrives, we all feel a little relief. But only a little. What I really need is another cook.

But I clearly can't find one of those now, so I keep my head down and stay focused. I'll rest after we close.

I'm fueled by caffeine and the vision of pulling the restaurant out of fast-moving quicksand.

As I flip pancakes, I think of all the bills piled up in the box on my desk. I mentally stack them one on top of another, in hopes that the lower ones will magically disappear.

With a few days like this, I can make a serious dent in them. Maybe I could start paying people back.

It's not lost on me that months, or even two consecutive and consistent weeks at this pace would be even better, but I force myself not to entertain Gram's idea.

Asking someone like me to pretend-date someone like Dallas was like asking me if I wanted a truckload of money. Asking someone like *him* to pretend-date someone like *me*, well. . .that was like being awarded the Cutco steak knives for third place in the talent portion of the Little Miss Loveland pageant.

Useful, but you know you're looking for a reason to re-gift those knives.

I'm flushed with humiliation all over again and comfort myself by picturing Dallas's bright blue eyes. He's got this sort of steely gaze, the kind that makes a person wonder what he's thinking, and when that gaze is trained on you, rational thought goes out the window.

"There's a customer out here demanding to see the chef." Selena stares at me from the doorway of the kitchen.

I look up at her, wearing my *are you kidding me?* expression and knowing full well that it *has* to be Margot.

"Can you explain that I'm a little busy right now?" I ask.

"Are you sure you want me to do that?" Selena's eyes are wide. Afraid. And I'm not surprised. Everyone is scared of Margot.

"Yes, Selena." I crack an egg into a bowl. "I'm so backed up in here, there's no way. Please kindly let whoever it is know that I'm up to my eyeballs, and I apologize, but I can't come out onto the floor at the moment."

She stands there, staring at me like I've just sent her to her public execution.

"Go on," I say.

Margot has been bullying me for as long as I can remember, but the fact of the matter is, I'm not a child. And I'm not going to let her get away with it anymore. Not in my own restaurant.

And in perfect Poppy fashion, I sent someone else to deal with her.

These omelets aren't going to cook themselves.

I crack another egg into the bowl. Then another. I begin to whisk. I'm overheating. I dab my forehead with my sleeve and pour the eggs into the pan when the kitchen door swings open again. I expect Nate, the busboy (because really, where is he?) but instead, Dallas saunters into my kitchen, looking as out of place as a horse in a library.

I straighten. "What are you doing here?"

Selena pushes through the door behind him and stands there, gawking. He smiles a boyish smile that doesn't seem to be trying.

"Well, I thought it might be good to swing by for a meal before I go to practice," he says, looking around. "But I can see you're swamped."

"*You're* the customer demanding to see the chef?"

He grimaces. "Guilty?"

I laugh. "It's your own fault I can't come out there and chat with you, so I don't feel bad about it anymore."

He grins. "How is this my fault?"

"Your post," I say. "Or they're all here on the off-chance they might run into you." I flip the omelet in the pan.

"I guess this is an off-chance kind of day," he says, leaning back against a fridge.

Is he flirting?

I meet his eyes. "You're only keeping the gossip going, you know that, right?"

He shrugs. "Let 'em talk. If it helps you, it's fine, right?"

I look away. It *does* help me. But it's a total fabrication. What does that make me? An image of Julia Roberts in thigh-high patent leather boots flashes through my mind.

"What are you really doing here?"

He walks over to my station and watches me for a few seconds, the same way he did the night before in his kitchen, with more interest than I know what to do with. "It's like you have choreography."

I laugh. "This is not choreography. It's madness."

"Well, you're good at it."

"Thanks."

He smiles. "I came to offer you a job."

I glance over my shoulder, thankful Miguel is engrossed in his own culinary chaos. "I thought you said the fake dating thing wasn't smart," I keep my voice low, just in case.

"Oh! No, not that," he says. "I thought you might cook for us. Me and Gram. I've got the PT and the nurse, but I realized last night, I don't have anyone to cook."

"Ah." I plate the food and set it on the shelf for the servers to pick up, not telling him that I had the same thought less than twenty-four hours ago. "Okay. Tell me more. I'm going to work while you talk, but I promise I'm listening."

"I was thinking you could come out like you did last night," he says. "Maybe make an extra meal or two for the fridge so you don't have to be there every night."

Right, because that would be terrible.

He continues. "She's not going to be able to get around very well to start with, and I thought maybe it would be good since she obviously likes you."

I walk over to the cooler and grab a basket of tomatoes. "She does?"

"She does," he says. "And your food is fantastic."

I mime a little curtsy as I turn away from the cooler. "Thank you. And I love your use of the word 'fantastic,'" I say. "A very underused adjective."

He laughs. "We can work out the details later if you think it might be doable?"

"If it's evenings only, it's doable."

He nods.

"Starting when?"

A shrug, then, "Tonight?"

I laugh. "Wow, last night's audition was a success then, huh?"

"Yeah." He smiles. "I suppose so."

The swinging door to the kitchen crashes open. "It's madness out there!" Selena is back, and she looks completely overwhelmed.

As I walk back to the stove, I give Dallas a smack on his chest and say, "Blame it on this guy." It's an in-the-moment reaction, and I'm shocked at how comfortable I am with him.

If we weren't contemplating fake-dating, we might be real friends.

Still, I instantly wish I could take it back. I'm not *that* familiar with him, and I have no business touching him at all.

Though that one little smack was enough to tell me that he doesn't skip chest day at the gym.

"I'll leave out the back," he says with a smile. "And. . .see you tonight?"

I nod. I smile. I can't help it—this is great for my career, even if I am his private chef and not his fake girlfriend. *Plus, I get to go back to that glorious kitchen.*

As soon as he leaves, I'm bombarded with questions and it becomes painfully obvious working for Dallas is only going to keep the rumors going. And I'm a little more okay with that than I should be.

Chapter Eleven

Dallas

After practice, I'm called into Coach's office. It was only a matter of time before we had this discussion. I'm honestly surprised it's taken him this long to address the issues with Mulligan.

I don't know what he's heard, I don't know what my teammates have said, but since I'm taking all the blame, I fully expect him to read me the riot act. I feel like I've used up all my chances.

I knock on the glass window of the door, and he waves me in.

Coach Turnrose is by far one of the best men I know, and it's not even close. He took a chance on me years ago, and, like Gram, saw something in me that I didn't see in myself. I want to make him proud.

Why is it so hard for me to do that?

"Burke, have a seat." He motions to the chair across from his desk.

I'm not one for excuses, so I wait for him to start the conversation.

"You looked good out there today," he says. "Strong. The work is paying off."

"Thanks, Coach."

"But what are we going to do about this?" He picks up the same magazine Gram had, and drops it on the desk facing me.

My gaze hits the floor.

"The team is barely keeping it together as it is, Burke, and you're the captain. This kind of fighting? This kind of press? It's a bad look."

I could argue that fighting is a part of hockey's culture, but I know where Turnrose stands on the subject.

"I'm sorry, Coach," I say. "It won't happen again."

"Yes, it will." He leans back in his chair. "Mulligan has it in for you."

"He blames me for Ricky," I say.

Coach studies me. "*You* blame you for Ricky. That's why he drives you to do crap like this." He motions to the magazine. "You have to find a way to forgive yourself and let it go, Dallas. If not for your sake, then for the team's."

I lean back in the chair, hands interlaced behind my head, trying not to replay all the things I could've done differently that night. I should've been more alert. Less distracted. Or maybe I should've listened to Mulligan, which is the part that burns me more than anything.

"We've been through this," Coach says. "It was the driver of that truck who was at fault."

I stand, instantly defensive. Not because he's wrong, but because I don't want to relive this. Any of it.

"*Mulligan told me to leave Ricky there*, Coach" I confess. "He told me to take his keys and make him sleep on the couch." I look at him. "I didn't listen. I acted like I knew better, and look what happened."

"You did exactly what you should've. You were trying to get a teammate and a friend home safe."

I bite the inside of my lip to keep any emotion from showing on my face. I hate talking about this. Ownership is still forcing me to attend bi-monthly therapy sessions—even nine months later—and I have to relive the accident over and over. The only thing I'm learning is how to talk about it detached and without emotion.

Coach knows me better than the therapist does.

And he has a way of hearing what I don't say.

"It's still affecting the way you play," he says now. "You used to be the leader on this team. You called the shots. Everyone listened. You don't do that anymore." He leans forward on his desk, leveling my gaze. "I need my captain back."

I hear him. I know what he's asking. I just don't know how to deliver.

I'd made a judgment call, and it had backfired in the worst way. How could I trust myself, let alone expect anyone to listen to anything I said after that? Especially with Mulligan reminding me of it every single day.

"And you've got to do something about the press," he says.

"I don't know what to do about that," I say.

"Stop giving them fuel, for one thing." He rubs a hand over his beard. "You and I both know that Mulligan's future here is uncertain. And I'm not deaf. I heard what he said to you. He deserved a beat down."

The words rush back. *If you'd listen to other people once in a while, Ricky would still be walking.*

"But you are too valuable to me and to this team to have something like this ruin your career." He pauses. "You said you've changed, Burke, and I believe you. But now it's time to prove it to everyone else."

I hear what he's saying, but I don't know how to fix it. I don't know how to make the negative press go away. I *did* hit Mulligan. I *was* driving the car when we got in the accident. I *am* responsible for the division on our team.

I think back to what Poppy said to me the night before, about the press getting it wrong about me. What was it that she saw in me that the rest of the world didn't? And how could I change their minds?

"Is the foundation still in the works?" Coach asks now.

"It's on hold," I say. "Until this all blows over."

"Then you've got a bigger reason than hockey to make sure it does."

"What am I supposed to do?" I ask. "The press isn't interested in my redemption story."

He shrugs. "I don't care what you do. Just do something. Talk to Alicia—they don't call her the Spin Doctor for nothing."

I sigh. I already know what Alicia wants me to do, and that plan has the capacity to blow up in my face.

The one thing that could potentially save my career and my reputation off the ice could also potentially hurt someone who, if I'm right, is legitimately a good person—someone who I could see becoming a genuine friend.

I'm figuratively driving down the road with a passenger in the car, headed for disaster all over again.

Chapter Twelve

Poppy

I keep the restaurant open an extra hour just to give customers time to finish. While my staff cleans up, I make a list of meals I can cook for Dallas and his grandma, and I can't help but feel a little giddy that he's invited me back.

It's not just *him* that's prompting these feelings—it's also the fact that I get to cook in a kitchen in a house. I haven't done that, not with this kind of joy, for a long, long time. It's like finding that favorite pair of jeans you thought you gave away, only to discover they still fit, and there's a $20 bill in the back pocket.

Never mind that I'm tired and sore and still have restaurant prep to do for the following day.

I set Miguel on it, because this is an opportunity I don't want to pass up. Maybe if it doesn't work out to be Dallas's fake girlfriend, I can be his real life private chef. Purely business.

Will there be speculation? Yes.

Will people chatter in hushed tones hunched over tables in my restaurant? Surely.

Will I care?

The jury's still out on that one.

I can't help what people say. And I can't help it if that speculation brings them into my restaurant.

When I get out to his house, I don't knock, per Dallas's instructions. Gram is home, but Dallas is still at practice, and he didn't want her to have to get up to answer the door.

But when I walk into the kitchen, I find Gram standing at the counter with a tall dark-haired woman wearing a black suit jacket over a crisp white blouse, jeans, and heeled boots. Her makeup is impeccable, and she's all sharp edges. Both women look at me.

"I'm so sorry," I say. "Dallas said to let myself in."

The woman I don't know smiles and walks toward me. She extends a hand. "Poppy Hart, in the flesh."

I shake her hand, feeling the confusion on my face.

"I'm Alicia Montgomery," she says. "Dallas's manager."

"Oh!" I say. "Right." I feel like I've walked in on a war room meeting that's being held behind Dallas's back.

"Sylvia told me about the idea you discussed last night," Alicia says.

I walk toward the counter. "Sorry, I just need to set this stuff down." I glance at Gram, whose name, I only now realize, is Sylvia. The fact that I'd been thinking of her as *Gram* suddenly seems very inappropriate, as if I'd adopted their family and made her my own.

I look at Sylvia. "Dallas told you I'm cooking for you tonight," a sideways take at Alicia, "right?"

"He did," she says. "I said you'd be back." She shifts her position, and I catch a nearly undetectable wince on her face.

"You should go sit down," I say.

"You're as bad as Dally," she says, and I smile again at the horrible nickname.

Secretly, I'm just hoping that the two of them will relocate to the living room so I can claim ignorance to whatever is happening here.

"Poppy, we have a proposition for you," Alicia says.

"If this is about the fake dating thing," I say, "I think you may be wasting your time. Dallas already said no."

"My grandson doesn't always know what's best for him," Gram says.

"That's why he hired me," Alicia adds.

"I don't want to go behind his back," I say. "The last thing I want is for him to be mad."

Alicia suddenly looks like she discovered who the killer was before turning the page in her novel. "Oh, no. You *are* wholesome."

I frown. Why does that sound like a condescending insult?

Maybe because it was.

"Which. . . is. . .why you are *perfect* for this," she adds, trying to spin my negative reaction into something positive. "I'm not going to go into the specifics when I know you've already been over it—"

"And it's pretty clear he wasn't for it," I interject, but it doesn't derail her like I had hoped, because she just keeps right on talking.

"—but I want to remind you how good this would be for your restaurant."

And there it is.

I pull a large jar of homemade marinara from my tote and set it on the counter. "I freely admit that. We're not drowning —" *okay, I'm understating it, but she doesn't need to know that—* "but we're not raking in money hand over fist." I look at Alicia, completely honest. "But I really would like my food to be the reason my restaurant is successful."

"Well," Alicia leans on the counter, a move that somehow

makes me instinctively lean back. "If nobody tastes it, it never will be."

Ouch.

"Dallas can bring people in the door." She stands straight, looking straight at me. "But it's you who has to make them stay."

I shake my head. "Miss Montgomery, nobody is going to believe that Dallas Burke is dating someone like me."

"Leave that to me." She's so certain when she says this, and I can only assume she has a PR plan to do just that.

I am not convinced. "Very doubtful. Have you seen him? He's like some ancient Greek guy carved him out of marble." My eyes dart to Sylvia. "Sorry."

She raises a shoulder, casually. "We have good genes."

I glance at the clock, and I'm starting to feel pressure. "Miss Montgomery—"

"Call me Alicia, please."

I slip into chef mode. "Miss Montgomery, Dallas won't be home from practice for another forty-five minutes. I'd hoped to have dinner on the table as he walked in the door. No offense, but—" I reach in the tote and begin to unpack the rest of the ingredients, "you're going to slow me down."

Now Alicia is the one to lean back.

"Food is important, and if it's not right, that means *I* didn't get it right. And that's not okay with me. "

Raya, eat your heart out.

Alicia looks at Sylvia, and they exchange a silent glance that looks like it harkens back to a conversation I wasn't privy to.

"Just hear me out," she says. "Dallas thinks that I'm just here to spin things in the present—but I actually look out for him in a bigger picture than that. A future picture."

"What do you mean? Like after he's done playing?"

"Exactly. Ultimately, we're hoping that when Dallas retires, he can move seamlessly into analysis or commentary. It's what a lot of professional athletes want to do, but very few of them get to do it. The only problem is that he's not going to get *anything* if he's only known as 'the bad boy of hockey.'"

Images of models draped on his arm flash before my mind's eye, and for a moment, I have a really hard time squaring that with the Dallas I've come to know in the short time I've been around him. He just doesn't seem like that guy.

"He needs to alter his image, win over the public, and more importantly, show the executives making these decisions that he's focused, clear-headed, and reliable. And to do that—" she picks up a bound group of spring onions, which I promptly take out of her hand and set back down—"he has to keep himself out of trouble. Maybe even prove he's a changed man. We can score a deal with HydroIce, the sports drink. Get him back on the right track. That would be huge for his career."

"How huge?" I glance at Sylvia.

"Very." Alicia gives me a knowing nod that seems to mean *more money than you could even imagine.*

Of course she wants him to get this deal. She'll get a cut of it, and odds are, even her small percentage is more money than I'll make in the next five years.

Alicia reaches into a bag and pulls out a few papers, stapled together. "I've taken the liberty of drawing up some paperwork. It's very standard." She flips the pages. "And *this*—" she points to a number at the bottom of the contract, "would be your payment."

My jaw goes slack.

"To start."

I can't even process this number. I could pay everyone back. I could take care of the rent for the next two years. I could even take a vacation.

And still have enough left over to add on to the restaurant.

"There's a standard NDA, of course," she says. "And there's room here for the two of you to add in your own terms of what you will and won't do."

I imagine the sound effect of a woman gulping as I try to swallow. My mouth is bone dry at the thought of *what I will or won't do* when it comes to Dallas and I force myself not to let my imagination run away.

"You can negotiate public appearances, like requiring Dallas to eat at your restaurant once a week or take you to any local events, and Dallas can do the same. Odds are, you'll be asked to attend a charity function or two, home games, maybe the occasional night out, but we may be able to drum up enough interest without too much of that. We can outline acceptable forms of PDA depending on what you're both comfortable with."

I'm blank, but I manage a weak "Wait. Forms of what?"

"Public displays of affection. Hand holding, kissing, the occasional back seat. . ."

"Whoa!" My mind is filling in *all* of the blanks now.

She looks at Sylvia and continues like this is all no big deal. "It's a pretty standard contract, but if you need time for your lawyers to look it over, I'm sure we can wait, what, a couple days?"

It's hilarious Alicia thinks I'm the kind of person who has "lawyers."

She folds the papers over to the last page and sets it down on the counter. She clicks open a pen, places it on top, and then slides the whole thing over to me.

I stare at the blank line with my name typed under it. Then I look at the pen.

This is wrong. I don't care *how* big that number is.

I look up. "Does Dallas even know you're here?"

Alicia's jaw snaps shut, but she quickly regroups. "He does not."

I slide the papers back to Alicia. "I don't feel comfortable discussing anything until he's home," I say.

I catch a quick glance between Sylvia and Alicia, and then the knowing eyebrow raise from the older woman. "Told ya."

Alicia gives her a nod.

"Told her what?" I ask, feeling like the C in their A-B conversation.

"That you're perfect," Gram says. "Most people would jump at the chance to make that kind of money. No matter who they hurt in the process."

"Well, I can't take that money," I say. "And I have no interest in hurting Dallas."

"That's good to hear." The male voice comes from the entry at the back of the house. Dallas must've parked in the garage and come in through the back door like a stealthy robber, and none of us heard a thing. He walks into the kitchen, takes one look around the room, and then his gaze lands on me. "Are you okay?"

"She's better than okay," Alicia says. "She's perfect."

"Alicia, can I see you in the other room?" Dallas's jaw muscles are doing that twitching thing again—it's like he's physically biting down on the words so they don't fly out of his mouth.

I pretend not to notice. I also pretend it's not attractive that he asked if I was okay. A voice inside of me is screaming, *No! I'm not okay! Take care of me forever*!

I need a vacation.

Alicia sighs, then follows Dallas out of the room.

"You have a good heart." Gram is still watching me. "That's why you'd be good for this. You're genuine."

"That's exactly why I'd be terrible at this," I say, realizing I got myself into this mess. "It's not honest."

"It's a business deal," she says. "I know it feels a little shady, but what business deal doesn't? If we can get the public to fall in love with you both, that will be very good for Dallas. And for you."

"Until it ends."

"Amicably," she says. "Alicia has a plan."

"I'm sure she does," I brood.

She's probably really good at her job, which means that her plan is probably really good, which means that it will probably work.

Yuck.

I think for a moment. What if I dug myself out of debt and my restaurant became a Loveland favorite? What if, for the first time in my life, people didn't see me as a complete loser?

Stop that right now, Poppy. I'm using my firmest inner voice.

Funny, it sounds like Raya.

What happens when I get attached to Dallas and his big life? I'm already attached to his big kitchen, and I know full well it's going to hurt when I have to give *that* up. If I can have these feelings over a room, how can I ever hope to stay neutral over a seemingly kindhearted, clearly misunderstood, and downright sexy man?

Gram walks off, leaving me alone to prepare the pasta and meatballs, which is good because I need space to think. I can't imagine what it would be like to have someone calling the shots of my life so openly like this. To walk in and find people plotting and planning about my next steps. To have every decision I made scrutinized and plotted, right down to who I fake date.

I shudder at the thought.

Could I actually stomach it to save my restaurant? To turn my own reputation around?

I've never been driven by fame or popularity or even money (hence *chef*), but the fact is my restaurant might not survive if something doesn't change.

Without this agreement, the intrigue will die down, the people will stop gossiping, the patrons will stop coming, and I'll be back to worrying how I'll make rent.

And if Poppy's Kitchen fails, I'd have to win the lottery to have any hope of paying my parents back.

Chapter Thirteen

Poppy

After a good half hour, Dallas returns to the kitchen. There's a weariness behind his eyes that wasn't there before.

He looks at me. "I'm so sorry they bombarded you."

"I'm fine," I say, resisting the urge to point out I'm the one who should be sorry. "Are you okay?"

He inhales a deep breath, then exhales on a sigh. "Nobody's asked me that in a long time." A pause. "I'm fine."

"Yeah, that was lame. I don't believe you."

He sits on the stool on the other side of the island and scrubs a hand down his face. "Tell me the truth. How much would this help you?"

I take the pot of cooked pasta off the burner and begin to strain it. "You said it was ridiculous."

"I know. I did say that," he says. "And it probably is."

My eyes flick to his.

"But. . ." he starts.

I nearly drop the strainer in the sink. "But what?"

He says this as if he's testing the water in an outdoor pool with his toes. "Maybe it

isn't?"

I stare, trying to figure out what he's actually suggesting.

"I mean," he continues, "would it help?"

The look on my face isn't changing. There's just silence, save for the soft bubbling of the meatballs in the sauce on the stovetop behind me.

I turn away from him. I've forgotten what I'm doing. I look down and realize that the pasta is still in the strainer, which is still in my hand, which is now dripping on the floor. The sight of food being ill-prepared snaps my mind into focus, and I quickly bring the pasta back to the sink.

A thought hits me.

"You do know they're playing us, right? Alicia pitched this as a way for *me* to help you. But to you, she pitched it as a way for *you* to help me."

"Maybe we should take that as a compliment." He smiles. "She knows that neither one of us is really in this for ourselves."

I begin to plate the pasta, healthy tong-fulls, leaving a crater in the middle for the meatballs, sauce, and cheese.

"I honestly would like to help you, Dallas," I say. "But I'm not convinced this is the way."

"What if it's like Gram said?" he asks. "Not fake?"

I laugh. "Okay, buddy. We both know you don't *actually* want to date me. The only way this works is if we're straight with each other from the start, so let's not pretend. At least not in private."

He looks away.

Why did he do that?

"What's on the line here for you?" I turn to get the pan of meatballs from the stovetop.

He shrugs. "Endorsement deals, I guess. A change in my 'direction,' maybe? Both of which are important for my future."

I tenderly offer, "Is that all?"

He hesitates. "It would be nice for people to start believing I've changed. If they do, maybe my teammates will start believing it. It's been. . .hard since the accident. There's more division on our team than any team should have, and it's. . .it's my fault." He looks at me.

I pause. "And?"

He smirks. "What makes you think there's more?"

"Gut feeling." I smile at him.

He pulls in a deep breath, then lets it out on a sigh. "You won't believe me."

"Try me," I say.

"I want to start a. . ." He stops. "You know what, let's get into it later."

I frown. Now I'm intrigued. "You don't trust me?"

His face falls. "I don't trust anybody."

I watch him for a moment. "We have that in common."

The air between us thickens. Two people who've been hurt one too many times finally acknowledging out loud that those hurts affected them.

Common ground.

Culinary expert James Beard once famously said, "Food is our common ground." And here we are, in the kitchen—the heart of the home.

James Beard also said that if he were ever forced to try cannibalism, he might manage it if there was enough tarragon around. So not all of his quotes are quotable.

After a pause, he asks, "And what's on the line for you?"

I pick up two plates and walk them over to the table. "Everything. My restaurant. The debt. It would be nice to have some breathing room." I set the plates down and turn to face him. "As it is, I usually feel like there's an elephant sitting on my chest. I'd love to get out from under it."

"Stress isn't good for the body," he says.

I laugh. "I know."

"So. . .this could ease your financial stress."

"Maybe?" I hear the question in my voice because I'm so unsure. An hour ago, I was convinced that the idea was utterly moronic. But now, everything is upside down. Alicia has pleaded a good case. Dallas is considering it, and now somehow *I* am considering it.

What is even happening right now?

I walk back over to my cooking station and give the salad another toss. "I think it's going to be hard for people to believe that someone like me would ever be with someone like you."

Why must I play devil's advocate? Why can't I just sign on the blank line with my name typed below it? I'm *this close* to getting the deal of a lifetime—something that would surely save my restaurant—but now that so many people are involved, it feels less like an innocent favor and more like a backroom deal.

"I think people already believe it," he says. "If the crowd at your restaurant today is any indication."

I walk the salad to the table. "Oh, I think that's more like morbid curiosity. Like an accident you can't look away from. People are showing up, pressing their nose to the glass to try and figure out what's really going on because everyone knows this—" I flick my hand back and forth between us— "doesn't make sense."

"Weren't you the one who grabbed my arm in the first place?" He laughs. "Now I'm the one trying to convince you."

"I didn't mean for it to turn into this!" I groan.

"I think we could sell it," he says. And then he smiles. And my knees buckle, and I melt into a puddle right there on his kitchen floor.

Oh look, there's me, waiting to be mopped up.

Because "selling it" with Dallas Burke conjures up all *kinds* of extracurricular activities, and every single one of them makes me blush.

I regain my composure, though I admit, not as quickly as I should, and then meet his eyes. "Being seen with me is not a prize, Dallas. You should know that straight off the bat."

"Okay, first, this self-loathing thing you've got going on is going to have to stop."

I laugh. It's probably so foreign to him to not be confident in one's own skin, but it's been my reality since puberty. That's when I discovered I wasn't going to be tall and wispy. That's when I got boobs and thick hips and when I stopped looking like most of the rail thin girls in my class. And it's impossibly hard to find fashionable clothes for a fifth grader in the women's section.

Every once in a while, Raya would give me a pep talk, usually after our grandma made a remark about me being "sturdy," but the truth is, I pretty much tuned her out. I'd accepted my curves. I knew my place, and I was totally fine with it.

I'd made peace with the fact that I wasn't meant to be beautiful a long time ago. Dallas was blind if he didn't see it.

"Don't sell yourself short," he says.

"Oh really? A lot of curvy chefs turn your head, do they?"

He shakes his head. "If the curves are in the right spots. . ." He says this next word right through me: "Yes."

The unexpected words contradict everything I know about the preferences of men, which, I only now realize is very little. Had my assumptions been wrong all along?

But no. I know what I know.

"I'm ordinary," I say, and then repeat it with a laugh. "I'm *so* ordinary. I'm average in every way. I don't look like *anyone* you've dated."

"What, fake?"

"No. Beautiful."

"You're so wrong," he says. "I would take bona fide over boob job any day of the week."

I gasp with laughter as I grab a dish towel and throw it at him.

"Look, I know it's a crazy idea," he says.

"I can't believe you said boob job. *Boob job*. Like, what?" I'm still giggling, which is partly due to my nerves.

"Poppy." He's trying to get me to focus.

"Dallas." I mimic his serious tone, but I break into a smile.

Then he points behind me.

The meatballs!

I turn and see the sauce bubbling. I quickly take them off the burner and shift them around in the pan—not burned, thank goodness.

He continues, "I *know* it's a crazy idea. But having someone in my corner who isn't trying to manipulate me or use me or get something out of me—that would be kind of nice."

"But I *would* be using you," I say.

"But I'd know about it," he says. "And I'd kind of be using you right back. If we're both okay with that, and we're honest from the start, then it's not a bad thing—right?" It makes twisted sense.

"Right," I say, spooning out two of the giant meatballs onto his plate, then ladling out sauce. "That's true."

He looks down and nods as if I were a blackjack dealer and he's saying *hit me*.

I slowly add another meatball.

He raises his eyebrows.

I add another one.

He nods. I shudder to think of this man's caloric intake.

"I guess that makes it less shady?" He sounds as if he's

convincing himself along with me. "Because we'd both be up-front about what we need right from the start."

I pull a block of parmesan cheese from the refrigerator and begin to grate it into a bowl. "A business arrangement."

"A business arrangement."

"For. . .fake dating."

"Exactly," he says. "No feelings to muddy the water. Just both of us doing what we need to do to turn things around."

I scrunch my nose. "Gotta be honest. Still feels a little shady."

"I know," he says with a sigh. "And I would never suggest it if I thought for one second it could hurt you, or worse, cost you your restaurant."

I'm strangely touched by this.

"Really?"

He smiles softly. "Really."

I finish out two plates, giving Sylvia one meatball.

"And if you're not up for it, I'm out. We call it off. But—I'll still show up at your restaurant while we're in town."

Maybe that would be enough. Do we really need to create a whole romance out of it?

But then, how would I pay him back? He wasn't going to let me cook for him without paying me, so I'd be just another person using him for his fame.

If we pretended to be a couple, he'd get something out of it too, at least according to Alicia. I don't really get what, but I guess there are things about being a public figure that don't make sense to me.

I want to help him. I do. Maybe even more than I want the benefits to my restaurant. But I can't square this crazy proposition with who I am as a person. I'm bound to mess this up, right?

"The food is getting cold," I say.

He gives me a nod. "Yep. Let's eat." He glances at the table. "Where's your plate?"

"I can't eat with you every time I cook for you," I say. "Which I'm happy to do, by the way, but we need to sort out the details."

"It's in the contract." Alicia is back, followed by Gram.

"Alicia wants to try your food," he says.

"Only if there's enough," she says. "And only if we can discuss the terms of this arrangement."

I quickly pull out another plate for Alicia, and after I set it on the table, I look at them all. I've put on a nonchalant mask for too long, and it's starting to crack at the edges.

"Excuse me one minute."

I step out of the room and down the hall, searching for a bathroom, which I'm sure is here somewhere. Finally, I locate it, slip inside, and lock the door. My heart is racing.

What is happening?

I'm alone for a grand total of eight seconds when there's a knock on the door. "Poppy?"

Dallas is on the other side, probably wanting to make sure I don't hyperventilate and pass out in his bathroom. The last thing he needs is an ambulance in his driveway.

"I'll be out in a minute."

Then, more quietly, he says, "Are you okay?"

I open the door and pull him inside, closing the door and instantly regretting it. The room is a half bath, larger than a normal person's half bath, but definitely not big enough for two people. Especially when one of them is as tall and solid as Dallas. All of the air has been sucked out from under the door.

"Is this what it's like for you?" I whisper.

"Being pulled into bathrooms by gorgeous women?" He grins. "I mean, I wouldn't say it happens often, but. . ."

I cross my arms over my chest and try not to linger on the fact that he just called me

gorgeous. And that he smells *fantastic*. Neither of those things are the point.

Still. . .gorgeous? Me?

"No, I mean people badgering you until you do what they say."

"Oh, that." He leans against the door. "Yep. That's pretty standard."

I frown. "So your life isn't your own. At all."

He shrugs. "It is and it isn't."

"Well, I don't function that way," I say. "I. . .*can't* function that way. I don't like to be told what to do."

Unless it's by Dallas Burke, apparently.

"You shouldn't like it either," I add, a bit exasperated.

"I don't. But I've proven that every time I make my own decisions, I mess them up."

I knew a little something about that.

He fidgets with his sleeve for a moment, then looks at me. "There is. . .something."

I narrow my gaze. "Did you decide I'm trustworthy?"

"Not yet," he says, a bit playfully. "But I have a feeling you are."

I shift. "I am, for the record." I know what it's like for secrets to get out, and, on a much smaller scale, for people to talk about your mistakes. I would never betray anyone's trust. Especially, for some reason, his.

"I have an idea," he says, and I can tell it's not easy for him.

I stay quiet.

His gaze falls to the floor. "I want to start a..." he takes a breath. "A foundation. For a worthy cause." Then, he looks at me. "Kind of stupid, right?"

I lean back on the sink. "I don't think that's stupid at all."

"You don't?"

"No. I think that makes perfect sense."

"You don't think it's a little unrealistic? It's the good guys in the league who do charity work. Not guys like me."

I laugh. "I thought *I* had self-esteem issues."

He rakes a hand through his hair. "I just think if I start it now, people will think my motives are about changing my image. Like it's a publicity stunt. I don't want to spin this."

"So. . .Alicia doesn't know," I say.

He shakes his head. "If she did, she'd have me on every talk show she can find, peddling the idea. I just want to start quietly and on my own terms. I don't even care if people know it's me doing it—in fact, I'd prefer it that way. But ultimately, I want my reputation to help the cause, not hurt it."

I go quiet. I can see years of regret built up behind his eyes. This isn't the same guy plastered on the covers of magazines.

"What's the cause?" I ask.

He presses his lips together, then his eyes find the ceiling. Even this part seems hard to say out loud.

"You don't have to tell me," I say.

"I will," he says. "Because it's. . ." he stops himself. "One day, I'll tell you all about it."

A pause. I nod. I don't want to push. I can see it's important to him.

"So. . ."

He raises his eyebrows. "So."

I take a deep breath. "If we do this...if we're *really* going to do this, won't both of our reputations be worse off if people find out?"

"That won't happen," he says. "And even if it does, it won't matter, because we'll know the truth."

I give him a look. "You obviously do not watch rom-coms."

"I obviously do not."

He waits a beat.

"Ultimately, it's your decision."

Another pause.

"Even if you are the one who gave Gram the idea in the first place."

I look up, and he's grinning.

I groan, wishing I could turn a circle in the small space, but there's not room. "If we do this"—I draw in a breath and I cannot believe these words are coming out of my mouth— "we do it on *our* terms. Not Gram's, not Alicia's, not *The Mill's*, not social media's, no one else's."

"I like the sound of that," he says. "We make up the rules."

"Right," I say. "Us."

He nods. "Me and you."

It hits different when he says that.

"All right." I stick my hand out, and Dallas's eyes drop to it. "You have a deal."

He slips his hand around mine, and there's that electrical current again. "*We* have a deal." The smile is slow as it crawls across his face. "Might as well have some fun with it, right?"

"I think you and I have very different ideas of fun," I say.

He turns to go, one hand on the doorknob, then stops. He glances at me. "Thanks for doing this, Poppy."

My heart sputters, and I wonder if I can make it a line item in the contract that requires him to say my name at least three times a day.

I blurt out something that sounds like, "Of course."

I also wonder if we should add *No alone time in small spaces* to our list of terms. Because in the grand scheme of things, NDAs and financial compensation were no match for what this whole arrangement might do to my heart.

Chapter Fourteen

Poppy

Dinner was delicious, but odd. Not tense, exactly, but I now kind of understand the dinner scene in the movie version of *Clue*.

Neither Dallas nor I told Alicia or Gram about our bathroom bargain, and it felt nice to have a secret between the two of us.

I also realize this is dangerous territory I'm in right now, like swimming out past the buoys in the ocean. If I'm not careful, I'll start believing the lie myself. Someone like me could fall head over heels for someone like Dallas.

Even with all the warnings ringing out like a tornado siren.

That's the Poppy way. In spite of everything, I still have so many *feelings*.

Once everyone is done eating, I stand to clear the dishes and he puts a hand on my arm. "You cook, I clean."

I go still, and Gram winks at me.

Alicia raises a brow.

"This is part of the job," I say.

"No," he says. "It's not." He takes the plates from me and nods emphatically at my seat.

So, I sit.

He clears the table, rinsing dishes and putting them in the dishwasher while I chat idly with Gram and Alicia wondering if this is real life. How is it that I'm in the home of a famous hockey player and *he* is cleaning up?

He turns the water off and looks at the table. "Poppy and I have decided we'll go along with your ridiculous scheme."

Alicia gives a pointed nod and Gram looks unimpressed, as if this is what she expected all along.

"But only on our terms," he adds.

I chime in. "Neither one of us is interested in being handled."

"But—"

"No." Dallas's firm voice silences his manager. "You can send over the list of public appearances I'm expected to attend, and we'll review them together, decide what Poppy will come to, and get back to you."

"There's a list in the paperwork," Alicia says.

"And I won't accept any payment." I silence Dallas with an upheld hand before he can argue. "The extra foot traffic at the restaurant is plenty."

He narrows his eyes at me, but doesn't object.

"And I won't lie to my family," I say.

"I'm afraid I must insist on keeping them in the dark," Alicia says.

"That's a deal breaker for me," I tell her. "It's going to be hard enough to pretend for the rest of the world, but I'll never lie to my sisters. Or my parents."

Alicia glances at Gram, who gives a little shrug. "Fine. But they will each be asked to sign an NDA." Then, to Dallas, "What else?"

"We'll let you know."

She stands. "Fair enough. Let me know tomorrow. I'll leave the paperwork. You can add your terms, and sign at the bottom in all the places I've marked."

Gram stands. "I'm going to bed."

I also stand because it seems like the thing to do. Seconds later, Alicia walks out the door. Gram goes to her room, and I'm left alone.

With Dallas.

"I didn't have time to make meals for tomorrow, but I have a plan," I say.

"I'll get you a house key so you can cook here if you want to," he says. "Gram's surgery is next week. I got the day off."

I walk over to the stove and begin to pack up the leftover meatballs.

"So, should we talk terms?" he asks, after the counter is thoroughly clean.

"Sure," I say. "There's just one thing. . .isn't this going to get in the way of your real love life?"

"I'm not interested in having a love life right now," he says. "Feelings make things complicated, and honestly, I don't have time to manage someone else's emotions."

"Oh. Well," I say, "nobody can say you're not forthcoming."

"That came out wrong," he says, trying again. "I just. . .don't have a great track record, and I'm not looking for a relationship right now."

"You've sworn off women," I say, remembering what Sylvia had said.

"Pretty much," he says with a heavy sigh. He sits on a stool and leans forward, hands folded on the counter in front of him. "This way, we both know why we're doing this. It's all laid out, and there are no questions." Then, definitively, "I'm paying you to perform a service."

I frown.

"Wait, that came out wrong too."

I laugh. "You are determined to turn me into Julia Roberts, aren't you?"

He shakes his head with a smile. It's shy. Almost embarrassed. And yet, somehow sexy.

And that is a very risky thought.

"Let's talk terms," I say.

"Yes." He stands. "But first, ice cream."

"Do professional athletes get to eat ice cream?" I ask.

He opens the freezer. "This one does." Within seconds, he's pulled out a carton of ice cream, caramel sauce, hot fudge, marshmallow, whipped cream, and cherries. "You like ice cream, right?"

"Who doesn't like ice cream?"

"Canadians," he says.

I laugh out loud, and we get to work dishing up the sundaes.

"Tell me about your family," he says. "You said you have sisters? Do they live here?"

I hadn't considered this part. The *getting-to-know-you* part. I suppose this was bound to happen if Dallas and I were going to spend time together.

"I have two sisters," I say. "My older sister Raya lives here in town but commutes to the city for work. She's smart and successful and beautiful and all the things I'm not."

"Stop it."

"I will. . .try to stop it." I smile. It's nice to have someone contradict my self-deprecation.

"My younger sister Eloise is spunky and fun and a total people person, but she struggles to stay focused, and she's had three different careers since she graduated college. Currently, she's working at an animal shelter."

"And your parents?" he asks.

"They live here," I say. "Always have. We're all pretty close, honestly. It's nice."

"It sounds nice." He eats his ice cream thoughtfully for a few seconds while I work up the courage to ask him about his family.

"Does this mean I get to ask you the same questions?" I ask.

"You didn't Google my whole life's story?" He smiles, and I swear the light overhead flickers its approval.

"Only the important stuff," I say with a smile. "Like 'Are Dallas Burke's abs photoshopped?'"

His laugh is so honest, I want to bottle it up and take it home with me. *I* made Dallas Burke laugh.

I feel very smug about this.

"The results on that search were inconclusive," I say, taking another bite. "So, you might want to set the record straight."

Without a word, he stands and lifts up his shirt.

I remember that women in olden days would wash their garments by rubbing them against a ribbed washboard. . .and I suddenly wish I was a cotton peasant top being gently scrubbed against his stomach somewhere on the Oregon Trail.

As if being pulled by some magnetic force, I reach out and touch his stomach. It's every bit as solid as I expected.

I meet his eyes and find him watching me, one brow raised in amusement. Only then do I realize my huge violation of his personal space. I pull my hand back. "I'm *so* sorry."

"Maybe we should add in a 'no touching' clause." He sits back down, and I can tell he's teasing me, but it does little to make me feel less humiliated.

"How embarrassing," I say.

"I'm kidding." Dallas covers my hand with his and squeezes it. "You don't have to be embarrassed around me, Poppy."

"It's nice of you to say that since so far that's just about all I've been around you."

"I find your honesty refreshing."

I look at him. "You do?"

"Yeah." Another squeeze, this one with a touch of pity. "People usually try to be whoever they think I want them to be, but you seem to just be yourself. That's rare."

"I don't know how to be anyone else," I say.

He looks at me, almost quizzically, as if he's trying to figure out a riddle. Then, he either solves it or deems it too complicated, and pulls his hand away. "We should figure out the terms of this contract."

"Right," I say. "Terms."

"Maybe we should get the hard stuff out of the way first," he says.

"The hard stuff?"

"Public displays of affection," he says nonchalantly. "What are you comfortable with? Holding hands? Peck on the cheek? Full on makeout sessions?" He grins at me like this whole thing is amusing all of a sudden.

If there was any moisture in my mouth at all, it's gone now. I might as well be sucking on cotton balls. "I hadn't thought about that."

"Well, according to Alicia, you should," he says. "She said if we're going to make people believe this is a real relationship, they'll expect some level of intimacy."

"In public?"

He shrugs.

I cover my face with my hands and let out a groan. "Maybe I'm not the right person for this."

When I finally emerge from behind my own hands, I find him watching me with a lop-sided grin on his face.

"You must think I'm an utter lunatic."

"I actually think you're kind of adorable." He stands, walks around to the sink, rinses his bowl out—and he does all of this like the fact that he just said I'm adorable didn't just stop the world from spinning on its axis.

Chapter Fifteen

Poppy

We relocate to the living room, and I beg my brain to get in the game.

Truth be told, it's still in the kitchen, wanting to ask Dallas if he could continue to hold my hand and please elaborate on what about me is so adorable.

Dallas turns on the gas fireplace, loads in some logs, and then sits on the overstuffed sectional. "You should sit in the corner. It's the best spot."

I do as he suggests, and warn myself not to fall asleep. The couch is so comfortable it practically swallows me whole. "This might be the best couch I've ever sat on."

"Where's your house?" he asks—a question that seems to come from nowhere even though it's very basic.

"I live in a Craftsman house near downtown," I say. "It's not huge, nothing like this palatial estate." Dallas shakes his head as I spread out my arms, miming a grand gesture. "When the weather is good, I can walk to the restaurant. It's not fancy, and the entire house could probably fit in two of your rooms, but I like it."

"I'd like to see it," he says. Then quickly adds, "I mean, I probably should if we're going to pull this off."

I smile. "Right." But even as I say it, I wonder just how much I'm willing to reveal to Dallas. Most of his probing questions feel personal, and I answer them honestly.

But that means he's getting to know me. The real me.

I don't know how to feel about that.

It's risky, to say the least. Because while he is probably immune to my nonexistent charms, I am clearly not immune to his. Even after everything, I'm still so willing to put my heart on the line.

That's the danger of wanting to be loved—you start to see possibilities everywhere.

Even where there are none.

"So. . ." he says, "you can look over this whole list of events Alicia mapped out for us." He slides the paper across the coffee table, and I pick it up.

"If I'm not working at the restaurant, I'll be working it with you," I say. My face heats. "Wait. That came out wrong."

He laughs.

I try my best to smear new bad words over the old bad words. "I just mean you have a busier schedule than I do, and I'm easy."

He puts his head down to stifle another laugh.

Good LORD.

I sigh. "Is this the way it's going to be? Like we're in middle school?"

"Apparently so, Pops."

I feign writing on the contract, and pretend to read what I'm writing. "Never. . .use. . .that. . .name. . .ever. . .again."

"Got it," he says.

There's a slight lull, but it's not awkward. I wonder if this is what elderly couples experience when they sit across from one another, after years of marriage, and don't say anything, content to simply be in each other's company.

"So—" Dallas's voice pulls me back to the present— "beyond this, what do you want from me?"

Now I laugh. "Might as well cut to the chase, right?"

He shrugs. "Might as well."

"Well. . ." I pull my knees to my chest and wrap my arms around them. "I should probably focus on what my restaurant needs, right?"

"You don't have to," he says. "Do you want me to be arm candy at that Valentine's Day festival thing of yours?"

I grin. "My right winger Valentine."

He raises a brow. "Well, well, someone's been studying."

"I'm trying to learn the lingo."

"I'm impressed."

My eyes dip to his lips, and I try to ignore the tingling on my own. Would it be presumptuous to add "*One breathless makeout session per week, steamed up car windows optional*" to this contract?

Practice does make perfect, after all.

"What can I say?" I grin. "I'm impressive."

"You have no idea, do you?" He props his feet up on the coffee table and watches me. There's a notebook in his lap.

"I was referring to your position, not politics, by the way," I say. "The right wing thing."

He smiles. "Yeah. I got that."

"Because I feel like I should tell you that, you know, in case you were confused."

Between his smile, his deep, blue eyes, and talk of PDA, I'm out of sorts and struggling to concentrate.

"Poppy."

"Yeah."

He taps his pencil on the pad of paper. "Terms."

"Right," I say. "Business." I sink deeper into the couch. "Don't let me fall asleep."

He chuckles. "If you start to fade, I'll throw things at you."

I grin, then straighten."I've got one! You have to meet my family. And sign a hockey puck for my dad. Do players sign pucks?"

"Yeah," he says. "Or a jersey."

"His name is Mick."

"That's easy." Dallas scribbles on the notepad. "And I'll eat at your restaurant once a week. That will be even easier. It's *so* good." He glances up. "Want me to write down the festival?"

I shake my head. "No. I don't think I'm going to go. Not to the dance, anyway. I'll obviously be at the Taste of Loveland because we have a booth, but that's different from the dance." At the mention of it, I think about Margot and her clones. The years of torment. The years of hiding.

"What are you thinking about?" Dallas asks.

"High school." I roll my eyes. "I probably think about it more than I should."

"What was it like?" he asks.

"I was not popular in high school," I say. "Let's leave it at that."

"I am absolutely not leaving it at that," he says. "You're a chef with your own restaurant. You must've done something right growing up."

I drop my head back onto the cushion behind me. "I had very warped ideas about what was cool."

"Okay. . ."

"You're really going to make me tell you?"

"How about I tell you one embarrassing high school story, and then you tell me one." He settles into the couch like this conversation would pass for entertainment, but I already know his most embarrassing story could never top mine.

"Okay," I say. "I guess that's fair. You go first."

His eyes scroll the air, as if searching through a very long list of options, but I know it's more likely he's having trouble coming up with anything embarrassing.

"Okay," he starts, "how about this one. It's freshman year, it's tryouts for the club hockey team—our high school didn't have one—and there's a senior from my high school that's been on the team all four years. Goalie. Super talented."

I sit a bit forward. I like hearing him talk about this, even though I have no clue about the sport. He's passionate about hockey, and he lights up the room when he talks about it.

"I'm on the second line, think of it as kind of the B team, and I snag a puck that someone on the opposite team was trying to clear. I skate in, around one of the other guys, and five hole it for a goal on the senior."

I want to share in his story, so I gently ask, "...five hole?"

"I shot it between his legs and made him look like an idiot."

I laugh out loud. "Oh my gosh, you what?!"

He's beaming. "Yep. This punk freshman scored on their star goalie."

He stops talking and just looks at me.

"And?" I ask. "What's the embarrassing part?"

He stops, and looks confused for a minute. "Oh. Well, I guess there isn't one in that story. Embarrassing for him, maybe? Does that count?"

"No, that absolutely does not count," I tell him.

"Yeah. Maybe not," he says. "So, it's your turn."

I rub my temples, wondering why I ever agreed to this in the first place.

Chapter Sixteen

Poppy

I draw in a deep breath, regretting this entire conversation before I even get the worst of it out. "I was a senior in high school."

Dallas tosses the notebook aside, far too eager to hear this story, which is so much worse than his.

"It was almost Valentine's Day, and the big final event of the Loveland Festival of Hearts is a formal dance. But it's like a Sadie Hawkins dance."

"Oh yeah, so girls ask guys."

"Right," I say. "I knew a lot of guys who'd asked girls to homecoming or prom and they did these big, elaborate promposals, and I thought it would be a good idea to do the same thing."

"You didn't."

I cringe.

"Uh-oh."

"Yeah." I shake my head. "I cannot believe I'm telling you this."

"Well, you're in it now, so you might as well keep going. I'm not going to tell anyone."

"Can I just go on record and say that in hindsight I DO know that this was the opposite of cool?" I say this on a groan because even just thinking back on it makes me squirm. "You're going to die of secondary embarrassment. I'm just warning you."

"You're stalling."

"I absolutely am. I was hoping the fire would leap from the fireplace and force us to evacuate."

"Spill it, Hart."

I draw in a deep breath. "I had this friend, Tyler Nelson. He was a super great guy, and even though we were just friends, I had a huge crush on him. Doodle-his-name-in-my-notebook-all-day-long kind of crush."

He nods in agreement. "For me, it was Allison Buckley in eighth grade. I think it was her hair that did me in. Carved her name on the bleachers."

I go on, surprisingly comfortable telling this ridiculous story. "So, I got the brilliant idea to ask the cheerleading coach if I could take over the Friday afternoon pep assembly so I could share a very special Valentine's Day message."

"She didn't ask you what it was?"

"Sadly, no, and I think if she had, she probably would've advised against it."

He looks like he's holding in a laugh, and I haven't even gotten to the embarrassing part yet.

"So, I worked really, really hard on this—I spent hours practicing what I was going to do, and the day came, and I took my spot in the locker room, and after the cheerleaders were done, the stage was mine.

"Mrs. Doane, the coach, introduced me over the microphone, and the rest is a blur. . ."

"I know that's not true."

"It's not," I say. "I remember every single detail in slow motion."

"You're killing me, but your delivery is excellent. I'm totally invested."

My eyes jump to his, and I shake my head. "I performed a whole routine to the song "Kiss You" by One Direction."

"Are you a dancer?"

"No."

"A singer?"

"No."

He tries to put it together. "So then, how did you. . ."

"I lip synced the entire thing. And at the end, I had a giant sign that said, '*Let Me Kiss You, Tyler, at the Festival of Hearts.*'"

For a long moment, he doesn't speak, but he's pressing his lips together in a way that makes me think the laugh is just itching to come out.

"Go ahead and laugh," I say.

And he does. "I'm so sorry. I tried to hold it in. I'm just trying to picture it." He laughs again. "You win major bravery points."

"I don't know what I was thinking. I worked out choreography and everything."

More laughter. "Oh, man."

"But haven't you ever been that crazy over someone?" I ask. "To make a complete fool of yourself?"

"No," he says. "I honestly don't think I have."

"Well, that's sad," I say. "I think it showed just how much I liked him."

"How did he react?"

"Oh, he was a total champ," I say. "He came out and gave me a hug in public and then let me down easy later, in private.

He just saw me as a friend. But hey, at least I tried. I would've always wondered if I hadn't."

Dallas nods. "That's probably the best story I've ever heard."

"Well, I'm happy to share my humiliation as long as it entertains."

He writes something down on the notepad.

"What did you write?"

"Go to the Loveland Festival of Hearts Dance."

"We really don't have to do that."

"I think we do." He shifts his position on the sofa. "I think we need to redeem the dance for you."

"I'm okay," I say. "That was a long time ago. And I've had plenty more embarrassing stories since then."

So many embarrassing stories. *But only one that still hurts.*

Avi.

When he left, everyone knew what happened. Correction—everyone *thought* they knew what happened. There was a police report. It was in the newspaper. The real one, not just *The Mill*. I wonder if anyone will ever forget. If my life were a book, I swear the title would be *Poppy Hart Fails Again*.

He watches me. Sometimes I get the impression he's doing more than watch—he studies. It should probably be unnerving, but for some reason, at the moment, I like being the subject of his attention.

"Let's move on," I say.

"Okay, but I'm leaving it on the list," he says. "It can be our last hurrah before we stage a breakup. You'll be dumping me, by the way. Not in public. Just a quiet, amicable separation."

I nod. That's the part I need to keep in mind.

This fake relationship has an expiration date.

"What do you want from me?" I ask, feeling emotionally naked in the wake of this entire conversation.

"What do I want from you. . ." He seems to be thinking, and then, with a completely straight face he says, "Hm. Yeah, I think I'm gonna need to see the choreography."

I take the pillow from behind me and chuck it at him. He catches it with a laugh, then tosses it back.

"Okay, let me think. . ."

I hug my knees closer to my chest and try to study him the way he studied me. In spite of a neat cut, his dark hair is purposely messy on top. His blue eyes glimmer as he gives thought to the question on the table. He drags a hand over his shadowed chin.

Again, my toes curl. I want him to drag that hand over me. Anywhere.

"I don't really want anything from you," he says. "If I'm honest, I just want your restaurant to take off." Then, after a pause, he adds, "No, wait. I got it. You have to keep cooking for me."

"But. . .that's easy. And fun."

He pumps a fist. "Good. I want to try everything. Chicken, pork, beef tips. . ."

"Slow down, you bottomless pit," I hold up the paper outlining Alicia's requirements. "I don't think you're going to get away with just wanting that."

He groans. "You know I don't care about this stuff."

"Well, maybe you should," I say. I look over the list. "Maybe being more intentional about how the public views you is smart?"

"I guess," he says. "If it could help with team dynamics, maybe it is."

"So, public appearances?" I ask.

"Sure," he says. "Only if you're okay with it. A few home games—you can bring whoever you want. If any interview requests come up, we can navigate those."

I nod. "Done. My life is yours for the next four weeks."

He cocks his head. "Ditto."

I laugh. "Your life isn't even *yours* so it's definitely not mine."

"That's true." He goes still. "And as far as the physical stuff —" He glances down at the notebook.

I almost swallow my tongue, thankful that he's content to fill in the blanks on this topic.

"Holding hands. Close contact at public events. Maybe a kiss or two if we need to sell it. Nothing too crazy." He's been writing as he says this, but my mind keeps stumbling on the words *a kiss or two.*

Can I up that number?

Obviously, I didn't plan for kissing or the way mentioning it has made my heart bounce around in my chest like a kindergartner in a ball pit.

When he's finished writing, his eyes meet mine. "You're okay with that?"

"Mmm-hmm."

"You're sure?"

I nod. "But only in public."

He returns to the notepad, reciting as he writes, "No messing around in private."

"Messing around. Ha. That's *such* a guy way to phrase it." I giggle.

"Okay, what would you call it?"

"Making out!" I blurt the words before I even realized they'd formed in my brain.

And now I wish the couch would come alive and swallow me whole.

He looks a bit shocked, slowly lowers his pencil, and mouths the words "Making...out..." as he writes it in his notebook. "Oh, yeah. That's *way* better."

"Can we just move on? Let's just move on and pretend I never said that."

He tucks his lips in his teeth and scrunches up his face, then nods. He will definitely not move on.

"I hate to even ask this. . .but. . .what about sleeping over? In the guest room, I mean?"

I swallow—or maybe it's more of a gulp. "Might not play well with your squeaky clean image?"

"Right," he says. "Good call." Then, to the notebook: "No sleeping over unless impaired."

I laugh. "I won't be impaired. I don't drink."

"You could get tired."

"Not tired enough to sleep over." I laugh again, probably because talking about this so openly makes me nervous. Or maybe because now I have "Kiss You" going through my head, and I'm trying not to burst out into song.

We spend a few more minutes perfecting our list. Dallas is an excellent scribe, but a slow one, and in the quiet, I close my eyes. I'm aware of the flickering fire. I'm aware of the scribbling pencil. I'm aware of how warm and cozy this couch is. And then, I'm aware of nothing.

Chapter Seventeen

Poppy

My eyes flutter. There's dim light streaming through the window.

Daylight.

It's morning.

My eyes shoot open wide.

It's MORNING.

My brain tries to calculate what time it is, as if I know these things based on how deep into sunrise we are. I feel around for my phone, abruptly sitting up. Only then do I realize I'm covered with a fluffy cream-colored blanket and Dallas is breathing softly on the opposite end of the couch.

Did he put this blanket on me last night? I wish I'd been awake to watch that happen. Nobody would believe that he has such a soft side.

But I don't have time to think about that right now, partly because I'm late and partly because I can't turn to mush before I've even started my day. I fumble with my phone, and when it finally comes to life I discover I have twenty minutes to get to work. I stand up, frantic, and when I do, Dallas opens his eyes.

"Hey." He stretches and I catch a glimpse of the underside of his bicep. *It's lovely.* Then, most likely noticing the panic on my face, he adds, "What's wrong?"

"I'm late," I say. "I need to get to work."

He stands. "Shoot! I'm so sorry—I thought I set an alarm." He looks at his phone. "I must not have."

I ruefully chuckle to myself as I hunt around for my shoes. "Remember when I said 'don't let me fall asleep'?"

"No, but I remember when you said 'I won't fall asleep.'" He says this in a high-pitched voice.

I stop and look at him. "Is that your Poppy voice?"

He shrugs.

I purposefully lower the pitch of my voice and say, "Because I don't sound like that."

He stifles a laugh. "Sorry. What can I do? How can I help?"

I take a breath and blow it out. "Nothing. It's okay. I'll text Miguel and—" I pull the elastic from my hair and smooth out the long, dark waves. "Actually, do you have an extra toothbrush?"

"In the drawer of the guest bathroom," he says. "My cleaning lady stocked it like a hotel."

I stare at him for a beat. "Thank you." I rush into the bathroom and try to salvage yesterday's makeup. The smudged mascara under my eyes is not a great look, and yet if I wipe it away my eyes will be bare, which is an even worse look. I lean toward the mirror.

I can pass this off as a smokey eye, right?

I hurry and brush my teeth, then search the cabinets for deodorant, which I apply with gusto before even giving it a sniff.

I look at the tube. It's *Old Spice Kraken.*

Oh, great, now I smell like a man. More specifically, I smell like Dallas, which is going to be distracting all day long.

When I'm finished, I hurry back into the kitchen, find my bag and realize I have all of last night's dinner supplies here. "Can I get this stuff later?"

"Of course." He hands me a travel mug.

"What's this?"

"Coffee." He picks up the peppermint creamer. "It's not a fancy one, but hopefully it's close."

"You made me peppermint coffee?"

"That's what you like, right?"

I look at the cup. It has the Chicago Comets logo on the side, and it's full of perfectly brewed hot peppermint goodness. "Thank you."

He nods. "I'll send Alicia the terms we came up with."

"And tonight is dinner with my family." I want to tell them as soon as possible. Nothing will feel right until they all know the truth about what is going on.

"I'll be there."

I start toward the front door and realize he's following me. I tug on my coat, then turn to look at him. "Um. . .goodbye? I guess? Have. . .er. . .a good day at practice."

He pulls the door open, and I head outside, the chill of the morning cooling the heat from my skin.

Behind me he mockingly shouts in his Poppy voice, "Have a good day at work, honey!"

I turn around to give him a mad look, but I can't help but laugh as I hiss at him to shut up.

The whole exchange felt a little too *morning after* for me, and as I start my car and pull away from his sprawling home, I can't help but realize that we've already broken a rule.

It's all downhill from here.

Terms for the Relationship Between Dallas Burke and Poppy Hart

Four-Week Plan. From now until Valentine's Day.

1. Dallas must meet the Hart family and sign a puck (or jersey) for Poppy's dad
2. Dallas must eat at Poppy's Kitchen once a week and post about it—positively—on social media.
3. Poppy will be the private chef for Gram (but make enough food for Dallas) because her food is amazing, and I might as well put it in the contract that I get to eat it. Dallas will pay for all supplies.
4. There is a separate payment for all culinary services.
5. Dallas reserves the right to ask for seconds and thirds at any time.
6. Poppy will attend at least four (4) home games, as her schedule allows.
7. Dallas will attend three (3) Loveland Festival of Hearts events, including the dance on Valentine's Day.
8. Formal attire required.
9. Dallas will look hot.
10. No touching/kissing etc. in private. Purely professional.
11. Acceptable PDA as needed: hand holding, light kissing. Poppy doesn't want to be trashy about it, though she freely admits that kissing Dallas could be an excellent way to pass the time.
12. Dallas returns the sentiment.

Text thread between Dallas & Alicia:

ALICIA

Got the terms. This will work. Make sure you sell it.

Let's get her to a game.

DALLAS

Let's wait. I don't want to throw her in the deep end.

ALICIA

The whole point is to be seen.

DALLAS

We will be. But it'll be here.

ALICIA

Where she'll get all the publicity, and you'll get none.

DALLAS

<shrugging emoji>

ALICIA

Take her out a few times, but we need to get her to a game.

DALLAS

We will. But not till she's ready.

Chapter Eighteen

Dallas

Poppy didn't ask me to help her explain this plan to her family, but I'm glad I'm going to be there when she does. I have a feeling it's not going to be easy for her. Essentially, we're selling a lie, and I know she has a strong moral objection to that.

I don't mind so much, because it will help someone else. It's for the greater good.

I drive back to Loveland after practice to pick up Gram. She meets me in the garage, and I plug the address to Poppy's parents' house into my GPS. Once she's settled in the passenger seat—after shooing me away because she "doesn't need help"— we head out of the long driveway.

I like that this house is private, but until the mystery of a professional hockey player living in a small town fades away, I do need to take security precautions. I hate that I do. I'd hoped that living here might be a nice change.

"What, no Gerard tonight?" Gram asks as I turn out onto the road.

"I don't want to seem too pretentious," I say. "These are very down to earth people."

"Smart," she says.

We sit in silence for several miles, and then she pulls something from her purse. "This came for you today."

I glance over and see she's holding an envelope. "What is it?"

She looks away. "It's from your dad."

I shake my head. "You can throw it out the window."

Gram nods and tucks the letter away.

Just knowing it's there in her purse grates on me. I know Gram feels obligated to share these things with me, but I won't change my mind.

When I was first drafted, my dad wasn't a problem. He didn't keep tabs on me, and I didn't keep tabs on him. Easy.

Family drama is a lot easier to deal with when there's no communication.

Thanks to Gram, his identity had remained a secret all these years. It helped that we changed my last name and he's not listed on my birth certificate.

But as my popularity grew, so did his interest. In me. In my career. And especially, in my money. I'd already given him more than I should've, because, I don't know, I felt. . .obligated or something.

But I'm done.

Done paying for a mistake I'd made when I was a kid. A mistake I'm not even sure qualifies as a mistake, because looking at it now, as an adult, I think I'd do it again.

But he held it over me. Like I owed him.

The man was a leech.

After the accident, I got a card in the mail. On it were the words: *Guess you're more like me than you thought.*

No signature, but I knew who it was from.

I rearranged some drywall in my place with a few fist-sized holes.

"Is he going to be a problem?" I ask Gram as I turn down a rural road flanked by brown, bare cornfields.

"I'll talk to Alicia," Gram says. "We'll make sure it's not."

The thought of that man reinserting himself in my life ties my stomach into a knot.

Gram pats my arm. "We'll make sure."

Up ahead, a quaint two-story farmhouse with a nice-sized yard comes into view. Two golden retrievers race around the grass at the sight of our car, running and barking and probably planning their slobber attack for the second we open the car doors.

Poppy appears on the porch. She's wearing jeans and a simple cream-colored sweater, and I realize I wasn't lying the day we met when I told that awful woman I loved Poppy's curves. There's something so unexpectedly attractive about her, and I don't know what to make of that.

I shouldn't be noticing it at all.

But I am.

"Well, this is a whole different world, isn't it?" Gram pipes up, interrupting my runaway fantasies with the important reminder that Poppy and I don't exist in the same universe.

"That's what's so great about her," Gram says.

"As long as being dragged into *my* world doesn't change her." I put the car in park and cut the engine.

"I think she's too smart for that," Gram says.

I look at Poppy again and see that both dogs now sit calmly at her side. She waves. She really is the girl-next-door. Pretending to be dating might not be the difficult part of this whole arrangement.

Not letting myself actually develop feelings for her is a bigger concern.

"What are we waiting for?" Gram asks.

I shake the thoughts away and get out of the car, waving at Poppy as I do.

"I'll keep the dogs back while you help your grandma out of the car," she calls out.

I run over to the passenger side of the car and offer Gram a hand. I'm shocked when she takes it, then holds onto my arm as we make our way up the sidewalk to the porch stairs. She stops at the bottom.

"You got this?" I ask.

She nods and grasps the railing as she ambles up toward where Poppy is standing.

Poppy greets her with a smile. Then, she looks at me, and her smile holds. "We're glad you're both here. Thursday night dinners are a regular thing in our house. You might get suckered into a few board games while you're here."

Was now a good time to tell her I'd never played a board game in my life? As different as my present-day world is from hers, my childhood world was a whole other kind of different. She didn't need to know about that, though. Nobody did.

"My mom is cooking tonight. She's making chicken fajitas, so I hope you're both hungry."

"I'm always hungry," I say, suddenly nervous to walk through the door and meet Poppy's family. I realize as I'm standing there, I want them to like me. As much as I want the general public to forget my mistakes and give me a second chance, I want the approval of these perfect strangers even more, and I'm not sure why.

"Who are these guys?" I ask, looking at the dogs who are very well-trained, but who clearly want to jump all over us.

"This is Charlie and this is Gus."

At the sound of their names, both dogs whimper. I rub their

ears simultaneously and wonder why I don't have a dog. I always wanted one.

"Let's go inside so you can meet everyone," Poppy says.

"Have you told them anything yet?" I ask.

She shakes her head. "I thought we could do it together."

"They're not going to go for this, are they?" I ask.

She shrugs, but judging by the look on her face, I'd say it's a no. I follow her inside. *Here goes nothing.*

Chapter Nineteen

Dallas

We walk inside, and I'm struck by a home that is everything my childhood home was not. There is a whole collection of family photos lining the wall of the staircase, and we're greeted by the smell of food cooking in the kitchen. I can hear voices in the other room, though I can't make out what they're saying. Someone laughs. Dishes clank. Is it possible to be nostalgic for something you never experienced?

"Everyone is back this way." Poppy motions for us to follow her, and we start off toward the voices.

We enter the bright yellow kitchen and everyone stops talking to stare at me. I should be used to it by now, but I'm not. It sends me back to elementary school when everyone stared at me for other reasons.

The dirty hair in desperate need of a cut. The worn-out shoes with holes in the toes. The ill-fitting clothes that weren't clean half the time.

Thank God Gram stepped in when she did.

I smile, hoping it covers the heartache I'm trying not to feel.

"Everyone, this is Dallas Burke and his grandma, Sylvia," Poppy says.

I lift a hand in a wave.

"Dallas, Sylvia, this is my sister Raya," Poppy says, motioning to a classically beautiful, dark-haired woman.

She doesn't smile when she nods a hello. "Nice to meet you both." Her expression tells me she's wholly unimpressed by my fame. I can already tell that she'll be the hardest to win over.

But I love a challenge.

"And this is Eloise," Poppy says.

A petite blonde with golden hair and Poppy's same big, blue eyes, jumps up and sticks her hand out.

I shake it and smile. "Nice to meet you, Eloise."

"Nice to meet *you*, Mr. Dallas—wait, can I just call you Dallas?"

"Well, I hope you weren't going to call him 'Mr. Dallas,'" Poppy says. "He's not a preschool teacher."

Eloise's laugh sounds nervous.

"You can call me Dallas, that's totally fine," I say.

She turns to Gram and takes her hand, holding it like it's something precious. "And it's so nice to meet you too. Poppy says you have surgery next week. If you want, I could bring one of our therapy dogs out afterwards. Not that a hip replacement is traumatic exactly, but Susie, my favorite black lab, is great at keeping people's spirits up."

Gram hates animals, but thankfully has the good sense not to say so.

"That would be kind," she says, probably smitten with Eloise's big blue eyes and genuine smile. Neither of us have met a lot of people like this in our lifetime.

"And this is my mom, Tammy." Poppy motions toward a woman standing at the stove, stirring something in a pan. She's got kind, mothering eyes, and her face is bright.

Tammy smiles. "We are so happy to have you both here for dinner."

"We're happy to be here," I say. "We appreciate the invitation."

"Though we are wondering what the big announcement is," Raya says, straight to the point.

"Raya." Poppy rolls her eyes. "Dallas, let's go meet my dad."

She leads us out of the room, then turns to me but keeps walking. "I didn't tell him you were coming." She grins. "I hope that's okay."

"Is he going to be okay with me being here?" I ask.

"He's going to freak out." Her giddiness is adorable, but I try not to notice. "Huge fan, remember?"

We follow Poppy into the living room, where her dad sits, watching the television. He looks at us and his eyes go wide. He leaps from the couch, making hooting sounds. He looks at Poppy and begins moving his hands frantically, mouth moving without saying any words.

"Dallas Burke? Here? In my house?" Poppy says, interpreting what I realize is her father's sign language. Then, to her dad, "In the flesh."

He puts his hands on either side of his head and makes an exaggerated shocked face. Poppy signs as she speaks. "And this is Sylvia, Dallas's grandma."

Gram smiles at him as I step forward to shake his hand. "It's good to meet you, sir."

He shakes my hand, then signs again while Poppy interprets.

"Please, call me Mick," she says.

"It's good to meet you, Mick."

"I can't believe it," Poppy says, interpreting. "The girls said Poppy had met you, but I never thought I'd see you here, in my own living room! Please, sit."

I sit in the armchair next to him, Poppy between us. "Poppy invited us for dinner."

"We have a few things we want to talk to you about," Poppy says.

I watch her hands as they move so quickly, enamored by this language that's so foreign to me, but clearly so comfortable to them.

"Things like. . .?"

Poppy points to the doorway, where Tammy is standing. "Mick, we'll discuss it at dinner," she says with her mouth and her hands. "Which is ready, by the way."

"It smells wonderful," I say.

Tammy smiles, then looks at Poppy. "Dallas Burke says my food smells wonderful." She gives her shoulders a little shimmy.

"He says that to all the girls," Poppy says.

Tammy swats her with a dish towel. "Hurry up before it gets cold."

We all gather around a large table in the dining room, and it occurs to me that I've never had a family dinner like this. Growing up, after I moved in with Gram, it was just the two of us, so we didn't have the chaos of several conversations going on at the same time. It was always quiet. Always boring. Especially for a kid who hated school and was dealing with a lot of anger.

But it was peaceful.

Poppy's parents' house isn't peaceful. Eloise and Raya are talking at the same time while Tammy jumps up every few minutes to get something she forgot in the kitchen. As she bustles around the table, she checks in with Mick. A hand on his shoulder. A quick signed comment meant just for him. She fusses over him in a way that says she loves him, and I feel humbled that I get to witness it.

When he's not interacting with his wife, Mick is peppering me with hockey questions, which Poppy says aloud. There's something about her posture that makes her feel like a bystander in this madness.

"So, you and Aaron Mulligan," Eloise says with a nod my way.

"El—" Poppy glares at her.

"What?" Eloise says and signs. "I'm trying to give him a chance to tell his side of the story."

"There's video of the fight, and he threw the first punch," Raya says, demonstrating with her fist. "Not sure what he can say to dispute that."

"Nothing," I say, honestly. "It was dumb. I shouldn't have lost my temper."

"Especially not over Jessie DeSoto," Eloise says. "She can't even sing."

I laugh. "My issues with Mulligan have nothing to do with her."

"What about the drunk driving?" Raya asks.

"Raya!" Poppy's cheeks are red. It's cute. And the fact that she's defensive of me is even cuter. As if I can't stand up for myself. As if I haven't heard it all before.

"I'm so sorry," Poppy says to me.

I smile and nod. "I'm a big boy, I can take it. This isn't half of what I have to deal with when it comes to the media. *That*," I reach for a bowl, "I have to take *on camera*."

Poppy then turns to her sister. "He wasn't drunk. I explained that to you."

Raya chews her food silently, unimpressed.

"We might as well get this out of the way." Poppy takes a breath. "Look, the real reason I wanted Dallas to come meet you all is because there's been a sort of. . .development." She signs this as she talks. I'm drawn in by the way they all communicate with Mick. It's amazing to watch each one of them sign like it's second nature. I want to learn it myself.

"What kind of development?" Tammy asks.

"One that's mutually beneficial. I hope." Poppy stands and pulls the contracts from her bag, then passes them around the table.

"What is this?" Raya asks.

"It's an NDA," Poppy says.

"Like a gag order?" Raya scoffs.

"Like a promise to keep your mouth shut," Poppy says.

"You're making us sign something?" Raya asks. "You don't trust us?"

"*I* trust you," Poppy says with her voice and her hands. "But Dallas's manager insisted on it. This is how they do things in the big leagues."

I sit back and watch, wondering what it was like to have siblings. Do you just automatically get instant friends?

And to have two parents who clearly loved each other —and you?

"I don't think professional hockey is called 'the big leagues'," Eloise says. Then, to me, "Right, *Dallas*?"

I glance at Poppy, who rolls her eyes so I choose not to answer.

"ANYway," she says. "Sign them."

Mick is first to sign his contract and slide it back. As he does, he signs something to Poppy.

"Dad says he won't say a word," Poppy says out loud. She grins over at him, and his face lights in a bright smile.

Raya is, not surprisingly, last to sign. After she does, she glares at me, then snaps her attention to Poppy.

"Tell us what's going on, Poppy," she says. "The truth."

"Okay." Poppy draws in a breath and meets my eyes from across the table. "This cannot leave this room."

"We got it," Eloise says. "You just made us sign a legal document, for crying in a bucket."

I have no idea what that means, but nobody else bats an eye.

Poppy sits. "Dallas and I are—business partners."

There's a pause followed by a barrage of questions, the most pressing, it seems, being: "Is he investing in the restaurant?"

That probably would've been better—I should've just offered to do that. But Alicia would've said no. How would that make me look reformed?

"No," Poppy says. "But it will *help* the restaurant." She turns to her dad. "It'll help me pay off my debts."

He pats Poppy's hand, then signs something to Poppy.

"There *is* a rush, Dad," she says aloud, hands moving. "I don't like owing money to anyone, but especially not to you and Mom."

"Poppy," Tammy says. "That's what family is for."

I go still.

That wasn't what my family was for.

I had a father trying to mooch off of me and a mother who'd walked out on me when I was still a kid. This was unlike any family I'd ever seen.

Poppy shakes her head. "It's already settled. I'm paying you guys back and that's final. And thanks to Dallas, I have a way to do it."

After a beat, all eyes are on me.

"Did you *Pretty Woman* our sister?" Raya asks.

"Did I what. . . ?"

Beside me, Gram chuckles, pointing a finger at Raya. "I like this one," she says.

"It's not like that, Raya," Poppy says. "Not exactly."

"I don't get it," Eloise says. "Maybe a more current reference, Ray?"

Raya rolls her eyes. "*Maid in Manhattan?*"

Eloise shakes her head.

"Me Before You?"

"Oh, my gosh, is that the one with Wolverine in it?

Poppy puts her head in her hands. "That's *Someone Like You,*" she says and signs without looking up. Then, she lifts her head and says, "How about *The Proposal.*"

Eloise claps her hands together, seemingly over the moon excited. "Fake marriage?!"

Poppy holds up her hands. "Kind of. Not that. . .far down the road."

Raya sits back in her chair, continuing to size up both the situation and me. "*Pretty Woman* is a classic, Eloise. Though, much of it is problematic."

"You think?" Tammy shakes her head.

Then the questions resume, hands signing so frantically I'm sure Mick can't keep up any better than I can.

Raya: "Are you his hired plaything?"

Tammy: "I don't know if I'm comfortable with *all* of that. . ."

Eloise: "Do you have to, like, consummate the relationship?"

"*I'm not selling my body*!" Poppy says loudly, silencing everyone at the table.

There's a brief pause.

"They're in a relationship," Gram says.

"A *fake* relationship," Poppy adds.

For the first time since we sat down, there's complete silence. It's almost eerie. And then, as if on cue, another bombardment of overlapping questions. It reminds me of the press after a game.

To me, Eloise asks, "Why would you need a *fake* girlfriend?"

To Poppy, Tammy asks, "Wouldn't you rather date someone for real? You're almost thirty. You're not getting any younger."

To Poppy, Mick signs, "Any chance you can score us tickets to a game?" Poppy says this so quietly I almost miss it.

To me, Raya says, "If you hurt her, I'm going to make your life miserable."

Poppy stands and lifts her arms. "Would everyone just let me explain, please?"

They go quiet again, and Poppy lays it all out for them. Listening to her explain, it really does sound like a ludicrous idea. And yet, as I watch Poppy, I'm struck all over again by how good and honest she is.

"It's mutually beneficial," she says after it's all out. "I help prove that Dallas has changed—and he gives my restaurant a much-needed boost. His reputation is fixed and I pay everyone back."

She seems to rest her case, sitting back in her chair and finally taking a bite of the food on her plate. I wait until she looks at me to give her a little nod that I hope communicates *Well done.*

Her face softens and I feel her relax from all the way across the table, and I realize that she and I really are partners in this.

Teammates. And something about that comforts me.

Who knew a fake relationship could do that?

The {Rumor} Mill

Spotted: *Poppy Hart skating away from Dallas Burke's house in the early hours of the morning...*

Things must be heating up for Loveland's hottest new couple because according to multiple sources, Dallas Burke's SUV was parked outside the Hart home yesterday for *quite* a while.

That's not really the big news around here, because Poppy was seen covering a whole shift at her overcrowded restaurant in *yesterday's* clothes!

What do you think...is it really a "walk of shame" if you're driving?

After multiple reports of hockey's favorite bad boy showing up at Poppy's Kitchen just yesterday, this Miller can only speculate that against all odds, our local chef really has caught the eye of the millionaire right winger.

I think we can safely say *nobody* saw this coming.

<Series of photos of Poppy Hart out and about around town. In every photo, Poppy is dressed in workout clothes, wearing no makeup, with her hair piled in a bun on top of her head.>

From these glamour shots, I guess nobody can say Dallas Burke is shallow.

Chapter Twenty

Poppy

A few days after our agreement is made, I get an email from Alicia with a list of possible "outings." I'm thankful she doesn't call them "dates."

"We'll stick close to Loveland to start with, gauge how the locals respond to you two, then we'll move on to a bigger stage, per Dallas's request."

I'm thankful we're easing into this.

The plan is for Alicia to sell the public on a "celebrity falls for ordinary girl" story, because apparently, people really love that.

"Every girl wants to believe she has a shot with someone famous," Alicia told me at one point. I want to tell her that the thought has never crossed my mind before now, but I'm in deep enough with the little white lies.

I can't see Dallas's hockey fans, a large percentage of whom are most likely men, caring about him being reformed or caring that he's dating a small town chef. But, according to Alicia, most advertising is geared toward women. "They're the ones we want to win over. The women and the execs."

But they aren't really the ones Dallas wants to win over.

Alicia might have big plans involving sports drinks and shoe companies, but Dallas is looking to make a more permanent mark doing work that means a whole lot more than money in his bank account. While I still don't understand what part I have to play in him accomplishing that goal, I know it's a worthy one, and I want to help if I can.

My instructions, per Alicia, are simple: She wants to show the world that I'm a wholesome, sweet, kind-hearted woman who sees a lot of good in Dallas.

The only problem is that I have no idea how to convey these things.

One reason I was feeling semi-okay about any of this is because I wasn't planning to do much pretending. I *do* like Dallas. I *do* think he's handsome. I *do* believe he's a good person, regardless of his reputation in the media. The only bit of faking I knew I'd have to do is the actual *falling in love*.

That, I remind myself, *has* to be fake.

I notice Dallas is also copied on the email and wish I felt comfortable enough with him to reach out and ask what he thinks of Alicia's "date" ideas. Most are things I cannot imagine Dallas doing, even if we *were* in love. I mean, what man wants to "sit in a bookstore and read while holding hands and drinking coffee for at least an hour"?

Because that's number ten on this list.

Now that I think about it, I wish I *did* know a man who wanted to do that with me. I'd marry him on the spot.

The day after we signed the contract, Dallas went on the road. After three days away, he's back now—so this is it.

Our first, official, real fake date.

I get through the Saturday morning rush with all the grace of an albatross, and about ten minutes after Serena flipped the sign on the door to *Closed*, Dallas shows up.

Unfortunately for him, there are still plenty of people finishing their meals, and I don't have the heart to kick anyone out.

We arranged to meet here instead of at one of our houses, mainly because it's more public. Now that he's sitting in my dining room, I feel the rise of fear and self-doubt.

I stare at him through the window in the kitchen door, marveling at the way he even makes *sitting there* look good.

But it's more than that, isn't it? *He's* more than that. He's not *just* a good-looking guy. He's a kind one. The way he cares for his grandmother. The way he didn't try anything when I fell asleep at his house.

And of course, the way he jumped right in to help me with Margot. I'd fake date him for a year just because of that.

I found a single article buried on the twenty-third page of Google results after typing in "*Is Dallas Burke a good guy?*"

I scrolled through twenty-three pages.

The article highlighted Dallas' work with underprivileged kids, through various organizations. I don't understand why the media seems intent on not writing about this side of him. If more people saw it, they'd fall in love with him.

Which is exactly what I will *not* do.

"Are you just going to stand back here gawking at him?" Kit inches up on her tiptoes to peer through the same window I'm looking through.

"What? *No,*" I say, huffing away. "Of course not. I'm just trying to work up the courage."

Serena pushes the door open and looks at me with an expression that seems to say "Are you going out there or what?"

"I still have to change," I say.

"Well, at least tell him," Kit says.

I muster up my courage and walk out into the dining room. I can feel the eyes of the few diners watching me as I make my way over to his table, which is, naturally, right in the middle of the restaurant.

"Whoever sat you here clearly wanted to put you on display," I say as I reach him.

He stands, reaches for my arm and leans in to kiss me on the cheek. The single, swift action fills my mind with images of forthcoming PDA, and my whole body tingles because of it.

"Please, sit," he says.

I do, and once we're eye-to-eye I'm reminded how very out of my league I am.

But then I decide it would be smart to think of Dallas as *just a friend* instead of thinking of him as *fantasy plaything*, and I remember we're in this together.

Business partners.

Teammates, kind of.

"So," I say, because I'm an excellent conversationalist.

He smiles. "How was your day?"

"Busy," I tell him. "Nonstop. It pays to have beautiful, famous friends." I regret the words as soon as they're out of my mouth. As if I could conceal the fact that I think he's beautiful. As if I'm the only one.

"Beautiful, huh?"

I look away, but not before his smirk registers. I swipe my hands down the sides of my pants. "I saw Alicia's list. Did you pick somewhere to go?"

He shakes his head. "I didn't read it."

I laugh. "Do you want me to tell you what was on it?"

Another shake. "Nah, I think we should come up with our own list."

I lean in. "Isn't the point here to show the world how *reformed* you are?"

"I think the point is to show this town what a good chef you are."

As soon as he says the words, it's obvious to me that his reasons for doing this have very little to do with him or what he wants.

I hold up my hands in a mock *whoa.* "Okay, buddy, if you want to break the rules, what do you have in mind?"

"Do you have different clothes?"

I laugh. "What, you don't want to be seen with me in my stained uniform?"

He looks amused. "You know, everyone thinks you're so sweet, but I'm starting to think that they're completely wrong."

"Oh, they are. I *absolutely* have a snarky side," I say.

"Good. Get changed."

I don't like to be bossed around.

Unless it's by Dallas Burke, apparently.

I turn toward the kitchen and see two pairs of eyeballs staring at me through the windows of the door.

Something about that makes me feel giddy.

I rush back to my office and pull the blinds, then change into jeans and a pale pink sweater. I take the elastic from my hair, touch up what little makeup I have on, and emerge from the office in record time. When I do, I find Dallas standing in the kitchen, talking with Miguel.

Judging by the smile on his face, Miguel is a fan, and there's a tiny part of me that feels grateful that my accidental word vomit and left arm accosting landed me here. It was like the day I brought Eloise into school for show-and-tell. All of the other kindergartners were as smitten with *my baby* as I was, and I felt so darn special being the one to bring that kind of joy into the classroom.

Dallas laughs at something Miguel says, and I see it, that spark of connection, the moment he wins a person over. It's a gift, really.

He notices me standing there, and his eyebrows pop up. "Wow, you look great."

I don't have to turn to see both Kit and Serena react to this comment, and I don't need a mirror to know that my cheeks are red because of it.

"Thanks," I say, hugging my coat as if it's a life preserver and I have no idea how to swim. "Ready?"

"Where are you guys headed?" Miguel asks, still smiling.

Dallas turns to me. "It's a surprise."

"Have fun, you two," Miguel says. "We'll see you tomorrow, Chef."

I smile at all three of my employees and follow Dallas out the door, through the restaurant, and onto the street. A few people milling about downtown stop to take note, trying—failing—to discreetly take photos on their phones. I start toward Dallas's car, but he grabs my hand.

I stop and stare at it, like I'm a palm reader and just found the most fascinating line.

"I thought we'd walk," he says.

"Oh, okay." I wish I'd had a chance to wipe my hand off before he grabbed it. My palms are clammy.

He gives me a little tug, and we start off down the street.

"People are staring," I say, feeling like we're on parade.

"Isn't that kind of the point?" He looks at me, but I keep my gaze forward, trying to pretend I don't mind pretending. "Are you okay?"

I nod as we walk past the hardware store. "Where are we going?"

"You'll see." Then, something across the street catches his eye. "What are they doing?"

I follow his gaze to a group of artists painting the windows of a boutique across the street. "Oh, they're getting ready for Valentine's Day." I point to the sidewalks. "See how they've been painted?" The faded hearts stretch out in front of us. "The hearts from last year will be painted over and new hearts will be painted in their place. Every year, people add their own sentiments, you know, like 'I love you, Bertie' or 'Here's to 25 years, Shirl.'"

"Bertie and Shirl? Are there cartoon characters living here?" He laughs.

"Don't knock it. The festival is a week-long celebration." I give him a serious look. "It's a *very* big deal."

"So you've said." His smirk tells me this whole small-town tradition amuses him.

"It's still weeks away," he says.

"Right, but why celebrate a single day when you can turn it into a month-long event?" I smile. "This town is Valentine crazy."

"Will you paint your windows?" he asks.

"I might, actually," I say. "It could be fun."

I didn't paint them last year. Last year wasn't fun.

Poppy's Kitchen was newly open and not doing well, and on principle, I don't celebrate Valentine's Day. This year, for whatever reason, my thoughts are less cynical.

I glance down at my hand, intertwined with his. *For whatever reason*, indeed.

"I was thinking of doing heart-shaped breakfast pizzas for the whole month of February," I say. "I don't usually get into this holiday, but if I'm going to be a part of the community, I should probably embrace what they love."

"Or you could go the opposite. Deck your place out with skulls and crossbones. Give people a place to *not* celebrate."

I laugh. "That's actually a great idea." Though, hating the holiday this year is probably not wise. Not when the whole town is supposed to be rooting for me and my famous boyfriend.

"Am I dressed okay? I wasn't sure," I say, mostly to fill space.

"You look perfect."

I read far more into that comment than I should for far too many seconds.

As we stroll down the main street of Loveland's downtown, Dallas looks around. I try to imagine seeing this place through the eyes of someone who didn't grow up here. It's quaint. It's charming. There's a gazebo in the town square and a group of women decorating it with strings of heart-shaped lights.

By this time next week, the entire "business district" will be decked out. Business district meaning the five blocks of Cupid Lane. Painted windows. Painted sidewalks. Love songs pumped through the speakers attached to the old-fashioned lamp posts. It's an inescapable celebration of love.

We walk, hand-in-hand, in silence, taking it all in, and then Dallas comes to an abrupt stop. "You know what, I think this is the place."

I glance up and see that we are standing in front of the Loveland Ice House.

"Here?"

"Yep."

"We're going ice skating?"

He drops my hand and backs away, toward the building. "Let's see what you've got, Hart."

"Most likely, a pair of broken ankles."

He stops. "Have you ever been?"

I laugh. "No, and I don't think you want to see me try."

The grin on his face is full of mischief. "No, I really do."

I shake my head, but take a couple of steps toward him. "Haven't I humiliated myself enough around you?"

"I can ask them to play One Direction to get you in the mood," he says with a teasing smirk.

I look away and groan, but can't help but smile. "I knew I shouldn't have told you that story."

He laughs, but before we can move, a boy walking out of the ice house with his mother runs over. "Dallas Burke!?"

Dallas turns toward the young fan and smiles.

"I can't believe it's really you!"

The boy's mom rushes toward us. "He's a huge fan."

"Then we should take a picture," Dallas says.

"And you'll sign my stick?"

"Heck yeah! What position do you play?"

I watch as Dallas strikes up an easy conversation, getting down on the boy's level and chatting with him about their mutual love for hockey. It's really something to watch, how he is with this kid.

Dallas poses with the boy, then graciously signs his hockey stick and helmet. As he does, I lift my phone and snap a photo.

This is the Dallas people need to see.

Once the boy has walked away, still freaking out from meeting Dallas, I post the image on my own social media account.

Dallas turns back to me. "So, Miss Hart," he says, "are you ready to go ice skating?"

I guarantee they will name it ice falling after I'm done.

Chapter Twenty-One

Poppy

Some people should not be allowed to ice skate.

I am one of those people.

As I lace up the rented skates, I glance over at Dallas, who's talking to a group of teenage hockey players. I can tell by the looks on these kids' faces that he's made their whole year.

Conversely, the joy they currently feel is directly proportional to the dread I feel.

Once my skates are tied, I scootch myself over to the end of the bench toward Dallas. He notices, tells the kids he has to go, then faces me.

"You can keep talking," I say. "Talk to them for the rest of the night if you want to. I don't have to skate. I can just sit here. And not move. At all."

"Nah." He sits next to me and leans in, *close*. "We've got a job to do."

I groan, in spite of the shiver that runs up my spine at his nearness. "I don't remember ice skating being a part of our deal."

He holds his hands out toward me, and when I take them, he pulls me up. Our eyes meet, and I find his attention calms me. "I'm not going to let you fall."

Sometimes there are moments when someone says something to you, and as soon as they say it, you're awash with a calm you didn't have before. A single sentence from a doctor telling you the scan is clear, a family member leaning in behind you, telling you "*you got this*" when you're looking at the empty building you just bought.

This is one of those moments. And I believe him.

We step out onto the ice, and he skates backwards, holding my hands as I wobble around, struggling to find my balance.

For a man who is just doing a job, he's surprisingly attentive to me and careful to stay true to his word to keep me upright. Tiny humans zip past us with so much speed it catches me off-guard.

"These kids make me look like a lost cause."

"They were probably born skating," he says.

"Were you?" We take the curve at a snail's pace, and I'm certain if it weren't for his steady and strong arms holding me up, I would've been flat on my butt the second my blades hit the ice.

He shakes his head. "I didn't start skating till I was twelve."

"Really?" I ask. "I thought most guys playing at your level had been playing since they were super young."

"Not me."

We're past the curve now, and I want to relax, but every muscle in my body is tense.

"What made you start?"

"Gram," he says. "She said I was too angry. Knew I needed an outlet."

"So, she's the one who raised you."

He nods. "For the most part."

"And she's the one who introduced you to hockey."

"Yep. I owe her everything." He picks up speed.

"You know," I joke, "I feel like it might be better if I let all my muscles go limp and you just dragged me around behind you."

He seems surprised by his own laugh, and I don't let on that I'm dead serious.

"What about your parents?" I ask.

"Out of the picture," he says, then glances at my feet. "You're doing great."

I scoff and make a mental note that he changed the subject. "I've literally transferred all of my weight to you, so really it's you who's doing great."

After about half an hour, some of the teenagers come onto the ice with hockey sticks and pucks. I notice there's a girl in the bunch, and I silently applaud her for playing this male-dominated sport, secretly hoping she can skate circles around these boys.

One of them skates over to Dallas. "It's public skate, but they told me to ask if you'd stay and do a stick and puck session with us in half an hour."

Dallas brings us to a stop, and I tighten my grip on his hands. "Sorry, guys, I'm on a date."

The disappointment that splashes across their faces is almost unbearable.

"I'm okay with it," I say. "I think I might be better at watching."

"Yeah, you're looking kind of rough out there," one of the boys says.

Another boy smacks him across the chest, and I laugh. Then, to Dallas, "It'll be fun."

He thinks about it for a moment, then gives a definitive

nod. "Fine, but we have a dinner reservation, so I can't stay too long."

The boys let out an energetic cheer, and once again, I marvel at the joy he so easily brings to other people's lives. Especially kids. It's a strange thing, fame. People can spew so much hatred out there on the internet, but in person, they can turn out to be just *lovely*.

Half an hour later, I'm blissfully back in my shoes and on non-frozen ground.

I watch Dallas move across the ice with a kind of strength and speed that makes everyone in the rink stop and stare. And film. So many phones pointed at the rink—this has to be good for his reputation. And his future plans.

I hold up my own phone and take a video, then post it with the words "Ditched for a bunch of young hockey players and couldn't be happier about it!"

"Do I have you to thank for bringing the best player in the league into my rink?" Burt Dobson, owner of the Ice House, is standing beside me, watching as Dallas stops to coach one of the boys on his puck-handling skills. At least, that's what I'm assuming he's coaching him on.

"Oh, this was all his idea," I say.

"Well, tell him it was a good one," he says.

I notice more people gather on the outer edge of the rink, and before long, Dallas is giving a full-on clinic to these kids.

And he's *good* at it.

The way he interacts with them. The way he encourages them and points out what they're doing well before giving them advice on how to get better. I can see the boys soaking up every word.

Some coaches might tend to beat a kid down, and I love that Dallas doesn't. It's like someone turned a light on inside him, and it's incredible to witness.

Burt walks out onto the ice (without wobbling, I notice) and snaps a few photos, which gives me time to text my video to Alicia.

She responds:

ALICIA

Great idea, Poppy! This is gold!

I frown. I didn't stage anything here. This is just Dallas in his natural environment. Alicia thought she had to concoct some big elaborate plan to make people see him as a good guy, when what she really needed was to let Dallas be himself.

Before we can leave, Dallas signs pucks and sticks and jerseys for over forty minutes, chatting with the fathers of these kids and with Burt and even with a few moms who seem to forget that they're A) too old for him and B) married.

I stand off to the side, watching him, thinking how great it is that he's so willing to give this time to these people he doesn't know.

He glances up and sees me, and he holds up his hands and points at me. "I've got a date, boys!"

There's a collective *ooooh* from all of them, and I'm sure I'm as red as the Valentine hearts strung around town. If this were a real date, I might be inclined to feel a little overlooked, but the truth is, I like getting a glimpse into who Dallas really is.

Because of that, I can safely and assuredly say that it's going to be much more difficult to keep my heart in check.

Chapter Twenty-Two

Poppy

The town of Loveland is in love with Dallas Burke.

And I can't even blame them, because I get it.

A few days after our ice skating date, Gram has her surgery. I go out to stock the fridge and end up staying with her the four days that Dallas is on the road. She's a terrible patient, cantankerous and stubborn, fiercely independent and outspoken, and I have to use my firm voice with her more than once.

The Mill reports that I'm spotted taking Sylvia to a doctor's appointment, and the comments section explodes with engagement talk. Apparently you only help people post-surgery if you're planning to join their family.

Alicia is busy doing her job, raising questions about our relationship even though we're apart, and at one point, Eloise sends me a video online with the caption: *Dallas Burke on the road and missing his new flame.*

It takes me a second to realize that *I* am the new flame, but I don't watch the video because I don't want to know what people are saying about us.

I'm focused on keeping up with both the restaurant and Gram. The latter wasn't part of the deal, not specifically, but I'm happy to do it. Eloise shows up with Susie the lab, and even though Gram claims not to like dogs, this one seems to win her over immediately.

I wonder to myself why I don't have a dog. I've always wanted one.

For four nights in a row, Dallas calls after his games. He and Gram hash out what he did well and what he needs to work on, and then she hands the phone to me. I wonder if he's lonely in a hotel room by himself, night after night, in city after city, but I don't ask because it feels too personal.

Instead of going on about what he's doing, he asks about the restaurant. I tell him that it's so busy I've brought in Miguel's wife, Gabi to help part-time in the kitchen, and two more servers. He sounds genuinely happy by this news.

I also tell him about the Loveland Valentine's explosion. "It'll be out in full effect by the time you get home." And he claims he "can't wait," but I hear the irony in his voice.

Twice, I've fallen asleep on the phone with him, and when I wake up in the middle of the night, I find the call still connected, even though we're both asleep.

When he returns, Gram is a week post-surgery and progressing faster than anticipated, which she announces to everyone in the room was her plan all along.

Alicia pounces immediately, but Dallas ignores her directive to get out in public and asks if I want to come over to watch *Downton Abbey* with him and Gram.

As dates go, it's one of the best ones I've ever had. The key perk being that he instructs me to wear pajamas "or you won't be let into the house."

I remind him that I have a key, and he reminds me that he's

stronger than me and can remove me from the premises if he wants to.

I show up in my comfiest clothes and knock on the door. When he answers it, I give him a once-over. Black pajama pants and a Comets hoodie. I approve. But then I snag on the way his eyes light up. I tell myself it means nothing, but I don't believe it.

He looks genuinely happy to see me.

We make popcorn and sit on the sectional (me in the corner, him one cushion away) while Gram dozes in the recliner. I'm overcome with a desire to nurse her back to health, even though I know absolutely no way to do this other than to feed her and stop her from trying to take two stairs at a time.

We do make the occasional coffee run or grab a quick meal in town so we can post about it and tell Alicia we're out there being seen, but other than the constant attention from *The Mill*, there's very little interest in our lives.

And I love it.

Still, is it really fair to Dallas if all of the positive press works for me and not for him?

Valentine's Day is just two weeks away, and by now, the town is fully decked out. I even let the local high school art club paint my windows, and I have to say, it does make me feel festive. For the first time in my entire life, I'm not dreading this sugary holiday.

I know this is all fake, and I remind myself of it daily, but I'm not sure my heart is listening to my head.

After more than two weeks of Loveland-based outings, Alicia puts her foot down via a text message that she sends to both Dallas and me.

ALICIA

It's time to take the relationship to the next level. Poppy, how do you feel about a hockey game this week?

I've been watching Dallas's games on television or the internet, and while I still don't understand the rules of hockey, I do understand that Dallas is very, very good at it. Watching him do it in person would be pretty amazing.

POPPY

I can make that work.

ALICIA

Great! Let me know if you want to bring anyone,

and I'll have VIP tickets ready for you.

POPPY

I'll just need two tickets. Thanks!

The night before the game, it hits me that tomorrow the insular protection of our little Loveland bubble will burst.

Granted, this is the point—to put our relationship out there to be speculated upon and hopefully cheered for—but now that it's here, I'm a ball of nerves. It hits me that I will very likely feel completely out of place at this game.

Dallas must pick up on it because after we eat the dinner I've made for him and Gram, I catch him watching me.

"What?" I ask, filing the plates away in the dishwasher.

"You're quiet," he says.

"Am I?"

He pulls the carton of ice cream from the freezer and fishes two bowls from the cupboard.

"I really think you eat too much of that," I say, knowing he burns my total daily caloric intake before 10 a.m.

He grins. "It's my guilty pleasure."

I finish loading the dishes, thankful that he stopped fighting me on cleaning up, but also thankful that he helps. When I'm finished, I turn to find him standing there with two sundaes. He's added hot fudge and marshmallow topping to mine, and I'm impressed that once again, he remembered what I like.

"You're a pretty good fake boyfriend," I say, taking the sundae.

"Am I?" He walks over to the table and sits, so I follow him.

"I mean, even my real boyfriends weren't as good at remembering the things I like as you are. How I take my coffee. How I like my ice cream."

He takes a bite. "I pay attention."

He pays attention. *To me.*

My nerves vie for my attention. "What should I know. . .about the game?"

"Like, you want to know the rules?"

"More like, what's going to happen there with you and. . .me," I say, avoiding his eyes.

"You're nervous," he says.

"Well, yeah," I say. "This is very new territory for me."

"You'll be fine." He leans back and props his feet up on the chair across from him. "You sit in the stands, cheer like a rabid fan, and afterwards, we'll go eat with some of the guys from the team."

My pulse starts ticking like a stopwatch. "Okay."

He finishes off his ice cream, then pulls his legs off the chair, leaning toward me. "You're going to be fine. I promise. I can't control a lot, but I can make sure you don't get left alone, or have to fend for yourself."

He had a lot of unwarranted faith in me. "It's time to see if this plan of Gram's is going to work, I guess." Then, a humiliating thought escapes. "What if they don't like me?"

He frowns. "Who?"

". . .Everyone?"

"Poppy, don't be ridiculous. They'll love you."

"Some of them won't," I say, "because what are the odds the whole of the Internet will love me?"

"Those people don't matter."

I groan. It's easy to say that, and while it's true, it won't stop me from agonizing over opinions of people I don't know and will never meet.

"We might need to. . ."

My eyes flick to his. "What?"

"Be a little—" it's like he's searching for the right word—"*cozier* than we are here in Loveland."

Cozier? My mind puts itself in park, and ratchets up the emergency brake.

"You mean the PDA."

He winces a smile.

He means the PDA.

More than just holding hands while walking down the street, or bumping into one another on an ice rink, or leaning into one another at a table at a restaurant. Now my pulse is racing dangerously fast, and I try to calculate how quickly we could get an ambulance out to this side of town.

Could I go ten minutes without oxygen?

"You're uncomfortable with this," he says, gently pushing his bowl out of the way.

I shake my head a little too enthusiastically. "No. Me? Pshh. *No,* I'm not."

He laughs. "Poppy, all the blood has drained from your cheeks. You're like ten shades paler than usual. And that's saying something because you're already very pale." He reaches over and pokes my cheek. "Just checking to make sure you're not secretly the walking dead."

I scoff. "I am not *that* pale, you bozo." The spot where he touched my cheek pulses with heat.

"I don't want you to be uncomfortable with this." He turns to face me. "Maybe we just get the first kiss out of the way."

When I frown, I feel the skin of my forehead pull like an accordion. "What do you mean?"

"If we're going to look like a couple and convince people we're really together, we're probably going to have to kiss."

Gulp.

"So, maybe we should. . .practice?"

"Practice kissing?" I'm sure my eyes are wide. "But this is in private. We said no kissing in private, right?"

"I'm just thinking so it's less awkward when we have to do it in public." He's so matter-of-fact when he says it, and I'm still trying to reel in my shock.

"You're serious," I say.

There's something earnest in his eyes. "Well, yeah. I'm not trying to get you to do anything, I'm just thinking if we're going to sell it out there. . .Might be less uncomfortable to do it here, when we're alone, without a bunch of people?"

My palms are sweating. Less uncomfortable, maybe, but far, *far* more dangerous.

He laughs. "You look like you just swallowed a bird."

"I'm not as open about this stuff as you are," I say. "I haven't dated a lot, and the guys I have dated have been a little less forward."

And a little less famous. And a little less wonderful. And a little less beautiful.

Dallas walks his empty ice cream bowl over to the sink and rinses it out, so I do the same, even though there's still a melty scoop floating around in my bowl. As if I could eat it now.

We're standing shoulder to shoulder at the sink, and once the bowls are clean, he turns off the water and faces me.

"I think being forward is smart when it comes to business," he says.

"Right," I say. "This is transactional."

"Right," he says.

"No messy feelings to get in the way," I say.

"None," he says. "I mean, we're friends, I think."

"On our way to becoming friends," I say.

"Yes," he says. "And. . .my world might be a shock to you. If it's too much, you can tap out."

When I agreed to this, I thought Dallas might whisk me around town, maybe put his arm around me, take me to the Festival of Hearts, grant me a slow dance. . .all very low-risk activities.

But he doesn't live in a low-risk world, and while I knew that, perhaps I'd failed to fully consider it. In order for this to be of any benefit to him, I have to leave my safe space and become a part of that world.

Am I prepared for that?

"So what do you think?" He wipes his hands on a nearby dishtowel, looking as nonchalant as anyone has ever looked. I survey his eyes for any indication he has ulterior motives and find none.

"We said nothing like this in private," I say, matter-of-factly. "I don't want to break the contract."

"True," he says. "Though, that list was just for us and is not legally binding."

I laugh. "So, a list of guidelines we can ignore if we want to."

"Basically." He shrugs, and a sweet expression settles on his face. "But, it's totally up to you. I don't want you to feel nervous about tomorrow."

"I will, regardless," I say. Then, after a beat, "But it might help to, you know, practice." I wonder how transparent I'm being right now. Is it obvious that kissing Dallas would rank in my *Top Three Activities of All-Time*? I slowly turn toward him, aware that he's watching me with all the confidence you'd expect from the right winger of a professional hockey team.

He waits until I lift my chin and our eyes meet. "It's just business."

I should probably think of myself like an actress in a movie, playing a part, but here's the thing. I'm not an actress in a movie. And to me, kissing means something. At the same time, I'd be crazy if I didn't *want* to kiss Dallas Burke.

In the short couple of weeks I've known him, I've dreamed of this very thing at least 578 times. Probably more like 578 x 10.

And I do see how getting used to it here, in the privacy of his home instead of *out there* with a thousand cameras trained on us, scrutinizing our every move, would be beneficial.

He must sense this because he smiles and says, "It's okay, we can work up to it. Or find a way around it. The last thing I want is for you to be uncomfortable."

"I'm not uncomfortable," I say. "I mean, it's *just* a kiss. *You've* done it lots of times, *I've* done it. . .not as many times, probably, and we *should* look like we're familiar with each other, right? So, how do we do this, I mean, do we just—"

He doesn't let me finish. He steps forward and silences me, bringing his lips to mine in one smooth motion. His lips are softer than I expected, but his kiss is every bit as confident as I'd imagined. Because I *had* imagined it. How could I not? His hands are at my waist and I flounder for a moment, unsure what to do with mine.

He pulls back and looks at me. "Are you okay?"

Get it together, Poppy. It's not like I've never done this before. I nod, aware that I'm not breathing.

I roll up the sleeves on my sweater and blow a puff of air at a loose strand of hair that's in my face.

"Let's try again," I say. Because I really, *really* want to try again.

"You're sure?" His eyebrow twitches up in a question.

"I'm sure," I say, determined. "I can do better."

"Well, let's hope," he says, then laughs.

I give him a shove. "You just caught me off-guard!"

"I told you we were going to practice!" His hands are still at my waist. Mine are still at my sides.

"I know, but you just kind of went for it," I say.

"I thought it would be better that way. Like ripping off a Band-Aid." He grins. "I promise I won't. . ."

I don't let him finish this time.

This time, I force my insecurity away and kiss him back properly. A little less "middle school Seven Minutes in Heaven" and a little more "Adult who has perfected the fine art of kissing."

Our lips move together so beautifully, it's like we both got notes on how to do this beforehand. I can feel his grip on my waist tighten, and my senses are heightened. I'm aware of the way he smells (like a woodsy forest), the way he feels (taut, firm), and the way he tastes (like caramel ice cream). I settle in as the kiss deepens, and I relax, also aware that I'm enjoying this kiss. A lot.

But then, he pulls away, head down, gaze on the floor. He lets out a hint of a laugh.

"Sorry, did I do something wrong?" I ask, taking a step back.

"Uh, no," he says, clearing his throat. "You're, uh. . ." He shakes his head again. "You're a little too good at that."

Flames shoot through me, heating my cheeks with a mix of pride and embarrassment. I smile. "Sorry."

He looks at me, then steps back. He's visibly shaken—and I've never seen him like this before.

Did I do that to him?

He weakly shakes a finger at me. "I'm going to have to be careful with you."

My nerves come out in a tense laugh. "Right. Another episode like that, and I'm going to have a hard time remembering this is fake."

He smiles. "Right." Then, his eyes narrow ever so slightly. "That was a good kiss."

I look away. How do I respond to that? It *was* a good kiss—a great kiss—but I can't say that out loud. Instead, I fear the blush in my cheeks responds in my silence.

"It's just business," I say. "Right?"

"Well, you're awfully good at your job." He leans back on the counter and studies me. "You, uh, feel okay then? About tomorrow?"

"Yep."

Nope.

If I'm not careful, kissing Dallas could become my new favorite pastime.

A hobby that I would like to perfect. A definite perk in this little arrangement of ours. And I only feel a tiny bit like Vivian Ward. Though her rule was *no* kissing on the lips, so if I am Dallas's own *Pretty Woman*, I'm a much more wholesome version.

At least that's what I'm telling myself.

Chapter Twenty-Three

Poppy

The next morning, I wake up to a text with instructions from Alicia.

ALICIA

> Game day! I'll email you the tickets. He'll find you after the game. You should leave together. Hold hands. If there are cameras, make sure they get a shot of you kissing. His friends have to buy this too, and assume you're always being filmed or photographed.

Ugh. What am I getting myself into?

I get my coffee and head straight to the restaurant, aware that I'm going to have another crazy day, but also thankful because I've been able to catch up on my rent and pay all outstanding bills. My dad insisted on me taking care of those before paying him a dime. Really, I think he's just putting me off. To my parents, that money wasn't a loan, it was a gift.

But I wouldn't accept it unless he let me pay them back.

There's no pressure like financial pressure, and once it's lifted, hope can breathe again.

After work, I'll run home and get ready, and Dallas is sending his driver over to pick me up and take my dad and me to the game.

Mid-way through the morning, Kit walks into the kitchen with an order. "That stuck-up blond lady is asking for you, Poppy."

"Margot is back?" This was the third day in a row she'd eaten here. I mean, her money spends as well as anyone else's, but I can't help but wonder what she's up to.

"I make a point not to remember the names of people I don't like," Kit says dryly. "Can you come talk to her?"

"No," I say. "I'm really backed up."

"This'll be fun." Kit rolls her eyes and leaves the kitchen, but returns seconds later and says, "She's coming back here."

Margot appears in the doorway. "Poppy! I saw Dallas walk in here the other day, so I thought it'd be okay for me to come say hi."

"Did you just compare yourself to Dallas Burke?" Kit asks.

And did you call him by his first name, like you two are friends?

"It's fine, Kit," I say. "I'm pretty swamped back here, Margot, what do you need?"

My waitress rolls her eyes and walks back into the dining room. Margot looks around the kitchen. "This is adorable back here. You've really done great things with this little place. And with so little money."

"What do you want, Margot?" I ask, scrambling eggs for a ham and cheese quiche.

"Gosh, Poppy, that sounded hostile." She lifts both hands. "I come in peace."

"You've never come in peace."

Whoa. Where'd I get this boldness from?

"Clearly you have a reason for being here."

Margot gives a little shrug. The giant ring on her left hand catches the light, and I'm reminded of the way she stole Raya's high school boyfriend right out from under all of our noses. I've always learned that villains don't *know* they're villains, but I don't think that applies to Margot. Some people, it seems, just enjoy being mean.

"You know we've been planning the Loveland Festival of Hearts since last February, and we're really looking for something to kind of 'wow' up the festival this year."

I know exactly where this is going, and I really don't like it.

"What a stroke of luck that a genuine professional hockey player has moved into our little town," she says.

I look up. "Yep. Lucky us."

Margot flicks that diamond-studded hand in the air with a laugh. "For some unknown reason you seem to have an in with Dallas."

"It's because he's her boyfriend," Miguel says from behind me.

I smile at the griddle of pancakes I'm watching and imagine Margot's face faltering.

"Of course," she says, less sing-songy than before. "Which is why we thought you could ask him if he'd be a part of the festivities."

I eye her. "I'm not asking Dallas to be in the kissing booth."

Margot's eyes widen. "I didn't say anything about the kissing booth." She feigns innocence. "But that would be *such* a great moneymaker."

"No, Margot."

"I understand not wanting to share him," Margot says. "Though I doubt you'll be able to keep him all to yourself for very long." She laughs. "You know how those pro athletes are with women throwing themselves at them all the time. Tell me you don't think you can keep a man like that satisfied for very long."

I set my spatula down. Something in me rises up, and normally, I tamp it down, but I seemed to have lost that filter at this moment.

"Margot. You have no idea what he's really like. But you know what? *I do.*" I start walking toward her, and she begins to back up.

"I need you to leave my kitchen now," I say. "I have work to do."

"Yes, I see that," she says, backing into the edge of the counter and giving a nervous laugh. "*Very* busy out there. A pity everyone is here hoping to see the hockey player and not to eat your food."

Miguel spins around, but I hold up a hand to stop him. "It's okay, Miguel."

Margot raises her eyebrows and gives Miguel a pointed look while still managing to keep her nose in the air. Then, to me, "We were just thinking he could judge the teddy bear decorating contest, or pose for photos for a few hours at the dance."

"I don't handle any of that for Dallas, Margot," I say. "You'll have to contact his manager if you want to hire him."

She frowns. "We were hoping he'd do it out of the goodness of his heart," she says. "We thought maybe you could convince him?" A pause. "Think it over, okay, Poppy? We're discussing the Taste of Loveland event next week, and I'd hate it if we didn't have a booth for your little restaurant."

I sigh. This is so petty.

A vision of me backhanding her with a frying pan flashes across my mind.

She smiles, then glances at Miguel, gives him a familiar, condescending once-over, and walks out the door.

Miguel and I stare at the air in the kitchen, searching for

the black cloud that she had to have left in her wake, then finally turn to each other. "Did that just happen?" he asks.

"Yep. And she actually threatened my spot at the Taste," I say.

"She can't do that," Miguel says.

"She can, actually." I sigh.

Margot's husband, Jeremy, came from a wealthy Loveland family. I know Jeremy well because he and Raya dated all through high school and their first year of college. I think that's one of the reasons Raya is so cold now—because when Jeremy dumped her and started dating Margot, it broke Raya's heart clean in two. Then, when she finally decided to try again with a guy she met at work. . .another disaster. One she doesn't talk about. Ever.

Now, it seems my sister is content with her single life.

Margot let the power of Jeremy's last name go to her head almost instantly.

I groan. "I can't ask Dallas to do this." *He's not even my real boyfriend!*

Miguel shrugs. "Worry about that another day. For now," he points at the sizzling griddles, "cook!"

I do. And as I do, I start to panic. Not about Margot or the festival or the Taste of Loveland. About the hockey game tonight. I can feel the sweat gathering at my hairline. I dab it with my sleeve, but it doesn't help. By 11 a.m., I'm an anxious mess.

In a rare (and short) lull, I pull out my phone.

POPPY

Raya, I need your help.

RAYA

Did he already screw this up? That was fast.

POPPY

Gosh, no. Nothing like that! I'm going to a hockey game tonight.

RAYA

. . .Okay

POPPY

So far, we've only really been out in Loveland.

This is much more public.

RAYA

I assume you knew you'd have to be seen in public when you agreed to this. That is the point.

POPPY

Of course. But this is so high pressure. You know I never think about my hair and makeup. Or clothes. What the heck am I supposed to wear?

RAYA

Calm down, Poppy. Dallas knows what you look like.

I chew the inside of my cheek as my thumbs hover over my phone.

POPPY

I don't want him to get made fun of for dating me.

I stare at the words before hitting send. They're raw and honest. And humiliating. This part, I hadn't thought through. In Loveland, this was all fun for me. But out there—at the stadium, in Dallas's world—we were both opening ourselves up to public scrutiny. I mean, that was the whole point, right?

RAYA

Poppy?

The phone vibrates in my hand as Raya's text comes in. I close my eyes and hit send.

Not six seconds later my phone buzzes.

RAYA

Eloise and I will help. We'll meet you at your house.

POPPY

Thanks, Ray.

RAYA

That's what sisters are for.

Chapter Twenty-Four

Poppy

"Poppy, when Dad sees this, you're dead." It's Eloise, sitting on my bed with her feet up on the wall, scrolling through the last week of entries on *The Mill.*

I assume she's landed on the one talking about me sleeping at Dallas's house.

"I thought you said this was fake," Raya says, flipping through my closet.

"It is," I say.

She turns to me. "It doesn't look fake."

"Plus you slept over at his *house*." Eloise flips over on her stomach, mouth agape in mock shock, eyes wide.

They seem to have forgotten why they're here.

"I fell asleep on the couch," I say. "That's all." After a pause, I add, "And you would've too if you felt this couch, it was like the softest thing I've ever sat on. And the fire was warm, and the blanket. . ."

I'm not helping my cause.

"I don't think you're that good of an actor, Poppy." Raya

turns and faces me again. I'm standing just outside my bathroom wearing a robe and eyeing the clock.

I'm starting to feel even more panicked. "You have a lot of work to do to get me ready—why are we talking about this?"

"Poppy. . ." Raya crosses her arms over her chest.

"What?" I hear the guilt in my own voice. "Nothing has happened with me and Dallas."

But even as I say the words, my cheeks flame with heat and I turn into Hades in the Hercules cartoon, my hair a swath of flames.

"Oh my *gosh,* you're *lying,*" Eloise says.

"I am *not*!" This comes out shrieky—a telltale sign that I am, in fact, lying.

My two sisters look at each other, then back at me. I'm caught.

"What happened, Poppy?" Raya looks like she might take the ring in a welterweight boxing championship, and even against Dallas, I have to say, my money would be on my sister.

"You guys, I have to look *hockey girlfriend* presentable in T-minus thirty-five minutes, so could we please talk about this later?"

"Absolutely not." Raya plops down on the bed next to Eloise.

I groan. "Fine, we had a—moment."

"A moment?" Raya asks.

"He kissed me," I whisper. "But it was just for practice."

Eloise lets out a squeal like we're middle schoolers and my crush just asked me to the eighth-grade dance. "He *what*?!"

"We have to be. . .you know. . .*comfortable* with each other for this to work," I say. "Tonight is very public."

"*That's* what he told you?" Raya rolls her eyes. "You've got to be kidding me."

"Raya, I swear, it wasn't a line. He isn't shady," I say this, aware that I'm protesting a little too much. I walk over to my closet, though absolutely nothing inside of it registers in my brain.

"Then why is he doing this?" she asks. "It's completely disproportionate what you're getting out of it and what he's getting out of it."

I stop moving and look at her. "Gee, thanks."

"You know what I mean." She looks at Eloise, who is fully sitting up now. "He might have. . .*expectations*."

"He doesn't," I say.

"He *kissed* you!" Raya has her *I know best* voice on. "If it's really a fake relationship, what the heck is he doing kissing you? Are you sure he doesn't expect you to sleep with him, Poppy?"

I shake my head. "Every detail has been written down. There is nothing at all about. . .that." I can't bring myself to say it out loud because then I'll start thinking about it, and once that happens, I'm a goner. I've already made enough questionable choices.

"I'm completely protected," I say.

Raya straightens. "Um, there's still the little matter of, oh, I don't know, your *feelings*. We all know how messed up those are."

My eyes flick to hers. I hate when Raya brings up Avi, even as subtext. I hate when anyone brings him up, but especially her. These days, she's too pragmatic to ever be drawn in by a man's charm. She saw through Avi the first time she met him, and she tried to warn me.

It was me who wouldn't listen.

"I'm not that naive anymore," I say quietly.

"And yet, here you are, in another relationship where a man is using you."

I'm a tire that's just deflated. "It's different."

"Is it?" Raya asks.

"Of course it is," Eloise says, ever the optimist.

"How?"

"Because this time, Poppy's not in the dark." Eloise stands and walks over to me. "This time, she's getting something out of it too." She gives me a quick squeeze.

That was true. My heart begins to settle. It's different this time. This isn't a repeat of what happened with Avi. My eyes are wide open. My heart is protected.

I turn to Raya, more defiant now. "Yeah. I am getting something out of it. I could pay *rent* this month, Raya. Do you have any idea what that means to me?"

Raya is unconvinced. "Just be careful, Poppy. Because if one of you is going to get hurt as a result of this little experiment, it's going to be you." She stands. "And I'm not saying this to be mean. I'm saying it because I'm your older sister, and I love you."

"And you don't think I can take care of myself," I say.

"I think your heart is big," she says. "And that's one of your best and worst qualities."

I frown. "I don't think that's true."

"I don't either," Eloise says.

"You both only see the good in everyone," Raya says.

"I think that's a great way to be," I say.

"But not everyone is good." Raya heaves her big bag onto my bed and opens it, and I wonder if she's thinking of her own love life or mine. "You know that."

"I'm an adult, Ray," I say. "You don't have to worry about me."

She pulls out a curling iron, then looks at me. Her expression seems to say *Who are you kidding?*

"Just *please* don't fall in love with this guy, Poppy," she says. "If you do, you're just asking for trouble."

Raya is almost always right.

Which means she's sometimes wrong, I try to tell myself.

I know I'd be smart to pay attention, but I don't want to. I *like* being around Dallas.

Raya has set up a salon in my bedroom and bathroom, and now motions for me to come sit down so she can get to work.

Once I'm seated, I draw in a breath, thankful my emotional intervention is officially over and we can move on to another topic.

But then Eloise plants herself right in front of me.

"Okay, but how good of a kisser is he?"

Chapter Twenty-Five

Poppy

The ride into the city is quiet. Dad is watching hockey videos, and Alicia is on her phone, which means I'm left alone with nothing but my wild imagination.

I'm *this close* to backing out of the whole thing when the car comes to a stop.

Alicia looks at me. "You and Dallas haven't been together long enough to get an invite to the Wives' Room, but you'll be sitting in the friends and family section so you'll meet them anyway."

I've never been diagnosed with social anxiety, but I'm pretty sure this is what it feels like.

Alicia puts a hand on my arm. "Hey. Relax. You'll be fine."

I swallow, wishing I was as sure of that fact.

My dad glances up from his phone, and he must sense my hesitation. He grins an open-mouthed smile, then emphatically signs, "We're going to have so much fun."

His excitement actually lifts my confidence a bit. At the very least, I get to share this whole experience with the biggest hockey fan I know.

We all exit the SUV. I follow Alicia through crowds of people and into the noisy stadium, careful to keep my dad close.

I try to pay attention to this noisy world around me. I've only ever been to one professional sporting event in my life, a baseball game with Dad, before he accepted the fact that he didn't have sons. As it is, I'm too concerned with getting lost in the crowd, and the low hum of nervous, anxious anticipation is growing inside me.

When we finally make our way through security and into the actual arena, I stop for a brief moment and look around. This is Dallas's world—his stage. It's an enormous, bright spectacle and full of energy.

Dad and Alicia don't stop, but thankfully I catch up with them after my quick gawking session. Fans weave in and out of their seats, most of them wearing Comets black and silver—and many of them wearing Dallas's number.

It's strange how his reputation off the rink can be so sordid, but his talent has never been in question.

According to a commentator on a hockey podcast I recently listened to—research, of course—Dallas is one of the best players in the league. Or at least he was, before the accident. Since then, he's been inconsistent, and the hockey world is concerned.

Alicia leads us to a section of seats right in the front. We're behind a thick plexiglass shield, but our view of the ice is unobstructed. The section is roped off, and I realize this is a VIP area. I'm surrounded by empty seats.

"When it gets closer, the other wives and girlfriends will join you, but they're all back in the Wives' Room right now. Girlfriends aren't allowed back there until they've been around at least a few months," Alicia says as I sign for my dad.

So, I'll never see the inside of the Wives' Room because

Dallas and I won't last that long. The thought brings an unexpected disappointment, but I briskly shove it aside.

"Even then, you have to be invited by one of the other wives," Alicia says. "There's a whole protocol, even for players' families."

"Good to know," I say under my breath, knowing it's not likely I'll get the hang of it any time soon. And I don't bother to sign that part.

"Okay, I'm off. If you're good—" Alicia says.

"Wait, you're not staying?" Why does the thought panic me? My hands move frantically as I loop Dad in.

"I'll be around," she says. "But I have some things to take care of. I'm not here to watch the game."

Dad puts a hand on my arm, then signs, "We'll be fine, Poppy. Let her go. Look at this place! Look at where we're sitting!" He stands and practically presses his face on the plexiglass.

I have to smile, I just love to see him so tickled to be here.

Alicia hurries off, and I sit, watching the busyness in the arena. Across the rink, I notice a man with a camera pointed right at me. I look away, but I fear it's too late. If the world really does care who Dallas is dating, a photo of me sitting rinkside in the VIP section is probably going to fetch at least a modest sum.

But that's what we want, isn't it? We want to get people interested. We want them to stop talking about Dallas's mistakes and start talking about his sweet, small-town girlfriend.

"You're going to do fine," Dad signs. "Stop fidgeting."

"I just don't want to embarrass him," I sign. "I'm still not convinced this was a good idea."

"You must be Poppy!" The excited voice comes from behind us, and when I turn, I find a tall, glamorous, and perfectly made-up woman with long, dark hair, wearing a tight black Comets shirt and a pair of jeans. She's accessorized her outfit with big hoop earrings and a rock on her left hand that could cause a celestial traffic jam.

"That's right," I say, standing, signing to my dad as I do.

"I'm Monica Stephens," she says. "Jericho's wife."

I don't know Jericho, but I assume he's another player. "It's nice to meet you."

She stops at the end of the row and glances at my dad, who gives the beautiful woman a once-over.

My father stands, and I introduce him while signing. "This is my dad, Mick."

Monica's smile widens. "First game?"

"First game this close to the ice," Dad signs back.

She gives his arm a squeeze. "You're going to have *so* much fun."

Monica glances at me, then nods toward the row of empty seats. "I'm next to you."

We inch back so she can get through, and once she does, she takes her seat. Dad is completely engrossed in the world around him, and I make a mental note to thank Dallas for the tickets. This is next-level, and I'm so excited to share it with someone I love and who really appreciates it. I wish Gram could be here too, but she's not quite up for the craziness of the arena. Soon, I hope we'll have a whole section of Dallas fans up here all together.

"The guys will be out to warm up in just a few minutes," Monica says.

"And the other wives are in their room?" I ask, trying to remember what Alicia told me.

Monica laughs. "Right."

"You don't want to be with them?"

"Dallas asked me to look out for you today," she says. "And

I don't want to miss a second of Jericho on the ice." She scrunches her face and gives a little shimmy. "It's so hot."

I laugh. "That was nice of Dallas, but I don't need you to look out for me."

"You haven't met the other wives yet," Monica says with a pointed nod.

"Oh," I say quietly, wondering if I'm in for yet another mean girls type of situation.

"Everyone is really nice, don't get me wrong," she says. "But all of them together can be a *bit* overwhelming."

My attention is drawn away from Monica when the lights in the arena go dark. The crowd cheers like a bunch of rowdy kids during a power outage at school. A loud drum beat reverberates through my rib cage, and I glance over to see my dad, wholly engaged. I wonder if he can feel the loud staccato as numbers on the jumbo screens above the ice begin to count down from sixty.

Lights flash. Drums bang. The numbers get lower and lower until finally, an announcer comes over the speaker, and with enthusiastic fanfare, introduces "The one, the ON-LY... CHICAGO COMETS!"

There's a flurry of activity on the ice as the players, dressed in Comets black and silver, rush out onto the rink. They each look double the size of a normal person thanks to their padding, but they move around the ice with the kind of speed and agility that deserves to be admired.

The crowd erupts, everyone on their feet, so I jump up too, mesmerized by the scene unfolding before me.

I search the ice for number 18, but the jumbo screen finds him before I do. My attention is drawn upwards where his face appears, and then I match the picture with the man moving on the ice. Now that I've locked onto him, I don't want to look away—it's stunning, the way he moves—so strong and confident —around the ice.

As the players take a few warm-up laps, one of them slows down as he skates past us. As he does, he points at Monica, then taps his chest. She leans forward in her seat and calls out, "Don't be good, be great!"

"Just for you, baby!" he brings his hand to his mouth, then points at her again as he skates off.

I glance at Monica and notice there's a fierce expression on her face. "Are you nervous?"

"I always get nervous before a game," she says. "I want him to win so he's in a good mood. I want him to play hard, but not get hurt." She pauses. "And most of all, I just want the women to stay away from him."

I turn.. "What do you mean?"

She looks at me, one eyebrow raised. "You find out that there's one major downside to this life, Poppy—the women. They don't care if your man is married, or engaged, or in a serious relationship. They all want to date a professional hockey player, and they'll do whatever they can to make that happen."

My eyes drift back to the rink, just in time to see Dallas whip the puck into the goal. He skates around the small net, and even without seeing his face, I can see how focused he is.

"How do you handle that?" I ask.

"Oh, he knows if he even entertains the idea, he'll be missing his man parts," Monica says.

I laugh, but I have the distinct impression she's serious.

Unlike Jericho, Dallas doesn't skate over to our section. He does interact with the other players, almost like he's the one calling the shots. He's not the oldest player on the team, but I'm starting to think maybe he is the best. Still, not everyone seems interested in listening. This must be the division he mentioned.

"What do you think of Dallas?" I ask Monica quietly, as if anyone might be eavesdropping.

Monica looks at me. "I think he's a really good guy. He's the captain. Jericho says he's the best. And he's a good friend, too. He'd do anything for any of these guys." She looks at the rink. "It's Mulligan that needs to go."

I follow her gaze, searching the backs of jerseys for the name "Mulligan." When I finally find him, Monica says, "I assume you know about the accident."

I nod.

"Dallas only drove Ricky home that night because Mulligan and Ricky were both too drunk. Ironic, right? The sober guy gets into an accident."

"People say Dallas paid off the cops," I say. "To keep from getting a DUI."

Monica shakes her head. "Not a chance. Dallas is a lot of things, but he's not a cheater."

"Then why does this Mulligan guy hate him so much?" I ask.

She shrugs. "He's jealous. In college, Mulligan was the star. He got here, and from day one, he's been strutting around like he owns the place. After his first season, it was pretty obvious he wasn't the one everyone was going to be talking about."

"But Dallas is."

"Right." She keeps her eyes on the ice. "He could have Mulligan traded if he wanted to. At least, I think he could. Jericho told him he should—but he won't do it."

"Why not?"

Monica shrugs. "Nobody knows. Maybe Dallas is one of those people who needs to save all the screwed-up guys who are making a mess of their lives."

Funny. That's the exact opposite of who the press wants everyone to think Dallas is.

Monica glances over at me. "I also think Mulligan feels guilty about Ricky. He was supposed to be the one that drove him home that night. Promised Ricky he wasn't drinking, and then got completely hammered."

"So, he takes it out on Dallas," I say. "Because he needs someone to blame."

"That's my theory," Monica says. "Jer thinks Mulligan is a first-class tool."

There's a commotion in the aisle as a group of well-dressed, perfectly coiffed women appear at the end of our row. They filter into the section we're sitting in, and Monica leans over to me. "Enter, the hockey wives."

My laugh is nervous. "You make it sound so ominous."

She bumps my shoulder with hers. "I know, and I'm kidding. You're with me, so you're going to be just fine."

As the women and children get situated, I glance up at the ice and find Dallas looking in our direction. The world around me goes quiet, and I feel like Kevin Costner on the mound, in the middle of pitching his perfect game.

He gives me a nod so small I almost miss it, but I'm sure he's just communicated something to me. I look down, then look back up at him and give him a little wave.

This man is far more complicated than I originally thought, and even though our relationship is phony, I find myself wanting to know him for real.

He holds his hand over his chest and acts like he's weak in the knees, wobbly on his skates. I laugh, and point to my head, signing *what is wrong with you?!* He cocks his head, smiles, then he skates off the ice.

Monica bumps my shoulder with hers. "Well, now. Someone's got it bad."

Yeah, Monica, I do.

Or wait. Did she mean him?

Chapter Twenty-Six

Dallas

It's the first intermission, and we're on fire. *I'm* on fire. We're up 3-0 and I've scored twice and assisted on the other one. I haven't felt this good about a game in a long time. We hit the locker room, a sweaty mass of adrenaline and testosterone.

"You showing off for your new girl or what, Burke?" Junior says, picking up a water bottle and taking a long drink.

"Maybe she's your good luck charm," Jericho says, speaking aloud the thoughts I'd been trying to ignore. "'Bout time you got your head outta your backside."

I'm not superstitious, and I don't really believe in luck, but knowing Poppy and her dad are in the stands, that there are people there cheering for me, not just nameless fans, but people who know me and really want me to succeed, it's settled something inside of me.

I don't know what to think of that, but I'm not questioning it. Until now, Gram's lived in Florida, and while she's been to games, she's not a regular in the stands. I've dated plenty of women, but rarely seriously, and I've never invited any of them to a game. To me, this is sacred, hallowed ground.

Still, when Alicia suggested a game as my first outside-of-Loveland outing with Poppy, I didn't give it a second thought. Somehow I knew Poppy would understand how much it means to me. She wasn't coming along to be seen, even though that was technically her end of the bargain.

It was a welcome change.

So often, it felt like so many people were just waiting for me to fail, but when I saw her sitting up there with the other wives and girlfriends, I had the strangest feeling knowing she was rooting for me.

And I'm not sure what to make of that.

I'm also not sure what to make of that kiss. If I think about it long enough I can feel it again.

I'd pulled away, because if I hadn't, it easily could've gone from business arrangement to steaming up the windows in about two seconds flat.

I thought I could kiss her without feeling anything. After all, kissing didn't mean much, not anymore.

Turns out, I was wrong.

Turns out, I want to kiss her again.

Poppy

"Dallas is *killing* it!" Monica says this as if I should be proud of it, like I have some right to claim his success in this game as my own.

Mostly, I'm just trying to figure out the rules of hockey. Everything moves so fast, it's hard to get my bearings. Beside me, my dad is fully invested in this game. He has more energy than anyone here, but twice I've asked him to explain something to me, and both times he's half-signed things because he can't look away.

I make a note to google the rules of hockey at some point before I come to another game. The hockey podcasts weren't doing the trick.

We're nearing the final moments, and Dallas and Jericho are working together to get the puck down to the other end of the rink. The energy in the arena is electric, and even I get caught up in it, in spite of not knowing what exactly is going on.

The crowd starts chanting Dallas's name, and I feel a sense of pride wash over me. He's *so* good at this. It's. . .well, it's really, really attractive. And whether or not the press or Alicia or even Dallas realize it, he still has many, many devoted fans.

Jericho and Dallas maneuver their way toward their goal, and the rest of the players become a blur. Jericho passes the puck to Dallas, he takes it and brings it around the back of him, behind his legs. He then guides it through his legs AND the legs of the opposing player, picking it up on the other side of him.

Everyone in the place jumps to their feet, me and Dad included, and I can actually *feel* the energy of the crowd in anticipation. The decibels get twice as loud, and Dallas shoots the puck toward the goal. I think it's way off—only to see Jericho skate in and take what is a perfect pass to flip it in the back of the net.

The whole arena goes bananas, the huge horn sounds again for the fifth time, Dad is jumping up and down and turns and hugs me hard, and I see complete strangers in the crowd high-fiving, hugging, yelling. The crowd counts down the final seconds of the game, then erupts in one last, huge, collective roar.

I've never felt anything like that in my entire life. My ears are ringing, I can't see straight, but I love Every. Single. Second.

A blonde named Lisa leans forward and puts a hand on my shoulder. "Looks like Dallas is showing off for you."

"Uh, yeah, you can come to every game," the woman next to her says.

"Oh, I don't think—"

"He's been in a slump, Poppy," Monica says. "A bad one. And now, *all of a sudden*, he's not. What do you make of that?"

I go quiet. I have watched several of Dallas's games, and I would hardly say he was in a slump, but I really didn't know what to look for.

He did play differently tonight. I wish I could take credit for that, but I know the truth.

The game ends, and I realize I'm not sure what's next. I only know I want to run to wherever he is and tell him how awesome he was tonight.

"You and Dallas are coming to dinner, right?" the blonde asks.

Before I can answer, Monica grabs onto my arm. "She'll be there."

The plans had already been made. I'd meet Dallas outside the locker room while Gerard drove my dad back to Loveland. We'd go out, be seen, look *cozier* than we do in Loveland, and then Dallas would drive me home.

Cozier.

The plan might be set, but now that it was time to see him, nerves start bubbling through my body.

Dallas *might* kiss me again. I *might* kiss Dallas. We *might* have another moment like the one in his kitchen last night, and I *might* be just a teeny tiny little bit excited about it.

Good thing we practiced.

I glance at my father, who is still beaming after what he just witnessed. Around us, there's the bustle of activity, but he stops and signs, "Poppy, please thank Dallas for me. This was so amazing! Tell him I loved watching him play."

The arena is buzzing, but I notice the flashing of a camera. Monica must notice it too, because she moves over, blocking the cameraman's view of me and my dad.

"Have fun tonight," Dad signs.

"I will. Thanks for coming with me." I smile. "Are you sure you're okay to go home alone? I can come with you."

He claps a hand over mine, then pulls back to sign: "Poppy, you're young. How many chances are you going to have to go out with a bunch of big shot athletes?" He squeezes my hand. "Have fun."

Did I tell him this wasn't my idea of fun? That I was already thinking about how early morning would come? That I was certain if I went out with these people I would make a complete fool of myself? And yet, I'd been sitting here the whole game, and I didn't feel like a fool yet.

"I'll talk to you later," Dad signs, then inches out into the aisle.

I tap his arm. "I should walk you out," I sign.

"I know my way around a hockey arena a lot better than you do," he signs with a wave. "I'll be just fine."

And I know he's right, so I nod, and watch as he walks off, feeling like a buoy floating alone in the ocean.

I turn to Monica, who is still standing beside me like a bouncer outside a club. "Thank you for shielding us from that photographer." I feel protective of my dad, even though he can more than take care of himself.

"Don't mention it." Monica links her arm around mine. "Let's go."

She leads me out of the arena to a hallway that feels like backstage at a concert.

"We'll have to wait a bit for the guys," Monica says. "They have a ritual they have to run through, post-game press conferences, showering, it's a whole thing."

Lisa walks up with another woman whose name I forget. Like Monica, they look like they just stepped off a runway. By contrast, even in Raya's slick leather jacket, I look exactly like the ordinary girl I am. But I suppose that's the point, isn't it? I'm meant to look like the girl-next-door.

As if I could look like anything else.

"So," Lisa says. "You and Dallas." She smiles.

"He could use a good woman," the dark-haired woman says. "Especially after that Jessie DeSoto mess."

"And everything else," Lisa says, ruefully.

"Lisa is married to the goalie, Krush," Monica says, nodding toward the blonde. "And Kari is dating Junior. He plays defense."

Lisa. Kari. (Car-ee) I say their names over in my mind to try and remember because Monica introduced me to both of them in the stands, and I'd already forgotten one of them.

"Your husband is named Krush?" I ask.

Lisa smiles. "Russ Krazinski. Krush is a nickname. And it's spelled with a 'K' but don't ask me why." Then, to Monica, "I like this one." Then, to me, "Most women that come through here try to fake their hockey knowledge—"

"—But we can always spot a fake," Kari interjects.

The word might as well be a neon sign flashing at the back of my mind. *Fake. Fake. Fake.* My laugh is high-pitched and nervous. "Well, I have absolutely no knowledge of hockey."

"We know," Lisa says with a laugh. "Thanks for not trying to pretend."

I look around for a fire extinguisher in case I spontaneously combust.

Monica links her arm through mine again like we're best

friends heading out to the playground for recess. My heart begins to settle. "Poppy owns a restaurant about an hour from here."

"I know," Kari says, excitedly. "We saw the post!"

I frown. "What post?"

She opens her phone and navigates to a post with the headline *Who is Poppy Hart*?

"I haven't seen this one," I say, staring at it. I scroll through, reading details about my own life, wondering if this journalist will uncover the fact that I had head gear in middle school and musically annihilated my high school prom-posal.

"It's a profile on *Hockey News*, a website dedicated to all things hockey," Lisa says. "They mention your restaurant by name, so that's good, right?"

"Yeah, that's..." I'm a bit taken aback, ". . .that's great, actually." Right at the top of the article, next to a photo of me from culinary school (not the worst choice, I'm relieved to say), is a line of bolded text that reads: *The owner of Poppy's Kitchen in downtown Loveland, Poppy Hart is spicing things up with Chicago Comets' star, Dallas Burke.*

I skim read what they've written, grateful to discover the profile is straightforward. And most of the details are correct. I make a mental note to call in a few extra servers this week—just in case. I hand Lisa her phone.

"Hey, you don't think. . ." Monica pulls me a bit closer.

I chuckle. "What?"

She slides her arm out and puts a hand on my shoulder. "Maybe you can cook for us sometime?"

The other women all voice their agreement, genuinely excited at the idea.

Monica's smile is warm and welcoming, and I find myself wondering if everything about this relationship with Dallas *had* to be fake. I like these women, and I'm surprised that I do.

"I'd love to!" I blurt, and without thinking, gush, "Typically, I feel like a fish out of water in social settings like this, but you all are so kind and beautiful, I don't know what I was expecting, but you're totally making me feel like I actually belong here, and," I'm shaking now, and for some reason, on the verge of tears, "it's just really, *really* nice."

The combined reactions—some with hands over their hearts, two of them coming in to hug me, the rest with an *aww* on their faces—makes me feel even better.

I get the sense that when you become one of them, you have a built-in support system, and though I already have that in my sisters, I love that they didn't dismiss me.

It's like they're good with letting me be whoever I am.

Monica says, "Honey, you have to understand—this group right here? It's all we have." The other women all nod. "Oh, we have our families, and kids, but when it comes to protecting one another, this sisterhood is unbreakable."

"That's really amazing," I say, wiping my eyes.

"But. . ." Lisa chimes in, "you're still going to cook for us, right?"

"I'd love that," I say. "My town has a big Valentine's Day festival that might be fun for all of you to come out for. There are a bunch of events, including a big Taste of Loveland. I'll have a booth there."

"Oh my gosh, that sounds so fun," Kari says. "It would be nice to get out of the city."

Lisa is engrossed in her phone. "Oh, look! There's a formal dance!"

I peer over at the screen and see she's pulled up Loveland's website. The others lean in and read over her shoulder.

"Can we come to that?" Monica asks, her eyes darting to mine.

"Uh, sure," I say. "I mean, everyone is welcome."

"You're going, right?" Kari asks. "With Dallas?"

Before I can answer, Monica interjects. "We're going. We'll have so much fun."

"I'll have to make sure it's. . ." I start to say, but nobody hears me because the door to the locker room opens and draws their attention away.

A freshly showered Jericho walks out. He saunters over to Monica and plants one on her. I look away, slightly embarrassed and a bit worried that this is part of the ritual for the players.

Another man walks out, and I assume he's the goalie, Krush, because he pulls Lisa into his arms and kisses her like he's been underwater and she has all the oxygen.

Two for two. Dallas is going to kiss me.

"Jericho, this is Poppy," Monica says.

He looks at me. "Dallas's girl."

Dallas's girl. Me.

"I don't know what spell you've cast on the man, but keep it up," Jericho says. "You're magic." I laugh and shove aside the desire to correct him, mostly because everyone else seems to agree.

"He wasn't even moody before the game," Krush says. "Can you come on the road with us?"

Everyone laughs, so I laugh, but I'm not sure how to feel about their unwarranted praise. If these people knew that Dallas and I weren't even a real couple they'd realize I had nothing to do with how he played. It feels so odd—and wrong—to let them believe otherwise.

Jericho drapes an arm around Monica, and Krush grabs Lisa's hand.

"We'll see you at the restaurant." Monica reaches out and squeezes my arm, then they turn to go.

One by one, the men pair off with the women waiting, and

eventually, I'm left on my own. I hug my purse as I lean back against a wall, wondering if I should've left with my dad.

But then the locker room door opens and Dallas walks out, looking like he just stepped off the pages of *People's* Sexiest Man Alive issue. It's not even fair.

And he's here with me. Fake or not, I'm going to enjoy this fantasy for a moment.

I manage to not drool on myself, but it takes some effort. Post-game Dallas, dressed in a bluish gray suit coat over a crisp white button-down shirt, is giving my sense of morality a run for its money. When he stops in front of me, I say a silent prayer of thanks for the wall I'm leaning against because it seems to be the only thing holding me up.

"Hey," I say.

He smiles. "Hey."

"That was kind of cool, I guess."

His smile broadens. "Kind of."

"You played pretty good," I say. "If you like that sort of thing."

He quirks a brow. "And do you? Like that sort of thing."

I grin and scrunch my nose. "I really, really do."

He laughs.

"I can't get over how easy you make it look," I say.

"Like you in the kitchen."

"Uh, no. The two things are not the same."

He leans in. "Poppy. It's *exactly* the same."

He starts walking down the hallway, toward the parking lot, and I fall into step beside him. My arm brushes against his, and without thinking I slide myself right underneath it the way Monica had done with Jericho.

But there was nobody else around. No reason to pretend.

We find Dallas's car and he punches in the address to the restaurant where we'll meet the rest of our party into his phone.

Before pulling away, Dallas pulls in a deep breath. "I almost wish we could just go back to my place."

My eyes go wide without my permission, and he laughs.

"That came out wrong," he says.

"That's starting to become a theme with us," I say.

"I don't usually have so much trouble saying what I mean." He laughs. "I just meant I wish we didn't have to go out and pretend."

"Do we have to pretend?"

SHOOT.

Now it was my turn. "That came out wrong."

He looks at me a bit curious, and I try to recover. "I mean, go *out* and pretend."

He opens his phone and shows me a text from Alicia:

ALICIA

Post-game dinner. You'll be photographed in the restaurant. All the other girlfriends and wives will be there.

Sell it.

"It'll be okay," he says. "This is why we're doing this, right?"

I nod. "Right."

"Okay, then let's go convince my teammates that we're a real-life couple."

My heart turns over at that because it conjures all kinds of thoughts on just how exactly we could accomplish this task.

Is it bad that I think we should practice on the car ride over?

Chapter Twenty-Seven

Poppy

We leave the car with the valet, who asks Dallas for an autograph, and then turn toward the restaurant. He looks at me and I can see the weariness behind his eyes.

"Are you okay?" I ask. "I thought you'd be on cloud nine tonight after the game you played."

He stares out into the darkness, over my head. "I'm good."

"I don't believe you, but I won't press," I say. "Raya is pushy that way, and it's annoying."

He laughs, then draws in a breath. "Are you ready to pretend to be completely smitten with me?"

The words stop my pulse for a three-count. "Yep."

He holds his hand out, and I take it, turning toward onlookers who've most likely already been alerted that several Chicago Comets are dining here tonight.

A man in a black suit meets us as soon as we walk inside. "Mr. Burke, I'll escort you back."

Dallas's hand loosens, and he presses it into the small of my back. I don't know that a man has ever guided me like this, but he does an excellent job of it. The only problem is, I'm so focused on the placement of his hand that I forget people are probably filming and photographing us, which means I'm not paying attention to my facial expressions. I'm just out here being normal, as if any of this is normal.

I can only imagine there will be more *Why on earth is Dallas Burke with this woman?* posts when I wake up the next morning.

When we reach the back room, the man in the suit pulls open the door and leads us inside.

It's slightly darker in here than it was in the main part of the restaurant, but I look around and see some familiar faces. Monica, Lisa, and Kari are all standing by the bar, while the men congregate on the opposite side of the room.

It feels a little like an eighth-grade dance with the boys on one side and the girls on the other. A few others are seated at tables, and for a moment, I feel like I'm on display.

When the men see Dallas, they all give a cheer. Jericho rushes over and puts his arms around him and lifts him off the ground—no easy feat—carrying him back to the rest of the team. I sense the absence of his hand on my back almost immediately. It's as if I were a tea kettle about to whistle and someone took me off of the burner a moment too soon.

But the burner was nice and warm and cozy, and I want to go back.

"How about this guy!?" Junior and a guy they call Kemp join the bro hug, and Monica rushes to my side.

"Come over here, Poppy," she says. "Have a drink."

"Oh, I have to work in the morning, so maybe just a Coke?"

She nods at the bartender, who miraculously heard my request over the noise in the room. He shoots Coke into a glass of ice and slides it over to me.

"We were just talking about you and Dallas," Kari says.

"Oh?"

"We think you're good for him," Lisa adds.

"We're still really new," I say.

"But he seems different. More mellow, somehow." Monica takes a sip of her drink. "A little like how Dallas used to be, you know, before."

Dallas glances our way.

"See? He checks on you," Kari says. "It's really sweet."

"He does not." I feel a blush rise to my cheeks.

Dallas looks away.

"Yes, he does," Lisa says.

I know she's right. What I don't know is why. Someone would have to be an Oscar-worthy actor to remember to "check up on my fake girlfriend by glancing over every so often."

I tell myself it's probably because he's a nice guy, and even though we aren't actually romantic partners, he doesn't want me to feel awkward.

"I'm sure he's like this with everyone he dates." I take a sip of the Coke.

A roar of laughter from the guys. They're so loud, but they're fun to watch. Like German Shepherd puppies, with their oversized paws, wrestling and knocking everything over.

"No, he's not," Monica says. "He's never invited a woman to a game before."

I turn to Monica, surprised. "That can't be right."

"It's right," Lisa says. "Dallas is a one-man show. He doesn't let anyone in. *Ever*."

"And he's such a Cinderella story," adds Kari.

I frown. Is that why Alicia insisted on me attending a game? Because she knew it would go further in selling us as a couple? "What do you mean he's a Cinderella story?"

Monica puts a hand on Lisa's arm. "Enough shop talk."

Something silent passes between them, and I get the

distinct impression that there are some secrets that my contract with Dallas doesn't entitle me to. I'm curious, but I like the way Monica protects him.

I realize there is a whole side of Dallas that I know nothing about.

And I want to know all of it.

I put that thought in check. *We are just friends.*

I turn my attention to the room. It's a lot to take in. The sheer amount of money represented here (from the salaries, to the designer shoes and handbags, to the amount of food and alcohol being consumed) is shocking. I see what they're ordering, I know what it costs wholesale, and I know the markup.

After about ten minutes, the room starts to feel warm and crowded. My body temperature climbs as a flash of heat washes over me.

"Excuse me," I say. "I need to use the ladies' room."

I slip out into the hallway, find the nearest restroom, and lock myself in one of the stalls where I practice deep breathing. Everyone is so nice. No one is making me feel out of place. With the exception of my runaway Dallas fantasies, I'm holding it together nicely.

I make the giant mistake of opening my phone, where I find a photo of Dallas and me walking into the restaurant just twenty minutes ago. He looks like he's walking a runway in Milan, while I look like one of the hyenas in *The Lion King*.

My mouth is agape and slightly contorted, and as I feared, the general consensus among commenters seems to be "What on earth is *he* doing with *her*?"

Raya didn't teach me a thing about being photographed from every angle at any moment. How do these people do this all the time? It's exhausting.

I step out of the stall and wash my hands, and when I re-enter the hallway, I smack into a pale-faced blond guy whose chest is almost as broad and firm as Dallas's. Almost.

He gives me a once-over, then a lazy smile crawls across his face. "You're Dallas's. . . flavor of the month." A statement, not a question.

I don't have to see my own face to know I'm frowning.

"I'm just teasing. Your name's Poppy, right? The chef?" The man grins, and something about it chills me from the inside out.

I instantly don't like him.

"I'd love for you to cook for me sometime."

"Uh, I have a restaurant," I say dumbly, wishing I could get away from him and not liking that he's boxing me in.

"But you're a *private* chef too, right? I think I heard Burke say something about that." He lingers on the word "private" in a way that makes my skin crawl. Or maybe I'm just imagining it. He takes a step toward me, and I inch back.

"We should be friends," he says. "I'm Aaron."

My mind spins. Aaron. . .I blurt out "Mulligan."

He looks taken aback for a moment. "So, you know who I am. . ."

"Um. . .I should get back in there. Dallas will be looking for me."

"He probably doesn't even know you're gone." Mulligan holds his smile, as if he hasn't just insulted me.

There's a pounding in my chest like the drums in the pregame fanfare. All I can think is that I want to get away from this guy.

But he's blocking my way.

I give the hallway a quick glance. I'm alone with a man who makes me uncomfortable, and I have no idea what to do. I can't make a scene and risk embarrassing Dallas.

He eyes me. "I admit, I'm surprised to see Burke with

someone like you, but I'm beginning to understand the appeal. You've got that sort of prudish, cute, girl-next-door thing going on."

I stare past him, not wanting to give him any encouragement, but he's blocking my view of the private room door.

Which is why I don't see Dallas come out.

The next thing I know, Mulligan is yanked away from me and shoved into the wall. I jump at the movement and rush out of the way.

While Mulligan is big, Dallas rises and stands a good four inches taller than him. He pushes a forearm into the other man's chest and growls, "*What* do you think you're doing?"

Mulligan smiles, hands up. "Are we really doing this again?"

Then lower, quieter, more threatening, Dallas says, "Stay. *Away*. From her." He gives Mulligan another shove, then backs away. He turns toward me. "You okay?"

I nod shakily.

He protected me.

Dallas reaches for my hand and leads me away from Mulligan, who sneers. "Careful driving her home, *Burke*."

I feel Dallas tense up and hesitate. I know instantly that he wants to turn around and throttle this guy. I'm way past pretending—this has become very real. I instinctively cling to his arm and pull him forward.

"Ignore him," I say. "He's not worth it."

He looks at me, fire behind his eyes, and then glares at Mulligan. I reach up and grab his face, forcing it to look at mine.

"Please," I plead. "*Please*."

His eyes soften. His breathing slows. His shoulders drop slightly, and for a moment he looks. . .ashamed. He looks right into my eyes, as if searching for a life preserver.

I nod slightly and rub his cheek. "It's okay," I say. "It's okay."

"Okay." he says. "Let's go."

I nod again. We grab our coats, say a quick goodbye, then walk out of the back room, through the restaurant, and out to the valet stand. Dallas stares off in the darkness, and I can't help but wonder if he'd rather be alone.

"What did he say to you?" Dallas asks.

"It doesn't matter," I tell him, knowing that any more detail on the subject would only serve as fuel to the fire. And at the moment, he is all fire.

But then, he faces me, intensely worried. "Tell me you're okay."

I take his hand, not caring about cameras or contracts. "Hey. I promise, I'm okay."

"You shouldn't have to deal with him," he says. "I should've warned you."

"Dallas, it's not your fault," I say.

"Yeah," he mutters as the valet returns with the car. "It's never my fault."

Chapter Twenty-Eight

Dallas

When I saw Mulligan had Poppy cornered, something inside me snapped.

We may be fake dating, but I feel like we're real friends.

And as her real friend, it's my job to protect her. From idiots like Mulligan. From the press. From this whole stupid world of mine.

I'm starting to think that this whole thing is going to backfire in one way or another. Especially since seeing Poppy in the stands, wearing my jersey, cheering me on—it was nice.

Life for me has never been stable. There was a brief stint of near-stability in middle school and high school when I lived with Gram, but before and after, my life has mostly been about upheaval. Change was the constant, and never a welcome one. What I realized in that moment of pulling Mulligan away from her was that I really need something I can fight for.

Or someone.

Someday, maybe.

I couldn't bear to bring Poppy into the craziness of my

world. It would be way too big of an ask. Even for a strong person like her.

I'm lost in my own thoughts, and we mostly drive in silence on the way back to Loveland.

"You must be hungry," Poppy says. "We left before we ate."

Boy, I've royally messed this whole date up. If it's fake, why do I care so much?

"I promised you dinner, and then I made us leave before you got it," I say. "I'm sorry."

"Oh, I'm not worried about me." She stares out the window. "I had a pretzel at the game. You probably need eleven or twelve of those."

I know she's trying to lighten the mood, but I'm having trouble releasing my grip on the memory of her cornered. "You don't have to worry about me either," I say.

She doesn't look at me. "Someone has to."

The words reach inside of me and squeeze. *Is this what it's like to not be alone?*

"Let me make you something to eat." She faces me.

"I'm sure that's the last thing you want to do," I say.

"I'm a chef, you doofus. I actually *like* cooking," she says. "And if we go to the restaurant now, it won't feel like work. It'll be nice and quiet." After a beat, she says, "It's been a while since I've been there by myself. It'll be fun."

I *am* hungry. But more than that, and I'm not sure what to make of this, I don't want to take her home yet.

Without making me explain, with ease and understanding, Poppy seems to get me in a way that's different from the guys on the team, or Alicia, or even Gram. Maybe things between us weren't romantic, but we'd both agreed we were, in her words, "on our way to becoming friends." There was nothing wrong with that, was there?

"Are you sure?" I ask.

She nods. "Hockey players need to refuel after a game. That kind of physical exertion does a number on your body."

I laugh, and the tightness in my neck begins to loosen. "Google?"

"Yes." She grins. "It's on the internet so it must be true."

I bite back a smile and turn to look at her. She looks back, raises her eyebrows, and shrugs.

And with that, we both laugh.

We park in the back of the restaurant, entering through a door that leads right to the kitchen. The space is dark, and when Poppy flips on a work light, it barely gives off enough light to see.

"I don't want anyone to know we're here," she says.

The dim atmosphere lends itself to a date more than it probably should.

I'll protect her at all costs, and I hope we can keep the negativity and unwanted advances far, far away. And then, once her restaurant has soaked up every bit of publicity it can, I'll quietly extract myself from her world. Already, I'm looking forward to that day. For her sake.

My phone buzzes with a text:

ALICIA

How are we supposed to sell this relationship if you go home right after the game?

I click the phone off without responding, leaving it looking unread on her end.

I know eating here after dark defeats the purpose of our agreement to go out and be seen, but I couldn't do it tonight. Not after catching Mulligan with Poppy.

Not after my conversation with Coach Turnrose. I find myself turning all of it over in my mind. Because it wasn't only my leadership on the team he wanted to discuss.

"You're quiet," Poppy says as she pulls a package of meat from the oversized refrigerator in the kitchen. "Shouldn't you be celebrating? You won. And you were the star of the game."

It did feel good to be on top again—I'd been in a bit of a slump. The guys didn't hide their theory as to why I'd been on fire tonight. The public may not have warmed up to the idea of Poppy and me as a couple, but my teammates seemed to approve. All but one of them, anyway.

I force a smile, struck by how in tune with my moods she is.

Tonight, I'm conflicted. And for whatever reason, I feel the need to tell Poppy about it. It's almost like. . .like I *have* to.

"Found out after the game they're retiring Ricky's number. There's a whole ceremony and everything." Most likely, she doesn't understand what this means for me. She wasn't a part of my life when Ricky was injured, after all.

I don't know what Poppy is making, but I'm glad it has her attention, otherwise I wouldn't have the courage to talk about this.

"It's a pretty big deal," I say. "Ricky hasn't been back since. . ." I can't even say the words. *The Accident.* It's so easy for other people to refer to it, but it would never be easy for me. "Coach asked me if I wanted to be a part of it."

Her eyes shoot to mine, but she keeps cooking the meat she's put into a pan on the stove, silently seasoning and stirring. "Do you want a drink?"

"I don't drink anymore," I remind her.

"Good, because I don't have a liquor license." Poppy points double finger guns at me. "*Breakfast restaurant.*" She wipes her hands on a towel and walks over to the refrigerator. "Pick your poison." She nods toward the open door. Inside are glass bottles of just about every soda you can imagine.

"Coke," I say.

"A purist. I like it." She grins, pulls out a bottle and opens it, hands it to me, and in a horrible Southern drawl, says, "Ya look like you could use one 'a these."

I stifle a laugh as I take the bottle. "What is wrong with you?"

"Oh, *so* many things, my friend. I'd need charts and graphs to show you, but we really don't have that kind of time." I smile and take a drink, aware that unlike most people, Poppy isn't trying to tell me what I need to do.

Or think. Or feel.

"Dallas, that game was. . .*amazing*." I can tell she's telling the truth, because she talks faster and moves her hands a lot when she's excited about something. "I know *zero* about hockey, but the crowd, the lights, the whole thing—it was bonkers. My dad *loved* it. He nearly passed out. And *you*," she points a wooden spoon at me, "you were the best one out there."

"This coming from a person who knows zero about the game?"

She moves around the kitchen like me on the ice; she knows where everything is, every nook and cranny, how everything should fit together and how to make something incredible. "Come on. You have to know. Like, come *on*."

I sigh. "Fine, you win. It *did* feel good out there tonight."

She's just letting me sit here in her kitchen as I wrestle with it all. How does she know to do that?

"So, what do they want you to do? For retiring the number?"

Strangely, I feel way more comfortable talking about it now. "They're doing a video tribute," I say. "If I don't film something, I'll look like a jerk, and if I do film something, I'll look like a jerk. There's no winning here."

"What do *you* want to do?"

I turn the cold bottle around in my hands, the condensation

wetting my palms. "Feels wrong not to say what Ricky means to me and to the team."

She's quiet for a moment. "I seem to remember someone telling me, 'It doesn't matter what other people think.'"

I set the bottle down. "Okay, not fair quoting me back to me." I wipe my hands on my pants. "This is different."

"I understand things work differently for you than they do for me," she says. "But some things are true, regardless of who you are. Saying something kind and from the heart is never a bad idea, and it's never the wrong thing to do."

It all sounded so simple when she said it.

"You like spaghetti with meat sauce, right? It doesn't really matter what you say because that's what I'm making you. I read that hockey players need a lot of carbs. And protein." She pulls a head of broccoli from the fridge. "And vegetables."

"You read this? When?" I'm starting to wonder if this woman sleeps anywhere other than my couch. I watch her continue to move around the space with speed and grace, taken in again by her confidence. I realize I like watching her. It soothes me somehow, and before long, the knot in my stomach unravels.

"If I'm going to cook for you, I want to make sure I'm making things that are good for you. I've never fueled a professional athlete before." She puts her hands on her hips. "It's probably not unlike feeding a horse."

"When did you get so funny?"

"It's after ten, I get funny after ten."

"Ah."

It's adorable how seriously she takes this job, though I have mixed feelings about her "job" being to take care of me.

"To answer your question, yes. I like spaghetti with meat sauce. I could do without the broccoli though."

She glares, and crosses her arms over her chest. "You haven't had mine."

I mimic her pose and give her my best *I doubt it* look, which she promptly ignores.

She goes back to cooking, but looks up at me from the stove. "You don't have to let them know your answer about the video tonight, which means you can sleep on it."

"True," I say.

"So, let's not think about it now," she says. "Just for tonight, can we celebrate your win? And then tomorrow we can worry about this."

We celebrate. Tomorrow, *we* can worry.

It's not lost on me that she's including herself in my highs and my lows.

Once Poppy finishes the food, she dishes it up, and we sit at the counter in her kitchen. I inhale the smell of the tomatoes and garlic and spices, wondering how she managed to elevate something as basic as spaghetti to a practically gourmet meal.

I could get used to this.

Before I can stop myself, I say, "It's been a long time since anyone has done anything like this for me."

She looks confused. "What, cook?"

I don't know how to articulate what I mean without spilling everything, all at once. Instead, I just say, "it's incredible, Poppy, thank you."

She hands me a napkin, then puts hers on her lap. "It's fun to cook dinner food. Breakfast is my favorite. I could eat it at any time of the day, but I miss dinner sometimes."

"You're really good at it," I tell her. I swirl the spaghetti around my fork and take a bite, letting out a little groan of appreciation for the flavor explosion in my mouth. Once I've swallowed, I bring my attention back to her. "Did you have an okay time tonight? I know it was a lot."

She smiles wide. "You have no idea how fun it was. And the wives were *so* nice! Monica is a-*ma*-zing, and she really helped me feel welcome. They all did." She looks right in my eyes. "I had a great time, Dallas, thank you."

When she says my name, it's like a tripwire inside of me. I like it. I want her to say it again.

I try to remind myself that my relationship with Poppy isn't real. At least not the romantic part.

There's nothing to say we can't be friends. Which is good because I really like being around her. Her personality, her willingness to be put in awkward situations for me, her ability to see what I need before I need it.

Does she see what I need might be her?

But no. It's not practical for me to be involved with anyone right now, but especially not someone as rooted in a place as Poppy is in Loveland. My contract is up at the end of this year.

I could be in Winnipeg next season.

"Oh, I forgot!" She pulls her phone out, clicks around on it, then slides it across the counter, face-up. On the screen is an article profiling Poppy and her restaurant. I skim it quickly, but judging by the look on her face, it's a positive profile, and that's all I need to know.

She takes a bite and talks with her mouth half full. "Almost makes up for the Walking Dead photos people took of me tonight in the restaurant." She swallows and laughs, but her words trouble me. I hadn't thought about that part. People were vicious online, and I didn't want to expose Poppy to that kind of ridicule. It was never fair.

"I think I have Alicia to thank for this?" she asks, tucking her phone away.

"Looks like her handiwork." Knowing Alicia, she was going to turn Poppy into a saint, and that's fine by me, because even after knowing her a very short time, I'm wondering if that's exactly what she is.

Poppy Hart. The patron saint of pasta.

Chapter Twenty-Nine

Poppy

I hadn't intended for us to stay so late here, in the restaurant.

I'd be back for morning service in just a handful of hours, and yet, something about being here after dark has the exact opposite feeling as being here on a busy, bustling morning.

In moments like this, I like to take a step back and look around and marvel at the fact that I *actually have a restaurant.* If I take a second and think about it, it's all a bit surreal.

Financial problems aside, I have my own restaurant, where I cook for people every single day.

It's hard, it's rewarding, and it humbles me daily. Lori Grenier was right when she said, "entrepreneurs are the only people who work eighty hour weeks to avoid working forty hour weeks." I don't care how hard it is, I just don't like being told what to do.

I glance at Dallas, knowing that isn't always true.

Still, I've built my life around this place. I can't bear the thought of losing it. And even though Dallas Burke is currently in my kitchen and shockingly in my life, that is still no guarantee I'll make it.

There's a moment of silence as we both chew our food, but it's not awkward, and I feel no need to fill the space. Well, that's not true. There *is* something weighing on me, and even though I doubt Dallas cares, I find myself wanting to share it.

What is it about this man that makes me want to bare my soul? It's not like he's an open book. I get the impression that Dallas is surrounded by people, but mostly alone.

I know I'm not the one to fill any sort of void in his life, but in typical Poppy fashion, I'm probably going to try.

Raya's warnings echo in my head. This is how I get myself into trouble. A wise woman would hold back and keep herself from getting too close. When you get too close, you get hurt.

This isn't a real relationship, after all.

Remember that, Poppy.

He's busy eating, and I'm at that same proverbial point of shutting my eyes, holding my breath, and plunging back into the cold water.

"I wasn't completely honest with you before."

He looks up and stops chewing.

Ugh, I'm such an oversharer.

It's a wonder I haven't come right out and told him that if he's looking for someone to bear his children I'd willingly volunteer my grandmother-approved child-bearing hips.

I inch out on this emotional branch one small step at a time.

"I told you I thought the reason my restaurant was struggling was because the town had their favorites, that they were hard to sway—old dogs and all that. But. . .it's. . .not exactly true."

Dallas sets down his fork, but doesn't respond. His face isn't confused, or annoyed. It's welcoming and kind.

"I don't talk about this often. Well, *never*, is more accurate. I just. . ." I'm floundering a bit.

"Hey," he says softly, "you'll get no judgment from me. What's going on?"

I don't make a point of reliving what Avi did to me, so words don't come out as smoothly as I'd like.

"The truth is, when I moved back here after culinary school, I brought someone with me." I take a drink of water. I need a moment. Maybe this was a bad idea.

"A boyfriend?" he asks.

I nod. "His name was Avi."

"Was this the guy that Margot lady was bullying you about the first day we met?"

He remembers that? Another nod.

"You loved him," he says.

"I did," I say, remembering. "At least, I thought I did. He was all charm, and promises, and flirtation." A pause. "Which is why I didn't see it coming when he conned me out of the very little money I had saved."

His face drops. "He *what*?"

Tears spring to my eyes. The pain of that betrayal is still so fresh. While my general rule is to feel everything fully, this one hurt too much. I loved Avi. And he broke my heart.

It was my roommate's birthday, which meant I had to trade in my yoga pants for club clothes. She insisted on going out for karaoke, of all things. We'd been there about an hour when I first noticed a tall, slender man in a tailored dark blue suit (no tie) sitting at the bar, watching me.

He had the confidence of Ryan Gosling in *Crazy, Stupid Love* and Lord knows I was a sucker for that.

After a few minutes of eye-flirting, he made his move. He walked over to our table and handed me a drink. "The bartender said you're drinking ginger ale tonight."

"I am," I said. "My roommate's birthday."

"DD?"

I nod. I liked being the designated driver. It let me off the hook from pretending I liked alcohol.

Avi sat down at the table next to me, and my friends barely paid attention.

"I haven't seen you here before," he said.

"I haven't seen *you* here before." I smiled over at him.

He barely moved, just studied me with an intensity that held me captive. "I'm Avi."

My smile held. "Poppy."

What happened next was your typical meeting/dating/falling-in-love story. And by the time I brought him home to meet my family, I was convinced he was the one. Only Raya disagreed, because she had zero tolerance for charm and flirtation. Also she had a nose for nonsense, and she could smell it on this guy a mile away.

I didn't listen.

I bought every bit of it.

I look at Dallas, wishing I hadn't told him. "This is the kind of thing that tabloid reporters are looking for, huh."

He looks angry. Angry at me for not telling?

"I wish I could find this guy in a dark alley," he says, clenching his fist on the countertop.

Oh. Not angry at me.

"I should've told you this sooner," I say. "Before we became..." I search for a word. "Business partners."

"Why? This is your personal life."

"But you know it could come out," I say. "And if anything that I did ruined anything for you, I just couldn't. . ."

I look down. Shame has a unique ability to make even the simplest eye contact uncomfortable.

"And then, when people learn about it, I'll look like a fool." I go still. "Because I *was* a fool."

"I think you're trusting," he says. "That's not the same thing."

I shake my head. "I feel like such an idiot. Is this going to make you look bad?"

"That doesn't matter."

"Stop saying that. Because *The Mill* has already written about it, so if Alicia is going to float my name around like she does, it's going to come out."

He sits forward. "The only thing that matters to me is that you don't get hurt in all this. I don't care how it affects me, or my career. None of that matters."

"But it *does* matter, Dallas!" I tell him. "You're so much more important than me!"

He stills. Then, without a word, he stands, walks around the counter, and sits next to me.

"Poppy."

I still can't look at him.

He softens. "Poppy, look at me."

I don't like being told what to do, and yet. . .

I look up at him. His eyes are kind, but strong.

"You have no *clue* what you've done for me these past weeks. It's never been about what I get out of this, and I'm certainly not more important than you."

My eyes are starting to brim with tears, I can feel them. "But that's why you're doing this." I'm struggling to get the words out without my voice breaking. "So you can show the world you've changed. So you can start your foundation."

He sighs, almost smiling. "That's not the only reason."

I go still. Was he saying that *I* was one of the reasons?

"What did this guy steal from you?" he asks.

"You mean besides my dignity?" I scoff. "Everything." I draw in a breath. "My grandparents aren't wealthy, but they started an account for each of us girls when we were born. I didn't know about it until I graduated culinary school. By then, I had a lot of debt, but I also had a dream—a big one."

"The restaurant."

"Right," I say. "I already had a plan for paying off my student loans, and even though it wasn't wise, I wanted to use the money from the fund to open a restaurant. And then Avi happened." I take a breath. I never realized how much I needed to get this out.

"He came into my life, claiming to know everything about the business side of things. 'You just be the chef, Poppy, I'll handle the rest,' he'd say. He was the one to find the location, do all of the paperwork, set up all of the accounts."

"Don't beat yourself up," he says. "You trusted him."

"And he sounded legit." I groan.

"I'm sorry, Poppy," he says. "Stuff like this shouldn't happen to people like you."

"It gets worse." I take another drink. "When Avi was here, he asked me for a list of the more well-off families in town. He said it would be good to convince them to invest in the restaurant."

Dallas sits back in his chair. "He didn't."

"Yeah, and I told him there were four or five families, and..."

This part is the hardest to admit. I stand, and start to pace.

"He had me meet with each family. I sat there, in the living rooms of people I had known all my life, and told them about my dream, how it would impact the community, and how it would maybe even bring a bit of tourism to this small town. I sold them on Avi, on how he was a whiz at the business side of things, and if they invested in getting it off the ground, they would hold a percentage of the profits for years afterward."

Dallas just sits, listening. Without saying a word, he's exactly what I need right now.

"Avi convinced me to lease everything ahead of time, before we even had the money. I scrounged enough for deposits and down payments, but we had contractors doing build-outs and kitchen equipment being delivered before we deposited one single check."

I stop pacing and put both hands on the counter to steady myself.

I look up at Dallas and say, "And two weeks later, after the final check was deposited and a week before the restaurant was set to open, Avi drained all of our accounts and left. Vanished. I never saw him again."

I stand straighter, hold up my hands in surrender, and let them flop to my sides. "I had no money. No way to continue. So, my parents loaned me what I needed, I took out what loans I could, and. . .well. . .here we are."

Then, silence. It's a lot for me to reveal, and probably even more for him to take in.

After a long moment, Dallas frowns. "I would think people would be sympathetic to you, maybe even support you out of pity?"

"Initially, the police didn't believe me. A lot of people thought I was in on it, especially when I opened the restaurant in spite of all this. But I saw no other way to pay any of these people back. Everyone was so angry, even though I was a victim, too. They didn't know how to blame him without blaming me, because he wasn't here."

Dallas gets a knowing look on his face. "So, instead of learning the truth, people just decided you were one way and stuck with that."

He understands.

"Yes. Exactly. People treated me like I deserved it. Like, if I was going to be *that* stupid, to trust in him, then it was all my fault."

"So, they didn't catch him?"

"I'm not even sure they looked." I sigh. "He's 'in the wind,' as they say. I've given up ever finding him now. He targeted me. Raya said it's because I'm too trusting, and maybe I was. I'm smarter now, I think, and stronger, but that doesn't change the past. I just need to pay everyone back, starting with my parents, and maybe with a little luck, people will forget and move on."

"They will," he says. "They have to."

I glance up. "Will they? Like people will forget about the 'bad boy of hockey'? I would give anything to make them see the Dallas Burke *I* see."

I mean that. It's a travesty that people don't know this guy for who he is.

His smile is weak. "I honestly don't know if people will *ever* forget that nickname."

I desperately feel the need to lighten the mood. "It *is* catchy."

I look at him, fishing for a glimmer of a smile—and I hook one.

I pause for a moment, aware I have no right to act like I'm an authority on anything, but still feeling like I have an opinion worth sharing. "I don't think you should wait to start your foundation."

He frowns. "You don't?"

I shake my head. "I understand why you felt like you should, but there's a lot of good inside of you. Why wait to let it out?"

He pushes a bit of food around on his plate. "I just want it to be accepted, you know? For people to buy into the whole idea."

"What is the idea?" I ask.

He goes still. "I want to start a youth foundation for kids who have at least one incarcerated parent."

I watch as his jaw twitches.

"But that would mean telling the world about my father."

The {Rumor} Mill

Spotted: *Poppy Hart cheering on Dallas Burke at last night's Comets' game, and wearing a sleek, updated look.*

It would seem by all accounts that local chef Poppy Hart and her boy toy, pro hockey player Dallas Burke, have made their romance rink-official! And that won Poppy a front-row, VIP seat, watching Burke come out of a fog that's left him without a goal or an assist for the last five games.

Thanks to hockey's favorite bad boy, last night's game was an absolute gong show, with the Comets shutting out Ottawa, 5-0. This Miller wonders what exactly Burke had been sampling off of Poppy's menu that had him skating better than ever. . .

We'd also like to know who styled the middle Hart sister—a valiant effort, though it does fall a little flat when you put her next to the other hockey wives.

It's nice to see Poppy is at least trying to fit in somewhere where she so obviously doesn't!

After the game, the pair were spotted at a swanky Chicago

restaurant, but they didn't stay long. Spectators said when they left, Dallas seemed agitated, which begs the question—how long till the fiery forward reveals his true colors? And is Poppy in for a rude awakening?

Chapter Thirty

Poppy

The next day, by some miracle, I wake up early in spite of the late night. I get ready and drive myself to the restaurant, skipping my morning Mo's Coffee trip, and when I pull around the corner I see a line of people looking like they're waiting for concert tickets to go on sale.

Only when I make the turn into the alley behind the restaurant do I realize they're actually lined up at my door.

I park the car and hurry inside where I find Miguel and his wife Gabi prepping for the morning.

"I had a feeling after we saw you at the hockey game last night that we might need to get an early start," Miguel says.

"You saw me at the hockey game?" I ask. Why hadn't my family told me?

Gabi grins. "You looked so pretty, Poppy! And so *chic* up there with the other wives and girlfriends. The camera zoomed in on you twice."

My throat is closing. I'm going to need to be intubated. Why didn't I know this? "What did they say about me?" Why did I ask? I don't even want to know.

"They were nice," Gabi says. "A lot nicer than *The Mill*."

Miguel shoots her a look I think is meant to be discreet, but absolutely isn't. "They mentioned the restaurant. It was good. I don't know what's going on with you and Dallas Burke, but if it keeps up, can I ask for a raise?"

I laugh and pull on my apron, tying it around my waist. "I might consider it just for you having the smarts to come in early today. Let's focus on getting through the morning, and then we can talk."

By the time we close that afternoon, Miguel, Gabi, and I collapse at the counter in the kitchen, completely spent. It's only now that I realize I still have to cook for Dallas and Sylvia.

Oddly, that thought energizes me.

Miguel and Gabi take off, with the former reminding me of his impending raise, and I start to make a shopping list. I'm about halfway through when Raya and Eloise walk into the kitchen.

Both of my sisters seem to be on a mission.

"We got no update last night!" Eloise practically squeals. "If our sister is going to date a famous hockey player, we darn well better be in the loop!"

"Didn't you watch the game?" I ask. "If you did, I think it's me who should've been looped in. Miguel said I was on TV."

Raya nods at the espresso machine. "Latte please."

I roll my eyes but make no comment about how they're using me for my caffeine. "I'm going to teach you both how to make these drinks so I don't have to wait on you anymore."

"We'll call it payback for getting you ready last night," Raya says.

I rethink my position. "That's fair."

Eloise opens her phone and shows me today's installment of *The Mill*. "Have you seen this?"

"You know I don't read that." Ever since Avi, I stay away

from the gossip site. No sense reliving my greatest humiliation through someone else's commentary.

"You are definitely the talk of the town," Raya says. "But Poppy, was this really what you wanted? Things had just started to die down after—" She pauses. She knows I don't like to rehash it. She knows because I've told her a million times. Raya was the least understanding about what happened, but also my fiercest defender. She chastised me in private and pointed out all of my mistakes, but in public, she did her best to protect me. It didn't always work, but I appreciated the effort.

I don't have a lot of friends, and the ones I did have had moved out of Loveland. But I never feel lonely thanks to these two. Built-in best friends.

"I know," I say, returning to Raya's unfinished question. "I told Dallas all of it last night."

"All of what?" Raya asks.

"About Avi," I say. "The whole sordid tale."

They exchange a glance, then back to me.

"What?" I ask. "Is this some conversation that you've had without me again?"

"Poppy," Eloise says, "are you sure that was smart?"

"He's going to find out," I say, feeling instantly defensive. "I wanted him to hear it from me, and not read it on some stupid website."

Raya slowly sets her coffee cup down on the counter and turns it so it is perfectly perpendicular with the edge. She calmly folds her hands, then squares off with me.

"You're doing it again."

"Doing what again?"

"Baring your soul?" Raya says it like I should know already. "Letting him in? The kiss was bad enough, but now you're sharing your feelings? And your history? The dating might be fake, but your feelings for him clearly aren't."

"I'm sorry I'm not completely closed off, Raya," I say, a bit cold.

Eloise giggles. "Ooh, shots fired."

Raya studies me, unaffected. "Do you have feelings for this hockey player?"

My eyes widen. "What? No. We're friends. Business partners, if you want to get technical."

"Business partners don't talk about personal things like being conned out of your life's savings," Raya says.

"When it will affect the other person, they absolutely do," I say, rising up a little.

She matches my tone. "No. They don't. Why can't you see that?"

"Maybe we could just talk about this later," Eloise tries to bring down the temperature in the room.

"No," I say. "We're talking about this now."

"Yes, Poppy," Raya stands. "Let's. Because I feel like I'm the only one in this room who cares about your feelings. Or your future!"

Our voices are getting louder than I'm sure we both intend, but this is sometimes the best way to break down the walls and get to the truth.

I stand. "You think I don't care about my future? It's wracked with debt because of my past!"

"And whose fault was that?"

I'm offended now. "Are you saying Avi was my fault?"

"No, but you're repeating the same mistakes all over again!"

I circle around the counter toward her. "Am I?"

"Yes! And you can't see it!"

"You weren't there last night, Raya! You didn't see what he did!"

"What in the world are you talking about?! Did that creep do something to you?"

"No!" I shout, exasperated. "He *saved me!*"

I'm trembling. What I just said hangs in the air.

I gather my nerves and tell both of them every detail of the previous night. The after-party, the bar, the expensive food, the sisterhood I *almost* felt like a part of, and finally, Mulligan cornering me outside the bathroom.

My voice breaks as I point at Raya and say, "I was *terrified.* And Dallas saved me. And it wasn't because of some contract, and it wasn't because of some photo op, and it wasn't because he had to. He pinned that complete waste of a human being to the wall and told him to leave me alone."

There's a moment of silence, save for my breathing.

"So we left. We left, and came back here, and I cooked for him, and I felt safe enough to confide in him, because I don't have *anyone* to do that with. I don't have *anyone*, Raya."

I crumple into a chair, even more spent now.

Raya moves toward me, and I hold up my hand. "Don't. Just. . .don't."

As is typical with her, she doesn't listen, and she kneels down in front of me and takes my hands.

"Poppy." I look at her and her eyes are glassy.

"You have me."

Eloise drags a chair over next to me, obnoxiously loud. "And me."

Raya takes a breath, and what comes out of her mouth is something I thought I would never hear.

"Maybe I judged him too quickly. Maybe I was. . .wrong about Dallas Burke."

I wipe my eyes and turn to Eloise.

"El, can you mark the date? I think I just heard Raya say she was wrong."

Eloise lays her head down on my arm.

"I'm sorry. I don't mean to be. . .me. . .but I just know that sharing too much is what got you in the mess with Avi in the first place," Raya says. "And that was heartbreaking to watch."

Eloise takes an even softer tone. "We just don't want you to get hurt."

"Dallas isn't like Avi," I say.

"No," Raya says. "I don't think he is." Then, after a pause, she adds, "But in some ways, there's a lot bigger chance of heartbreak with Dallas than there ever was with that skinny little dweeb."

I laugh. "Skinny little dweeb? You should come with me to a hockey game, you'd learn *way* better insults there."

There's a pause, and then Raya's pragmatism returns. "I just think you'd be wise to hold back a little. Keep a bit of yourself to yourself. Don't share everything."

"Plus," Eloise adds, "a hockey life is no life for someone like you."

I frown. "What do you mean?"

"It's not that stable. They can get traded without warning, have to pack everything up and move to a different city."

"And your life is here," Raya says.

My stomach twists. "I didn't know that." I sniff. "Good thing we're not a real couple, then, huh?" I say, though I think I'm doing a terrible job of meaning it.

They know me well, and they know that when it comes to matters of the heart, I'm just not good at holding back.

Even after Avi.

I put an arm around Eloise and squeeze Raya's hand. "We're friends. I like him. He's kind, and thoughtful," I tell them, "but I'm not going to fall in love. I can't. Our worlds are so different. If there's one thing that the situation with Avi taught me, it's to look before I leap."

I'm afraid, though, that I might've already jumped.

Chapter Thirty-One

Dallas

The day after the game—and the night at Poppy's restaurant—I go to practice and the atmosphere is already different. It's not like everyone is suddenly going to listen to me after one good game, but nobody comments on me being "washed up."

Mulligan doesn't say a word.

In addition to getting Poppy that profile, Alicia also got several sites to post photos of Poppy, in my jersey, cheering me on. The hockey world seems to be asking *Who is Poppy Hart?* and my manager is thrilled.

I, on the other hand, am beginning to see the recklessness of this entire plan. There are real feelings involved in this fake relationship, and I'm starting to worry that one of us is going to get hurt.

After practice, I'm sitting on a bench in front of my locker, getting ready to shower when Jericho strolls in. He's got a towel, but for some reason he's got it over his shoulder instead of around his waist.

I shake my head. "Dude, put some clothes on."

He stands directly beside me. "You jealous?"

"Nobody wants to see that, buddy," Krush says. He and Kemp are on the opposite side of the locker room, and I'm thankful for the back-up.

"Don't knock it till you try it, fellas." And then Jericho does a little dance that none of us asked to see. I stand up quick and snap him with the wet end of a towel.

"Yow!" He grabs his rear end as the other guys howl their approval.

"Get that out of my face." I hold up a fist and Junior, walking past, hits it with his own.

Jericho goose-steps away toward his locker, complaining that it's "gonna leave a welt."

"Is your girl coming to the game tomorrow?" Kemp asks, rightfully ignoring our streaking teammate.

My girl.

I pull my shirt up over my head and toss it into my bag. "I don't think so."

Jericho, who has taken his towel and made a head wrap out of it, says, "Why not? Monica said they all loved her. The ladies think she's good for you."

I shake my head. "This life is a lot for a woman to adjust to. You guys know that. And Poppy is. . ." the only word that comes to mind is *special*, which I don't dare utter aloud. Instead, I say, ". . .different."

"Shoot, I think she should come to every game, you haven't played that well since—" Krush stops mid-sentence, but I know where he was headed. Since the accident.

"Come on, guys. That wasn't because of her," I say.

Judging by the looks on all three of their faces, and then by their unanimous scoffs, they aren't buying it.

"Well, if you're embarrassed of *us*, you're out of luck," Jericho says. "Monica is planning for a bunch of us to come to

Loveland for some Valentine's Day shindig with you guys." He looks at the other guys. "You guys'll be invited. We can meet up at Dallas's new place."

"You're inviting people to my house?"

Jericho holds up his hands. "Not me, my man. You know I just do whatever my wife tells me to do."

I laugh, but I'm not fully on board with Monica's plan. Mixing my life with Poppy's didn't seem like the best idea. It would be best to keep our relationship in Loveland as much as possible. Poppy still gets the benefit of whatever it is people are responding to there, and I can keep her away from the prying eyes and situations like the one with Mulligan.

Kemp and Krush both stroll off to the showers, leaving me with a half-naked Jericho and my thoughts.

"What's bugging you?" he asks. "You want to keep her for yourself? You afraid all of this—" he waves his hands out—"will scare her off?"

"I think all of that—" I wave a hand in the general direction of his lower half—"would scare her off."

Jericho laughs.

"I can't talk to you until you put some clothes on."

He grabs the towel from off his head and wraps it around his waist. "You saw the way the guys responded to you today, man. It was like old times. Even Mulligan seemed to be on his best behavior."

I couldn't deny it. I noticed it immediately. They were listening again. For the first time in a long time, we felt like a team. Almost.

Mulligan was determined to be a thorn in my side.

"I caught him cornering Poppy last night," I tell Jericho. "No idea what he said to her, but I didn't like it. I don't want her to have to deal with any of that."

Jericho lets out an audible sigh. "Aw, man, that guy needs to learn."

"Tell me about it."

"It's not just about Ricky, and you know it," he says. "He just wants to be the star. And as long as you're here, he never will be."

"He blames me," I say thoughtlessly, caring less about Mulligan's opinion and more about what the rift is doing to the team. "For what twisted reason, I have no clue."

"But nobody else blames you," Jericho says.

I look at him. "You sure about that?"

I replay the moment of impact in my mind. Ricky was messing with the radio, and I was trying to get him to stop. He didn't have his seatbelt on, and he was hanging out the window, sloppy drunk, so trying to contain him was difficult, to say the least. I'd been looking at him at the point of impact—not at the road. If I hadn't been, would I have been able to stop in time or swerve out of the way? These are things I think but don't say. These are things nobody else needs to know. Not even Jericho.

"Take the win, man." Jericho stands. "You're back. Took you long enough."

"Shut up." I smile.

"And there's a good chance your girl got you there."

I look around, just to make sure no one else is within earshot.

"Yeah. You actually might be right. She's. . .she's something, Jer."

I can't tell him the truth about Poppy and me, and I hate that I can't.

He starts to walk out, toward the showers, but stops and turns. "You hear they're retiring Ricky's number?"

My gaze hits the floor. "Yeah."

There's a pause. "Coach asked you to film something."

I nod without looking up.

"You gonna?"

"Not sure yet," I say. "Feels a little like showing up to a party I wasn't invited to."

"That's crap and you know it."

"That night is all about Ricky," I say. "I don't want to take away from that."

"You won't."

"Won't I?" I grab the towel from my locker. "He won't want me to be a part of it."

"Ricky's just mad at the world right now," Jericho says. "This is a good chance to put it all behind you."

I stand. "Do I deserve that?" I'm more conflicted about this than even I realized.

"Don't be a martyr, Dallas." He pauses. "What's Poppy say?"

I shake my head and chuckle. "You really want to know what she said?"

"Yeah."

I cock my head a little, close my eyes, and repeat her advice verbatim—because it's stuck with me ever since she said it. "'Some things are true, regardless of who you are. Saying something kind and from the heart is never a bad idea, and it's never the wrong thing to do.'"

I open my eyes, and Jericho holds his arms out wide, as if I just stated the secret of the universe. "Bro, you need to *wife* that girl immediately."

I laugh, absently thinking *that's not in the contract.*

"Monica is the same way. *So* smart when it comes to this stuff. I just do what she says."

"That's because you're whipped."

"And proud of it!" He grins. "That woman is my best friend. No offense."

"None taken. She's better looking than I am."

"Ha. She's the one person in the world who will never steer me wrong." Then, after a beat, "I have a feeling Poppy could be that for you too. If you get your head out of your—"

"Ooo-kay," I cut him off. "You made your point. Now go shower, you smell like a herd of goats."

He strolls off, leaving me alone in the locker room with a lot to chew on. I envy what Jericho and Monica have, but it's something I've always convinced myself I don't want. A partnership. Someone in my corner with no ulterior motives.

Poppy isn't that person. Right?

She can't be. Her coming into this world would be like transplanting a rose into a bed of poison ivy.

Saying something kind and from the heart is never a bad idea, and it's never the wrong thing to do.

She's right. And I think I know what I have to do.

I just don't know if I can.

Text Message from Dallas to Poppy

DALLAS

Was thinking maybe we keep things close to home for a while.

My world is so public, and it might be better to take a step back.

I don't want you to get overwhelmed.

POPPY

Right. Probably smart.

Small town living involves a lot of prying eyes, but those eyes don't have access to a 24-hr. news cycle 🙂

Chapter Thirty-Two

Poppy

I stare at the text exchange. Am I sensing regret?

I can't imagine that his teammates were horrible to him about me, but it seems like his tone has definitely changed. I don't know him well enough yet to know these things for certain, so instead, I'll jump to conclusions and fill in the blanks.

This is my way.

I can only guess there were more posts or tweets or responses questioning his taste in dating someone like me. I get it. The plan for me to bolster his reformed image isn't exactly working, so he's pivoting.

He wants to keep me here, in Loveland, where we're less likely to be photographed. Makes sense.

If I needed a reminder that I do not belong in his world, this was it. And it did a good job of knocking some sense into me. Never mind that Alicia also texted to find out my plans for the home game tomorrow. And that she has not been updated on Dallas's change of heart. I decide to skip the game and focus instead on catching up on meals.

Maybe Raya was right. Stop oversharing. I could stand to refocus.

Over the next few days, I make myself scarce. Dallas goes back on the road and is gone for a few days, so I stock meals for Sylvia and give the restaurant all my attention. Business isn't exactly slowing down.

By Dallas's third day away, I realize I miss him. Not in a super romantic way. . .just his company. He brings a strange excitement to my life, and I tell myself that's all this gnawing feeling is.

On his first night on the road, I watch the highlights of the game on my computer in bed only to discover the Comets lost in overtime. I feel terrible that I haven't reached out to him sooner. It's not part of the contract but *is* part of being a decent human.

I watch an interview with Dallas after the game, and I try to read how he's feeling through the pixels on the screen. It's difficult, but I can see a weight on his shoulders. He's taking the brunt of the blame for the loss.

I pull out my phone and text him:

POPPY
Hey
DALLAS
Hi
POPPY
I'm sorry about the game.
DALLAS
You saw it?
POPPY
I watched the highlights.

Overtime, wow.

Looked like a tough loss.

DALLAS

Yeah, it was a rough one.

POPPY

I'm going to have a watch party for the next one. Me and Raya and Eloise are crashing Mom & Dad's house, and we'll be cheering you on!

DALLAS

I'll try to play better.

POPPY

I know you're going to be awesome.

DALLAS

Thanks Poppy.

I stare at the words, assigning more weight to them than I should. All he said was thanks.

But, he'd also added my name. In his mind, he must've said it as he typed it. And that meant he was thinking about me.

And I'm thinking a little too much about him.

And I continue to think a little too much about him for the next few days.

But I also do other things while he's away. Big girl things.

I tell Margot that she can't bully me into making Dallas part of the Festival of Hearts. She threatens my spot at the Taste of Loveland, but Cara Carson sticks up for me, and soon the whole committee has secured my spot, whether Dallas is a part of the activities or not.

It's a small thing, but it feels like a turning point. I'm proud of myself, and I find I want Dallas to be proud of me too. I want to tell him about the look on Margot's face when I finally stood up to her.

I want to tell him all the small things.

The Comets win their next two games on the road. My family (even Raya) watches the games together. I do nothing to hide my enthusiasm when in the first game, Dallas scores the winning goal and, in the second, he steals the puck from the other team, thus stopping a potential tying goal in the final seconds. Dad and I were high-fiving, hooting and hollering, while my mom and sisters looked on in amusement.

After the second game, we watch the post-game commentary with the captions on. Two men sit behind a desk, both wearing suits. One is a former hockey player named Chuck Martin. The other, a journalist named Mariano Flores.

Chuck Martin: "Welcome back to the post-game, and what a game that was for the Chicago Comets. I think we can safely say that Dallas Burke is back, and he's proving a lot of naysayers wrong out there on the ice."

Mariano Flores: "So right, Chuck, over the last three games, he's had five goals, four assists, he's locked it down on defense—one has to wonder if it's what's been on the menu lately."

Chuck Martin: "You might be right, partner, maybe his new girlfriend, a chef from Loveland, Illinois, has figured out what to cook the guy."

Mariano Flores: "Lots of veggies, lots of carbs, and a whole lotta protein! I tell you, Burke looks like his engine is in top form out there."

Chuck Martin: "I couldn't agree more, Burke hasn't looked like this since he joined the league at the age of twenty-two."

Mariano Flores: "You know what they say about the

way to a man's heart is through his stomach! Let's see if his new good-luck charm can keep cooking up wins for both Dallas Burke, and the Chicago Comets."

"Poppy, *you* are Dallas's good luck charm!" Eloise squeals.

A look passes between Mom and Raya, and I can read it instantly. "That's what his manager told them to call me," I preempt their complaints, halting any concerns that my actions or thoughts are headed in a romantic direction.

Even though they totally are.

"She orchestrated the whole thing," I add.

After we clean up from the night, Mom pulls me aside. "I don't like this, Poppy. You're playing with fire."

"It's fine," I tell her, though, even I don't believe me.

"But is it?" She studies me. "Tell me it didn't make your heart skip a beat hearing those men credit you with Dallas's success tonight."

I shrug. "Maybe a little."

"And that's what worries me," she says. "I've never been comfortable with this plan. Not only because of the obvious deception, but because you, my darling daughter, fall hard and fast."

"I'm a realist, Mom. There is no way I'm going to be delusional enough to think any of this is real."

She takes me by the shoulders. "Protect your heart, Poppy."

The words are heavy and they hang there, like a storm cloud waiting for the precise moment to rain down a torrent and ruin a perfectly beautiful day.

Sunday evening, I'm in pajamas and ready for bed by 8 p.m. At 8:15, there's a knock at my door, so I do what I always do when someone knocks on my door—pretend I'm not home.

But then, a text comes in from Dallas.

DALLAS

I just saw you run out of the living room through the window.

Or. . .do you just not want to be bothered?

I chuck my phone aside and run for the door. When I open it, a little out of breath, I find him standing on the porch wearing a North Face hoodie, a pair of gray sweatpants, and a stocking cap.

A rush of heat washes over me in spite of the fact that it's thirty degrees outside.

He grins. "You were hiding."

"I didn't know it was you."

"Who'd you think it was?"

"Girl Scouts."

The grin widens. "Can I come in?"

I move away from the door and let him through, repeating my mother's warning in my head over and over again. *Protect Your Heart.*

There was just one problem. I had no idea how to do that.

Okay, two problems. I'm also not sure I want to.

Chapter Thirty-Three

Dallas

I don't know why I'm here.

I got back to town an hour ago, found Gram already asleep in the recliner, and couldn't think of anything else to do.

That's not true. I wanted to see Poppy.

She's standing in front of me in pajamas, with her dark hair in a bun on her head and not a stitch of makeup on, and she's never looked more beautiful.

I stuff my hands in the pocket of my hoodie and look around her quaint Craftsman, instantly struck by a single word that pulses through my mind. *Home.*

I fight off the desire to pull her close, unsure where all of this is coming from. I'm a loner. I do better by myself.

"Come in," she says. "Do you want something to eat?"

I shake my head. "I don't want you to do anything."

She crosses her arms over her chest, her baggy sweatshirt shifting as she does.

"So, this is your house," I say.

She eyes me, probably wondering why I'm here. I wish I

knew. If she asks, I'm doomed, because I couldn't explain it if I tried. I'm not willing to admit to her that I missed her.

"Do you want a tour?"

"Uh, yeah. Sure." I say this mostly because I'm curious.

"Well, my grandparents lived here, and I rent from them. They retired to Arizona right around the time I moved home to open the restaurant. Thankfully, they let me decorate how I want, but most of the furniture was here."

I look around the room. The wood floors appear to have been restored, and there's a worn-in beige sofa next to a matching armchair. They're facing a wall of built-in shelves, books stacked on each one, and her muted television is at the center, paused on two people mid conversation.

She turns a small circle around the room we're standing in. "This is the living room." The space opens to a dining room with a large wooden table and two walls of windows. She flips on the light, and I see a photo of an older couple hanging on the wall.

"Your grandparents?" I ask.

She nods. "I almost never use this room. No fun eating. . .um. . .by yourself. . ." She pauses. "Okay, that sounded pathetic."

The way she says it makes me chuckle.

She leads me into the kitchen. It's a little cramped, and while the house is charming, it seems a shame that someone with Poppy's culinary talent doesn't have room in her own house to show it off.

"You can see why I envy your kitchen so much," she says.

The walls are painted a buttery yellow, and there are flowers at the center of a small table that's part of a built-in, surrounded by windows. "It's a great house."

She opens the refrigerator. "You sure you're not hungry?"

"I'm sure," I say, peeking in the fridge. "But I'd take a bottle of water."

She hands it to me, and I open it, taking a long, cool drink, hoping that hydration is what I need to explain why I'm here, when truthfully, I don't really know.

I lean against the counter and the ticking of a small clock hanging on the wall catches my attention. "You probably want to know what I'm doing here."

She leans against the counter opposite me. "The thought did cross my mind."

I cap the water bottle. "Can we go back to the living room?"

There's the hint of a frown on her face, then she pushes herself upright and nods. "Of course."

I follow her, wondering if I should tell her the truth. That I missed her. I wanted to see her. I haven't stopped thinking about her.

I can't. Not yet anyway.

"I thought about what you said," I say as we sit on the couch.

"About what?"

"Ricky's ceremony." I drape my arm across the back of her sofa. "I recorded a video."

She grins, looking a little pleased with herself. She reaches out and covers my hand with her own. Her touch stirs something inside me. "I'm so glad! I think you made a good choice."

I nod. "I think so."

A pause.

"That's not why you came here, though."

I just look at her.

"What's bothering you?"

My eyes hit the floor. Again, she knows, without me having to say a word.

Her hand is still on mine. I move closer, turn to face her,

and take her hand in both of mine—more intentional than a casual touch. I rub my thumb along hers in a fluid motion, feeling the softness of her skin under the pads of my fingers.

Don't cross this line.

"The foundation," I finally say, still looking at our hands, clasped together.

"What about it?" she asks.

Our eyes meet. "I want to go for it."

She smiles. "Good. I think you should."

"But if I'm going to do that, I need to come clean."

Her smile fades. "About what?"

I pull my hands away and take another drink of the bottled water.

"About my father."

I turn away, realizing that this is harder than I thought it was going to be.

Did I think this would be easy? Really?

"We've managed to keep his name from being associated with mine, and I'm afraid allowing people to make the connection could undo everything."

She frowns. "You choose your friends, Dallas, not your parents. You're not responsible for him."

"I know," I say.

She inches closer. "I *hear* you saying that, but you don't believe it. Just like when you say you don't believe the accident was your fault."

I stare at the paused image on the television and clench my fists. She's right. I don't believe it. And as much as I want to, I don't know how to process these feelings. I know what people tell me I'm *supposed* to do, or how I'm *supposed* to feel, but I just get angry. The guilt over my dad, with the accident, the rift in the team. . . I learned at an early age how to use anger as a response. It's not as effective when you're an adult, punching the world, trying to ward off the ghosts of your past.

She reaches for my hand. "Why are you trying to fight the whole world?"

I bring my eyes to hers.

"I can see it on your face," she says. "The weariness."

I don't respond, and I don't look away. And as she holds my gaze, I feel like she's reading my innermost thoughts. And I want to let her.

"My mom left." The words are out before I can stop them.

Poppy pulls her feet up and sits cross-legged on the couch, facing me.

"She left us when I was really young. Like seven or eight. That left me alone with someone who really wasn't fit to be a father."

She sits, quietly, listening, holding my hand, and in the silence, I feel her encouraging me to go on. Without saying a word, she is exactly what I need right now.

It goes against everything I believe about relationships, but Poppy is safe. In a way nobody else in the world is safe.

"I didn't know it at the time, because every kid wants to idolize their dad, but he was a criminal," I say. "By the time I turned ten, I'd been a sort of accomplice in at least a dozen of his crimes."

Her eyes widen for a flicker of a moment, but then she returns her face to neutral.

"When I turned eleven, he finally got caught and thrown in jail. That's when Gram stepped in. Turns out, she'd been trying to get my dad to let her raise me for years." I pause. "He refused. Not because he wanted a kid, but because I made him look more legitimate."

I let go of her hand and reach for my water bottle, but I don't take another drink. I need to squeeze something, hard.

"Gram sat me down and told me the truth of what was really going on. She encouraged me to tell the police everything I knew, which, as it turns out, was enough to get him convicted." I look at her. "My testimony put him at the scene of an open case—a homicide."

She reaches out and puts a hand on my forearm.

My smile is forced. "I was there, Poppy. I was his lookout in the next room while he was killing some guy, and I didn't even know."

I wrench the water bottle, making a plasticky *crunch* sound, and toss it on the ground.

"We changed my last name to my grandma's maiden name, and she adopted me. Said we were putting him behind me, once and for all. But I couldn't." I laugh ruefully, turning to Poppy. "Turns out I was an angry kid. Who knew?"

She takes my hand again. I'm grateful for that touch. It's a much-needed talisman.

"I started to get into trouble, pick fights, bully other kids, and Gram put her foot down. Said if I was going to live with her, she wasn't going to put up with it. She'd let my dad get away with too much over the years, and she wouldn't make that mistake again. So, she steered me toward the only thing I showed any interest in at that age."

"Hockey." Poppy smiles softly.

I nod. "She's also kept my dad away. Wasn't hard because he was in jail." I pause, thinking back on it. "But with hockey—I got good. Really good, really fast. I never paid that much attention, I just tried to hit the puck as hard as I could. I was All-State in high school all four years, and we won the state championships three years in a row. Then I got drafted, and that's when he started to make threats."

"From prison? He knew where you guys were the whole time?"

I nod. "He saw that we changed my name, and he didn't like it. He threatened to tell everyone who he was, who I really was, and how I helped him with the crime, but got away with it because I was just a kid."

"Oh my gosh."

"Yeah. He's a *winner*." I turn away for a moment. Picturing his face tenses up every fiber in my whole body.

"What did he want from you?" Poppy asks.

I scoff. "Money. He finds out his kid gets drafted by the NHL, and all he sees are dollar signs. A bank account in his name for when he gets out." I pause. "And I did it, because I knew he could sell his story to some trashy tabloid, and I'd be that kid again."

"What kid?"

My vision goes blurry as my eyes unfocus, hating to talk about it, hating that it still has any effect on me, hating everything.

I angrily push her hands away, not meaning to. "You ever know any kids who showed up to school with clothes that didn't fit? Kids with dirt in their hair because they didn't shower that week? Kids who smell, kids you avoid, kids everyone whispered about when they walked in the room?" I stop. "That was me."

Poppy is watching me, and when I find her eyes, I don't see pity in her expression, but genuine concern.

I feel anger kick in, this time at myself. "This is so stupid, to feel this way about something that happened when I was a kid. I know I'm not that kid anymore, but I can't get past some stupid crap that happened when I was ten."

My eyes burn. My voice hitches. I'm so angry that I can't change any of it, and even angrier that I'm letting these stupid emotions get the better of me.

"I don't want to be that kid anymore."

She shifts, situating herself so our bodies are touching. She nestles her head just under my chin, resting it on my chest, and wraps her arms around me in the strongest, longest hug I've ever had.

The message I got loud and clear growing up is that guys don't cry. We just don't. We pick ourselves up off the ice and skate on. It's better to channel emotions like this into fuel to check the other guy into the boards.

But here, in this moment, I finally. . .*finally*. . .let go. I feel embarrassed and dumb and vulnerable and safe all at the same time. I pinch my eyes shut and try not to care that the tears are probably wetting Poppy's hair below my chin.

We sit like that for a long time.

In the quiet, I feel a calm step in. My breathing slows, and my shoulders relax.

I shift and wrap my arms around her, and we fit perfectly together. I sink a bit farther into the couch, and soon, the dark weight of the world completely drifts away.

Chapter Thirty-Four

Poppy

Oh, no. I did it again.

I drifted to sleep on the couch in the middle of a conversation.

I crack open my eyes to find light pouring through the windows, the television still paused, and Dallas sleeping quietly next to me.

Somehow, in the middle of the night, we shifted, and now we're both sprawled out on the couch, each of our bodies sideways, my head on his chest and his arms wrapped around me.

In other circumstances, this would feel like a very intimate sort of position, but knowing what I know about my relationship with Dallas, this feels exactly like what it is—one friend comforting another.

I don't want to wake him, so I don't move, but my bladder is raising its hand from the back of the room, demanding attention.

I replay our conversation from the night before. My heart still aches, after hearing about his childhood. I wish I could turn back time and make sure he never went through what he went through.

My childhood was so different from his, the complete opposite really. How lucky I am to have the parents I have. I feel a twinge of guilt and sadness that he didn't have that.

Finally, to stop me from actually wetting my pants, I shift, and Dallas stirs. I sit up and his eyes flutter open. And while I find him crazy attractive, even in the morning, what I really can't stop thinking about is how much I *like* him.

I like him—a lot.

"What time is it?" he asks.

"Early," I say. "But probably not early enough to keep the town gossips from spinning a big story about you sleeping over."

He sits up. "I should go."

We both stand, and Dallas folds the afghan that was half-draped over both of us all night long. I hope it smells like him.

I search his eyes for the familiar weariness, but I don't see it. He seems brighter this morning, in spite of the awkward sleeping arrangements.

"I'm sorry I stayed so late," he says. "I didn't want to wake you, and—" he pauses, "I didn't want to leave."

My heart stops beating and I hear the sound of it flatlining somewhere in the back of my mind.

I quickly reel in my thoughts before they run away from me.

He just needed a friend. He asked to keep your dates in Loveland. He's embarrassed of you.

And even though I feel a little like his dirty secret, I still manage to say, "I'm glad you stayed."

He puts his shoes on and grabs his coat, then walks toward the door. I follow him, like a puppy.

He stops in the entryway. "I. . .guess I talked a lot, huh?"

"Yeah, you did. Are you. . .okay with that?"

He looks pensive for a moment, then a realization comes across his face. "Yeah. Yeah, I think I am. I don't usually talk about that stuff. Ever. But, I guess I. . .needed to." He looks at me. "I guess I needed a friend."

I love hearing him say that. And I make a face and say, "Well, maybe that's the best thing that will come out of this fake dating," I joke, "and all of this real sleeping over."

He grins. "Thanks for everything, Poppy."

"Anytime," I say.

He turns to go.

"And Dallas?"

He faces me, one hand still on the doorknob. "Yeah?"

"For what it's worth, I think you should be honest about your dad," I say.

"You do? Why?"

I shrug. "You have this secret. It's a big one from your past. Believe me, I know about trying to get out from under things from the past."

"Yeah, you certainly do."

"I'm ashamed of mine, and you're ashamed of yours. And it kind of has this hold on you, like it's made you a prisoner. You live fearing that someday it'll come out."

He doesn't respond, just gives a slow nod of agreement.

"The only way I know for something like that to lose its power is to shine a light on it. To speak it out loud. To call it what it is, and to own it. That way, it can't torture you anymore."

He reaches for my hand and gives it a tug, pulling my body to his in one smooth movement. "I know we're just friends, Poppy, but I'm really glad I met you."

I drag my gaze past his chin, past his lips, and finally land on his eyes. "Me too."

"I feel like you're in my corner, and I need that right now." He leans down and places a single, sweet kiss to my forehead, which sets off an explosion of fireworks throughout my entire body. Vivid memories of our practice kiss roll through my mind like a slideshow I have no interest in turning off.

He pulls back and looks at me. "You've got work."

"Mmm-hmm," I say.

He pulls open the door and looks back at me. "I'll call you later." He squeezes my hand, then turns to go, leaving me standing in the entryway, watching like a lovesick teenager peering through the window at the boy she just porch-kissed.

The {Rumor} Mill

Spotted: *Dallas Burke leaving the home of Poppy Hart in the wee, small hours of the morning.*

<Image: Dallas walking out of Poppy's house, while Poppy stands in the doorway and watches him go.>

While Loveland's own Miss Hart has not been spotted in the stands cheering on her favorite Chicago Comet as of late, it looks like the pair is keeping it close to home and as cozy as ever.

Having returned from a stint on the road, the hockey sensation must've stopped over at Poppy's right when he got back to town, which is where he spent the *entire* evening, according to multiple neighborhood sources.

Things sure seem to be heating up for this pair of lovebirds, and Dallas seems to have given up his partying ways in favor of quiet nights with our favorite local chef, whose restaurant continues to be the hottest spot in town.

While it's still early, this Miller is rooting for the couple. . .and wondering if Poppy wants to invite her hunk of a boyfriend's tantalizing teammates to town for the Festival of Hearts. ;)

Text thread in the Hart sister chat group:

RAYA

You did it again, Poppy.

POPPY

Did what? <confused face emoji>

A photo pops up onto the screen, and I'm assaulted by the image of my disheveled self pining after Dallas, walking away from my house that very morning.

ELOISE

<dancing woman emoji>

Go, Poppy!

RAYA

Eloise. Do not encourage her.

POPPY

It's not what it looks like. As usual.

ELOISE

Looks like you've got a big fat crush on that fine-looking man.

POPPY

We're friends. Full stop.

RAYA

So what was this, a slumber party?

POPPY

He's going through some stuff, Raya.

I'm just trying to be there for him.

ELOISE

I think it's sweet, Poppy.

Even if I don't believe a word you're texting.

POPPY

<eyeroll emoji>

Chapter Thirty-Five

Poppy

Back to cooking. My happy place.

I let myself into Dallas's house after work a few days after *The Mill* runs the photo of the two of us. I've got two totes of fresh produce and a list of meals I'm going to make. When I walk in, I find Gram and Alicia standing there, and I'm struck with a strong sense of deja vu.

They look at me the same way they did on the day the wheels of this whole wild idea were first set into motion.

I stand in the doorway and they stare at me.

"Poppy," Alicia says. "Just the woman I wanted to see."

I set the bags on the counter and look at Gram. "How are you feeling?"

"Better," she says. "Good enough that I let the live-in nurse go."

"Sylvia," I say.

She holds up a pointed finger. "Don't start with me. I already got an earful from Dallas."

"It's going to be weeks before you're back to your old self. Having someone help you is not a bad thing."

She waves me off. "Pfft. I'm doing my PT. My physical therapist is a handsome young guy named Dex. Isn't that just the best name? Dex."

"Dex Marshall," I say. "I know him. He's a great guy and one of Eloise's best friends. But he doesn't live here, and you really need someone around when Dallas goes on the road."

"This is not why you're here," she says.

"No, I'm here to cook." I give Alicia a pointed look and start unpacking my groceries.

"You're also here to get ready for the game," she says.

The Comets are playing at home tonight, and while I'd hoped Dallas would invite me, he didn't. "I'm not going." I move around the kitchen with familiarity. "Dallas wants to keep our relationship here, in Loveland." I don't say anything else about this, but I notice Sylvia watching me.

She narrows her gaze. "Why do you suppose that is?"

I pull out a cutting board and an onion and start slicing. I force my emotions to detach. "I'm guessing he got some grief the last time we went out with the team, and he doesn't want to deal with it. Maybe they teased him about his boring, plain, homely girlfriend."

The wrinkles in Sylvia's forehead deepen. "Wow, someone did a number on you, honey. Ex-boyfriend?"

She's good.

I ignore her and keep on talking. "I told you both from the beginning that his reputation could actually take a hit, and I was probably right."

"What do you mean 'probably'?" Sylvia asks.

"I'm assuming," I say. "I don't read anything they write about us unless one of my sisters screenshots it and sends it to me."

"So, you have no idea." Alicia looks at Gram.

"No idea about what?"

Alicia pulls out her phone, scrolls for a moment, then holds the screen up to my face. It's opened up to a page she'd clearly already visited. It's a Google search for Dallas's name, followed by several headlines in a row about "Hockey's Reformed Bad Boy."

"It's working, Poppy," Alicia says. "All of these articles mention you, even credit you with Dallas's performance on the ice, with his calmer demeanor, even his mood with the media post-game. They even mentioned the photo that showed up on that local site, the one of Dallas leaving your house the other morning—"

Gram gives me a pointed look.

"Nothing happened," I say.

Her expression doesn't change.

"Sylvia. Nothing *happened.*"

"Uh huh."

"The idea that Dallas would trade in the parties and the women for a quiet night at home is making the rounds," Alicia pulls her phone back, "and it's a very good thing."

I go back to the onion chopping. I don't know what to think about any of this.

Alicia's phone rings. "Oh, I bet this is an interview request. I need to take this." She walks out of the room, leaving me standing there under Sylvia's watchful eye.

"You can't really think that's why Dallas said you should keep things here," she says.

"Can't I?" I flash her an ironic smile.

"Don't you know him better than that by now?"

Whatever she's about to tell me is going to challenge my resolve to stop fantasizing about her grandson, I can already tell.

"He told me Mulligan cornered you."

I look away. "It wasn't a big deal."

"It was to Dallas," she says. "He feels protective of you. He told me he doesn't want to expose you to that side of his life."

"But that's why we're doing this, isn't it?"

"That was never why Dallas is doing this," she says. "And I think you know that."

I pull out a green pepper and start chopping it up.

"And he needs you tonight, whether he wants to admit it or not."

I frown. "Why? What's so important about tonight?"

"Tonight they'll retire Ricky's number. There will be a ceremony before the game."

I stop chopping. "That's tonight?"

"It'll be the first time Dallas has seen Ricky since the day after the accident when Ricky ordered him out of the hospital room."

"He did that?"

"He did," Gram says. "I think it was the worst day of Dallas's life. And he's had plenty of bad days."

I think about everything I now know about this man. This beautiful, good, kind, misjudged man, and I want to take the ten-year-old boy with the mismatched clothes and hold him and tell him everything is going to be okay.

But another thought demands my attention. "If Dallas wanted me there, he would've asked me." I pick my knife back up and slice through the pepper. I'm not trying to be melodramatic. I just want to be clear where I belong. And where I don't.

"Dallas prides himself on not needing anybody," she says. "But he's not an island. And I can see the difference you've made in his life."

"I think you're giving me too much credit."

"I don't," she says. "You should be there tonight. If for no other reason than to make sure I don't fall down the stairs."

My eyes go wide. "You're going?"
"My first outing with my new hip."
I frown. "Is it safe?"
She shrugs. "You should probably come along to be sure."
"This is not fair." I groan.
"But you'll come?"
"Fine," I say.
She grins. "Good girl."

Chapter Thirty-Six

Dallas

It's two hours before the game, and I'm sitting in the locker room, my knee bouncing with nervous energy.

There's been an unwanted hum inside of me all day. Like a radio frequency only I can hear. Tonight I'll come face-to-face with Ricky for the first time since the accident.

I'm not afraid of confrontation. I'm not even afraid of doing the hard thing.

But this. . .this sucks.

I don't know if I'll mend the fence or burn down the bridge. Most guys I know don't sit around and talk about their emotions. Myself included. But I care about Ricky, and I care about making things right. I just have no idea how he's going to take it.

Yeah. This sucks.

I've got to get a grip. We have a game. We need the win.

I pull out my phone, knowing that one call will iron these nerves right out of me, but I can't bring myself to make it. I'm unsure about relying on Poppy too much. I haven't relied on anyone but myself for most of my life.

It was safer that way.

But it was also lonelier. And harder.

The doors to the locker room open, and several of the guys walk in. I brace myself for Ricky, but he's not with them. I start my typical pregame ritual as the noise picks up, and then, everything goes quiet.

I turn and find Coach Turnrose standing in the locker room beside Ricky, who is seated in a wheelchair. His wife Layla stands behind him.

Ricky is thinner now, and there's a strange expression on his face as he looks around the locker room. It has to be surreal being back here, and while I'm usually pretty good at warding off unwanted emotions, I notice there's a lump that's formed at the back of my throat.

After a few seconds of silence, the guys move toward Ricky, all of them talking loudly at once, welcoming him, joking, laughing. Layla takes a step back, and when she does, her eyes find mine.

I expect to see anger, but there's no trace of it. Only a silent understanding that we've both been through something traumatic.

I look away.

"All right, all right, good grief, give the man of the hour some room," Coach says. "You guys need to go get ready." He looks at me—a glance that seems meant to encourage me, but I won't ruin Ricky's night by inserting myself somewhere I don't belong. I was already nervous about my part on that video.

I turn toward my locker and rummage through my duffel, when I hear a voice behind me. "Burke."

Silence settles on the entire locker room, and I can only imagine what the guys are tuning in for. Angry, cross words—the moment I finally get chewed out by the man whose life I ruined.

But when I turn around, I see that Ricky is wearing an expression that matches the one his wife wore only moments before. *Understanding.*

Or, maybe to put it more correctly—*grace.*

Or, maybe even. . .*forgiveness.*

"Ricky," I say, trying to keep my voice steady.

"I saw the video they put together for tonight," he says.

I sit on the bench in front of my locker so I'm eye level with my former teammate.

"I watched the whole thing."

I brace.

"And I have never. . .*ever*. . .in my whole life...witnessed such a huge load of horse crap."

I blink. *Wait. What?*

He beams a huge smile. "All that stuff about what a great player I was? The best teammate?" He laughs a genuine laugh. "That I was an even better friend—" He scoffs.

I laugh. "I meant every word."

"Who wrote that for you, your new girlfriend?" he teases, and there are muffled laughs from the rest of the guys. "Someone get her a job in PR, I swear. . ."

There's a long, weighty pause, and most of the guys start toward their lockers, getting ready. Layla moves a few steps away, to give us space.

My gaze hits the floor. "Ricky." I breathe through the words, hoping they won't crack. "Man, I'm so, so sorry."

He reaches out and puts a hand on my shoulder. "It wasn't your fault."

At that, we have the attention of the room again.

I look up at him. "But at the hospital, you said—"

"I was freaking out. Mad at myself. Worried about the future." Ricky leans back. "I took it out on you, and I'm sorry."

"*You're* sorry?" It doesn't register. "I keep replaying that moment. I should've been a more defensive driver."

"I was drunk, and even I know that truck came out of nowhere," Ricky says, then he seems to wait for my full attention when he repeats, "It wasn't your fault."

The words stop time.

Ricky glances around the room, and then raises his voice louder. "You guys hear that? *It wasn't Dallas who caused that accident.* He didn't try to buy anyone off! He wasn't drunk! And he wasn't even supposed to be watching out for me that night. He did that—" he turns to me— "because he's a good friend."

Nobody is moving. The air is thick, as if everything has frozen.

"Stop letting this ruin our team," he says. "Stop acting like Dallas doesn't deserve your full support. Stop taking a single second of your time on that ice for granted, because one day, maybe sooner than you think, it'll all be gone."

The lump at the back of my throat grows, and I force myself to choke back the tears welling there.

"Now, I've seen the guys from Detroit close up," he's talking about our opponent tonight, "and I swear on a friggin' pogo stick, if you don't go out there and hit them right in the mouth I'm going to get out of this wheelchair and do it myself! Quit moping, put on the pads, and go win this game!" Ricky lifts a fist with a shout, and the rest of the guys erupt with a cheer. Everyone except me because I'm too overcome with emotion to make a single move.

Someone flips on Guns N' Roses' "Welcome to the Jungle," and the locker room explodes in pounding and chanting and cheering, but for me, everything goes to slow motion.

When Ricky notices that I haven't moved, he pushes his chair a little closer. "Time to go, Cap."

"I need to know you forgive me." I can't look at him when I speak.

He claps a hand on my shoulder and leans in until our foreheads are touching. "There's nothing to forgive, brother."

My throat closes, but I manage to say, "The team isn't the same without you."

Ricky's hand squeezes the back of my neck. "They need *you*, Burke. You're the only one that can lead them." He pushes me away to look at me in the face. "Time to stop beating yourself up and do your friggin' job."

I smile through the tears.

"And after watching you last game, I think I can move faster than you in this chair, what do you think? Lady chef got you fat?"

I shake my head and point my finger at him, then close my fist in front of him. He closes his fist and knocks it against mine.

"Go get 'em!"

The arena is full of Ricky's biggest fans. Of the team's biggest fans. Around the rink, there are banners, displays, and large, cut-out photos of him in what will turn out to be his glory days. And while the entire setting is bittersweet, I find I'm filled with gratitude.

Ricky forgave me.

I'd never been forgiven for something so monumental, and that forgiveness cracked something open inside me. I felt motivated in a way I've never felt before. Not to play this game, but to live life on purpose. *With* purpose.

Ricky was right—none of us is promised another day, another game, another moment out here. All of it is a gift.

I've been taking things for granted for far too long.

We're about to take the ice to warm up, when Jericho bumps my side. "You good, Cap?"

I look at him. "I'm good."

He nods. "Then let's do this!"

There's a shout, a release of testosterone, and then we barrel out onto the ice. The crowd is already electric in anticipation of this game, and they stand to their feet the second we hit the ice, cheering and screaming.

Everything blurs to the background as I skate out into the center of the rink, then around behind our goal. Ricky is sitting rinkside, right next to Coach, and as I pass by him, I stop and hold out my hand. "This one's for you, West."

He grabs it, and with a crazed grin, says, "Tear 'em apart, Burke!"

I keep my head down through the warm-ups, and once we're finished, I make my way back over to our bench. A kid hands me a bottle, and I shoot a stream of water into my mouth. As I do, my eyes land on the VIP section. There, sitting with Monica, Gram and the other wives, is Poppy.

And she's looking right at me, nodding and smiling.

She signs something to me, and while I haven't picked up a ton by being around her and her father, I know what this one means.

You got this.

"Your girl's back," Jericho says, stopping at my side.

I give her a nod and press my fingers to my chin and move them out, meaning *thank you*. Then, without thinking, I put my hand on my chest and point to her. It's a small gesture, barely noticeable, but she sees it, and that's all that matters.

Poppy is here.

She found out tonight is the ceremony, and she came.

I'm so thankful to have an ally in the stands tonight. The

rest of this crowd has no idea that Ricky forgives me, and when they see me on that video, they're bound to have opinions. It's nice to know that, no matter what, at least one person out there is on my side.

And it's even nicer that that person is Poppy.

Chapter Thirty-Seven

Poppy

Dallas saw me.

He pays attention to how I like my coffee, and now he's picked up some sign language?

He saw me, and he acknowledged me in the sweetest, most subtle way. Maybe someone caught it on video, but I hope not. I don't want that moment to be shared.

Fake dating but real friends. I know I'm supposed to remind myself it's all a show. But I don't. Because I like him.

My chest fills with heat at the admission, even though I haven't said a word out loud. Telling this to myself is the riskiest thing of all. And the words are on repeat in my mind.

I like him. I really, really like him.

Raya and Eloise are going to kill me.

But I can't help it. He's funny and charming and kind and attentive and thoughtful and good-looking. And misunderstood. He's *so* misunderstood.

The players leave the ice after the warm-up, and the lights fade. A video pops up on the screen—Ricky West, slow motion, in his heyday. He shoots a goal, and Dallas, his beloved team captain and friend, is there to celebrate with him. The two men embrace on the screen, and my eyes dart down to where the team now stands, searching for him, anxious to make sure he's okay.

And then, Dallas's face appears on the screen. This is the part he was nervous about. How would this arena respond, with sympathy or judgment?

Dallas speaks for a few minutes about his friendship with Ricky and his grief over the accident. He holds back his emotion in a way that almost seems cold, but I recognize a defense mechanism when I see it. And then, right on the screen in front of me and tens of thousands of other people, Dallas's voice cracks and he looks away from the camera.

He gathers himself, and says, "Ricky West will never be forgotten by me or any of the Chicago Comets. He's one of us, always has been, always will be." He looks directly into the camera and says, "We love you, man."

The video fades to black, and when the lights come back up, Ricky is at the side of the ice alongside the coach and several guys in suits. Off to the side, the two competing teams stand in solemn rows, and my gaze falls to Dallas, who is turned toward Ricky, but too far away for me to assess his emotional state.

An announcer introduces the former Comet, listing a number of accolades and painting a clear picture that Ricky West was in the prime of his life at the time of that accident, and my chest squeezes as I imagine how all of this is making Dallas feel right now.

Ricky speaks for a few minutes, and the crowd is so kind and encouraging. The speech is inspiring, even for me, because he talks about not wasting a single moment, not taking any bit of this life for granted. And I'm guilty of both of those things.

Several minutes into the speech, Ricky goes quiet. The

pause is so lengthy, the men in suits start to look at each other. His wife steps forward and puts a hand on Ricky's shoulder. He touches it and nods, and it's so beautiful to witness that moment, the way she gives him strength when his runs out.

Could I ever do that for someone?

Could I ever do that for Dallas?

Ricky clears his throat. "I'm so glad to be here because there's something else really important that needs to be said publicly."

The crowd is silent.

"Dallas Burke was driving the car the night of my accident."

Beside me, I feel Sylvia tense. Inside me, I feel my own muscles do the same.

"He was taking me home because I was in no state to drive, and unlike me, he hadn't been drinking that night. He did that because he's a good friend. More like a brother, really. He watched out for me, the same way he watches out for everyone on the team. And I know a lot's been said and written about Burke since that night, but I want to set the record straight. What happened wasn't Burke's fault. It was an accident. There was no way he could've prevented it."

Ricky looks over at the crowd, and the guys on the team follow his gaze to Dallas, standing in the center of them. His face appears on the large screen overhead, and I see his jaw twitching as he clearly tries to hold back his emotion.

I want to run out there and hold him, to make sure he knows he doesn't have to go through any of this alone.

But I also know there are some storms we have to weather on our own.

"Dallas Burke is more than a great hockey player; he's a great friend, and I'm honored and grateful to know him." He points at Dallas, who shakes his head and points back.

"Detroit's in for a rough time tonight, boy!" The arena explodes in cheers at this, and Ricky, over the din, shouts at the Detroit players, *"Welcome to the Jungle, Ice Hawks!"* And at that moment, Guns N' Roses rips through the speakers, sending the crowd into a boisterous frenzy. Ricky hands the microphone back to the announcer, who directs us to turn our attention to where a large banner with Ricky's name and number is being raised from one end of the arena to the rafters.

The rest of the ceremony is a noisy blur because all I can think about is Dallas.

After the game, Alicia and Gram leave to find Gerard, and I leave with Monica to wait for Dallas and Jericho.

"I think it's sweet how you worry about him," Monica says.

I glance up. "I'm not worried."

Monica pulls a compact out of her bag and tosses me an *Okay, sure* look.

"So, your big festival is coming up soon, right?" Monica says, like we're sharing a secret. "I got a new dress for the *dance*."

It occurs to me that if she and Kari and Lisa really do come to the dance, they will make everyone else there look like trolls. Including me. Still, I couldn't fault them for being beautiful. Or rich.

And it would be *so lovely* if Margot wasn't the queen for a night.

I don't feel bad at all for thinking that. I should, but I don't.

It also hits me that my contract with Dallas is coming to an end. Valentine's Day will be our last night as a fake couple.

It's going to be a lot harder than I thought to let him go.

The door to the locker room swings open, interrupting my thoughts. Jericho walks out and heads straight for Monica. He wraps his arms around her, picks her up and spins her around. I'm still watching them when he goes in for a kiss, and it turns sexy fast, so I look away.

Before long, I'm standing in a clump of hyped-up men who just won their game and the women they love. It's like Valentine's Day a week early, and I'm caught in the middle of it.

And then, the door opens and Dallas walks out. Last time I met him back here, everyone else was gone. This time, we're surrounded by teammates and girlfriends and wives. The door closes behind him, and I swear the world turns to slow motion as he locks eyes with me, walking with a purpose.

I stand completely still, the sound of my heart beating in my ears. I'm unsure how to act with this particular audience, so I decide I'll follow his lead.

He stops in front of me. "You came." A smile. No weariness. No weight.

"I know you said we should stick closer to Loveland, but I wanted to be here tonight. I hope it's okay."

"I only said that because I didn't want to subject you to all of this," he says. "I just want to keep you safe."

"I'm not going to break in half, Dallas," I say. "I'm stronger than I look."

"Oh, I know," he says. But it doesn't feel like he believes it.

I *was* strong enough to handle it. I could fit in here. *Right?*

Behind him, I notice some of the others are watching us, like we're an exhibit in a museum, on display. "*Dallas in Love*" isn't a sight anyone is used to. And if I had to guess, at the moment, it's causing some head scratching.

I bring my eyes to his and smile, realizing how I can prove to him that I'm stronger than I seem.

I wrap my hands up around his neck, giving him my best *go*

with it look. He drops his duffel bag to the floor and wraps his arms around my waist. Our bodies press against each other, his eyes searching mine for permission, which I silently give.

He leans in as I go up on my tiptoes, and then his lips are on mine. The kiss isn't chaste. Or polite. This is a post-game, heat's up, three goal kiss. And I'm here for all of it.

There's emotion trapped inside of him, I can feel it in the way he kisses me, and that same desire to hold him, to make sure he knows he's not alone, returns and intensifies.

His hands press into my back, pulling me even closer, and it's still not close enough. I would trade just about anything to stay in this moment forever.

When he finally pulls away, I've almost forgotten we aren't practicing in his kitchen, just the two of us. But it doesn't seem to matter to Dallas. He presses his forehead to mine, and I want to look down to see if I'm levitating because I don't feel the floor under my feet.

"Hey," he says, his voice low and husky, his breath shallow. "You okay?"

I can't answer. Not with words. All I can do is move my head up and down in a nod against his.

"Yeah," he whispers. "Me too."

It doesn't feel fake at all. Is he really this good at pretending?

Jericho smacks a hand on Dallas's shoulder, breaking the spell. "Yo! You coming to dinner?"

Dallas's eyes are on me as if he doesn't want to leave this moment behind quite yet.

Maybe that's just me projecting, because I could live right here in his arms.

"Sure," he finally says. "If Poppy wants to."

He's asking if I want to go out and pretend to be in love with a man I may already be in love with? *Yes, please.*

I can practically feel a tiny Raya appear on my shoulder in a poof. She's sitting on a cloud, there to remind me not to fall for this guy. And then, there's my mother on the opposite shoulder, sing-songing "Protect your heart" over and over in a voice that sounds like one of the Chipmunks. Why did I get two tiny naysayers and no one cheering me on?

I close my eyes and Eloise pops in my head. She's wearing the same red dress as the dancing lady emoji, doing the salsa like she doesn't care who's looking, and giving me two thumbs up.

There. That's better.

Tonight is not a night for logic or reason. Tonight is a night where I get to experience what it's like to be Dallas Burke's girlfriend. . .and all that entails.

Chapter Thirty-Eight

Dallas

I *wonder if she felt what I just felt.*

I take Poppy's hand as we all walk into the parking garage toward our cars. I tell myself that I'm selling a story, mugging to a crowd, playing a role, but even I know better.

When I saw her in the stands, my heart turned over in my chest. The ally I needed was there, and she was only there for me. Even if Ricky hadn't forgiven me, she still would've been there. Even if my world imploded tonight, she still would've been there.

And I'm pretty sure our contract has nothing to do with it.

After the game, the thoughts spinning around inside me had my head jumbled up. We won, so there was excitement, but seeing Ricky and discovering that he forgave me offset that excitement with a bittersweet emotion I couldn't name. But then I saw Poppy standing there outside the locker room, and something inside me settled.

She didn't have to do a thing. Her presence was exactly what I needed.

On the way to the restaurant, she asks about Ricky, and I'm shocked I hold it together when I tell her what happened in the locker room before the game.

"Ricky forgave me," I say, pulling into a parking space in the lot beside the restaurant. "It was unlike any feeling I've ever experienced."

I put the car in park, and Poppy turns to me. She watches me so intently I feel like she can see straight through my crap and right into my soul.

Nobody else has even bothered to look before.

She reaches over and takes my hands. "Now it's time to forgive yourself, Dallas."

My eyes dip from her eyes to her lips and back, and all I can think about is how badly I want to kiss her again. I know there's no one around. I know the contract forbids it. I know it will only confuse things. But I reach out and let my hand rest behind her neck, stroking her face with my thumb. "You first."

She places her hand on my arm. "Not fair," she says with a coy smile. "You're *so* not fair."

I watch her for a long moment, thinking that she's helped me see a different side of myself in only a handful of weeks of knowing her. She makes me want to be better. She makes me believe I can be.

"Thanks for being there tonight, Poppy."

She smiles, and I feel it under my hand. Her skin is soft, and her eyes sparkle in the faint light of a street lamp outside.

"Thanks for letting me be here." Then, she grins and widens her eyes. "And thanks for that fake kiss back there outside the locker room." She fans herself dramatically. "Think it convinced some people? I understand now why 'weak in the knees' fits!"

The moment had gotten heavy, and I'm grateful for the

levity. Grateful she reminded me to stay on track—we're just friends pretending to be more.

"My pleasure," I say cheekily, pulling my hand away. "You're fun to kiss."

She looks at me. "I am?"

I grin over at her. "Yep."

Jericho and Monica walk by my car, and Jericho knocks on the window.

I look at Poppy. "You ready?"

She hasn't moved, and I wonder if I shocked her. I wouldn't mind if I did. I know our lives are just about as opposite as possible, but I don't even care.

Now that I know what it feels like to have her cheering me on, not only on the rink, but in my life—I'm not sure I want to give it up.

Finally, she nods and looks away, grabs her purse and gets out of the car. Monica meets her, and the two take off toward the restaurant, which makes me rethink my stance that Poppy doesn't fit in my world. . .because my world seems to like her a whole lot already.

I fall into step next to Jericho, who pushes me. I push him back, and he puts his hands up like a prize fighter. "You think you got what it takes? Throw hands, old man!"

I laugh. "I could throw you on the roof of this building before you threw the first punch, sucker."

Jer lifts one hand up in surrender and I high five and hold it. He softens a bit, but adds, "You're still a scrub, though."

"Shut up," I say as I shove him again. I love this guy.

"Tonight was a big win, man," he says. "And not just for the team."

I know what he means. "Ricky."

I can still feel the effects of that moment before the game.

It makes me think of what Poppy said about saying out loud

the thing that you're desperately trying to keep secret. Ricky's words stitched something up inside of me, and I wonder if speaking the truth about my past could heal something else.

"It was a good night," I say.

"And Poppy?"

"What about her?" I stuff my hands in the pockets of my dress pants as she tosses me a look over her shoulder. She smiles, and it feels like I just got zapped with a laser gun.

"I've seen you date a lot of women, Burke," Jericho says. "A *lot* of women."

"Easy, buddy."

He continues, "But I've never seen you like this."

"Like what?"

"Like the way I was when I started dating Monica."

To me, Jericho and Monica have the kind of relationship everyone aspires to and few people find. The comparison was bold, but it didn't feel completely off-base.

"You're falling for her," he says.

I shake my head. "Poppy's great. But we're still new."

"I proposed to Monica two weeks after I met her," he says with a resigned shrug. "When you know, you know."

But you don't know everything, *buddy*.

My thoughts are conflicting, and I know I should talk to Poppy about all of it. I *want* to talk to Poppy about all of it.

Say we start a real relationship. I'm a free agent next year, and could land anywhere in the country. Chicago doesn't match other offers, and I'm thousands of miles away. No way we're doing long distance. No way she's leaving Loveland.

No way I would let her.

When the hostess seats us at a dark booth in the back corner, and I slide in next to her and inhale the sweet vanilla scent I've grown to crave, all logic and reason exit my brain.

I take her hand under the table, purposely keeping it

hidden in hopes that she'll see I don't care about my public image at all.

We spend the night talking about the game and about Ricky, but it's when we talk about the Festival of Hearts dance that I get an idea.

It's insane, but once it's in my head, I can't get it out.

After we eat, I pull Monica aside and ask her opinion on it. She's all in, and she's willing to help wherever she can.

"The guys are gonna flip out, you know that?" She shakes her head in disbelief.

"Oh, I know—but it needs to be done, right?"

She grins. "Definitely."

On the drive home, Poppy is quiet—and I wonder if being out in public like this is taking its toll.

It's a lot.

We reach her house, and all of the pretense falls away. It's just Poppy and me. No cameras. No teammates. No spectators.

This is when I need to keep my hands to myself. But I really, really don't want to.

Poppy picks her purse up off the floor of the car and sets it in her lap. "Oh, hey, good game tonight, by the way."

I smile over at her. Her adorable awkward side is making an appearance, and even though it's cute, I don't want her to ever feel anything but comfortable around me.

I wonder if she's fighting any of the same feelings I am.

I wonder if I should just tell her.

I wonder if it will only make everything harder when it all ends.

I'm not the type to overthink things. I see a crease, I angle my skates and power through it. I see a five-inch opening above the left shoulder of the goalie, I shoot. I find someone I care about is cornered in a dark hallway, I react.

With this, though, it can't be that heavy-handed. It can't

just be, "here it is, this is what I want. Let's do it." Most, if not all, of my decisions have been singular in focus: how they affect me. I have leaned on the fact that I couldn't care less about what others thought of me.

But that's not true anymore. Not when I find I care a lot about what Poppy thinks of me.

How do I protect her from the pitfalls of being a professional hockey player's girlfriend? How do I ask her to be with me when there's a very real possibility that my living situation could change in a heartbeat?

How? How do I do that?

You can't.

I sigh. And there it is. Making something work means asking her for impossible, selfish things. It's not fair.

"Thanks for dinner," she says.

"Thanks for coming tonight."

She smiles. "You already thanked me." Her hand is on the door handle.

I should let her go. Why can't I let her go?

"Hey, um, do you want to come in and watch the next episode of *Downton Abbey*?" she asks.

I don't even like the show, but that doesn't stop me from saying, "Sure."

Her smile widens. "Okay, but no falling asleep this time."

I laugh. I'm bone tired. And there's something awfully appealing about drifting off to sleep with Poppy in my arms.

Chapter Thirty-Nine

Poppy

And now he's back in my house.

This night has not been good for my resolve.

I'm more smitten with Dallas than ever, and that's saying something, because I was a hot ball of flames from the moment I grabbed his arm in that line at the coffee shop.

Now that I know him, now that he's allowed me into his life, allowed me to see a side of him I don't think he shows to a lot of people—it's ten times worse.

Or better, depending on your perspective.

And I know when he walks away from me, it's really, *really* going to hurt.

I think, though, that we'll remain friends. At least I hope we do. But once the contract expires, once Sylvia is rehabbed, he won't have a reason to come out here as often.

But I don't want to think about that right now.

When we get in the house, I pop a bag of microwave popcorn, willing my emotions to *please behave.* I turn around to find Dallas, standing in my living room, changing out of his dress shirt and into a hoodie he had stuffed in his duffel.

The view is *lovely*. He's all rippling muscles and firm skin, and I try to control my pulse, but it's a lost cause. I don't know why I even bother.

Maybe this was a bad idea.

"I'll be right back." I race upstairs into the bathroom and close the door behind me. I pull out my phone and open my chat with Eloise and Raya.

POPPY

You guys were right. I like him.

I like him a lot. DANG IT.

RAYA

Shocker <eyeroll emoji>

POPPY

Don't judge me right now. Tell me how to fix this!

ELOISE

You're a goner.

We saw that little moment you two had at the game tonight.

Did you teach Dallas sign language?

POPPY

You saw that?

RAYA

It was on television, Poppy. Everyone saw it.

POPPY

It was very subtle. I hardly even noticed.

ELOISE

<eyeroll emoji>

You're a terrible liar, even over text.

POPPY

Whatever! I'm sure Alicia told him to do something like that.

RAYA

Look, Poppy, it's been an emotional night for him. You'd be smart to call it a night and let it all settle. Otherwise you might do something really stupid.

ELOISE

If something stupid is making out with Dallas Burke, I think you should ignore Raya and do that.

<red lips emoji> <dancing lady emoji> <heart eyes emoji>

POPPY

You're not helping, El.

ELOISE

What's the big deal? You like him. He's a good guy, right?

RAYA

He's a professional athlete, Eloise.

ELOISE

So what? Don't stereotype him.

RAYA

I don't have to.

POPPY

You guys! Focus!

Right now, there is a beautiful, sweet, wonderful man who had EMOTIONS tonight and I'm feeling things. So, help me out here!

RAYA

Kick him out.

ELOISE

Go for it!

I groan and turn my phone over in my hand, setting it down on the sink. This isn't helping.

My phone buzzes, and I stupidly pick it up.

RAYA

Remember this is all for show, Poppy. He's doing all the right things because he knows how to do all the right things to make people believe this is real. But it's not real. Just keep that in mind, and you'll be okay.

Right. Raya is right. It's all for show.

I keep repeating that to myself as I change my clothes, then walk back downstairs and find Dallas in my kitchen, pouring the popcorn into a bowl. He's now fully clothed and looks completely comfortable moving around my space.

I watch him for a few seconds (*this is all for show, this is all for show*) when he glances up and smiles.

"You look cute," he says.

And with that, tiny Raya disappears off of my shoulder in a poof.

"Is it the lack of makeup or the uncombed hair that's doing it for you?"

"A little from Column A, and a little from Column B." Gotta give him points for playing along.

"I've got the show cued up where we left off," he says. "But I'm not watching any episodes where any main characters die."

"Dude! Spoiler!" I join him in the kitchen and pull out the salt, shaking it generously over the popcorn.

"You've seen it before," he says.

"You haven't?"

He winces. "I hate to break it to you, but this really isn't my kind of show."

I feign shock. Then, after a beat, "We can watch something else."

"No, it's fine," he says. "You like it. But remember, you're the one who said 'no falling asleep.' I make no guarantees if those women in the kitchen start complaining about the war again."

"Oh, don't worry, I'll keep you awake." As soon as the words are out in the atmosphere, I feel blood rush to my face and a gasp closes my mouth.

He watches me, an amused expression on his face. "That came out wrong?"

I nod, and we both laugh. I should be used to making a fool of myself in front of this man, but even though he always lets me off the hook, it never gets easier.

I walk into the living room and sit on the couch, propping my feet up on the coffee table. When he sits down next to me, I notice he's closer than usual, and that sends a wave of tingles across my skin.

I try to rub the goosebumps away.

"Are you cold?" He turns and pulls my grandmother's afghan off the back of the couch, then spreads it over our legs.

In my head, I think of my mom's directive to Raya, whenever she had Jeremy over in high school. *No blanket sharing! Feet on the floor! Lights on at all times!*

I'm disobeying all of these rules, which meant by morning I'll be married.

I shove the thoughts aside as Dallas turns on the show. It's horribly depressing, and the plot moves so slow it's like a lullaby, rocking us both to sleep.

Our hands occasionally meet in the popcorn bowl, and I pretend not to notice, even though I start to watch for ways to make it happen again.

Every once in a while, I take a handful and flip it up at his face.

He responds by soundlessly taking a handful and dropping pieces in my hair.

It all feels very couple-y.

After a while, Dallas sets the bowl on the table and leans back against the couch, our shoulders touching, our hands dangerously close to doing the same without popcorn as a reason.

During some long, protracted wide shot of the outside of the Crawley family's massive estate, he quietly says, "I'm going to take your advice."

"About what?" I ask, peering over at him.

"The foundation." He looks at me. "I'm going to tell the truth."

Even though I feel the weight of his gaze, I don't look away. And when he reaches over and lets his hand rest in the crook of my neck, I stop breathing altogether.

I want to warn him that if he doesn't stop it right now he'll have to figure out how to dispose of my lifeless body. Instead I ask, "What made you change your mind?"

He shrugs. "You."

The word is so simple, so honest, I want to bottle it up and save it. "Me?"

"You don't have a hidden agenda," he says. "And I trust you."

My muscles tense at this.

The corner of his mouth twitches in the hint of a smile. "I know, I'm surprised too."

He trusts me.

In one of our first real conversations he told me he doesn't trust anyone.

I could relate. At the time.

And now, he trusts me. . .and I can relate to that too.

Because as crazy as it is for me to say, I trust Dallas. I honestly believe he'd do anything to make sure my restaurant succeeds—and even more than that, to make sure nothing and no one ever hurt me again.

His thumb moves across my cheek in the softest, sweetest motion.

I warn myself not to get awkward. Not to make any sudden moves. I want him to kiss me. In private. Not to check a box on Alicia's To-Do list.

But before this heated, heavy moment can evolve, my living room brightens with a flash at the window. Then another, and another.

Was that. . .a camera?

Dallas yanks his hand away, jumps up from the couch, and rushes toward the front door. I follow, mentally chastising myself for not pulling the curtains closed when we first got home.

But who thinks of that?

He flings the front door open and runs outside just in time to see a figure in black race off down the street.

He turns and looks at me, breathless. "I can probably catch him."

I put a hand on his arm. "No, don't bother."

He faces me. "Are you okay?"

I wrap my arms around myself, feeling oddly violated in my own home. I nod.

He reaches for me, holding my body to his, giving me perfect access to where I fit.

"This is just the kind of thing I wanted to protect you from," he says. "This part can get really ugly."

When he pulls away, I see something on his face has shifted.

"I should go home," he says.

I want to protest, but I can't. He should go home. He *should've* gone home already.

Raya, again, completely right.

In a flash, there was never a clearer reminder that Dallas and I are a wrong fit, no matter how much I wish it weren't true.

Protect your heart, Poppy.

He grabs his bag from the living room, turns, and looks as if he wants to say something, and doesn't. He shakes his head, and the next moment, he's gone.

Chapter Forty

Dallas

The room buzzes with the low hum of voices as I take my seat at a table in front of a Chicago Comets step-and-repeat banner.

Lights flick on all over the room, and the reporters I've gathered together wait for my announcement. I search the small crowd and only see the faces of strangers.

My phone buzzes.

When I pull it from my pocket, I see a text.

ALICIA

Why did I just get a notification that you're holding a press conference?

DALLAS

Because I'm holding a press conference.

ALICIA

Without consulting me first?

DALLAS

Yeah, sometimes I like to make my own decisions.

ALICIA

Dallas, wait for me. We need to talk about whatever it is you're planning to say.

DALLAS

I've got it, Alicia. We'll catch up after.

The door to the hallway opens, and Layla holds it as Ricky comes through. He grins at me as he takes his place next to me at the table.

Now we can start.

Coach slips in the side door and stands next to Layla. I wish Poppy was standing here too. After all, she's the reason I'm doing this. But after last night, it felt wrong to ask her to come.

"Ladies and gentlemen," I say into the microphone. "On behalf of my teammate Ricky West and I, I want to thank you for joining us today." I clear my throat. "Many of you have written about me over the years—some good things, some not so good. I'm looking at you, Brian."

There's a quiet ripple of laughter.

"To be fair, most of it was warranted, " I say. "But some of it wasn't. You did the media thing and blew things out of proportion to get reads and views—I get it. But ever since the accident Ricky and I were involved in, I've felt like my life needed an overhaul. Last night, at the game, Ricky encouraged us all to live in the moment, and I realized I haven't been doing that."

I stop. A camera clicks. A light flickers. Poppy's words rush back at me.

The only way I know for something like that to lose its power is to shine a light on it.

I inhale. "Someone really special to me encouraged me to be honest about my story. She said I shouldn't be ashamed of things that happened when I was younger because I've grown up a lot since then, and I took those words to heart. I can't be the only guy who's made mistakes, and I want to prove that we can forgive ourselves and move past them. And I want to start by coming clean with a secret I've held onto since I was eleven years old."

The room is silent. Red lights on cameras blink at me.

I adjust the microphone in front of me. "Most of you know I was raised by my grandma, something I'm supremely grateful for, but you may not know why. My mom left when I was young, and. . .my dad is a criminal." I pause. "And it was my testimony that put him in jail."

More clicking. More flashing lights. I imagine Poppy out there on the other side of that camera, and I try to absorb strength from the thought of her.

I tell the whole story. I confess the shame that's kept me locked up right alongside my father for as long as I can remember. I talk about my role in his crimes. The anger I felt. The way I tried to hide it all because I was humiliated and ashamed. And once it's all out there, I let it settle for a moment before going on.

"I've been very fortunate in my life, because those humble beginnings haven't stopped me from accomplishing what I always dreamed of," I say. "But what's the point if I don't use what I've learned to do any good?"

I glance over at Ricky. He upward nods at me, and says, "Do it already, my butt hurts sitting here."

More laughter.

I indicate to Ricky. "You all know the comedian over here, right?"

The press pool waves, and there's a murmur of anticipation in the room.

"So, I've asked my good friend Ricky to be a part of something we're going to build together. We want to make a difference for kids in situations like mine. Today, and together, we're announcing the Sylvia Burke Foundation."

A round of camera clicks as I unveil the logo—a single hand, holding up a pointer finger in a "number one."

"If we get one kid out of one bad situation and give them one chance—it could change their life. My Gram did that for me, and we're going to work to do that for as many kids with incarcerated parents as possible."

Ricky wheels over next to me, and I lean the mic down so he can be heard. "We'll work to raise money, create programs, teach skills, and of course, train them to play hockey—" another ripple of chuckles— "that will give these kids a fighting chance."

I pick up where he leaves off. "Because I can say, from experience, they won't all have a grandma, or an awesome high school coach, or," I slap a hand on Ricky's shoulder, "a great teammate to tell them to get their head out of their rear ends."

The reporters laugh their approval, and I add, "But they sure as heck need one."

I look out at all of the people gathered there.

"We want to be those people for them."

In the front, a female reporter with brown hair and a made-up face raises her hand. I point to her.

"How do we know this isn't just a publicity stunt?" she asks. "You've had your name dragged through the mud quite a lot lately—maybe this is simply a way to make yourself look good?"

"You can believe that if you want to," I say into the microphone. "I can't control that. But—and I mean no offense—I also really couldn't care less. People are going to say what they want and believe what they want. What I care about is what the people who really know me say and believe. And how I think of myself. You want to judge me? Judge what I do from here on out."

Another reporter raises a hand. "I gotta say, this version of Dallas Burke is very different from the one we're used to. To what do you credit such a drastic turnaround?"

"I grew up," I say. "Life changed me. I had some hard knocks, and instead of getting angrier, I learned from them." I pause. "And I found someone who believes there's good in me."

Several reporters overlap similar questions, and one wins out.

"Are you talking about Poppy Hart?" a reporter asks. "Is she the 'special person' who encouraged you to tell the truth?"

I run a hand over my face, my whiskers scratching my palm. Alicia would want me to say something sweet and romantic, to use my relationship with Poppy the way she intended it to be used. But there's not one part of me interested in doing that.

"I think. . ." I smile, "that is none of your business."

The reporters laugh, as the one who asked the question says, "Fair enough."

There are more questions—some for Ricky, some for our coach, and some for me—but the rest of the press conference is a blur. All I can think of is calling Poppy and telling her that I did the thing I thought I was too afraid to do.

And it was all thanks to her.

Chapter Forty-One

Dallas

"We can spin this." Alicia is on the other end of the line as I walk into my house and hang my keys by the back door.

"We're not spinning anything," I say. "I said what I said, and I meant all of it. Leave it alone."

"You really jumped the gun here," she says. "You should've run this by me before you made this announcement. We're still in damage control mode. The press about you has shifted, but it was too soon."

"I don't care," I tell her. "I'm not waiting another day to do something good. People can think what they want."

She goes quiet for so long I wonder if she's hung up.

"Did you get the itinerary I sent over?" Her tone is clipped, the way it always is when I don't do exactly what she says.

"Sometimes I think you forget that you work for me and not the other way around."

"Dallas." She sounds exasperated.

"Okay, okay." I open my email and find the list of events she's committed me to.

I'm on the road for a few days this week, but every second I'm not practicing or playing a game, I'm going to be at the Loveland Festival of Hearts. With Poppy.

And maybe the creeper in her yard should be enough to knock some sense into me, but it isn't. I still want to see her.

"This is a lot," I say as I scroll her email.

"That's the point," she says. "You and Poppy really need to sell it after your little stunt today."

"What good will that do?"

"It's your last chance to convince people that you're as good-hearted as you say, before the contract is up."

"What if they already believe that?" I ask. "What if they saw that I was being honest today, and that matters more than who I'm dating."

"They won't. Read to the bottom of the list."

I frown as my eyes fall to the last sentence on this itinerary.

Announce amicable break-up.

"So, we get everyone to love us as a couple. . .and then stage our break-up?" Gram walks into the room as I pull out one of the meals Poppy has prepared for us.

"It does sound like a dumb idea," Gram says. "Why don't you just keep it going a little longer?"

Alicia on the phone: "You don't get it, Dallas. The plan was to get people to change their opinion of you, using Poppy."

"Watch it."

She sighs. "You know what I meant, I like her too. I'm not being mean, that was just always the plan. Change people's opinions, get through Valentine's Day, amicably break up, and *then* announce whatever you want. You could've said she really inspired you, changed your life, whatever. But now?"

She *did* inspire me. And she's well on her way to changing my life.

"What were you thinking holding a press conference? Telling the whole world about your dad?"

"I was thinking I was sick of hiding from it. Always worried someone would find out. Figured it was best to confront it head-on and try to use it to do something good."

"Fine," she says. "But you should've talked to *me* about it!"

Maybe I should've. But I didn't.

It felt good.

"A quiet split was always the plan, Dallas," Alicia says.

I shake my head. "We'll figure it out later. For now, can you tell me how I ended up judging a teddy bear decorating contest?"

She doesn't talk for a good five seconds.

"Alicia?"

She huffs. "Can you think of anything better to solidify your reputation as a wholesome do-gooder than spending an hour looking at teddy bears with Poppy?"

I can think of a thousand reasons I don't give a rip about that anymore, but I keep them all to myself. "We'll talk about that later, too. I'll let you know which of these things I'm actually willing to do."

"But Dallas, you're already commit—"

"Bye, Alicia." I hang up the phone and find Gram smiling at me. "What?"

"She's good for you," Gram says.

"Alicia?" I scoff her name as I pull out a bottle of water and walk over to the table.

She laughs. "Not Alicia. *Poppy*."

I sit down. "I don't follow."

"Oh, quit it with the '*I'm a dumb jock*' act," she says. "There was something about that girl from the first day she came in here to cook for you, and you can't hide it from me any more than you can hide it from yourself."

I shake my head. "Poppy and I are friends."

"Pfft." She shakes her head. "You're falling for her, if you haven't already."

I know there's no point in arguing with Gram. She's got her mind made up, and frankly, she's right. What difference did it make if I admitted it?

I draw in a deep breath and let it out on a sigh. I sit, hold up my hands in surrender, and let them fall on my lap.

She smiles a knowing smile. "When did you know?"

I think for a moment. "Well, I knew instantly that we would be friends. It was so easy being around her, no work to have a conversation, she even knew what I needed before I did."

"But when did you *know*, Dallas?"

I knew exactly when. I could pinpoint the exact moment.

"When she came to the game on Ricky's night. I looked up and saw her in the stands. . .and I knew."

I look at Gram with helpless eyes.

"Oh good Lord, you've got it bad. First time in love or what? Get out of here with that look." She's not one for sentiment or romance.

I shrug. "It doesn't matter. There are a million reasons it won't work."

Gram's eyes narrow, the way they always do when she thinks I've said something stupid. "Why?"

"Because she's got a life here, and it's really different from mine."

"Maybe that's good."

I scoff. "Gram. Poppy's great. But our worlds don't fit. You know that. I don't want her privacy to be invaded every time she walks out the door. My life doesn't exactly leave room for another person, and you know it. Not someone with a career and a life of their own anyway."

"Have you talked to her about this?" Gram asks.

"I don't see the point," I tell her. "These are facts."

"So you're deciding for her." She scowls. "Just like a man."

"I could be skating in a completely different *country* next season! I can't ask her to dig up her roots here and follow me, that would be totally selfish!"

"You're not giving her a choice even though you've obviously got feelings for each other." She leans in. "And she's good for you."

"You said that already."

"You looked like you needed the reminder."

"But am I good for her?" I don't have to wait for Gram to respond to know the answer, but I find myself hoping she can give me some reason—any reason at all—that maybe I've got it wrong.

She stares at me for a few seconds. "I don't think you're thinking clearly."

I shake my head. "I've thought this whole thing through, Gram."

"Not all the way through."

I frown. "What are you talking about?"

"That woman shows up for you. She convinced you to defy Alicia and hold your press conference because it was good for you—not for your career—for *you*."

"Okay."

"How many people in your life would do that? How many other people do you know who care more about Dallas Burke the person than Dallas Burke the hockey player?"

I go still. "Only one. You."

"That's right," she says. "And ya can't marry *me*, so. . ."

She stands without wincing. She's more mobile as of late, and she's a bit worked up. She comes right over to me and says, "Think about what concerns you the most. The distance? The family history? The women on the road vying for your attention? Think about *all* of that—and then figure out how to make it work."

I know she's already worked out the solution for herself, but Gram was never one to give me the answers to any test. She watches me as I obey her instructions, and then I see her point.

Maybe. Maybe there is a way.

"If you love this girl," she says, "or even think you might be able to love her— you owe it to yourself to try." She reaches out and puts a hand on my shoulder in a rare sentimental moment. "You deserve to be happy, Dallas, no matter the lies you've repeated in your head over the years. I did not raise you to think less of yourself."

She looks right at me. "I raised you so someone like her could find you."

I look at this woman, this old, wise woman who I owe everything to, and I know she is doing what she always does.

She's speaking truth.

And I want the chance to prove her right.

Hart Sisters Group Chat

RAYA

Poppy, did you see the press conference?

POPPY

What press conference?

RAYA

Dallas's press conference.

POPPY

I'm up to my eyeballs in maple syrup over here. I haven't left my kitchen all day.

ELOISE

He didn't get traded, did he?

RAYA

No, he's starting a foundation for kids whose parents are incarcerated.

POPPY

WHAT?! He announced it?

ELOISE

Wow. That's oddly specific.

RAYA

Turns out, his dad killed someone.

He's in jail. I looked him up.

ELOISE

<surprised face emoji>

POPPY

I can't believe he announced it.

RAYA

He said someone special encouraged him to tell the truth. I can only assume he meant you?

POPPY

<shrugging emoji> Maybe it was his grandma?

RAYA

<eye roll emoji>

Okay, Poppy.

ELOISE

Aw, our little Poppy. . . "someone special."

<kissing lips emoji> <dancing lady emoji> <heart eyes emoji>

POPPY

OMG. I'm going. I've got work.

RAYA

Okay. But just be careful.

ELOISE

She jumped right over careful a long time ago.

Chapter Forty-Two

Poppy

The Taste of Loveland falls on a Monday, the first day of the Festival of Hearts.

The first day of my last week with Dallas.

Any hint of real feelings seems to have been doused thanks to some perv taking pictures in my yard, but I suppose I should be grateful. It was just the wake-up call I needed.

Never mind that Dallas held a press conference and called me "someone special." He didn't even tell me he was holding it. Or invite me to come. He may have some feelings for me, but he's distancing himself. I can sense it.

Miguel and I head over to the town square after a full morning of service. We were slammed, and three times I overheard someone use the words "someone special," as if they wanted to know if there was any truth to Dallas's claim.

On the way over, I notice the painted hearts on the sidewalks, each one professing a love that will last forever.

I stop by a giant purple heart in front of Beads and Baubles and notice the words: I'll be yours forever Eloise.

Loveland isn't a large town, and Eloise isn't a common name. I snap a photo and send it to my sister.

POPPY

What is this is all about?

ELOISE

I have no idea! Where is that?

POPPY

In front of Beads & Baubles

ELOISE

<chin scratching emoji>

POPPY

You really don't know?

ELOISE

No clue!

POPPY

So you have a secret admirer!

ELOISE

How exciting!

POPPY

This mystery must be solved.

ELOISE

It was probably one of the high school kids I work with.

I choose not to tell Eloise she should look for a job that a high schooler isn't qualified for and tuck my phone away, heading off in the direction of the booths. Margot got outvoted, so I can only assume I've still got a spot.

We cross the street under the strings of hearts attached from one side to the other, like Christmas lights. Everything is red and white and pink, and through the speakers affixed at various points along Cupid Lane, Frank Sinatra croons about flying to the moon and playing among the stars.

Ahead, at the center of town, there are tents set up all around the gazebo. Large banners soar overhead that read: *Welcome to the Taste of Loveland*, and then, underneath, in bright red lettering, *Sponsored by Poppy's Kitchen.*

I stop walking and stare at the sign. "What in the world?"

Miguel follows my gaze up to the banner. "You sponsored the whole event?"

I look at him. "I didn't."

He grins. "Bet I know who did."

I snap a picture of it and send it to Dallas.

POPPY

Did you forget to tell me something?

DALLAS

About the press conference?

Oops. I didn't realize my question had a double meaning. My plan not to address the fact that I wasn't invited to the press conference officially backfires.

POPPY

Well, that, yes, but that's not what I was talking about. Read the banner. . .

DALLAS

Oh, that. Yeah, I did that. <smiling emoji>

POPPY

You didn't have to! I'll pay you back!

DALLAS

No, you won't. It was the only way I could think of to get out of judging some teddy bear decorating contest.

I laugh out loud as we enter the square, looking around for our booth. I don't see it, but I do see a very handsome hockey player staring down at his phone.

POPPY

Aww, the elementary schoolers are going to be very disappointed.

I watch as he reads the text, smiling as he texts back.

DALLAS

I mean, I love kids, but I'm much more interested in not disappointing you.

The text comes in at the same time Dallas looks up and sees me. The words are like a warm hug on a cold day, and I want them to mean more than they probably do.

His smile is steady as he waves me over. "You're over here." He points to the biggest tent of the bunch, positioned right at the main entrance.

"Did you also buy my spot?"

He shrugs. "It is possible a deal was struck."

I shake my head. "What the heck, Burke?"

"My motives were purely selfish, I swear." He laughs. "Remember. . .the teddy bears. . .?"

I don't believe him for a second. "You didn't have to do that, but thanks. What are you doing here anyway?"

He holds my gaze. "I came to support my best girl."

The words land sideways, with our break-up looming, and I try not to let them penetrate the wall I've been meticulously building around myself since he left my house the night before.

Surely, he's still pretending. But a quick look around the square tells me there's nobody to pretend for.

I hurry over to the tent and see that the small wood-fired oven I've rented for the night has been delivered and hooked up. I've prepped plenty of heart-shaped pizza crusts for the event, and I've planned for a mix of regular and breakfast pizzas, both of which are on my brunch menu through the month of February.

Dallas and Miguel unload the supplies. The two of them pull out the tablecloths and start setting up the tent. I stand back, dumbly, for a long moment, hardly believing that he's even here, helping.

He looks up and finds me staring. "You okay?"

I motion for him to step aside with me, though there's really nowhere private among a bunch of open air tents. He follows me a few feet away, to where I think we're out of earshot of almost everyone out here.

"What are you really doing here?" I ask.

He frowns. "Do you want me to go?"

"No, of course not." Goodness knows his presence would be good for business. "I just—can't figure you out."

And frankly, it was getting harder and harder to try.

"Alicia sent me a whole itinerary," he says. "I thought you were copied on it. Tonight, I was supposed to come down here and help you serve food to locals, sign some autographs, pose for pictures. You didn't read that?"

I cross my arms over my chest. "No, I didn't." But it makes a lot more sense to me now. Alicia set this up. Of course she did.

"The email outlines the whole week. I did refuse to judge anything, but I donated some money and they altered the banner at the last minute to make you a sponsor."

I kick at a rock, careful to avoid his eyes.

"Did I do something wrong?"

I shake my head. "*No,*" I say, feeling a little silly. "Of course not." Of *course* not. He was holding up his end of the bargain. It didn't matter that my emotional knot was tightening. This was the deal.

"Okay," he says. "I'm sorry about the press conference. I didn't want to burden you with it."

My eyes flick to his. "It wouldn't have been a burden. I could've, I don't know, been there for you. I'm sure it wasn't easy."

He holds my gaze, and something silent passes between us. I thought he trusted me—why would he leave me out of something so important?

Because this isn't real.

"I'm sorry," he says. "Honestly. I should've told you. Especially since you're the reason I had the guts to do it in the first place." He reaches out and takes my hand. "Thank you."

How am I supposed to convince myself this is all pretend when he's so sweet?

"Chef?" Miguel calls out. "We need to get moving."

I nod. Then, back to Dallas. "Duty calls." I pull my hand from his and force all the pestering thoughts from my mind, which is no small feat considering that he stands right beside me all night long. Our arms graze, our hands touch, he scoots past me so closely it almost feels intentional, like our bodies are two magnets drawn together.

Or two doomed goldfish circling the drain.

By the end of the night, I'm gobsmacked by our success and a bit slap-happy from sheer exhaustion. Dallas served pizzas, made small talk, signed autographs, posed for photos, and single-handedly tripled my income.

It was all working just like Alicia and Gram said it would.

I'm in the process of a quick and dirty calculation on how much I can pay my parents back when Margot stops at my tent.

"I hope the night went well for you, Poppy," she says. I think it was physically painful for her to fake the kind tone.

"It went wonderfully," I say.

"Seems like everything's coming up roses for you these days." Margot leans toward me. "I just wonder how much longer you can keep up this act."

I frown. "What are you talking about?"

"You and Dallas," she says. "How much longer do you think you can pretend to be an interesting person? It seems like the attraction is waning, and someone like that needs a woman who knows how to keep a man's attention." She gives her hair a flip that reminds me of the Margot I knew back in high school.

Everything inside of me wants to spit fire, but all at once, something inside me shifts, and I realize I feel *sorry* for her. "Margot, I just want to say how sorry I am."

She frowns. "For what?"

"Whatever it is that makes you so miserable," I say, honestly. "For as long as I've known you, you've been mean and ugly to just about everyone we know. Even your friends. Even Jeremy. Only really unhappy people take pleasure in making other people miserable, don't you think?"

"I'm not miserable, Poppy. I've got everything I could possibly want." She scoffs. "You enjoy this fifteen minutes of fame because everyone can see it's about to come to an end."

At that moment, Dallas grabs my hand and tugs me toward him. He takes my face in his hands and kisses me like his life depends on it.

If a crowd gathers, I don't even care, this might be the last time I get to kiss this man, so I'm going to kiss him like I mean it. I've got two fistfuls of his sweatshirt balled up in my hands, and I shut my eyes, using my other four senses to experience this mind-blowing, knee-buckling kiss.

Dallas clings to me so tightly, it's like I'm the lifeboat in the middle of a storm. I haven't kissed him enough for it to feel familiar, and while I'd love to kiss him every day for the rest of my life, I want to believe that it will always feel as new and exciting as it does in this moment.

When he finally pulls away, I wait a moment before I open my eyes.

When I do, he's grinning at me, and the remnants of my tiny, half-built wall crumbles into rubble on the ground around me.

Around us, people begin to whistle and cheer. Some of them point their phones in our direction, surely filming that little show.

Margot is nowhere to be seen, but she's the last thing I'm thinking about right now.

Dallas smiles. "We're getting good at that."

I can't really talk. I just nod.

We *are* getting good at it.

How good do we need to get at it before it becomes really bad?

Chapter Forty-Three

Poppy

That night, in the quiet of my bedroom, I replay the kiss over and over, wanting to turn it into one of those memories I can call back up at any moment.

I'm mid-makeout memory for the fifty-second time, when there's a rustling outside followed by the *clink* of a rock against my bedroom window.

I sit up and listen and—yep—there it is again. *Clink.*

I slide out from under the covers and go to the window. I peek around the curtains and see Dallas standing in my yard. I open the window, and he waves.

"What are you, fifteen?" I hiss down, so as not to wake the neighbors. "You don't have a boom box down there, do you?"

He laughs, and I shush him. "*I wanted to see you!*" he yell/whispers at me.

The words are an arrow straight to my wobbly heart, but I try to cover it with humor.

I strike a slanted, unflattering pose up against the window frame and try a Scottish accent. "Feast yer eyes!"

He stands there, shaking his head.

I whisper down, "I know, my Scottish needs work!"

"Can we talk for a minute?"

My heart skips a beat. "I'll be right down." I grab a sweatshirt and pull it on over my pajamas, then flip on the porch light as I open the front door. "I could've called the cops on you, you know that?"

"I know," he says. "Sorry."

"Why didn't you just call?" I lean against the door jamb.

He shrugs, looking slightly sheepish. "Isn't it more romantic this way?"

I scoff. "Does it need to be romantic with you and me?"

The expression on his face shifts.

"I mean, since we're pretending," I add, quietly.

He watches me with an intense gaze. "Are we? Pretending?"

I'm not sure what to say.

He takes a breath. "Sometimes it doesn't feel like it."

Oh. My. Gosh. My heart is a race car on its final lap at the Indy 500.

What is he saying? "What are you saying?"

"I guess I just wondered how you're feeling," he says.

I look at him blankly. "About. . .?"

"About everything. About. . .this. About us." He reaches for my hand, and I let him take it, standing in a mental fog. He could've taken my arm and raised it over my head, and I probably would've just left it there, hanging in the air.

A pause. "I didn't see you coming, Poppy. You took me by surprise."

I shake my head. I go to speak, and I shake it again. "I can't believe that's true. That *can't be true.*"

Oh, how I want it to be true.

"It is. I wasn't looking for anything," he says. "You know that."

"Me either. I wanted coffee and for Margot to go away."

"But instead you found me. And tonight, just like every other night lately, I found myself missing you." He laughs. "It got to the point where I would be in some hotel room in some city hundreds of miles away, thinking about how I just wanted to be here, pretending to watch *Downton Abbey*. With you."

"But. . .wait." I stammer, trying to rope in this runaway conversation. "Dallas. Your life isn't here," I say. "Not *really*. Not with *me*. It's not even with a. . .*version* of me." I use my free hand to gesture wildly. "It's out there. Hundreds of miles away. In hotel rooms."

He takes a breath. "And I can deal with that, *if* I have you to come home to."

I go completely still. My muscles aren't tense, but they're frozen. I want to ask him to repeat himself, but I'm afraid if he does, he'll change the words and I'll realize I've heard him wrong.

I do anyway.

I say, quietly, "Can you please repeat that?"

"You don't have to respond now. I know it's a lot. I'm. . .a lot. My life is a lot. I get it."

I know he's saying words, and those words are probably making grammatical sense, but I can't seem to focus.

"My world is wild and unpredictable, and it's not fair for me to ask you any of this, but I'm asking anyway."

All the voices I've been trying to silence over the last several weeks are back, and they have a million questions. They're logical and practical and they remind me that I don't fit in Dallas's glitzy, glamorous world. I am plain and simple and ordinary, and I can't leave Loveland.

And I certainly can't ask him to stay.

"Say something," he says.

"We fit," I blurt out.

He looks confused for a moment. "What?"

"On the couch when we fall asleep. When I hug you when you're hurting. When you protect me from the world." I look up at him. "We fit."

He takes my face in his hands. "We do fit."

I cover his hands with my own. "And as much as I want to say yes—as much as I've been wanting this since we had our first real conversation in the coffee shop. . ."

"Wait. Since then? You. . ."

"Quiet," I cut him off, "never mind that. I need to think, Dallas. And you need to think—about what you'd be giving up to be with someone like me."

"I'm only thinking about what I'll gain."

"Which is what?"

"You," he says simply. "You are all I want."

He leans in and brushes a sweet, soft kiss on my lips, holding it for a few seconds before pulling away and studying me. "Just think about it, okay? I'm on the road the next three days, but I'll be back in time to take you to that dance on Friday night." He kisses me again. "Maybe by then you'll have an answer for me?"

"I'm sorry, what exactly is the question?" I ask because I need him to speak clear, short sentences in order to wrap my brain around this.

"Would you like to date me for real?" he asks. "No contracts. No business. Just you and me."

I press my lips together, and try not to melt.

"I'll see you when I get back." Another kiss, this one on my cheek. "And I'll call you from the road." Another kiss, on the opposite cheek.

I nod. I can't speak or stop looking at him.

And then, as if to make sure I know exactly what he's offering, he pulls my body to his and kisses me again, this time a little more spicy than sweet, leaving me bewildered and out of breath.

"Goodnight, Poppy," he says, his lips still touching mine.

"Goodnight, Dallas." I smile against his mouth, then finally pull away.

And when I close the door, I wish I'd recorded that whole conversation because even I don't believe it actually happened.

I'm not going to sleep at all tonight.

The next few days feel like eight weeks. I haven't told anyone about Dallas's late night visit, and while *The Mill* had a lovely write-up about our town square make-out session, that moment on the porch seems to have been only between us.

Thank God.

I attend most of the Valentine festivities, and for the first time, I begin to understand the appeal.

Valentine's Day, shockingly, is way less horrible when you're actually in love.

That thought stops me in my tracks. *Love.*

I run out of heart-shaped pizzas early for the second day in a row, and spend my evenings with my parents and sisters, watching Dallas play on TV. Gram joins us one of the nights, and I make sure she's got meals to get her through the week.

I write my parents a substantial check, which my dad tries to give back to me, but I explain that while I appreciate what they did for me, it's important to me to stand on my own two feet. I'm also able to pay back a small portion of what I owe the other families Avi conned.

I'm finally starting to feel like I'm on the other side of despair.

I'm supposed to have an answer for Dallas when he comes back. A well thought out, emotionally mature, completely logical answer.

The question? *Do I want to date him for real?*

The answer? *Yes.*

However, as soon as the question enters my mind and my answer follows, I'm bombarded by a whole laundry list of reasons I should not pursue this relationship, no matter how strongly I feel for him.

Strangely, they're all in Raya's voice.

1. Because he's famous and I like my privacy.

2. Because I don't want to be photographed by strangers.

3. Because I would worry I will never be enough for someone as beautiful as him.

4. Because he could get traded, and I can't leave my restaurant or my family.

But as quickly as these problems enter my mind, they're replaced by possible solutions. They're all in Eloise's voice.

1. The interest in me and Dallas will die down. Hockey players aren't as famous as other pro athletes.

2. Being photographed by strangers might be good for my business.

3. Oddly, the fact that I'm at best a six and he's definitely a 10 (okay, 12), doesn't seem to matter.

4. . .

I'm hung up on number four. That might be the deal breaker.

Dallas's professional life, from what I've read, is unpredictable, and even if he was the best player in the league, he could still get traded. Or not get re-signed and go into free agency. Then literally *any* team in the league could pay him enough, and he'd have to go. And then what? I close down the restaurant and move away?

I can't. My home is here, in Loveland.

Then, a third voice, separate from Raya's or Eloise's in my head, says one simple word.

Try.

This one sounds like my voice.

Chapter Forty-Four

Poppy

Friday arrives like every other day, but I quickly remember that this is not like every other day.

Tonight Dallas comes home and we go to the dance and then tomorrow morning, we're supposed to part ways.

Forever.

Never mind the fact that I've been counting down the seconds until he gets back home. Or the fact that only a few days ago, my inner voice had convinced me to give us a shot. In the light of day, logic stepped in.

I have to stop romanticizing. I have to stop imagining his arms wrapped around my waist or the casual, easy kisses that meet me in my dreams.

I have given his question a lot of thought—both with my heart *and* my head. Here's the best, most adult answer I could come up with.

I like him. A lot. Heck, I might even almost love him. But I have a life here I like, a lot. We've both worked hard to get where we are, and for a time, we helped each other achieve more than we could on our own. He might have to leave and I can't go with him. Contract ends, we're still friends, no matter what. In the future, who knows, but for now, it's best to part ways on a high note.

So.

I have one plan, in two parts, for the evening—first, look gorgeous. And second, say goodbye to Dallas Burke.

Pssh. Piece of cake. *How hard could it be?*

The festival has been good for business. Dallas has been good for business. People are curious, and my restaurant has benefited. For his part, Dallas is getting great press. He'd hired Ricky to head up his foundation, a move that has nothing to do with publicity, and everything to do with his giant heart. People are intrigued by these two men, who survived something unthinkable, and who are still able to stand side-by-side for the good of others.

Our plan had worked. *We* had worked. I only hope that everything doesn't fall into the foggy place where memories live when we go our separate ways.

At the end of Friday morning's service, I leave the locking up to Miguel and hurry home, where I'm meeting Raya and Eloise so we can all get ready together.

Eloise is going to the dance with a firefighter she swears is just a friend (but I've seen his photo, and I'm not buying it for a second.) Raya is going solo, because she is apparently auditioning for the role of "spinster" in our little town. My parents, along with several of Dallas's teammates and their wives will also be there.

I'm determined to make the most of my last night with Dallas.

I'm glad I met him and glad I agreed to Gram's crazy plan, even if it has to end.

It was an exciting four weeks, and though I know now not

to pretend to be dating strangers in coffee shops, I can't help but think it was quite the adventure. And a lot of fun while it lasted.

I'm forcing myself to think about all of these things in the past tense. In my mind, it will make it easier if I already think it's done.

But the kissing.

I'm ruined on kissing now. I'll remember the way he kissed me for the rest of my life.

I'm home for about three minutes when my doorbell rings. I'm expecting Eloise and Raya, but when I open it, I find Truman Keys, with a flower delivery.

"This one's for you, Miss Poppy," the older man says kindly. "Special order."

I take the large bouquet of gorgeous pink tulips from him and fish around in my pocket for a five dollar bill I tucked away.

"Tip's already covered," he says. "Mr. Burke sure is a nice guy."

I smile at him as he turns to go, and then pull the card from the wrapping.

Poppy,
Had a few things to take care of in the city. I'll meet you at the dance.
I'll be the one staring at you like a lovesick puppy.
—Dallas

I press my lips together to hold in a smile as Eloise pulls up in her old, yellow VW beetle. She gets out and slams the door, which is always risky because at any moment, the entire car could fall apart like a cheap watch. She calls over the roof, "You got flowers!?"

Seconds later, Raya parks her sleek Altima right behind Eloise. I can't help but think the cars they drive are excellent visual representations of them both. Raya joins our sister on the short trek to my front door.

"Poppy got flowers." Eloise studies the bouquet from a distance. "Tulips! You love tulips!"

"I do love tulips." I wonder out loud, "How did Dallas know that?"

Raya's eyes flick to the porch, where I feel like a burglar caught with sacks of cash, sneaking out the back of the bank. I deflect, and hold them up, giving them a little shake. "He asked to meet me at the *dance,*" I say, in a sing-songy tone.

Eloise snatches the card from my hand.

"Hey! That's private!" I try to snatch it back, but she holds it out of my reach.

"A lovesick puppy?" Eloise and her wide eyes bore a hole straight through me. "Did he plan on having this note published?"

I frown. "I don't think so."

"Then *why* is he writing romantic things?" Raya asks pointedly.

I take the note, tuck it back under the ribbon, and walk inside, aware that I'm being followed.

"Poppy," Raya says.

I pretend I don't hear her.

"Tonight is the end of your contract, right?"

"Of course." I fish my scissors from my junk drawer and find a vase under the sink.

"She's acting weird," Eloise says.

"She *is* acting weird," Raya agrees.

"Which means. . ."

Both at the same time: "She's hiding something."

I cut the ends of the stems off and toss them in the trash can, then fill the vase with water.

"Something about Dallas?" Eloise points at me, saying it like trying to guess at charades.

I give her a look.

She gasps. "It *is* about Dallas!"

"And she thinks we aren't going to figure it out," Raya adds.

I tear open the flower food and sprinkle it into the vase, trying to ignore both of them and my pounding heart at the same time.

"But she forgets that we are experts at seeing through her *lies*," Eloise says, playfully. "Like, if I say, '*I think her feelings for Dallas have gotten very, very real*—" she pauses, peering at me with one eye shut, and I try to keep my face neutral.

"Or if I say that it's very likely a certain hockey player reciprocates said feelings—" Raya pauses and makes the same one-eyed stare.

My eyes betray me. I told them to focus on the flowers, but they darted right over to Raya, whose eyebrows pop up as if to say *Caught ya*!

"I knew it."

"She can't hide from us," Eloise adds.

"Do you think she didn't tell us any of this because she knows it's crazy?" Raya asks.

Eloise frowns. "I don't think it's crazy."

"You don't?" Raya and I say, in unison.

She shakes her head. "I think it's romantic."

I pick up the vase and walk it back to the entryway, where I set it down on the center of the table there. It is romantic, but I can hardly say so.

"Poppy, your face gave you away," Raya says. "What is going on?"

I have nothing else to occupy my hands, so I walk back into

the living room and face them. "I do have feelings for him, which you already know."

"Right," Raya says. "You told us you liked him."

"Right." I pause. "I do like him."

"But it's more than that," Raya says.

I don't respond. I feel like I'm on a tightrope made of fishing line.

"Did you tell him?" Eloise asks.

"No." I drop into my oversized armchair. "But he told me he has feelings for me."

Eloise squeals, then jumps onto the ottoman in front of me. "Tell. Me. Everything."

Raya stands, unmoving, a line of concern knit in her brow.

"He wants us to try dating. For real," I say.

"And you said. . .?" My little sister props her fists under her chin in eager anticipation.

"Nothing. I'm supposed to give him an answer tonight," I say. "He wanted me to think about it."

"Uh, what is there to think about?" Eloise asks. "When someone like Dallas Burke asks you out, you don't think —you go!"

"It's not that simple." I run through my list of pros and cons, and when I finish, I hear something come out of my older sister's mouth I thought I would never hear.

"I'm proud of you, Poppy," she says.

I do an actual, real-life double take.

"I'm sorry, what?"

"You're using your head—not just your heart—to make a really important decision. I'll support whatever you decide." She walks upstairs, presumably to get ready, leaving me in a stupor.

I look over at Eloise. "Did she actually say she'd leave it up to me?"

Eloise shakes her head. "Yep. She must have hit her head."

I laugh. "What do you think?"

"Well. . ." she says, "I guess it's great that you're using your head and all, but. . . I can't help but think that as smart as Raya is, all of her advice comes from a place of hurt."

"But I got hurt, too," I say. Did I need to remind her what Avi had done?

"Everyone gets hurt," she says. "Until they heal. And then it's time to try again." She stands, picks up her bag and the dress she carried in on a hanger. "Otherwise, we'd all end up sad and alone." She walks up the stairs, disappearing from my view.

Well, that was maddeningly unhelpful. I thought I had it figured out. I thought I had decided. I was thinking about Dallas and I in the past tense. Done. Over. And now, the two people who I lean on for a balance between free spirit and old maid, are close to agreeing.

I guess it really is up to me.

Chapter Forty-Five

Poppy

After two hours of primping, my sisters and I are ready to take the town by storm. Or at least to stay awake past 9 p.m.

Raya is wearing the most stunning long, black gown. She doesn't say so, but I think her goal for these town functions is always to make Jeremy regret his stupid decision to dump her for Margot.

It's the perfect choice for a revenge dress.

Eloise is wearing a hot pink cocktail dress, which seems to say, "I'm just here to have a good time!"

And I picked out a red dress that hits my knees in the front and my ankles in the back. It cinches around my waist, and according to the saleslady "accentuates my curves."

I figure if I have curves, they might as well be accentuated.

Once again, Raya does my hair and makeup, and then, when we're all ready, we each go our separate ways.

Eloise's firefighter, a guy named Tyson who is very, *very* cute, shows up at my door, and Raya gives him such a stare-down, I'm shocked he doesn't wet his pants. Eloise pushes our sister aside and waves to me as she takes his arm. "See you there!"

Raya turns to me, giving me a once-over, looking less at my features and more at the job she's done getting me ready. "I want you to look hot if this is your last night with him." She moves a strand of my hair from one side of my head to the other. "Leave him wanting more."

"What if it's not?"

Her eyes dip to mine. "Not what?"

"Our last night together?"

"Poppy," she says, her voice softer than usual. "When it comes to choosing between your feelings over someone else's, I will always pick you. Every time. I want what's best for you, and if it's him—great. If not, you know what you need to do. For the sake of your heart."

"But that's just it," I say. "My heart is going to break no matter what."

"Well, then it's better you're the one doing the breaking," she pats my cheek and smiles, "because being on the other end sucks."

"I think your mere presence tonight is going to make Jeremy regret his worst decision," I say. "You're gorgeous."

"Well, I hope so, because I'm going to the dance with our parents since I have the greatest non-existent love life the world has ever known. Mom's already texted me three times, so I have to go. I'll see you there."

Once a year, the Loveland Community Center is transformed into "the most romantic place in the nation," or so claims the local paper. The theme is always different, but you can count on white twinkle lights, lots of crepe paper hearts, tulle covering any bare surface, and the most eclectic playlist imaginable, from *The Bodyguard* to *The Lion King*.

I walk in the double doors at the front of the building, and my nerves march double time in my belly. I wonder if Dallas is here yet.

I check my coat, then make my way through the lobby and into the main space, a large room with hardwood floors and a wide stage on one side.

Inside, the lights twinkle and spin. Several couples are already out on the dance floor, bouncing around to the B-52's. I pull my phone from my small clutch, but I don't have any new texts.

I wander over to the punch table and take a glass as more people arrive, and the room begins to feel crowded.

I inch back against the wall, out of the way, where I'm comfortable. There's a row of chairs that seems designed for people who came alone. I sit, setting my purse on my lap. I take a drink of punch and scan the room for any sign of Dallas.

It's not only that I feel a little awkward sitting here by myself, I also really want to see him. I glance at my phone again. *Nothing.*

I don't want to panic, but what if Dallas decided not to come?

That's dumb, Poppy. He sent you flowers.

"What are you doing sitting back here alone?"

I glance up and see Monica, Kari, and Lisa walking toward me. They look like they just stepped off of a magazine shoot, and the people of Loveland are noticing.

I stand up and tuck my phone away. "You all made it."

Monica leans in and kisses the air beside my cheek. "You look beautiful, Poppy."

"You all look like models!" I say. "Where are the guys?"

"Who knows?" Kari says. "Where's the punch?"

I nod in the direction of the table, and Kari and Lisa walk away. They'll probably give someone a heart attack on their way over there.

"They probably hope it's spiked," Monica says.

"Ladies and gentlemen, may I have your attention, please?" Mayor Hermes stands on the platform, smack at the center of a circle of light. He taps the microphone twice, and the people in the crowd begin to quiet down. Out of the corner of my eye, I see Raya and my parents walk in, so I wave them over. Dad hugs Monica like they're best friends after watching a game together a few weeks ago, and I introduce her to my mom and Raya.

"As you know, here in Loveland, on this particular day, we love to celebrate love. This week alone, we had thirteen couples marry in the Loveland chapel, and I'm told there's another ceremony scheduled for after the dance."

Someone on the other side of the room lets out a whoop, and a laugh ripples through the crowd.

"But tonight, we're all going to celebrate the joy of young love with a very special presentation. This one goes out to you, Poppy Hart!"

Monica grins over at me and says, "I just want you to know I did the best with what I had to work with."

"You. . .what?" I frown, but there's no time to ask her to clarify. The lights go off, and in the darkness, everyone leaves me standing on the dance floor. Alone.

I look around, but all I see are people scurrying away.

And then, the music starts, and in .3 seconds I recognize the song. The opening lick of "Kiss You" by One Direction is forever burned into my brain, a core memory that still haunts me. Every time I hear the song, I'm instantly back on that gym floor, making a fool of myself for Tyler Nelson in front of God and everybody.

Panic rises up inside me. Is someone playing a terrible joke on me?

I'm assaulted by a blinding spotlight, then another light

flashes on over the stage. I squint up and see Dallas standing at the center of it. Next to him are Jericho, Kemp, Krush, and Junior.

And as soon as the first verse starts, all five of them start to dance.

Their moves are choreographed. They have parts. They shake their hips and lip sync along with the boy band like they're going to be judged for their performance, and there's a Stanley Cup on the line.

The crowd goes absolutely bananas, rushing the stage like it's a concert—but leaving an aisle between me and where Dallas is currently shaking what God gave him.

I cover my mouth to try and contain a giggle, but before long, I am all smiles.

Shockingly, they aren't half bad. When they hit the first chorus, Dallas looks right at me and grins. Seconds later, all five guys are shaking their hips and earning all kinds of catcalls from the crowd.

They all jump off the stage and the lights follow them, and by the second chorus, Monica, Kari, and Lisa join in. *When did they have time to put this all together?*

By the time they reach the end, the Chicago Comets invasion of Loveland is complete, and the entire room is jumping and dancing and laughing and singing, and just before the song ends, Dallas holds up a huge poster board sign with the words *Let Me Kiss You, Poppy, at the Festival of Hearts* handwritten in thick black marker.

They all strike a pose and the crowd erupts in a huge cheer, and Dallas is at the center of it all.

Mr. Hermes is back on the mic in seconds. "I think we all know what Poppy's answer is going to be, don't we folks?" Another cheer. "Let's hear it one more time for Dallas Burke and the guys and gals from the Chicago Comets!"

The crowd roars, the music kicks back up with a new song, and Dallas and the others are inundated with people, high-fiving, pointing and laughing, hugging, and taking selfies.

I watch as he holds his hands up to stop others from asking him for things, and points in my direction.

He's telling them he needs to talk to me. He's choosing me.

Dallas holds out his arms in a wide shrug as he walks over to where I'm standing.

He's wearing a neatly tailored gray suit with a blue tie that makes his eyes look like they've been run through a SnapChat filter. And the rest of the room seems to disappear.

"I cannot be-*lieve* you did that," I gasp.

He smiles. "Haven't you ever been that crazy over someone? That you were willing to make a complete fool of yourself?"

My own words hang between us.

His hands are on my arms, burning straight through my skin. "What did you think? Did we do okay?"

There isn't a drop of moisture in my mouth, that's what I think. "When did you have time to—?"

"Monica used to be a professional cheerleader," he says. "She did it all. The choreography, I mean, not the part where we made fools of ourselves."

I smile. "You have good friends."

"They like you," he says. "They think you're good for me."

The music shifts to "This Night", by Billy Joel, circa 1983, and he holds out a hand. "I happen to agree. Do you want to dance?"

More than anything. I take his hand and float out to the middle of the dance floor.

The lyrics. Billy is singing our whole relationship, and just like the song, I want this night to last forever.

After a few slow dances, Dallas and I take a break. He stops by the punch table, as Raya walks over. Dallas hands me a glass, and then, without thinking, gives Raya the one he got for himself.

"Thanks." She takes it, and stares him down as he gets another for himself. "I was there for the first rendition of 'Kiss You.'"

"Oh?" He glances at me, then back at Raya.

"Yours was much, much better than Poppy's." Raya's expression remains the same.

Dallas's smile is tentative.

"That was cool what you did." Then, with a smile that would chill a corpse, she says, "But if you hurt her, I'll kill you."

And with that, she walks away.

"She secretly likes you," I tell him.

"If that's her version of liking someone, I'd hate to be on her bad side."

The dance floor is covered with couples of every age and walk of life. It's the only time during the year that the teenagers will hang out with their parents and nobody cares if it's cool or not.

I spot Eloise on the opposite side of the room. Her cute firefighter is talking to someone nearby, and Eloise is making eyes at Dallas's teammate Kemp. Trouble is, he's making them right back.

My two sisters couldn't be more different. Raya is guarded and stand-offish to the point where I feel she'll end up alone. Eloise is looking for every opportunity to jump into something new—and when she jumps, she'll offer her whole heart, no matter how many times it shatters.

I suppose it's fitting that I'm somewhere in the middle. Guarded, but not as much as Raya. Open, but not as much as Eloise.

Am I really ready to jump into something new? "Dallas, I—"

The photographer takes a photo that flashes right in my eyes. It blinds me for a good five seconds. Dallas takes my hand. "Let's get some air."

It's freezing outside, but I'm burning up, so I gladly follow him without complaint. He leads me out to a small courtyard at the side of the building, and thankfully it has a tall, outdoor patio heater.

Once we're alone he turns toward me and smiles. "I missed you."

"I missed you too." I wrap my arms around myself and inch toward the glowing heater, the cool winter air chilling me.

He slips off his suit coat and drapes it around my shoulders. "You look beautiful tonight."

"What, this old thing?" I say with a slight curtsy, then quickly realize how very uncool that was. "I don't know why I just did that."

He laughs. "I think you're adorable." After a beat, his face turns serious. "Have you thought about what I asked?"

"Yeah," I say.

"And?"

I had an answer. I had it all planned out. I had a pro/con list with one insurmountable "con," but that list is currently not accessible to me. The only thing running around in my brain is that there is no way I want to let him go.

The voice I'd silenced returns. It's quiet, but I hear it. It's mine. *Try.* I look at him and realize that's all I want to do. And yet. . .

"I'm scared." I tell my voice to hold steady, but it betrays me with the wobble of emotion.

He takes a step closer. "Me too. I've never really done this before."

"You don't seem like a guy who spooks easily."

"I'm not scared of, like, spiders or mice." His gaze is steady. "I'm scared of what tomorrow is going to feel like if you're not there. I'm scared of going another day without telling you how I really feel."

"How do you really feel?" I nearly choke on the words.

"I think you know."

I smile. "I want to hear you say it."

"Well, this whole thing hasn't been phony for me for a long time."

"I don't think it was ever phony for me," I whisper.

He takes my hands and presses his lips to them. "I was so concerned with protecting you from the ugliness of my world that I failed to see you don't need protecting. You fit right in."

"It's not just the differences in the way we live, Dallas, there are other issues," I say, clarity coming over me now that my body has cooled off. "I don't know much about hockey, but what if you get traded? What if you have to move away? I can't leave Loveland—my whole life is here."

"I know," he says. "And I would never ask you to."

"So, how does that work? I cook for you over Zoom? We Facetime while falling asleep?"

"You've really been thinking about this, haven't you?"

I close my eyes and shake my head, willing away the smile that I can't seem to keep from crawling across my face. "It's all I've been thinking about."

He leans in and brushes his lips across mine, sending a shiver straight down my spine. "*You're* all I've been thinking about." Another kiss.

Had I really thought I could reject his offer? My willpower would never hold up against this.

"You don't know a lot about hockey contracts, I'm guessing?"

"Zero."

"When you first come into the league, you sign one. It's for a certain number of years for a certain amount of money." He pauses. "You. . .don't know what mine was, do you?"

"I never looked. I didn't care."

He shakes his head. "Another reason why you're so, *so* perfect."

He breathes in the night air. "As a rookie, I signed for the league minimum. A basic, two-year entry level contract, but it was still a lot of money."

He doesn't have to give me a number for me to understand —it's more than I can comprehend.

"After a few years on the rookie contract, players—if they're good—can renegotiate their contracts for longer terms and more money. I did that for my third year in the league."

I look at him. "And?"

"I signed a six-year contract." I pauses. "For a lot more."

I want to ask for specifics, but I'm afraid if he tells me, I'll be so intimidated I'll run away.

He takes my hands and pulls me a bit closer.

"This week, I re-negotiated my contract," he says.

"You did? Why?"

He holds my hands close to his chest. "I asked them to add a no-trade clause."

I'm confused at the terminology at the start, but then I put two and two together. "Wait. No trade? Meaning you can't be traded? Ever? How did you do that? Why would they agree to that?"

"I told them I wanted to finish my career in Chicago. So, I

signed a new ten-year contract and spread out the payments to take less money."

"But why would you. . .?"

He lets my hands go and puts his on my waist. He pulls me into him, like he did on the porch, or the couch, or the hallway, or the dance floor.

"Because," he says, "you fit."

I fit.

Close to him. It's as if there's a Poppy-shaped cut-out on his body, and every time I step into it, I'm finally complete.

We hold each other in the warm orange glow of the heater for not nearly long enough.

He pulls away and says, "Heck, we've known each other two whole weeks longer than Jericho and Monica knew each other before they got engaged."

I laugh.

He doesn't. "There's something here, Poppy. You feel it, right?"

I nod. "Yeah, I just never dreamed you felt it too."

"I felt it that first day we met," he says.

"Whatever! I ran into the granola bars and pretended we were dating. Nobody has ever made a worse first impression."

"I thought you were cute. And cutting the potatoes...*whew!*"

I quirk a brow. "You like my knife skills?"

"They're sexy," he says.

I cover my mouth as a laugh escapes. "You're crazy."

"Crazy about you," he says.

We stare at each other for a few seconds, then both start laughing at the same time.

"That was cheesy." He laughs at himself and looks away, that sweet shyness ıeturning.

"*So* cheesy." I'm still laughing.

"But also, true." He studies me.

I like being the subject of his attention. The moment sizzles between us, and I realize now that even if I wanted to, I could never let him go.

I inch up on my tiptoes, take his face in my hands, and kiss him with such purpose I feel it in my toes. My muscles tense as everything inside of me stirs. I remember the way he reacted to our practice kiss, so I try to recreate it as best I can (not hard since I've had that moment on repeat for weeks now).

This time, he doesn't pull away. Instead, he deepens the kiss, and I fear I may never want to leave this exact moment. It is, without question, one of the best of my life.

After several minutes of moonlight and makeouts, we come apart, dazed and breathless.

"You're really, really good at that," he says.

"I practice on my pillow."

He laughs.

"We should go back in, I guess," I say.

"I guess we should." And I get the distinct impression that neither of us actually wants to go.

I give him one more quick kiss, then turn away. "You know, if we're going to be dating for real, we need to talk about your dance moves. When you're committing to making a complete fool of yourself over a girl, it's important to note that you *cannot* look sexy while doing it."

He drapes an arm around me and we start toward the building. "You think I looked sexy?"

"That hip shake thing? Are you kidding me?" I shudder. "Hot!"

He laughs out loud, then presses his lips to my hand. "There's plenty more where that came from."

I follow him back inside with a smile. "I can't wait to discover it all."

Epilogue

Poppy

The breeze off of the turquoise ocean is warm and inviting.

The small beachfront cafe is one of Dallas's favorite places in the Bahamas, and now that he's brought me here, I'm pretty sure it will also be one of mine.

The season ended on a high. The team's record was a winning one, but they lost a tough series in the playoffs. And, since Dallas was able to renegotiate his contract, the team now has more money to spend on getting more players. He's made the team even better.

To celebrate, Dallas convinced me to take a trip with him to the Bahamas. I insisted on bringing both of my sisters, and before long, we had a whole party camping out in a huge house right on the ocean. Monica and Jericho, Lisa and Krush, Kari and Junior, Kemp, a guy they called "Torpedo," and my two sisters all joined us for a once-in-a-lifetime tropical experience.

The vacation has been a dream, and I'm shocked to report that even Raya seems to be having a good time.

After the night of the dance, Dallas and I took the "fake"

descriptor off of our relationship, which basically meant we told my family and his grandma that we weren't faking anymore. Everyone was happy for us, but Sylvia seemed unfazed.

"It was only a matter of time," she'd said, making me wonder if this was her plan all along.

Now, as we near the end of our Bahamian vacation, I'm struck with the kind of contented relaxation that doesn't come around very often. I kick my feet up on a chair, when I spot a commotion on the sidewalk across the street from the cafe. Two police officers appear, practically out of nowhere, and at the sight of them, a lanky man wearing a Hawaiian button-down shirt, takes off running—straight into the chest of another officer.

I frown. "I wonder what's going on."

"Justice, I think," Dallas says, from the chair next to me.

I laugh. "You sound so sure."

"I am sure." Then, he leans toward me. "Look closer."

As the cops handcuff the man, they turn toward us, and that's when I get a good look.

It's Avi.

I stand. The officers are heading in our direction. One of them looks at Dallas.

Avi looks at me and scoffs. "You? What are you doing here?"

I'm too stunned to speak. I always wondered what I would say if I ever came face-to-face with Avi again. Turns out—nothing. I'm too shocked to utter a coherent word.

"Looks like she's having you arrested," Dallas says in my weakness. "And it sounds like you're going to do a lot of time."

"Who are *you*?"

Dallas looks at me, then stands to his feet. He straightens up even taller, and looks down at Avi, who shrinks just a little.

"I'm the guy who helped her find you." He turns to me. "Anything to add?" I give Avi a once-over and realize I have nothing at all to say to him. "Get this piece of trash out of my sight."

Dallas puts a protective arm around me, and Avi raises a brow.

"We'll take him down to the station, Mr. Burke," one of the officers says. "And then we'll turn him over to the Feds."

"The Feds?" Avi actually looks scared. I hope he wets his pants.

"You're wanted in eight states and three different countries, Mr. Palmer," the cop says. "Like Mr. Burke said, you're gonna do a lot of time."

"Poppy, baby, come on." Avi looks at me. "I had good reasons for leaving when I did. I was always going to come back! Why would you do this to me?"

But Dallas steps in front of me. "Get him out of here."

They cart him off, and I look at Dallas. "You did this?"

"You deserve to have some closure, Poppy."

"But. . .how?"

"I put out some feelers," he says. "We've got a lot of fans who are cops, some who deal with federal crime and Interpol, and they helped out."

I turn toward the blue-green ocean and draw in a deliberate, deep breath.

"Just one thing. . ." Dallas starts. I can tell by the tone that he thinks he's going to be funny.

I turn and look at him, waiting. He's scrunching up his face.

"Him? You picked *him?*"

"Shut up right now if you know what's good for you."

"I mean, maybe with the lights off, or from far away, *maybe*, but up close?" he shudders.

"That's it. You're on lockdown."

He gets on his knees. "Wait! No! I was kidding! I. . ."

I hold up a hand. "Nope." I take my pointer finger and circle my face and torso. "This? All of this? Now off limits."

He grabs my waist. "But not this part right?" He hoists me up over his shoulder and carries me, fireman style, toward the water.

"*Dallas. Patrick. Burke. Don't. You. DARE.*" I'm almost laughing too hard to get the words out.

Dallas laughs, puts me down, then pulls me into a warm, wonderful, sunlit hug. He kisses my forehead and I look up, fixing my sincerest expression on my face.

"Thank you, Dallas," I say. "For giving me closure."

His arm rests across my shoulders as we start back in the direction of the beach house. "I think it's important to do everything we can for the people we love."

My shoulders drop at the mention of the word. "Did that come out wrong?" I look up at him, his shadow a shield from the bright, midday sun.

He stops moving and takes my hands. "No, Poppy. That definitely didn't come out wrong."

"But you said—"

"I said I love you." He kisses me. "And I meant it."

My cheeks are as hot as the sun-baked sand, but there's no possible way to keep from letting my feelings out. "I love you too, Dallas. And I always, always will."

THE END

A Love Letter
From the Author

Dear Reader,

Like with any creative endeavor, there are times when a story just works. There are other times when it simply does not. After months and months of wrestling with a book that would not work, I decided I needed a little creative palate cleanser. A *just-for-fun, just-for-me,* low pressure story with only one purpose: to evoke JOY.

Creative play is something we often abandon as adults, but I'm a huge fan of it. It keeps me from loathing this work that I love. It brings back that spark of imagination and honestly, reminds me why I started doing this in the first place.

With this book, you've got a whole lot of what I love all poured into a single story because I realized that I want to write the stories I want to read. I'm not trying to be clever in writing this novel. I simply wanted to have fun. To fill the book with all the things I love. And to hopefully help you forget your troubles for a few hours.

Thank you so much for reading my books. You have literally thousands of options, so it's not lost on me how very much it means that you would choose to spend time reading mine.

For every single reader who reads this book, shares it with a friend, requests it at a local library, reviews it online, talks about it to anyone, anywhere. . .THANK YOU. You are why I get to keep doing this.

And I am forever grateful.

Please don't hesitate to catch up with me via email: courtney@courtneywalshwrites.com I love to chat with my readers & make new friends!

I'll be the one standing at the back of the room, holding the half-full glass of punch and lip syncing to "Kiss You."

Courtney

Acknowledgments

Adam—Always and always and always. Me + You.

Mom–Thanks for always being my first reader. And for still buying a paperback copy. I'm so thankful for you. You're a good one!

Sophia—Turns out you're a pretty fabulous co-worker. Thanks for helping me with my last minute book project. I think you're pretty awesome.

Ethan—Thank you for always reminding me that my phone camera is dirty. And for being a genuinely good human. I see so much good in you.

Sam—Thank you for making me laugh. And for being one of the most authentic souls I know.

Becky Wade & Katie Ganshert—Thanks for not telling me I'm crazy for writing and releasing this book. Even though I am. I'm so glad we're doing life together.

Melissa Tagg—Always such a good friend. I'm so very grateful for you.

Our Studio Kids & Families—Do you have any idea how special you are? You make my "day job" nothing but pure joy. I'm so thankful for each one of you!

Denise Harmer—No idea how you pulled it off, but thank you for being an awesome proofreader/copyeditor. I'm so thankful for you!

About the Author

Courtney Walsh is the Carol award-winning author of seventeen novels and two novellas. Her debut novel, *A Sweethaven Summer*, was a *New York Times* and *USA Today* e-book best-seller and a Carol Award finalist in the debut author category. In addition, she has written two craft books and several full-length musicals. Courtney lives with her husband and three children in Illinois, where she co-owns a performing arts studio and youth theatre with her business partner and best friend—her husband.

Visit her online at www.courtneywalshwrites.com

Made in the USA
Columbia, SC
24 November 2024